PUBLIC LIBRARY
TOWN OF BOSCAWEN
1913

THE WIZARD'S DAUGHTER

THE WIZARD'S DAUGHTER

BARBARA MICHAELS

Thorndike Press • Chivers Press
Thorndike, Maine USA   Bath, England

This Large Print edition is published by Thorndike Press, USA and by Chivers Press, England.

Published in 1997 in the U.S. by arrangement with Chivers Press Ltd.

Published in 1997 in the U.K. by arrangement with Severn House Publishers Ltd.

U.S. Hardcover 0-7862-1025-7 (Americana Series Edition)
U.K. Hardcover 0-7540-1029-5 (Windsor Large Print)
U.K. Softcover 0-7540-2013-4 (Paragon Large Print)

The text of this Large Print edition is unabridged.
Other aspects of the book may vary from the original edition.

Set in 16 pt. Plantin by Minnie B. Raven.

Printed in the United States on permanent paper.

British Library Cataloguing in Publication Data available

Library of Congress Cataloging in Publication Data

Michaels, Barbara, 1927–
The wizard's daughter / Barbara Michaels.
p. cm.
ISBN 0-7862-1025-7 (lg. print : hc : alk. paper)
1. Large type books. I. Title.
[PS3563.E747W5 1997] 96-53155

THE WIZARD'S DAUGHTER

AUTHOR'S NOTE

With one exception, all the characters in this book are solely the products of the author's imagination and bear no resemblance to any persons living or dead. Readers who are familiar with the history of spiritualism will realize that *David Holmes* was inspired by Daniel Dunglas Home, the most famous physical medium of the nineteenth century and, perhaps, of all time. The likeness is purely superficial. Mr. Home's performances were far more fantastic than any I would dare attribute to a fictional character, and his career was quite unlike the melodramatic fate I have invented for my Mr. Holmes.

PROLOGUE

She was the most beautiful woman of her time. Fashionable ladies tried in vain to imitate the elegance of her slim figure, her gliding walk, her exquisite auburn hair. Once she had been a humble little Spanish girl attending convent school in Paris. Now she was every inch an Empress; and most men would have quailed before the fury in her eyes as she stood in the majesty of offended pride, her plumy fan snapping, the priceless lace at her breast trembling with each sharp breath.

"You dare, sir, to complain of the group that has assembled to honor you — the wealth and nobility of France?"

The gentleman she addressed was tall and slight, almost boyish in appearance. He was the only man in that glittering crowd who did not wear a gold-braided uniform or the ribbon of some distinguished Order. His only unusual feature was his thick wavy hair, so fair that it shone like silver in the light of the hundreds of candles. Yet his features showed no alarm, only courteous regret. He spread his hands in an apologetic gesture and murmured, "Your Imperial Highness, I am aware of the condescension you and the Emperor do me, a poor citizen of the United States. It is not I, it is those I serve who insist that this is not a theatrical performance. They will not appear to any group larger than six or eight. And even then, you understand, I cannot guarantee results."

A concerted gasp went up from the watching throng. They knew their Empress; and they were not surprised when, after a moment of frozen silence, she turned on her heel and swept out of the room, so rapidly that the footmen in their powdered wigs and satin knee breeches had barely time to open the doors before she reached them.

A soft cough broke the appalled silence, and all eyes turned toward the short, stout man who stood facing the young American. His uniform was the most elaborate in the room — gold epaulets, rows of ribbons covering his breast, a court sword whose hilt blazed with rainbow jewels. Fierce black mustaches and a neat beard masked half his face. He had been, in his time, adventurer, gambler, exile, and dealer in dubious trades; but he was now the self-proclaimed Emperor of France, and his courtiers waited apprehensively to see how he would deal with the impertinent nobody who had insulted the Empress.

For a moment they studied one another, the slight young visitor and the most powerful man in Europe.

"Clear the room," said Napoleon III.

Six people remained — the Duchess of Alba, Prince Murat, the Comte Tasher de la Pagerie, General Espinasse, the Emperor himself — and Mr. David J. Holmes, private citizen of the United States of America, on whose behalf the noble courtiers had been dismissed and the Empress humiliated. Yet Mr. Holmes was not a diplomat or a millionaire or a famous painter, novelist, or musician. What precisely he was might be difficult to define.

At the Emperor's suggestion he seated himself and proceeded with the activity that had already made him notorious enough to warrant an invitation to the imperial court. Matters had not gone far before Napoleon, his hard black eyes even blanker than usual, sent for the Empress. Eugénie did not dare disobey, but her lovely face was decidedly sullen as she took her place in the circle that had formed around the table.

Her pouting lips relaxed and her eyes widened as a pale, luminous cloud began to form a few inches above the tabletop. It shaped itself into a hand — a man's hand, blunt-fingered, short, and square. The fingers curled in a quick, impatient gesture, then seemed to reach out. The bizarre object glided slowly across the table toward the Duchess of Alba, who shrieked and shrank back.

"Moi, je n'ai pas peur." Despite her brave claim, Eugénie's slim white hand trembled slightly as she extended it. The disembodied object changed course, as if it had heard and understood. Its outstretched fingers touched those of the Empress. She changed color visibly, then, with a sudden convulsive movement, clasped the dreadful thing in her hand.

For a space nothing could be heard except the measured tick of the enameled porcelain clock. Even breath was suspended. Then, as quickly as it had formed, the ghostly hand was gone. From Eugénie's throat came a painful whisper. *"Papa. C'etait mon père."* She hid her face in her hands.

Napoleon's exotic career had included some years in the United States. He had not wasted his time; among other things, he was a skilled amateur magician and a good poker player. The expressionless face necessary to financial success in this latter activity had often stood him in good stead. It did not change now; but for once his opaque, squinting eyes had a rather pensive look. He nodded. "Yes," he said. "There was a certain physical peculiarity. It was the hand of Don Cipriano."

From the homely farm kitchens of Pennsylvania to the drawing rooms of fashionable London and the salons of Paris Mr. David J. Holmes of America, twenty-two years old, had carried his message: There is no death, there is only change; the spirit lives forever. It is the one message all the world aches to hear, the colonel's lady and Mollie O'Grady, and the Empress of France. On Friday the thirteenth of May, 1857, Mr. Holmes carried the good tidings to the imperial court of France.

Napoleon was not the first or the last to be convinced that Holmes's powers were genuine, but he was certainly one of the shrewdest and most cynical converts. Perhaps he wondered, in the light of later events, whether Holmes's spirit guides had informed him on that eventful May night that he had less than five years to live. But, to be sure, when a man is convinced of the existence of a world after death, the date of his passing cannot be of much concern to him.

CHAPTER ONE

"Fifty pounds! But, dear Mrs. Jay, I was told that poor dear papa had left nothing at all. Fifty pounds is a great deal of money!"

Marianne's blue eyes sparkled; her silver-gilt curls, escaping from the net, glittered like imprisoned sunbeams; and the dimples that had dazzled so many susceptible Yorkshire youths returned to the places they had abandoned a week earlier, after the death of Squire Ransom.

Mrs. Jay's lips tightened as she viewed her godchild with something less than her usual doting fondness. She did not blame Marianne for the tossing curls or the dimples. The child had mourned her father properly; indeed, Mrs. Jay privately conceded, she had shed more tears for that rude, crude male creature than he had earned.

Perhaps Squire Ransom would have displayed more fatherly interest in a son, who, in good time, might have shared his interests: hunting, drinking, gambling, and . . . Mrs. Jay's thoughts came to a dead halt. The year was 1880, and Victoria had been on the throne for over forty years; the widow of a clergyman could not even contemplate the squire's favorite hobby without wincing. There was no acceptable euphemism for it.

In any event, the late Mrs. Ransom had not produced a red-faced, thick-set male infant to mirror its father's appearance. (Even in his declining years the squire looked alarmingly like a huge overdressed baby, especially when drink had smoothed out the lines in his moon of a face.) Instead she had born a girl, a delicate pink-and-white creature so unlike her sire that she might have been a changeling from fairyland. Within a few months the dark fuzz common to most infants had been replaced by a cap of soft silvery curls, and the ambiguous newborn blue of the baby's eyes had turned to a startling shade of aquamarine. And she had been as good as she was lovely; instead of howling vigorously when the baptismal water expelled the demons, as so many babies did, the little Marianne had opened her eyes wide and smiled.

Almost eighteen years ago . . . Mrs. Jay's grim expression as she remembered that perfect day, a day of soft sunshine and gentle breezes, when she had stood as sponsor to the child and her beloved husband had performed the ceremony of baptism. Dear Mr.

Jay, now passed to his heavenly reward. She had never addressed her husband by his first name, and still thought of him in formal terms.

Then she realized that Marianne had seen her frown, and that fresh tears had flooded the sea-blue eyes. Young girls were supposed to be full of sensibility and tender emotion, but some of Mrs. Jay's original ill humor remained, and she spoke more sharply than was her wont.

"It is not a great deal of money, Marianne. I only wish it were."

She did not add, as she might with reason have done, that eight pounds of the fifty had been her own contribution, from a life savings that could ill afford any diminution. The remainder of the sum had been made up of similar contributions from neighbors and friends. Squire Ransom had left his orphaned daughter nothing but debts.

There was another fact unknown to Marianne that Mrs. Jay could not explain. As a Christian woman her fortitude ought to have been equal to the task, but it was not. She had only recently learned of the malignant thing that was gnawing at her life and would soon end it; she had faced the fact and the increasing pain without flinching. But she could not tell her darling of her approaching death. It had tried her faith to a degree she would not have believed possible, not because she was afraid of dying, even in the dreadful manner experience had told her she could expect, but because just at the time when she might have hoped to be of use to the girl, who was as dear to her as a daughter, she could offer no help. She had no means of her own. If she took Marianne into her tiny home, within three months the girl would have to face the prospect she faced now, with the additional burden of having watched her old friend die an agonizing death. No. Better for Marianne to take the necessary action at once.

"You have no notion of money, naturally," she went on. "How could you have, when your father, despite his advantages of age and masculine intelligence, spent his income faster than it came in?"

"He spent generously on my account," Marianne said. "I cannot reproach him for extravagance when he denied me nothing."

"Hmph." Mrs. Jay said no more, but she had her own opinions about the squire's generosity. She had long been a reluctant observer of human nature, and she suspected that Squire Ransom's willingness to spend money on his daughter was an effort to make up for his neglect in other areas.

"At any rate," she said, more cheerfully, "you are well equipped with clothing and other necessities. That will not be a charge on your wealth. Did not Mrs. Maclean complete your new winter wardrobe only last week?"

"She completed it," said Marianne calmly, "and she is presently removing it."

"I beg your pardon?"

"One can hardly blame her. It appears the garments were not paid for. She hopes to alter them in order to resell them."

"Yes, yes, I understand. But what a callous thing to do!"

"Not at all. She has her living to earn."

Mrs. Jay lifted her hands helplessly. The girl's calm acceptance dismayed her. She would have attributed it to the indifference of shock had not Marianne displayed considerable emotion over other matters. She could only conclude that the child did not understand the desperation of her plight, so desperate that even the loss of a few pieces of clothing constituted a major disaster. The bare necessities for the approaching winter would make a sizable hole in the fifty pounds.

The golden fall sunlight pouring in the open windows gave no hint of the bleak months ahead, but it showed, with pitiless accuracy, how badly the squire had neglected his family home. The drawing room's decay was all the more apparent now that the furniture had been carried off by creditors. Fifty years earlier the walls had been hung with imported yellow damask. Bright unfaded squares, where paintings had once hung, contrasted painfully with the shredded remains of the once lovely fabric, stained with damp from the leaking roof. The hardwood floors had been gouged by hunting boots and stained by spilled wine. Over the years Mrs. Jay had mourned the room's deterioration, but on this occasion its ruin seemed to her like viewing the corpse of an old friend. She had not had the courage to inspect the rest of the house, having come only to escort Marianne home with her. Fortunately — for she could not afford to keep a carriage — the cottage was within walking distance, at the near end of the village. Billy Turnbull waited outside with his pony cart for Marianne's boxes and personal possessions. Mrs. Jay reflected, wryly, that his services might not have been needed after all.

They were sitting side by side on one of the window seats. Every stick of furniture in the room had been removed, and through the open doors Mrs. Jay could hear the heavy footsteps and rough voices of the carters who were even then carrying away the last of the squire's property. The late-afternoon sunlight caressed Marianne's curls. No painted saint had ever had such a halo; as the breeze stirred the loosened tendrils they sparkled and flashed. Even her swollen eyelids, reddened by weeping, could not mar the girl's exquisite prettiness, and the somber black frock, hastily dyed by Mrs. Jay, set off her slim figure and delicate coloring. She sat quietly, hands folded in her lap, thick golden lashes shadowing her cheeks; and Mrs. Jay, watching her, felt a pang even more severe than the gnawing ache she had lived with for months. How could she let this child, her heart's darling, go out into the world alone? Her beauty made her even more vulnerable than an ordinary young girl of good family would be. Mrs. Jay reluctantly conceded that the squire had kept his daughter's innocence untarnished; he had not brought his — er — women friends to the house, and even in his cups he was careful of his language. He had once kicked a drinking companion clear through the window when the man forgot himself and bellowed out a vehement "damn."

Only a life of service to God kept Mrs. Jay from cursing His cruelty. If she had only had a year — one little year! She could have used the time to prepare the girl for useful work, or even found her a husband — a gentle young curate or honest tradesman. Her hands clasped tightly and her lips moved in silent prayer. "Thy will be done," she told herself, and half believed it.

A voice separated itself from the general uproar upstairs. It grew louder and more strident as the speaker descended the stairs.

"Take care, you stupid girl, you are letting the flounces touch the floor. If they are dusty you shan't have supper tonight. Now the sash is trailing. How can you be so incompetent? I rue the day I ever took you on. Be careful of the turn there."

Through the open double doors which gave onto the hall Mrs. Jay saw the mute object of these reproaches stagger by. Presumably it was one of Mrs. Maclean's apprentices, but her identity could only be surmised, for she was virtually concealed by a towering stack of dresses. Her own skimpy homespun skirts and heavy shoes looked like an ambulatory gray column under that rainbow assortment: pink ruffles, like cream stained by floating strawberries, a flounce of green gauze the precise shade of young spring leaves, heaps of ice-blue satin and mandarin-yellow silk.

The anonymous bearer shuffled past and disappeared. Her figure was replaced, in the doorway's frame, by the much more substantial shape of Mrs. Maclean. The village dressmaker's skill with the needle was not matched by her personal taste; her brown taffeta gown was trimmed with flounces of a shrieking purple, and her bonnet of the same brown taffeta had birds' wings on either side. Her face was bright red and shining with perspiration; it formed a perfect circle, unbroken except for her false front of auburn hair. Draped carefully over her arms was a ball gown of coral faille, its ivory Sicilienne scarf and train folded up over the full skirt. Atop this elegant heap were a pair of white kid gloves, an ivory fan, and — toes turned in pathetically — two little satin slippers.

Marianne emitted a small, quickly suppressed sound, like the squeak of a mouse under a cat's claws. Her eyes were fixed on the coral-colored heap, and her lower lip trembled. She had tried to harden herself to her loss, but seeing this favorite gown her fortitude had given away; and although Mrs. Jay deplored the exhibition of sensibility over anything as frivolous as a ball gown, she could not help remembering how Marianne had looked in the dress the one and only time she had worn it. Sir Albert Martin's ball, only last month . . . Marianne had been the undoubted belle, despite the presence of several haughty young ladies from the metropolis of York. Sir Albert's son and heir had been assiduous in his intentions. Mrs. Jay had hoped . . .

But the loss of Marianne's inheritance had deprived her of that means of being relieved of the poverty that was its result. Sir Albert and the other country gentry would never permit their sons to marry a penniless girl.

Mrs. Maclean paused, her squinting eyes avoiding those of the two women sitting in the window.

"There are two more boxes," she said abruptly. "I shall return for those directly."

"Very well," Marianne said.

That was all she said; but Mrs. Maclean gathered the stiff folds more closely to her bosom as she correctly appraised the girl's hungry look.

"I will lose a great deal of money," she grumbled. "I must sell these at a loss, supposing I am fortunate enough to find a purchaser. Perhaps . . ." She hesitated for a moment, and then, remembering that Marianne would not patronize her establishment again, and that the vicar's widow had never been a good customer, she added belligerently, "I will take the blue coat and muff as compensation."

Marianne's yelp of distress was quite audible this time. Mrs. Jay rose to her full height, swollen with righteous indignation.

"You most certainly will not. The coat and muff were purchased in London, they were not made by you. Come, Marianne; we had better go through your wardrobe to make sure nothing was stolen."

Mrs. Maclean retreated as the vicar's widow advanced on her.

"But I will suffer a loss —"

"I doubt that. And if you did, it would be trivial compared with the sums the squire has paid you over the years. I always suspected you overcharged him; and goodness knows your profits have not been spent on those starved, overworked girls you employ."

She continued to move forward, and Mrs. Maclean, recognizing a superior will, beat a hasty and undignified retreat. She was muttering to herself as she flounced out, and she took care to make her comments audible.

"Paupers . . . charity . . . taking advantage. . . ."

Marianne slipped her hand into Mrs. Jay's.

"You were wonderful! I would never have

had the courage to stand up to her. She was always friendly and respectful; who would have supposed she could be so unkind?"

"You will find that adversity brings out the true nature of false acquaintances," Mrs. Jay replied. "And you must learn to defend your rights, Marianne. That coat is far too frivolous for your new station in life, but at least it is warm, and you will need it. Now let us do as I suggested and see what that wretch has left you. I wouldn't put it past her to take things that are not rightfully hers."

Resolutely ignoring the desolation around her, and the rude voices of the workmen, she started up the stairs. In this small way at least she could be useful.

There were after all quite a number of boxes to be taken away. Not all the squire's creditors were as hardhearted as Mrs. Maclean, and the trinkets and frivolities so dear to the heart of a young girl had little monetary value. By the time Marianne's possessions had been transferred to Mrs. Jay's house and put away, the old lady was more than ready for her tea.

There could not have been a greater contrast between two places than the rotting elegance of the manor house and the neat, overcrowded parlor of the cottage. Every table was decently swathed in cloths of heavy plush, and every surface was covered with ornaments, photographs, and the memorabilia of a long, active life. The windows had been sealed against the unhealthy night air, and Mrs. Jay had ordered the fire to be lighted. She felt the cold rather more than she used to.

Marianne found the room uncomfortably stuffy, though of course she did not say so. The day had been unusually warm for the beginning of October. A beautiful day — the last day in her childhood home. She tried to feel sad, but even her memories of "poor dear papa" could not quench her rising spirits. It is hard, she told herself sagely, to think of winter when the sun is shining. Then she smiled. I do believe, she thought, that I have composed an epigram!

Guiltily conscious that she should not have smiled, she glanced at Mrs. Jay. That lady, worn out by woe and emotion, and by another cause Marianne was unaware of, had nodded off, her head resting against the worn leather of the highbacked chair. In her white lacy cap and black gown she resembled the engravings Marianne had seen of a more famous widow, the royal widow of Windsor, who had been mourning her German prince for twenty years. Except, Marianne told herself disloyally, Mrs. Jay had a much more pleasant face than did the Queen. Once she must have been a pretty girl.

A strange little chill ran through her body, despite the excessive warmth of the room, as she contemplated the inevitable tragedy of time; but she was too young to think of disagreeable matters for long, and much too young to believe that such a tragedy could happen to her. Surely, she knew that one day she would grow old; but that would not be for a long, long time. Before her hair whitened and her cheeks grew withered (oh, impossible!) there was a great exciting world to be explored and conquered.

Of course it was very sad that poor dear Papa had died so suddenly. She had enjoyed her first eighteen years of life enormously, for her father was no disciplinarian, and she would have run quite wild had it not been for the admonitions of Mrs. Jay. Marianne loved her godmother and was always amenable to the old lady's suggestions; but Mrs. Jay had been a busy woman, as the wife of the pastor of a large parish always is, and during Marianne's childhood she had not had time to interfere unduly.

Marianne's father had taught her to ride — it was the one skill he did teach her —

and he had not objected to her playing with the village children, though Mrs. Jay never failed to point out that they were beneath Marianne's station in life. As a child Marianne had never understood why this should be so. Billy Turnbull and Jack Daws and the others were far cleverer than she. They had taught her many useful things — how to set a snare for a hare (though they never could persuade her to take the poor thing out of the snare), how to fish with a bit of string and a pin, how to play ball and jacks and marbles.

Then, when she was thirteen, Mr. Jay had died, and Mrs. Jay had been free to devote all her time to her goddaughter. She had spent hours coaching Marianne in the manners and skills required of a young lady. Thanks to Marianne's instinctive gentility and affectionate disposition, this task had not proved as difficult as one might have supposed it would be, after thirteen years of neglect. The squire had also neglected the girl's formal education. Her governesses had been of two types: distressed gentlewomen, who found it impossible to adapt to the squire's boisterous life-style and invariably departed in a huff after a few weeks, and women of quite another sort, who adapted only too well and had, thereafter, little time for their pupil.

Fortunately, Marianne liked to read. She had acquired this skill early and had improved it by daily practice. At thirteen she had had no other educational advantages, but the squire, intimidated by the icy courtesy of the vicar's lady, was easily persuaded to make up the deficiencies. "Anything for a quiet life" was his motto. So they came and went — drawing masters, French masters, instructors in dancing and music and German. At eighteen Marianne had the usual young lady's repertoire of half-developed talents: a smattering of French, a soupçon of German, the ability to sketch a pretty stretch of woodland (if the drawing master outlined it first). She had also embroidered half a dozen fire screens and five pairs of house slippers for dear Papa. The squire never wore the slippers, but he thanked her for them nicely, after studying their patterns of pansies and forget-me-nots with poorly concealed astonishment.

Since she had never been told that children are entitled to develop their own personalities, Marianne had accepted the change of routine docilely. She really was a nice girl, with an affectionate heart; and if a bright October afternoon, crisp with frosty sunlight, made her yearn to be out playing tag with Billy and Jack instead of conjugating *servir* in all its possible tenses, she never said so. The new regime had its compensations. The changes in her body and heart, which coincided with Mrs. Jay's full-time tutelage, made it easier for her to abandon childish pursuits; performing prodigies of Berlin work, she dreamed of the young curate's soulful looks. (This was no adolescent fantasy; the curate was the first of many victims, and Mrs. Jay had been obliged to lecture him about his behavior.)

And there was music.

The squire had, upon demand, bought his daughter the finest available pianoforte, of carved rosewood with puckered silk panels and gold candleholders. Why should he not? He never paid for it, although, to do him justice, he fully intended to do so. If the piano dealer had not gone bankrupt first . . . Before that, Marianne had heard no music except for birdsong and the earnest but untrained efforts of the church choir. When M. George, the music master, flipped up his coattails, seated himself, and plunged into a Mozart sonatina, Marianne knew what she had been missing all her life. She made astonishing progress with her music, and for several years the squire avoided his own drawing room during the hours of Marianne's practice. She practiced quite a lot, and classical music made him want to howl like one of his own hounds.

The inadvertent mixture of educational styles had, in fact, produced a rather remarkable personality. From Mrs. Jay Marianne had learned that a lady did not acknowledge the existence of her own nether limbs — never to be thought of, much less referred to, as "legs." But before Mrs. Jay took over her education Marianne had watched the stable cats copulate and had been present when the squire's favorite bitch had her litters. Mrs. Jay had told her that ladies swooned at the sight of blood; but in childhood she had often torn up a petticoat to bind the scrapes and bruises she and her playmates incurred. Once she had even cut a fish hook from Billy's "nether limb."

How, one might ask, did Marianne manage to reconcile these opposing viewpoints in her own mind? In the same way most human beings are able to accept the shocking discrepancy between the ideal and the actual; as the merchant is able to nod piously at Sunday sermons adjuring him to relieve the poor and suffering, and on Monday watch complacently as his overworked, underpaid factory children drowse over their looms. As Mrs. Jay herself could trust in the loving kindness of the Creator after beholding countless examples of that same Creator's failure to relieve death, suffering, and pain.

When dusk was far advanced, the vicar's widow roused herself and ordered the candles to be brought in. Gas lighting devices had not reached the village, and if they had, Mrs. Jay would not have tolerated them. On this particular evening the pale, limited light seemed scarcely to relieve the darkness; Mrs. Jay had to force herself to reach for one of the pieces of fabric laid out on the table. Black thread on black fabric — difficult even for young, strong eyes to see. But the work had to be done, especially now, in view of the unexpected diminution of Marianne's wardrobe. Mrs. Jay had bought the black wool herself when the shocking news of the squire's financial situation had become known. At least the girl would have a few decent black gowns to wear when she left for . . . where? That was the question, and Mrs. Jay applied herself to it with her customary fortitude.

"We must discuss your future," she said.

Marianne, her head bent over a seemingly endless pattern of black braid, did not stop sewing.

"I must find work, I suppose," she said.

"You have, I take it, no other — er — option?" Mrs. Jay inquired. She was sure Marianne did not. The girl had always confided in her.

This belief was, of course, an illusion. No young girl is foolish enough to tell a strict older woman about her romantic daydreams and adventures. Marianne's encounters had been innocent enough; all the same, the flush that spread over her averted face would have been a dead giveaway if the light had been stronger and the vicar's widow had not been distracted.

It would have been better for Marianne if she could have forced herself to tell Mrs. Jay about the particular incident that had caused the blush. The older woman would certainly have interpreted the occurrence correctly, and she might have been shocked into giving her goddaughter a few useful hints.

It had happened that very morning. Marianne had insisted on spending the last night in her old home, and Mrs. Jay had reluctantly agreed, since a few of the servants still remained. The girl had arisen early and had gone for a solitary walk through the grounds, bidding a sentimental farewell to her favorite spots. When she returned to the house she found a visitor waiting.

John Bruton was a neighbor, the son of one of the squire's favorite drinking and hunting cronies. Mr. Bruton was of the new gentry; having made his fortune by the efficient exploitation of child labor in his mills, he had been able to retire from trade and purchase gentility, in the form of a country seat, which he promptly renamed Bruton Hall. His eldest son, John, had been one of Marianne's playmates until he was sent away to school. Returning, he had been astonished to find the hoydenish child grown into a beautiful woman. The fathers had talked vaguely of a possible match, and John had been enthusiastic. Marianne had not. Her dream hero, like that of most young ladies of that period, was dark and slim and melancholy. John's round pink face and plump, sweating hands roused no tremor in her heart.

Still, he was an old friend, and when she entered the hall and found him pacing up and down, irritably switching at the dying plants with his riding crop, she was glad to see him.

"Dear John, how good of you to come," she exclaimed, giving him her hand. "I trust your mother is better today?"

"Nothing wrong with the old lady but overeating. Now you — by Gad, you look absolutely first-rate today, Marianne."

"I don't feel first-rate." With some difficulty Marianne freed her hand and wiped it surreptitiously on her skirt. "Papa's creditors will be here soon — or their agents — I don't really understand what is going to happen, except that they will take everything. These are the final hours. I must leave the home of my childhood, never to return."

"Oh, well — Gad — yes, that's so. You always do put things so well, Marianne."

His eyes fixed themselves on her face with a look she had learned to know, and dislike, over the past months. Marianne turned away. He followed as she walked toward the drawing room.

"Yes," she went on musingly, "the end has come. I will see my ancestral halls no more. The orphaned child must wander, seeking her fortune in the cold, unfeeling world."

This touching sentiment ended in an inappropriate grunt as two arms wrapped around her waist so vigorously that the air was expelled from her lungs. The young man's moist cheek flattened the curls at her temple; his hot breath stirred the tendrils of hair above her ear as he whispered, "It don't have to be that way, m'dear. Er — that is — demmit, I can't talk elegant like you, but

— er — I mean — I'll take care of you. No need to wander, eh? Pa don't ask what I do with my allowance, he gives me all I want, enough for a nice little house with a garden — you're fond of flowers and all that — even a carriage, if I can screw a bit more out of the old . . . oh, Marianne . . ."

It was not the first time Marianne had felt a young man's arms around her; but when John's hand groped for her breast, encased as it was in layers of corset, camisole, and bodice, a violent thrill of outraged modesty ran through her. She wrenched herself away. Turning, she faced the young man with flashing eyes and a look of such indignant innocence that he actually fell back a step.

Seeing his confusion, Marianne's quick temper subsided. Perhaps, she thought charitably, he had been reaching for his pocket handkerchief.

"I forgive you," she said coolly. "So long as you promise never to do such a thing again. I esteem you as a friend, but I could never marry you."

John's fleshy mouth dropped open. "Marry?" he began.

A rumble of wheels outside, on the graveled drive, announced the arrival of the first of the carters who had come to carry away the squire's mortgaged property, thus sparing the young man the necessity of an explanation that would have been painful to all concerned.

Marianne remembered this incident as she bent more closely over her sewing. She was not experienced enough to understand why John Bruton's fumbling hands had offended her, as the tentative embraces of other enamored youths had not. Victorian young ladies were not as stupid as their elders fondly believed, but they were, for the most part, armored against rude behavior by the social conventions that made ladies immune from the sexual demands their female inferiors had to accept. What Marianne did not realize was that the death of her father had not only robbed her of a male protector, it had removed the social status that had made her sacrosanct. She only knew that her former playmate's proposal, as she believed it, had been unacceptable — and that she had better not mention it to Mrs. Jay.

Mrs. Jay took her silence for a negative reply and went on with her speech.

"I thought not. Well, one can hardly blame your father for not having made arrangements; you are quite young. And without a dowry, it is most unlikely . . . I fear that you must indeed consider some means of earning a livelihood."

"I understand that Lady Verill is looking for a companion."

"Out of the question!" In her agitation Mrs. Jay stabbed her needle into her thumb. "Lady Verill is always looking for a companion. She is . . . Her affliction is of a nature that . . . It would not do for you."

Lady Verill drank. This fact was well known to all the neighborhood, as was the corollary, that her companions were expected to see that she was supplied with just enough brandy to keep her in a mild stupor. It was no easy task to judge this correctly, and the consequences of misjudgment were horrendous. If sober, the lady fell into deep melancholy and attempted suicide; if too drunk, she flew into a maniacal rage and attempted homicide upon Lord Verill.

"I only suggested it," Marianne explained, "because it would be one means of my remaining in the neighborhood. I see no other opportunities here — unless I attend the next Mop Fair, displaying the proper uniform for the trade in which I seek employment. If cooks wear colored aprons and nursery maids white linen, what is the symbol for a companion, I wonder? A genteel but worn morning dress of gray cambric, adorned only by a neat white collar and cuffs? I might borrow Lady Verill's lap dog."

Mrs. Jay let her ramble on in this vein while she marshaled her arguments. She had no intention of explaining her real reasons for wishing Marianne out of the area. Luckily there were others.

"There are no opportunities in this backward country region. And it would be too humiliating for your neighbors to see you reduced to such a position. I have given the matter much thought, I assure you, and I see no help for it. Your only chance of finding a suitable situation is in a large city."

Marianne dropped her sewing and clasped her hands.

"London?"

"You needn't look so pleased," Mrs. Jay said, with some asperity. "I suppose that like all girls you think of London as gay and exciting. It is a great filthy hive, riddled with sin and vice and crime. However, it happens that I have a friend there who has turned her home into a boarding house for young ladies in your position — those of respectable family, but reduced circumstances. The need for such establishments is so great, and the supply is so limited, that her rooms are in constant demand, but I feel sure that if I ask she will find a place for you."

"Oh," Marianne said.

Mrs. Jay did not notice the flat tone. She

was sincerely pleased with her plan; indeed, the recollection of her old friend, so conveniently situated to do Marianne good, was the only bright spot in an otherwise dreadful state of affairs, and it never occurred to her that her description, with its reiteration of "respectable," might not thrill her auditor.

"She also has connections which enable her to place young ladies in respectable situations. It is an excellent opportunity, Marianne, and I can go to my rest — my nightly rest, I mean — with greater peace of mind, knowing you will be in her care."

"It is very kind," Marianne murmured.

"You might accept a position as companion, if the establishment were of the best quality. And, as I have reason to know, your accomplishments qualify you to instruct the young. Then there is your music —"

"My music," Marianne repeated, visibly startled.

"Yes, you play quite nicely. Eventually you might hope to set up as a music teacher, if you are very frugal and save your earnings. That would be pleasant, would it not? Your own rooms, where pupils could come to you?"

"Oh, certainly." Again Marianne bent over her sewing. Unseen by Mrs. Jay, she let out her breath in a sigh of relief. She would not have been at all surprised to find that Mrs. Jay had been reading her secret thoughts; often in the past, when she had meditated some improper act, the vicar's lady had seemed to know precisely what she intended — and had, of course, forbidden it.

She would certainly forbid Marianne to develop the plan she had formulated after the first shock of her father's death had passed and she had realized she was on her own. The girl was not above dramatizing the tragedy of her situation; references to poor orphans and cold, cruel worlds were romantically thrilling; but in fact Marianne was more pleased than intimidated by her freedom. She had the careless self-confidence of a young person who has never been hurt or deprived, and she yearned for excitement. Of course it was sad about poor dear Papa, and seeing her favorite ball dress carried away had been exceedingly painful; but now she could carry out the daring scheme that had oft occurred to her when, angered by some small punishment or frustration, she had vowed to run away from home and seek her fortune. She did play the piano well, and her singing voice had been much admired. The preceding fall, when a well-known mezzo soprano had visited Ripon — had not several gentlemen assured her that she sang the *Che farò* with much more feeling than did Madame Belledame?

Daunted, at first, by Mrs. Jay's suggestion, Marianne soon realized that the plan would provide no real obstacle to her ambition. The lady who managed the boarding house could hardly chaperone every single one of the respectable young ladies every hour of every day. Once she was actually in London . . .

A dazzling vision filled her imagination: an elegant theater, marble-columned without, red plush and gilt within; distinguished patrons in formal evening dress, the ladies glittering with diamonds; the Royal Box — and on the stage, the focus of a hundred footlights, she herself (pale blue satin and pearls, ostrich plumes in her hair) bowing, as thrown blossoms littered the boards around her and the applause deafened her, and the Prince of Wales leaned forward, the Garter ribbon across his breast. . . .

Her needle continued to flash in and out, sewing the black braid in a complex scrollwork; but she had learned, long since, to carry out work of this sort while her imagination soared free. So absorbed was she in her fantasy ("Ah, Miss Ransom," the Prince exclaimed, tears moistening his beautiful eyes, "never have I heard . . .") that she scarcely heard Mrs. Jay's voice extolling the advantages of the genteel boarding house.

The poor lady had her own vision, and it was, needless to say, considerably more realistic than Marianne's. All she dared hope for her darling was a comfortable small apartment, with a genteel pianoforte and genteel students, a canary bird, and perhaps a genteel kitten. Marianne did not notice when Mrs. Jay suddenly stopped speaking, nor did she observe the older woman's pallor.

Later that evening, after they had retired to their rooms, Mrs. Jay unlocked a small cabinet and took out a dark, sticky-looking syrup. She stood holding it for a few moments, an expression of distaste on her face. The doctor had pressed the laudanum upon her in spite of her insistence that she would never resort to drugs. If God chose to afflict her, she would bear the pain. It was not pain that weakened her resolve, but her determination that Marianne should not have worry about her godmother added to her other troubles. Her hand was quite steady as she measured out a careful dose. It was a sin, no doubt. If so, she would suffer the consequences.

CHAPTER TWO

Fortunately for Marianne, darkness was well advanced when the North Britain express pulled into King's Cross Station and she got her first look at the city she had dreamed of with such romantic hopes — fortunately, because night hid the soot and dirt and concealed the most wretched victims of a great nation's indifference.

She had resigned herself to being accompanied, knowing full well that Mrs. Jay would never allow her to make such a long journey unchaperoned. It had not been an easy task to find a traveling companion, for the residents of Wulfingham seldom had occasion to visit London. Mrs. Jay had finally been forced to extend her inquiries as far as York. Here she had found success, in the form of Mrs. Wackford, the wife of a schoolmaster. The school was known for its strictness, even in an age when education was not supposed to be fun. It had an excellent reputation among parents who were not at all amused by Mr. Dickens' savage satires on Yorkshire schools, being particularly popular with those who served the Queen in the jungles of the East. Mrs. Wackford was journeying to London to meet two such unfortunates, sent from India by their widowed papa; and as soon as Marianne set eyes on the lady she pitied the unknown children with all her heart. The schoolmaster's wife looked like a tall thin knobby iron column. Rusty ringlets, as rigid as sculptured bronze, lined the rim of her black bonnet. The only muscles on her face that moved were the ones necessary to open her mouth the barest slit when she was obliged to speak.

Marianne never knew whether Mrs. Wackford took an instant dislike to her personally, or whether she simply disliked everyone on principle. Certainly she displayed no warmth toward anyone they encountered, not even toward Mrs. Jay. That good lady had arisen at two A.M. and had endured the uncomfortable ride into York with her goddaughter; but not even the laudanum, which she had been taking regularly, could make this final parting endurable. After a quick, desperate embrace she fled, knowing she would betray herself if she stayed. Billy, who had driven the hired carriage from Wulfingham and carried Marianne's modest luggage into the station, lingered just long enough to give Marianne a most improper wink and press a small packet into her hand.

Marianne bit her lip hard and managed not to cry. Excitement had prevented her from sleeping the previous night, and she was bewildered by the new sights around her. She had never traveled by train before; the echoing station with its noisy crowds and snorting steel monsters was terrifying. She was not given time to indulge in tears. With a sniff and a jerk of her head, Mrs. Wackford indicated a nearby carriage.

The novelty soon wore off and was succeeded by tedium. Mrs. Wackford had a "Ladies Only" sign tacked on their compartment, so there were no other travelers to entertain them; for all the other ladies seemed to be accompanied by gentlemen. The only thing that cheered Marianne was Billy's gift — a twopenny's worth of bulls' eyes, rather squashed and dusty-looking, but recalling the sweets they had so often shared. She might have wept then, but seeing Mrs. Wackford's outraged glance at the grubby little offering, she was moved to mischief instead. Leaning forward, she proffered the sticky sweet and said demurely, "Do have one, ma'am."

This gesture effectively ended any possible communication between the two. Marianne dozed and woke and looked out the window and dozed again. The sky was cloudy, and it soon began to rain. Even her fertile imagination was daunted by the dreariness inside and out, and for the first time she began to entertain doubts of the future.

If the station at York had awed her, the magnificence of King's Cross made her wish she were back in Mrs. Jay's cozy parlor. The noise, amplified a thousandfold by the lofty ceiling, made her head ache. Everyone in London seemed to shout, and everyone except Marianne herself seemed to know where he was going and was in a great hurry to get there.

In an alarming foghorn bellow Mrs. Wackford summoned a porter and started out along the platform, shoving and pushing with as much abandon as the others. Marianne followed. She was glad to collapse into the cab, although it smelled like musty straw inside. Followed by the heated comments of the porter, who clearly felt that he had been inadequately compensated for his efforts, the cab creaked out of the station and onto the city streets.

Tired as she was, Marianne could not resist peeking out the window. Accustomed to the darkness of country lanes, she was dazzled by the gas lamps that illumined the main thoroughfares, and was amazed to note that though the hour was late the streets were crowded with people.

"How elegantly ladies dress here," she exclaimed.

Mrs. Wackford leaned forward to look. It was not difficult for her to pick out the particular "lady" who had roused Marianne's interest; her gaudy red satin skirts gleamed like stained glass in the lamplight, and her pelisse was thrown back from her shoulders, displaying a broad white bosom and the flash of what Marianne had naively believed to be diamonds. As Mrs. Wackford stared, a man in evening dress strolled up to the red-satin lady, doffed his top hat with a flourish, and offered her his arm.

Marianne felt herself pulled away from the window and shoved back into her corner.

"That," said Mrs. Wackford, "is no lady. I am responsible for you, miss, until we reach your boarding house, so I must insist that you pay no attention to such — er — persons."

"Is it a fallen woman?" Marianne asked, breathless with excitement.

Her companion gasped. "What is the world coming to? A modest young woman of my time would never have asked such a question!"

Marianne subsided. She did not dare

move out of her corner, but by craning her neck she caught occasional glimpses of shop windows displaying a luxurious assortment of goods, walls placarded with garish signs advertising pills and potions, corsets and coal scuttles, and more people than she had ever seen gathered together in one place. She did not see the beggars and the pickpockets, and she failed to recognize the harlots.

Eventually the cab turned off the brightly lighted street and passed into a quiet area of small houses.

"At last," said Mrs. Wackford, as the cab came to a stop. "Make haste, Miss Ransom, if you please; I have still some distance to travel and the hour is late."

Marianne was glad to oblige. Much as she dreaded the strange faces and places awaiting her, nothing could be more unpleasant than the company of Mrs. Wackford.

The house before which they had stopped was one of a row of similar structures, tall and narrow, each separated from its neighbors by a slitlike passageway. A flight of steps led up to the front door. The door opened; a form was seen silhouetted against the glow of lamplight within.

"Is it Miss Ransom?" a voice inquired.

Marianne could see nothing of the speaker

except her outline — that of a stout, short lady wearing a frilled cap of such extravagant proportions that her head resembled a cabbage — but she liked the sound of the low, pleasant voice. She started to reply, but was forestalled by Mrs. Wackford, still in the carriage.

"It is. You, madam, are Mrs. Shortbody? Then, madam, I have fulfilled my responsibilities and I bid you good night. Driver, we will proceed immediately to the Tavistock Hotel."

" 'old your 'orses," the driver replied. "I'll just 'elp the young lady wif her boxes."

"Thank you," Marianne said.

The driver grinned broadly at her, displaying brown, rotting teeth.

"There won't be no change out o' 'er," he said cryptically. "You go on, miss; I'll just take me time 'ere."

Marianne started up the stairs. Mrs. Wackford's furious criticisms of the driver formed a loud background accompaniment, though it had no perceptible effect on its object.

Mrs. Shortbody stepped forward as Marianne reached the top of the steps and held out both hands. Her grasp was warm, and her face, framed by the frills of her cap, was as smiling and pleasant as her voice.

"Welcome to London, my dear."
Marianne burst into tears.

II

As was to be expected, the seats inside the omnibus were all taken. There was room on top; but no lady ever attempted to mount the perpendicular iron ladder to that lofty region. If her long skirts had not prevented such an exercise, the possibility of exposing petticoats and pantalettes to the bold gazes of men below would have been unthinkable.

If it had been raining, even chivalry might not have prompted any of the men to exchange their inside seats for a place on the unroofed top of the bus. Fortunately for Marianne the day was fair, and one young man — a clerk on an errand, to judge by his neat but shabby attire and the large parcel he carried — was susceptible to melting turquoise-blue eyes. Marianne was not unaware of the charming picture she presented, slim and pathetic in her black gown, a few tendrils of sunny hair escaping the confines of her black bonnet; and it is to be feared that she allowed her eyes to linger on the young man's face for an instant before lowering them in modest confusion. An instant was all that was required. The young clerk leaped to his feet and bowed Marianne into his vacated seat.

Marianne relaxed as much as the hard wooden bench would allow and pushed her curls back into place with her gloved hand. It would be at least half an hour before she reached her destination; time to collect her thoughts and complete her plans.

She could hardly believe she had been in London only two days. The quiet country village from which she had come seemed like another world, and she felt herself quite a different person from the simple girl who had wept with weariness and nerves at the first kind word.

The omnibus made slow progress. Traffic was heavy, and if there were rules of the road, no one paid the slightest attention to them. Heavy drays, pushcarts and wagons, hansom cabs and carriages contended with pedestrians for the right-of-way.

A young man tossed a handful of bright-purple papers in through the window. Most of the passengers ignored them or brushed them irritably aside; but Marianne picked one up. She was intrigued by this form of advertising, quite unknown and indeed unnecessary in Wulfingham. This handbill told the pathetic yet encouraging story of a young man of Exeter who had been "effectively cured in a single night of insanity by swallowing the whole contents of a thirteen-penny-half-penny box of Number Two Pills."

Marianne of course believed every word of this. She marveled at the wonders of modern medicine and decided that perhaps the Number Two Pills might help Lady Verill. Next time she wrote Mrs. Jay she would mention them.

Yes, London was certainly a marvelous place! The city still frightened her a little; it was so very large and so exceedingly dirty. Dust and mud she was accustomed to, but the sticky soot that clung like oil to her clothing and skin disgusted her. However, the people were very kind, quite unlike the picture she had formed from the warnings of her friends back home. She had gotten the impression that Londoners were too busy to be civil or helpful to a stranger. She had certainly not found it so. Everyone had been most pleasant, especially the gentlemen.

Of course, she reminded herself, she had as yet seen only a minute fraction of the population. She had spent the preceding two days settling in, getting acquainted with her landlady and the other young ladies, and — somewhat surreptitiously — collecting as much information as she could about the city. Her complacent smile faded as she remembered some of the things she had said and done. Yes, she had changed — and not for the better. She had not told any out-and-out lies. . . . But that was equivocating, and Marianne knew it. Her silence had been a form of lying, her efforts to discover what she needed to know had been sly and lacking in candor.

Yet what else could she have done? If she had told Mrs. Shortbody what she intended, her landlady would have forbidden it in no uncertain terms. Mrs. Shortbody's genial face and round, comfortable figure had led Marianne to hope that her views would be more liberal than those of her old friend, but to her disappointment Mrs. Shortbody was just as narrow-minded and old-fashioned as Mrs. Jay, especially in her opinions about the theater. After all, the Queen had attended innumerable theatrical performances before her husband's death sent her into the voluntary retirement from which she had not emerged for years. She and Prince Albert had even acted themselves, in the privacy of the royal parlor. Mrs. Shortbody had admitted, in response to Marianne's adroit questioning, that she enjoyed a good performance of Shakespeare as much as anyone. However, she had added, most actors and actresses were people of immoral habits — not the sort one would ever invite into one's home.

Marianne did not remain gloomy for long. She assured herself that she would tell Mrs. Shortbody the truth as soon as she had secured a position as a singer; and surely, when the good lady saw how thoroughly respectable the situation was, she would accept it. ("My dear Miss Ransom, if I had but known . . . You were right, and I was quite wrong.")

Such pleasant visions, including the now classic daydream of the Prince of Wales bowing with tears in his eyes, occupied Marianne quite happily until she reached her destination. She would have missed the stop if the driver had not descended from his high seat to throw open the door and announce, "The Strand," as he nodded benignly at her. Unaware of how remarkable this behavior was, Marianne thanked him prettily and accepted his hand as she descended.

Though the theater she had selected was not far away, it took her some time to find it. Finally she stopped a constable and asked directions.

The facade of the Imperial Theater was all she had ever imagined. It had been recently remodeled in the latest classical mode, and the soot of London had as yet made comparatively small impression upon the Corinthian columns and the modestly draped caryatids. The lobby, with its massive bronze chandeliers and thick plum-colored carpeting, was as imposing as the exterior. Seeing no one about, Marianne pushed through the doors leading to the auditorium.

Later she would realize what a fortuitous chain of circumstances had conspired to lead her, unquestioned and unhindered, to the stage of that most prestigious of theaters. A rehearsal had been called for that morning, and she happened to arrive just after the doors were opened and just before the cast had assembled. The humbler employees were occupied with various errands, so the vast auditorium was unoccupied. The stage was alight and waiting.

As if mesmerized Marianne moved slowly down the aisle. It took her only a moment to find the steps that led to the stage. She moved out into the center and turned to face the rows of empty seats.

She did not see the two men who had entered while she was making her way to the stage. In their dark suits they were scarcely visible to eyes dazzled by the footlights, and Marianne's imagination was in full flower, supplying an orchestra in the pit and a glittering group of royalty in the nearest stage box. It is doubtful that she would have behaved differently if she had seen the small audience of two, for this was precisely the situation she had dreamed of — the young, unknown singer, the skeptical manager. . . .

She clasped her hands, lifted her eyes to what she (mistakenly) believed to be the Royal Box, and began to sing.

> "I dreamed that I dwelt in marble halls,
> With vassals and serfs at my side. . . ."

The two men listened in silence. The taller and stouter of them had been in a bad mood to begin with; the frown that darkened his normally affable face deepened when he saw the interloper, and Marianne's song did not lessen its severity.

The other man's slight, foppishly dressed figure made him seem, at first glance, considerably younger than his companion. Coal-black hair and luxuriant whiskers framed a face of luminous pallor — the face of a man who seldom goes abroad under the sun. It was a singularly expressionless countenance, and it remained so; but the narrow dark eyes, so black that they appeared pupilless, narrowed still more as they examined the dainty little figure on the stage.

"Your new nightingale, Nubbles?" he asked softly.

"Never saw the gel in my life. Some stage-struck chit from the country, no doubt. Well, Wilson, there is nothing more to be said. I believe our business is concluded."

The slighter dark man looked amused.

"It never actually began, Nubbles. You gave me no opportunity to enlarge upon my proposal."

"No need," Nubbles said gruffly. "Must I be blunt? You and I are not interested in the same aspects of the theatrical profession."

"Perhaps not. Very well. If you should change your mind . . ."

"Not likely."

"Good day to you, then."

With a mocking inclination of his head Wilson started toward the door. Nubbles, his eyes fixed on the stage where Marianne, carried away by her own performance, postured and swayed as she sang, did not observe that Wilson paused briefly to inspect the girl once again before he went through the door.

Despite his scowl, Mr. Nubbles was not immune to the charm of the young performer. Once the other man had left, his scowl relaxed into a faint smile, though he shook his head and sighed as he listened. He let Marianne finish her song before he started down the aisle.

"Now then," he shouted, brandishing his walking stick like a club. "That will be enough of that, young lady. Come down from there, if you please."

Marianne had been so deep in her dream-world that the gruff voice struck like a blow. She jumped.

"Oh, dear," she gasped.

"Oh, dear, indeed," said Mr. Nubbles, advancing. "Come here, miss."

Marianne tried to obey, but in her confusion she lost all sense of direction, and Mr. Nubbles had to indicate where she was to go. When they finally met in the central aisle, Mr. Nubbles was no longer smiling. His heavy eyebrows and bulky form were so forbidding that the speech Marianne had prepared in hopes of some such encounter went completely out of her head. She could only stare speechlessly up into his grim face.

Had she but known it, poor Mr. Nubbles was as uncomfortable as she. His suburban home in Islington sheltered three little daughters who adored their papa and knew him for what he was: the most sentimental and softhearted of men. In order to survive in his profession Mr. Nubbles had learned to suppress or at least conceal these attributes, for theatrical management is not an occupation for the tender-hearted. Over the years he had become more or less hardened to the necessity of discouraging eager young aspirants to the stage; at first he was at a loss to understand why this girl should affect him so strongly.

To be sure, she was uncommonly pretty. Her big, melting eyes were an unusual shade of sea-blue, and her hair had reflected the footlights like silver ribbons. Her figure, too . . . Yes, she was beautiful, but it was more than that. That was something about her that made him feel paternal, protective, reluctant to hurt her. A quality of innocence.

Because he had to struggle so hard to overcome his weakness, his voice was even gruffer than usual.

"Well, young lady? What is the reason for this intrusion?"

Marianne's thick honey-gold lashes veiled her eyes. Her mouth trembled. Mr. Nubbles resisted the impulse to fling himself at her feet and beg her to be his. (He had been a widower for five years.) But he was not moved to beg her to accept a leading role in his next production. Sentiment and business were two different things. He did not even ask her to sit down. That would only have prolonged a painful interview.

"You came here intending to perform, if you could," he said, seeing the roll of music that peeped out of her bag. "I suppose someone told you that you sing very nicely?"

"Yes, sir."

"You do. Very nicely. But a professional singer, my dear, must have more than a *nice* voice."

"Oh!" Marianne gasped as if she had been doused in cold water. Mr. Nubbles hurried on with his speech. If she started to cry he didn't know what he might do.

"My dear young lady, do you have any idea how many girls aspire to a career on the stage? Do you know how few succeed? You haven't even come to the right theater. It is true that we do sometimes produce musical plays, but just now we are dedicated to the classical drama. And," he added hastily, as Marianne's eyes lit up, "don't, I beg, offer to give me Juliet's balcony speech or 'The quality of mercy is not strained.' And don't offer to serve as Miss Terry's understudy. I assure you, it is a harsh, demanding profession, not one I would like to see one of my daughters attempt. Do your friends know you came here today?"

Marianne stared at him in shocked surprise. Still reeling mentally from the abrupt destruction of her lovely daydream, this last question added insult to injury. She drew herself up to her full height (a good inch over five feet).

"That, sir, is not your concern," she said. "Good day."

Mr. Nubbles might have gone after her. But the actors were arriving; someone asked him a question that had to be dealt with immediately. When he turned again, the slight little figure in black had disappeared. She took with her Mr. Nubbles' peace of mind. He was in a foul mood during the rehearsal and the cast of *Titus Andronicus* called him hard names behind his back.

By the time Marianne reached the door her eyes were flooded with tears. She could scarcely see where she was going. Blindly she pushed through the doors into the lobby. She was hurrying toward the exit when a hand caught her arm.

"I beg your pardon," said a smooth, soft voice. "I called to see Mr. Nubbles on a matter of business, and I could not help overhearing . . . everything. My name is Wilson. I am the owner and proprietor of the Alhambra Supper Club; and I am prepared to offer you employment, starting tonight."

CHAPTER THREE

Marianne decided that some good angel must be watching over her. She was not so much impressed at the offer of a singing job, for she had expected that; coming as it did after such a crushing disappointment only made the triumph sweeter. However, only a series of fortunate accidents made it possible for her to fulfill the engagement without a long, boring argument with Mrs. Shortbody. A summons from an old friend, taken suddenly ill, had prevented the landlady from accompanying Marianne that morning, and the emergency kept her from home that same night. (Marianne's definition of "fortunate" was as egocentric as that of most eighteen-year-olds.)

Marianne was able to creep out unobserved and meet the carriage Mr. Wilson had sent for her. Her excitement received a slight check when she saw the back regions of the theater where she was to perform. There were no chandeliers or plum velvet carpets backstage, only a dusty, noisy clutter; and the dressing rooms occupied by the artistes were less well furnished and far dirtier than the maids' quarters at home had been. For reasons of his own Mr. Wilson had given her a room to herself. She had no idea this was unheard-of for a beginner, nor did she know that two of his "star turns" had been evicted in order to accommodate her.

The room contained no furniture except a few hard chairs and a long counter that served as a dressing table. A faded curtain, strung on a rope, served as a wardrobe. The streaked mirror was illumined by flaring gas jets.

As Marianne and Wilson entered, a woman turned from the mirror and stood facing them, her hands clasped in front of her. Her clothing was commonplace; a plain brown alpaca dress and a white apron, with an old-fashioned frilled cap covering her hair. But her face . . . The left side from chin to brow was a livid, puckered mask of horror. A narrow slit of blank white eyeball showed through eyelids frozen in a permanent squint.

Marianne managed to turn her gasp of surprise into a cough, covering her mouth with her hand to hide her consternation. Her subterfuge failed; the woman's right eye narrowed until it matched the other, and the unmarred side of her mouth curled in a contemptuous smile. She made no attempt to hide her dreadful face. Instead she moved a little closer to the light.

"This is Maggie," Mr. Wilson said. "She'll help you dress and make up. Miss Ransom is new at this, Maggie, so show her what to do. She'll go on after the Magnificent Mazzinis."

He went out, leaving the two women alone.

Marianne felt as if she had been transported into the pages of one of the Gothic novels she had read with shivering delight. The ghastly figure before her stood as still and silent as one of the waxen images from the horror chamber at Madame Tussaud's. A wave of faintness swept over Marianne. "It is warm here, is it not?" she murmured.

"No."

Marianne managed to smile. "I am sorry. You must be patient. This is all new and strange to me. Tell me what I must do and I'll try my best."

The tragic mask of Maggie's face was ill-suited to any emotion except malevolence, but Marianne had the impression that her speech had surprised the other. After a moment Maggie said, "First the dress. It'll be in need of fitting. Martine's a good deal stouter than you."

She took Marianne's cloak; and as the girl stood uncertain she let out a cackle of sardonic laughter. "I s'pose you allus had a maid. Can you undo a button or d'you need to be undressed, like a babby?"

"I can do it," Marianne said.

In her voluminous petticoats and modest, ribboned corset cover she was no more unclothed than in a low-cut evening dress, but she felt indecent. Maggie paid no heed to her blushes, but gave her undergarments a critical appraisal.

"You must come from th' country. That crinoline's ten year out o' style. An' nobody wears flannel petticoats. Take 'em off."

"Isn't there a screen?" Marianne asked, with an anguished glance at the door. "What if someone —"

Her protests were in vain. Maggie had her out of the petticoats in a trice. Marianne did not relax until the new dress was on and Maggie was fastening up the back. Made of shiny black satin and imitation Chantilly lace, it was pulled tight across the front and draped in huge flounces on either side. A lace overskirt ended in a train in back, and the entire mass of fabric was caught up here and there with red velvet roses.

Marianne thought the dress quite magnificent, but she had an uneasy feeling that de-

drawn up into a coiffure far more sophisticated than any she had ever worn. A heap of sausage curls on top was surmounted by a black ostrich feather pinned by a diamond spray — as the naive wearer believed. The stones were paste, but in the gaslight they sparkled brilliantly. Loose ringlets cascaded down her back and over one bare shoulder.

To Marianne's disappointment Maggie rejected most of the fascinating little pots and boxes of cosmetics that littered the dressing table. She did pluck Marianne's eyebrows, a process that drew a series of anguished squeaks from the victim, and darkened its new, high arch. A delicate application of rouge and a touch of lip salve completed the process.

Maggie had been warned not to spoil the girl's ingenue look. Even the bright-scarlet mouth only gave the impression of a sweet young maiden who is playing at home theatricals.

Marianne sighed with pleasure. She thought she looked quite mature and sophisticated.

Then, beside the exquisite smiling face that stared back at her from the mirror, another face came into view, like a hideous mask hanging over the curve of her white shoulder. The two faces, one so lovely, the

spite its somber color it did not suggest the mourning costume she ought by rights to be wearing. Gazing down, she beheld an alarming vista of bare white skin, and she clutched at the narrow bands of black lace that were supposed to hold the bodice in place.

"Too big, like I said," Maggie remarked, from behind her. "Stand still if you don't want to be pricked."

The shoulder straps were pulled tight and whipped into place. Then Maggie took tucks on either side of the bodice, and in front, narrowing the waist. Marianne was jabbed several times, though she stood as still as she could. Finally Maggie said, "There. Sit down an' I'll do your 'air."

Marianne let out a gasp as she saw her reflection in the mirror. Evening dress was permitted to be décolleté, but Mrs. Jay had her own views of what was proper for a young girl, and Marianne had never worn anything that showed so much of her upper body. The dress was not really daring, by the standards of London society; but the contrast of the black lace against the girl's white skin was almost as wickedly suggestive as Marianne thought it was.

She forgot her qualms and watched, fascinated, as Maggie's trained fingers transformed her appearance. First her hair was drawn up into a coiffure far more sophisticated than any she had ever worn. A heap of sausage curls on top was surmounted by a black ostrich feather pinned by a diamond spray — as the naive wearer believed. The stones were paste, but in the gaslight they sparkled brilliantly. Loose ringlets cascaded down her back and over one bare shoulder.

To Marianne's disappointment Maggie rejected most of the fascinating little pots and boxes of cosmetics that littered the dressing table. She did pluck Marianne's eyebrows, a process that drew a series of anguished squeaks from the victim, and darkened its new, high arch. A delicate application of rouge and a touch of lip salve completed the process.

Maggie had been warned not to spoil the girl's ingenue look. Even the bright-scarlet mouth only gave the impression of a sweet young maiden who is playing at home theatricals.

Marianne sighed with pleasure. She thought she looked quite mature and sophisticated.

Then, beside the exquisite smiling face that stared back at her from the mirror, another face came into view, like a hideous mask hanging over the curve of her white shoulder. The two faces, one so lovely, the

temptuous smile. She made no attempt to hide her dreadful face. Instead she moved a little closer to the light.

"This is Maggie," Mr. Wilson said. "She'll help you dress and make up. Miss Ransom is new at this, Maggie, so show her what to do. She'll go on after the Magnificent Mazzinis."

He went out, leaving the two women alone.

Marianne felt as if she had been transported into the pages of one of the Gothic novels she had read with shivering delight. The ghastly figure before her stood as still and silent as one of the waxen images from the horror chamber at Madame Tussaud's. A wave of faintness swept over Marianne. "It is warm here, is it not?" she murmured.

"No."

Marianne managed to smile. "I am sorry. You must be patient. This is all new and strange to me. Tell me what I must do and I'll try my best."

The tragic mask of Maggie's face was ill-suited to any emotion except malevolence, but Marianne had the impression that her speech had surprised the other. After a moment Maggie said, "First the dress. It'll be in need of fitting. Martine's a good deal stouter than you."

She took Marianne's cloak; and as the girl stood uncertain she let out a cackle of sardonic laughter. "I s'pose you allus had a maid. Can you undo a button or d'you need to be undressed, like a babby?"

"I can do it," Marianne said.

In her voluminous petticoats and modest, ribboned corset cover she was no more unclothed than in a low-cut evening dress, but she felt indecent. Maggie paid no heed to her blushes, but gave her undergarments a critical appraisal.

"You must come from th' country. That crinoline's ten year out o' style. An' nobody wears flannel petticoats. Take 'em off."

"Isn't there a screen?" Marianne asked, with an anguished glance at the door. "What if someone —"

Her protests were in vain. Maggie had her out of the petticoats in a trice. Marianne did not relax until the new dress was on and Maggie was fastening up the back. Made of shiny black satin and imitation Chantilly lace, it was pulled tight across the front and draped in huge flounces on either side. A lace overskirt ended in a train in back, and the entire mass of fabric was caught up here and there with red velvet roses.

Marianne thought the dress quite magnificent, but she had an uneasy feeling that de-

spite its somber color it did not suggest mourning costume she ought by rights to b wearing. Gazing down, she beheld an alarming vista of bare white skin, and she clutched at the narrow bands of black lace that were supposed to hold the bodice in place.

"Too big, like I said," Maggie remarked, from behind her. "Stand still if you don't want to be pricked."

The shoulder straps were pulled tight and whipped into place. Then Maggie took tucks on either side of the bodice, and in front, narrowing the waist. Marianne was jabbed several times, though she stood as still as she could. Finally Maggie said, "There. Sit down an' I'll do your 'air."

Marianne let out a gasp as she saw her reflection in the mirror. Evening dress was permitted to be décolleté, but Mrs. Jay had her own views of what was proper for a young girl, and Marianne had never worn anything that showed so much of her upper body. The dress was not really daring, by the standards of London society; but the contrast of the black lace against the girl' white skin was almost as wickedly suggesti as Marianne thought it was.

She forgot her qualms and watched, f cinated, as Maggie's trained fingers tr formed her appearance. First her hair

other so hideous, might have inspired one of the story paintings so popular in that sentimental age: the princess and the witch, or youth and old age.

Marianne had been brought up on morality tales. Mrs. Jay would have approved the way she reacted now. "There but for the grace of God . . ." She was too well bred and too kindhearted to express this sentiment aloud; instead she said in a gentle voice, "How clever you are! I never imagined I could look so well. Thank you, Maggie."

Maggie's grotesque face vanished abruptly. From behind Marianne her stifled voice said, "I looked like that onct. Not so pretty as you, maybe, but there was a gentleman-a-waiting for me after I sung, beggin' for a flower from my bokay, and ready to set me up in my own 'ouse, too."

Marianne paid no attention to the last part of this speech, which would have shocked Mrs. Jay out of her senses. She heard only the pain in the hoarse voice. Turning, she reached out impulsively and took Maggie's hand in hers. "I am so sorry; truly I am. What happened? Or would you rather not —"

"It wos a fire. We 'ad candles then. It wosn't a place like the Alhambra; the Canterbury wos respectable, it wos. I was a ingenoo. *The Moor's Bride*. I wos the bride, wif a white veil. . . ."

Marianne squeezed the limp hand. "I am so very sorry," she repeated helplessly.

Maggie pulled her hand away. "Stand up and let's 'ave a look. I ain't so sure about them roses."

Marianne obeyed. She wished, humbly, that she could remember some of the fine religious sentiments Mrs. Jay had taught her, about beauty being skin-deep, and a good heart being more important than a pretty face. But she doubted that she could have expressed these ideas with conviction. She knew, and Maggie knew, that a pretty face was important.

Maggie decided against the roses, and removed them. Then Marianne sat down again while the woman put the finishing touches on her hair and makeup.

"That'll do," Maggie said finally. "Come along, you'll be going on in a few minutes."

She opened the door. Marianne heard thumping strains of music somewhere in the distance. She became aware of a peculiar sensation in her insides. "Oh," she gasped, putting her hands on her stomach.

"Come along," Maggie repeated.

"I — I can't. Oh . . . I really feel most unwell!"

Maggie emitted a hoarse sound that might have been a laugh. "Stage fright. You'll get over it when you're out there."

At least, she added to herself, I hope so. She had not believed Wilson when he told her the girl was a beginner. Amateurs were not welcome at the Alhambra. Now, having seen Marianne's total ignorance and uncharacteristic gentleness of manner, she realized that the manager had been telling the truth. A sentiment so long foreign to her heart that she did not recognize it made her voice softer than usual as she added, "I'll come down wif you. Don't worry now."

Marianne was convinced she was going to be sick, but she had been taught to face her duty with a stiff upper lip. She tottered toward the door, where she was met by Mr. Wilson, who had come to fetch her. He nodded with satisfaction. Then recognizing the significance of her pale cheeks and trembling mouth, he smiled faintly.

"You look utterly lovely, Miss Ransom. Don't be nervous; sing as I heard you sing this afternoon, and you will win all hearts. Just nod at the conductor when you are ready to begin."

Taking her icy hand in his, he led her along the corridor and down the steep iron stairs. Neither he nor Marianne noticed

Maggie skulking along behind them.

Marianne was also happily unaware of the looks and murmurs that followed her progress. Wilson's presence, as he knew, was the one thing that saved her from some of the unsavory practical jokes that were often practiced on unpopular performers by their fellow actors: the rude placard on the back, the foot outstretched to trip, the slashed gown. The music battered at her ears, and as they reached the wings and she looked out on the stage she saw only a dazzle of light, with dim figures moving in it. The music ended in a crash, blending with an unenthusiastic spatter of applause, and the acrobats who had finished their turn ran offstage, their makeup streaked from the hot lights and violent exercise.

"Now then, my dear," Wilson said, and led her onto the stage.

She scarcely heard his introductory phrases, nor the half-ironical applause that followed it; the thundering beat of her heart drowned out most other sound. But she did hear the orchestra. As always, music had the power to make her forget herself, and this was the first time she had sung to any accompaniment other than harp or pianoforte. Catching the leader's eye, she began to sing.

After a few bars Mr. Wilson, in the wings,

relaxed and allowed a smile to curl his lips. It had worked! He was not listening to, or looking at, Marianne; he was watching the audience.

It was a somber-looking crowd. Almost the only shade of color visible was the dead black of masculine evening attire. A splash of violent magenta or brilliant red marked the places of the few women who were present. Waiters trotted back and forth serving the customers, who sat at small tables scattered about the floor; the eating and drinking continued unabated through the entire performance. But, Mr. Wilson observed gloatingly, most of the men had stopped drinking to stare.

They had never seen anything quite like Marianne on the stage of the Alhambra. Maggie had been right to rip off the offending roses; the severe black gown was now, in design, what any well-bred young lady might wear to an evening party. What made it shocking and subtly perverse was its color; for no young lady wore black unless she was in mourning, and no young lady in mourning carried on an active social life. The stark, unrelieved black framed Marianne's white shoulders, curved with reflected highlights over her breasts, and reduced her waist to nothing. Her manner was perfect. No winks, no smiles, no suggestion of double entendre in the simple, sentimental words of the ballad. She looked like a lady and acted like a lady, and there she stood, in a place where no lady would have dreamed of appearing.

Mr. Wilson rubbed his thin white hands together. She was a sensation, a novelty. Of course the novelty would wear off, it always did; but while it lasted the Alhambra would retain its hold on the most dissipated and sophisticated members of London's haut monde. And when they tired of Marianne he would find something else.

When Marianne crept into the house several hours later she was in such a happy daze she did not even feel tired. It had been just as she had seen it in her daydreams. Of course the Prince of Wales had not been there; but no doubt he would come, another night. She had sung a second time, and on that occasion she had been scarcely troubled by stage fright, so that she had been cool enough to survey the audience while she sang. What a rich, elegant crowd they were! The snowy linen and diamond studs of the gentlemen, the satin-lined evening capes and gold-headed canes . . . She had been a trifle surprised to note that people kept drinking and eating while she sang, but concluded that this must be the mode in London. Some of the men had been quite nice-looking. One especially, sitting at a table to the right of the stage, had looked just like the Byronic hero of her dreams — a thin, clean-shaven face with curving dark brows and high cheekbones. She had not been able to judge his height, since he had been sitting, but she was positive he must be tall. And he had never taken his eyes off her the entire time.

She hoped to dream of the handsome Unknown; instead she dreamed of Mrs. Jay scolding her for some childish misdemeanor, and woke in a sweat of terror, because Mrs. Jay's distorted face had been so terrible.

II

Marianne's luck held — though in retrospect it would be hard to say whether that luck was good or bad. Her landlady's friend did not improve, so Mrs. Shortbody remained away from home. Had she been there, Marianne would never have been able to continue her career without explanations, since her schedule necessitated her leaving the house late in the evening, after the other residents had retired. She was able to do this because the overworked housemaid and cook went to bed early, and because her room was next to the back stairs. Marianne was able to creep down them unobserved, unlatch the kitchen door, and pass out. It was a miracle that none of the enterprising denizens of London's extensive underworld happened to try that unlocked back door. No doubt something of the sort would have happened sooner or later; but Marianne's career was over sooner rather than later.

It may seem incredible that Marianne should continue to be unaware of the real nature of the establishment in which she was performing. That she did may be attributed to two factors: first, the abysmal ignorance of a young lady of that period, and second, the assiduous efforts of Mr. Wilson to keep her ignorant. Even he underestimated her naivety; he felt sure that when she discovered that the "theater" was one of London's most infamous clubs, pandering to the jaded appetites of titled and wealthy roués, she would be too pleased by her success to object. However, he knew full well that her greatest charm — aside from her undeniable beauty — was in her innocence, and he did his best to maintain it as long as possible.

On the first night he managed to spirit her out of the place before any of the habitués could locate her. The task became harder on each succeeding night, but Wilson kept the would-be suitors at bay, insisting, in the face of ribald remarks, proffered bribes, and incredulous laughter, that the girl was precisely what she appeared to be, and that he could not permit an innocent young lady to be harassed. As he was well aware, the possibility that this might be true only made the suitors more eager.

Marianne had been appearing for slightly over a week when the inevitable happened.

She was a trifle preoccupied that evening, since she had learned that Mrs. Shortbody's friend was recovering nicely, and that the landlady hoped to return home within a day or two. When that happened, she would be forced to tell Mrs. Shortbody the truth. Though she did not feel she was doing anything wrong, she had a vague, uneasy feeling that Mrs. Shortbody might not share that opinion, and she was not looking forward to telling her.

However, when she arrived at the club her spirits soared, as they always did at the prospect of performing. The applause had gone to her head; she was fast becoming stagestruck. Mr. Wilson was waiting for her, as he always was, and on his arm she swept past the crowd waiting at the stage door.

Maggie returned Marianne's smiling greeting with her usual gruff nod. The woman's manner was never effusive; Marianne did not notice that she seemed disturbed about something, nor did she pay attention when Maggie drew Wilson aside and spoke urgently to him. The manager interrupted her after a few sentences with a wave of his hand and a curt dismissal.

Marianne had gotten over her stage fright by now; she moved onto the stage with cool assurance, her dimples very much in evidence. As the orchestra played her introduction she let her eyes wander over the audience, and her heart leaped as she recognized a face she had not seen since the first night — that of the dark, Byronic gentleman. She scarcely noticed the man who was with him. The latter was stout, gray-haired — too elderly and plain to be interesting.

As she sang she let her eyes wander over the audience in professional style; and the slightest of frowns puckered her forehead when she saw another familiar face. This man had been there every night, at the same table, one of those in the row nearest to the stage — from which she deduced, correctly, that he was a favored customer. He was dressed with a richness conspicuous even in that haunt of the wealthy; the studs on his shirtfront were rubies so large as to verge on vulgarity. The gaslights brought out the lines and wrinkles on his sallow face. He was bald, except for a fringe of dark hair. His eyes were dark too, though they were so sunk in pouches of flesh that their color was scarcely discernible.

Perhaps because she was nervous about the forthcoming interview with Mrs. Shortbody the unknown's unwinking regard affected her even more unpleasantly than usual, and when she had finished her song she left the stage at once instead of acknowledging the applause as she usually did. She was annoyed to find that Maggie was not waiting with her wrap. It was the first time she had had to go to her dressing room unaccompanied, though Wilson had not continued his escort service after the first night. He had made it eminently plain to the other performers that the slightest gesture against his star would be repaid with interest. So, although Marianne's progress was followed by stares and mutters, no one molested her as she made her way back to her room.

Maggie was not there. Grumbling at the inconvenience, Marianne got out of her dress — no easy task, since it had several dozen fasteners down the back — and hung it up to prevent its creasing. She was about to slip into her cotton wrapper when the dressing-room door was opened.

Marianne did not even glance up. "So there you are! I wondered what had —"

She saw the man reflected in the mirror, and shock stopped her speaking. The rubies in his shirtfront reflected the light like drops of liquid blood.

Marianne whirled around, clutching the dressing gown to her breast. The intruder smiled, if it could be called that; a spasmodic movement of the lips that did not alter his cold, hard stare.

"Nicely done," he said in a drawl. "And quite unrehearsed! Is it possible, I wonder, that Wilson could have been telling the truth after all?"

Marianne recovered enough breath to speak. Though frightened and angry, she still did not comprehend the full extent of her danger.

"How dare you!" she exclaimed.

The man's unpleasant smile intensified. He extended a gloved hand and closed the door.

"Sir, if you do not leave immediately . . ." Marianne began.

"Very well, very well; you needn't play the innocent with me; I am the Honorable Percival Bagstock, and I can well afford your price. We may as well come to a private arrangement, eh? Saves paying Wilson his cut."

Marianne let out a wavering shriek.

Terror constricted her breath, so the scream was not very loud; but it had a remarkable effect on Bagstock. His face darkened with fury. Gripping his gold-headed cane, he lunged at her, moved as much by anger as by lust, for he honestly believed that Marianne's outrage was pretense, designed to raise the price of what he desired. His violent, vicious rages were well known in his own circle; even his peers tried not to irritate Bagstock. And what had he to fear from a cheap performer?

Marianne's strength was no match for his. He had her pinioned in his arms before she could scream again.

"Very well," he snarled. "If this is how you prefer it —"

Marianne felt her senses leaving her. The dark, ugly face bending over her grew blurred. Then the hard arms relaxed and Bagstock's expression changed from anger to blank astonishment. He collapsed in an ungainly heap; and there stood Maggie, the gold-headed cane still raised in the gesture with which she had struck him down.

Marianne's knees gave way. Maggie did not allow her to fall; dropping her weapon, she seized the girl's bare arms in a grip that left bruises, and shook her violently.

"Quick! Make a run for it, now, 'afore he comes to. Where's your gown? Here . . . No time to fasten it, throw your cloak over. . . . Come, quick."

Automatically Marianne obeyed the commanding voice, the hasty, fumbling hands that helped her dress. Maggie pushed her out of the room and guided her down the stairs. When they reached the stage door, the doorkeeper looked up.

" 'Ere! Where do'ye think you're going?"

"A breath of air," Maggie answered, and propelled Marianne through the door before the man could reply.

The night air was not salubrious. It was thick with fog — not the black, choking peasouper common in the later winter months, when millions of coal fires added their poisonous fumes to the dampness, but heavy enough to blur the outlines of objects and shroud the streetlights in a white veil. Supporting Marianne's swaying form, Maggie headed toward the light at the end of the alleyway. "You got money?" she demanded.

"I . . . My bag. I left it —"

" 'Ere it is." Maggie looped the ribbons over her limp arm. " 'Old on to it, for Gawd's sake. Curse 'im, I shoulda known.

. . . Seen 'im watching you, shoulda known it was a false message. . . . Look 'ere, take 'old o' yourself, don't faint nor nothing. You know what you gotta do?"

Marianne groaned.

"Gawd 'elp you," Maggie muttered. "If you an't even more 'elpless than I thought. . . ."

They reached the main thoroughfare. To Marianne's dazed eyes it seemed like a scene from a nightmare, a dark landscape through which shrouded forms moved like ghosts. Maggie, peering through the fog with keen, accustomed eyes, put her fingers to her mouth and let out a shrill whistle. Marianne jumped. Maggie shook her again.

"Listen," she said breathlessly. "Go straight 'ome and stay there till you can get out o' London. Wilson won't look for you, 'e's not that kind, but if Bagshot finds out where you live. . . . 'E didn't see me, but 'e'll know who done it. 'E allus knows. They say 'e's in league wif the Devil. Old 'Arry'll take me in. I 'ope. . . . 'Ere's the cab. D'you 'ear me? D'you understand what I'm saying?"

Marianne nodded dumbly. With a quick, violent gesture Maggie pulled the hood of the girl's cloak up to cover her head; but before the folds settled into place her hard, rough hands briefly stroked the golden curls.

Then she turned to look at the driver of the hansom cab that had pulled up beside them. It was just as well Marianne did not see the look on the man's face as he studied her, or hear the brief exchange between Maggie and the driver. He thought, of course, that she was a streetwalker heading for home after a meeting with a generous patron. Still in a stupor she supplied the information that was demanded and sat like a wooden statue during the long, jolting ride. How she got into the house she could never remember; but seemingly she had wits enough to lock up, and undress. Not until she was in bed did the full reaction strike; she lay shivering, her teeth chattering, for what seemed like hours, until sleep, or unconsciousness, overcame her.

CHAPTER FOUR

As Marianne sat on the window seat looking out, she could not help but be struck by the difference between the view before her and her memory of her last night in London: the eerie, distorted sounds, the blurred forms moving through veils of fog, and the sickening terror that had turned her into a walking puppet.

The view from the window was lovely — green lawns like emerald velvet, flower beds glowing with chrysanthemums and late roses, and beyond, the gleaming water of the Thames. Here at Richmond the water was not so foul as it was in the city, where it served as a watery trashbin for every form of debris. Mr. Pettibone was a successful merchant who had married money, and he lived up to his income.

Unfortunately the handsome house and grounds were the only attractive part of the position Marianne had been forced to accept. Her lips tightened as she heard sounds from the adjoining room, where Master Cyril Pettibone and Miss Abigail Pettibone were supposedly at their lessons. It was clear that Master Cyril was up to his usual tricks. She ought to go back and stop him from doing whatever he was doing to Abigail; in fact, she had soon learned that it was unwise to leave Master Cyril unsupervised for any length of time. But after four days of Cyril she simply had to get away from him occasionally. Having set sums for the two children, she had escaped into the night nursery to enjoy the illusion of privacy for a few moments. She was seldom allowed that luxury. After a long day with the children she was expected to serve as companion and errand girl for her mistress, doing everything from winding wool to playing whist when Mrs. Pettibone had no better partner.

Now she understood why there had been no competition for what had seemed such an ideal position. The only women who would accept a situation so poorly paid and so fraught with unpleasantness were the elderly and desperate; and Mrs. Pettibone would not have employed such a person. She wanted someone young and healthy enough to do the hard work she expected — and put up with Cyril. Mrs. Shortbody, who had accompanied Marianne to Mrs. Hunt's employment agency in Marylebone, had not been enthusiastic about the position. She had heard of the Pettibones, and had tried to warn Marianne with expressive nods and winks and frowns. But Marianne had been almost hysterically determined. Richmond was sufficiently distant from London to be safe, and she could begin work at once.

Marianne grimaced at the sound of a slap and a yelp from Abigail. Cyril was bullying his sister again, no other victim being at hand. She was not moved to interfere. Abigail was not as actively vicious as her brother, but she was a whining, unpleasant child. And Marianne had a great deal on her mind.

Being young and resilient, she had recovered from her experience, except for a certain degree of self-contempt for her own stupidity, and she was fully cognizant of how lucky she was to have come out of the experience as well as she had. The thing that worried her to the point of sleeplessness was the thought of Maggie. She had been too distracted that night to think coherently; not until the next day did she realize that Maggie had risked not only her job but her safety in coming to Marianne's defense. If Bagshot knew who had struck him down, neither moral scruples nor fear of retaliation would prevent him from crushing Maggie as he would have stepped on an insect. Marianne's only comfort was the hope that Bagshot had not seen his assailant, and that he would be too humiliated to admit what had happened. Maggie was not stupid; she had warned Marianne of her danger, surely she must realize that her own was even greater.

The hardest thing for Marianne to bear was her own impotence. The lowest of wage slaves herself, she had nothing to offer Maggie in the way of help or security. She could not even inquire about her without risking discovery for both of them.

Wrapped in these now familiar but nonetheless disquieting thoughts, Marianne had stopped listening to the increasing uproar from the next room. She was roused from her reverie by a loud strident voice — that of Mrs. Pettibone.

"Miss Ransom! What have you gotten to? How dare you leave the children alone? I employed you to teach them, not to — Oh, there you are. What, pray tell, are you doing here?"

Marianne turned from the window. Swollen with righteous indignation, and with well-fed flesh that even her tight corsets could not contain, Mrs. Pettibone stood in the doorway.

"I set them sums to do, Mrs. Pettibone," Marianne said. "I merely came in here to rest for a moment."

"I do not pay you to rest. Return to your duties at once." She stepped aside as Marianne came toward her, adding, "You of all people, Miss Ransom, cannot afford to be slack. You are far from succeeding in your task. You do not inspire from my darlings the respect and affection it is your duty to inspire. I wonder, Miss Ransom, if you are capable of inspiring it."

Marianne wondered too. She doubted that Cyril was capable of being inspired to any positive act or emotion. Certainly no governess could hope to control the boy when his mother was constantly pointing out her inadequacies. She looked steadily at Cyril, trying not to let her dislike show. Cyril had no such compunction; the smirk on his fat, pasty, freckled face made her itch to shake him.

"Have you finished the sums, Cyril?" she asked.

Cyril turned to his mother. "She didn't say 'Master Cyril,' Mother. Isn't she supposed to say —"

"Certainly she is," Mrs. Pettibone said sharply. "Miss Ransom, how often must I —"

"I forgot," Marianne said.

"Don't forget again. I want you to take

the children for a walk now. It is too fine a day for them to be inside."

"The sums —"

"Do as I tell you. Cyril has worked quite hard enough for today. As I have repeatedly told you, Cyril is delicate. Too much mental effort can bring on brain fever."

Cyril grinned. He looked, Marianne thought, like one of the turnip faces children carved on Guy Fawkes Day, all wide mouth and pale, doughy face. He had every reason to look pleased. Not only was he excused from the sums, which he undoubtedly had not done, but the walk would give him a chance to practice his favorite activity — tearing something to shreds. If Cyril could not find an animal or bird on which to operate, he would tear the petals off flowers.

"Very well," Marianne said. "Children —"

"Put on your jacket, Cyril," Mrs. Pettibone interrupted. "And heavier boots. Must I constantly remind you of your responsibilities, Miss Ransom?"

After a prolonged period of idiotic, meaningless wrangling, Marianne finally got the children out of the house, and Mrs. Pettibone returned to the drawing room to harass the housemaid.

Watching Cyril chase his sister, brandishing a stick, Marianne thanked heaven she had only two young Pettibones to watch over. Three of the same species would have left her gibbering. Really, she thought, trying to find some humor, however ironic, in the situation, the Pettibones were like another species, made of flour and water, like underbaked gingerbread people. She had seen very little of Mr. Pettibone, but he appeared to be as doughy as the rest of the family, like a great bag of suet pudding molded into shape by his trousers and coat, his small gray eyes as blank as currants in his pale face.

The two children plodded along ahead of her. Overfed and underexercised, they did not even run like normal children. Cyril made a dark, squat blot on the grass. His legs were like sausages stuffed into his tight trousers. Abigail, wearing a blue velvet coat — Marianne knew she would be blamed for every spot on that coat — emitted squeals of terror as her brother pursued her. She had reason to be afraid. Cyril had no imagination, his routine never varied, and both Abigail and Marianne knew what it would be. First he would trip his sister, then he would fall on her, inflicting as many bruises as he could before someone dragged him off. If scolded, he would claim that the fall had been an accident.

The fall duly followed. Abigail's shrieks rose to high heaven. Marianne caught Cyril by the collar and jerked him to his feet. No wonder Mrs. Pettibone insisted on a young governess. Cyril was a solid mass of bone and fat.

As she lifted him, he kicked out at her. This was another unvarying part of the performance, and Marianne had learned to watch for it, though not before her shins had acquired several livid bruises.

She stepped briskly aside and Cyril, caught off balance, landed with a thud on his well-padded posterior. Abigail was still on her back, kicking like an overturned beetle and screaming like an engine whistle.

Marianne looked about for a weapon. Really, it was like dealing with a pair of mad dogs! They had reached the edge of a small copse of trees that bounded one side of the property, and although Mrs. Pettibone inspected this grove daily and lectured the gardener about any negligence, there were sometimes a few fallen branches to be found. On this occasion she was lucky. She was able to pick up a stout stick, which she held in one hand as she addressed Cyril.

"Get up and leave your sister alone."

Like a dog, Cyril had an instinctive skill in judging how far he could go. Something in Marianne's voice and expression — not to mention the stout stick — told him he had lost this round. He got to his feet, eyeing her balefully, and Marianne knew she would have to be on her guard the rest of the day.

She lifted Abigail up. The little girl's eyes were quite dry, but her nose was running. It usually was running. The concept of allergies was far in the future, so Marianne had attributed Abigail's running rose to general ghastliness, and indeed, who is to say she was wrong? She wiped the nose, dusted off the blue velvet coat as best she could, and they went on, with Abigail clinging close to her side.

Sunlight filtered through the branches onto the well-trimmed path they followed. Nothing on Mrs. Pettibone's property was allowed to grow naturally; even the undergrowth was restrained. Yet the grove did shelter animal life, the only place on the property where it could live, and Mrs. Pettibone did not allow traps to be set because of the children. For this reason the grove was Cyril's favorite walk. He was too slow to catch a normal bird or animal, but occasionally he would find one that was sick or hurt; and in spring — oh, bliss! — there were often nestlings fallen to the ground.

On the first day of Marianne's employment they had gone walking in this grove. Cyril had run ahead of her while she was trying to console the howling Abigail — and nursing the pain of her bruised calf. When she caught up with him, he had found a small animal. There had not been enough left of it for her to identify its species; in fact, after the first appalled glance she had turned aside and been sick, not because of the condition of the creature — as a country girl she had seen animals mangled in various unpleasant ways — but because of the fact that Cyril had obviously enjoyed mangling it.

Now she quickened her pace slightly, dragging the reluctant Abigail with her, as Cyril ran ahead. She was so tired, physically and emotionally, that even slow movement was an effort. With incredulous disbelief she remembered spring mornings when she had run like a deer through the fresh green grass. It seemed like centuries ago.

The angry cries of the birds warned her of what was happening, and suddenly, quite without warning, a great wave of fury swept away her fatigue. Dropping Abigail, she bounded forward, around the curve in the path that had hidden Cyril from her sight.

The bird was a robin. How Cyril had managed to catch it she never knew; perhaps it was old and sick and ready to die . . . but not at Cyril's hands. Its breast heaved and its beak opened and closed as Cyril jerked the feathers from its tail.

Marianne was on him so quickly he had no chance to escape. In the relief of allowing the suppressed rage of days to show, she felt abnormally alert; as she plucked the bird from his hands she thought it did not appear much hurt, and she placed it carefully to one side before twisting her hand in Cyril's collar and dragging him down the path, far enough from the bird so that no carefully calculated kick could strike it.

What she did next was done quite deliberately. She stood still for several long moments, automatically avoiding Cyril's kicks, while she contemplated her intentions. Then she sat down on a picturesque, moss-covered log, and arranged Cyril over her knee.

Country bred, she was much stronger than her fragile appearance led people to expect, and on this occasion anger lent power to her muscles. The stick came down with a thoroughly satisfactory thwack on the seat of Cyril's trousers; and the first blow astonished him so much that he stopped squirming, so the succeeding blows landed right on target. In an era where regular caning, on the naked backside, was an accepted part of educational training, the beating she gave Cyril was trivial, but he shrieked as if he were being skinned alive. He was unaccustomed to physical chastisement and, like most bullies, did not even try to defend himself against a stronger opponent.

How long Marianne would have gone on spanking him if nothing had happened to stop her is debatable. However, the interruption occurred before she had gotten her anger out of her system. A cry of outrage, louder even than Cyril's howls, echoed through the grove. Marianne, who had been watching the dust rising from Cyril's trousers with genuine enjoyment, looked up to see that she had an audience — not only Mrs. Pettibone, but a strange gentleman.

Marianne released Cyril, who rolled away like a hedgehog, and rose to face her employer.

"I must ask you to accept my notice," she said coldly. "Effective immediately."

"Notice? Notice?" The words were barely intelligible; Mrs. Pettibone — as she was to tell her husband later — was gasping with motherly indignation. She took a few deep whooping breaths and recovered herself sufficiently to continue. "You give me notice? I give you one hour in which to remove yourself! How dare you, you . . . I shall give you in charge! Not an hour, not five minutes

. . . Cyril, darling, come to Mama."

Cyril started to snivel. He crawled to his mother.

"She hit me. She beat me, Mama. I'm bleeding, Mama. Cyril hurt!"

Mrs. Pettibone caught Cyril to the maternal bosom. Fixing Marianne with one last, terrible look, she swept away. She had forgotten Abigail. The child stood with one finger in her mouth for a few seconds; then she scuttled off after her mother.

Reaction left Marianne shaking. She dropped back onto the log. What had she done? Back to London, with its manifold terrors, and the specter of Bagshot hovering over her.

"It was worth it," she said aloud.

"I certainly hope so," said a voice. "I have never seen bridges more thoroughly burned."

After the first quick look, Marianne had completely forgotten the strange gentleman, who had effaced himself behind a tree trunk, from which vantage point he had watched the confrontation with considerable interest. She had thought herself alone; the shock of hearing a stranger made her start. An even greater shock ran through her when the gentleman stepped out from behind the tree, and she recognized him. The Alhambra, the table to the right of the stage, on the last night . . . She had thought him handsome then — a dark, Byronic hero.

Now all she could think was that Bagshot had tracked her down. Her first mindless instinct was to flee; and she had actually turned, poised for running, before common sense returned. For whither could she flee? There was no refuge nearby. Mrs. Pettibone would be happy to assist any enemy of hers.

Turning back, she faced her adversary, as she thought him. Her chin was high and her shoulders were straight, but the pallor of her face and the terror that darkened her blue eyes were not lost on the man who watched her.

"Return to Mr. Bagshot and tell him to leave me alone," Marianne said. "If he persecutes me, I will proclaim his infamy to the world. There is a law in England to protect the weak and helpless."

The unknown gentleman's lips pursed in a silent whistle. Then he began to laugh. "Good heavens, you *are* naive, to talk of the protection of the law to a legal practitioner. Never mind; I now perceive your difficulty. It arises, I assure you, from a misapprehension. So Mr. Bagshot is connected with your sudden disappearance, is he? I need not ask how; his pursuits are notorious." Then, seeing that Marianne's anxiety prevented her from following his meaning, he added, slowly and clearly, "I do not know Mr. Bagshot personally. I am not in his employ. He did not send me to find you. I am acting for another person, who wishes only to help and protect you. Will you allow me to take you to that person?"

Marianne eyed him distrustfully, and after a moment he went on, "Here is my card. If you like, I will drive you to the house of your friend, Mrs. Shortbody; she has seen my credentials and will assure you that I am respectable."

Marianne took the card he held out to her. The name, Roger Carlton, meant nothing to her; but there is something inherently conventional about a printed name and a calling card. Somewhat reassured, though far from convinced, she began walking toward the house. Carlton followed.

"I see no reason why I should trust you," she said. "Once in your carriage . . ."

He grinned and twirled a nonexistent mustache.

". . . I will whip up the horses and carry you off to a fate worse than death! My dear young lady, it appears to me that you have no option but to trust me."

They neared the house. As if in emphatic

punctuation of Carlton's last comment, the front door opened and Marianne's portmanteau landed with a thud on the steps. It was followed by a rain of miscellaneous garments.

Marianne let out a shriek of indignation and began to run. Grinning more broadly, Carlton went after her. He was amused to observe that the threat of damage to her wardrobe could arouse a female even more than a threat to her person. He had sobered, however, by the time they reached the house, and when Mrs. Pettibone appeared, her arms full of Marianne's property, he spoke sternly.

"One moment, madam! I am this lady's attorney, and I assure you that you are accountable in law for any damage to her belongings. She must be given time to pack them and remove them."

Mrs. Pettibone, who had been on the verge of tossing the remainder of Marianne's things onto the steps, was visibly affected by this reference to the law. She looked so foolish standing there with her arms loaded down like a slovenly housemaid that Marianne almost laughed.

Mr. Carlton took out his watch and glanced at it. "One hour," he said.

It did not take Marianne as long as that.

She was as anxious to leave as Mrs. Pettibone was to be rid of her. Carlton stayed with her while she gathered up her possessions and good-naturedly helped her carry her boxes out. No one else offered to do so.

Waiting on the circle before the house was a carriage. It was the most elegant equipage Marianne had ever seen, drawn by a pair of matched gray horses whose coats shone like satin. The carriage itself was varnished to a high degree, and painted a rich but subdued green. On the door was a gilded and enameled coat of arms.

The sight of the carriage stopped Marianne for a moment. Mrs. Jay's tutelage had not emphasized the ancient and honorable art of heraldry, so she was unable to read the charges on the shield; but upon seeing the coronet emblazoned above, she realized it could not belong to a mere "Honorable." So, with the dismal feeling that the last bridge had indeed been burned, she allowed herself to be helped into the coach. When Carlton asked if she wished to be driven to Mrs. Shortbody's, she replied wearily, "What difference does it make? Take me where you will."

Carlton shook his head in exasperation. "How very dramatic you are! Well, I refuse to drive any distance with a quivering, nervous female who may burst into hysterical screams at the slightest provocation. Here — Wilkins . . ." The coachman, having stowed away Marianne's boxes, came to the door of the carriage, his hat in his hand. "Sir?" he said.

"Are you familiar with the Honorable Percival Bagshot?" Carlton asked.

"Now sir," was the reproachful reply, "you know us don't associate with such as he. Her Grace would never —"

"That will do," Carlton interrupted. "Well, Miss Ransom?"

Marianne was too vexed at his insulting comments to appreciate his efforts to reassure her. "Proceed, sir," she said haughtily. "Only spare me your conversation during the drive and I will endure what befalls me."

Her companion looked as if he wished to slam the carriage door, but the coachman performed that office and then mounted the box. They were off; and despite her lingering apprehension Marianne could not help feeling relieved at seeing the last of Pettibone Manor.

Carlton observed her request to the letter. He did not utter a word, and although there were many questions Marianne wanted to ask, pride prevented her from beginning a conversation. Her nervousness increased as the city closed in around them. The dirt and grime, the pinched faces of beggars, and the raucous, vulgar shouts of street vendors brought back only too vividly the scenes from which she had fled.

After the usual delays the carriage left the teeming streets and turned into a drive flanked by high stone columns. No house was visible, only clusters of tall chimneys lifting up over the tops of the evergreens that lined the drive.

Though the Ransom family was of good blood, they and their country neighbors had no claim to noble titles or great wealth. One really cannot blame Marianne for being aroused to the liveliest feelings of apprehension by the grandeur that surrounded her from the moment the carriage passed between the gilded iron gates. When it stopped before the facade of a mansion so large that its farthest wing was dwarfed by distance, only courage and her newborn sense of fatalism enabled her to accept Carlton's hand and descend from the conveyance.

Carlton, on his part, was not unmoved by her pallor and the coldness of the hand he held. Knowing Bagshot by reputation, he had some comprehension of her feelings. But his sympathy was diluted by his masculine impatience with female vapors and by other antagonistic sentiments of which Marianne knew nothing. He also realized that the quickest way of relieving the girl's fears was to show her what awaited her. In silence, therefore, he led her to the door.

It appeared that they were expected. Before Carlton could ring, the door was opened by a butler of impressive proportions and dignified visage. Carlton delivered his hat into the possession of this personage.

"Her Grace . . . ?"

"Awaits you in the small blue parlor," replied the butler.

A footman in powdered wig and green satin knee breeches opened a door to the right. The entrance hallway, floored in a pattern of green malachite and yellow marble, was so large it seemed to take forever to cross it. Carlton took Marianne's arm, more in the manner of a warder leading a prisoner than that of a gentleman escorting a lady. He propelled her through the door; it closed smoothly behind them.

Marianne found herself in a room even larger than the hall; dazedly, she wondered what the size of the *large* blue parlor might be. The walls were hung with damask. Chandeliers like frozen waterfalls tinkled in the breeze of the closing door. All the furnishings, from the curved and gilded loveseat upholstered in blue velvet to the innumerable porcelain and crystal ornaments scattered about, were of the lightest and most delicate nature. The pale colors and vast, shimmering expanse of waxed flooring created an impression of cold, though fires blazed at either end of the room.

This vast, chilly expanse was occupied by three living creatures. One was as out of place as a bear in a boudoir; red-faced, corpulent, his wiry gray hair standing up on end, he stroked his bushy mustache with one finger and glared at Marianne through a pair of gold-rimmed spectacles that had come to rest on the bulbous tip of his nose. The other occupants suited the decor. One was a dog, or so Marianne deduced, though only a blue bow distinguished the front end from the back end of the mop of long white hair.

The lady who held the dog was a larger, living version of the Meissen shepherdess that stood on the mantel beside her. Snowy hair, exquisitely coiffed, framed a face from which all color had fled. Marianne had a confused impression of soft, pale fabrics, rich with lace and embroidery, enfolding her slender frame.

Carlton cleared his throat. Before he could speak the dog let out a sharp, piercing yelp, as if the lady's white hands had contracted around its body. Dropping the animal unceremoniously onto a nearby chair, the lady glided toward Marianne, her arms extended. The color had rushed hectically into her face.

"My darling child," she cried. "Found at last! So long lost, so happily returned to my arms. Found at last!"

It was too much for Marianne. Nervous apprehension, bewilderment — and the more prosaic fact that the Pettibone parsimony and the unpleasant table manners of Cyril had prevented her from eating that day — all combined to bring on an attack of giddiness. The room slipped to one side, the lady's face blurred into a featureless white oval, and she felt herself falling into darkness.

CHAPTER FIVE

When Marianne came to her senses she did not at first understand where she was. She lay on a surface so soft it felt like floating, surrounded by clouds of the palest rosy pink. It was as if she had been lifted up into the sunset. She tried to raise her hand to her swimming head and found that her wrist was held. Fingers moved and pressed and then released her; a voice said, "Drink this."

A glass was held to her lips; she swallowed automatically. The liquid was thick and rather sweet. Then the same voice said, "She will do. It was merely a swoon — or a pretty counterfeit of one."

The gruff masculine tones assured Marianne that she was still in the land of the living — and that, if she had died, Paradise was not quite what she had expected. The comment was answered by a woman's voice, soft and refined, but thrilling with indignation.

"Horace, how often must I tell you to refrain from such statements? You will strain our friendship if you persist."

This voice was the one Marianne had heard just before she fainted. The details of that amazing encounter came back to her. She opened her eyes and realized she was lying on a bed canopied in pink chiffon, the hangings held back by twists of silk roses. Turning her head, she saw the porcelain lady leaning over her.

"Are you better, my child?" she asked tenderly. "Roger has told me of the dreadful place in which he found you, and of . . . But I will not speak of that, and you must never recall it. How could I have rushed at you so! I blame myself. Naturally you are bewildered. You can know nothing of your true history."

A growl, so heavy with cynicism that it required no words, came from the tall, stout man standing beside the lady. His gold-rimmed glasses had slipped even farther toward the end of his nose. It required no great effort of intelligence for Marianne to deduce that it was he who had expressed doubt as to the genuineness of her faint. Had his fingers touched her hand? The fact that he was in the act of returning a gold watch to his pocket confirmed her theory that he might be a doctor. Whatever he was, he was plainly hostile toward her. Thankfully she turned her eyes to the gentle face of the lady.

"I don't understand, ma'am," she began.

The doctor — for such, Marianne soon discovered, he truly was — gave another snort of outrage. "Ignorant girl," he exclaimed, "you are addressing the Dowager Duchess of Devenbrook. Kindly use the proper —"

"Horace." The Duchess spoke gently but firmly. "One more word and I will ask you to leave."

"Honoria, you know I speak out of concern for you. The state of your health . . . The feverish excitement of this meeting — of the past few days —"

"But my anxieties are now relieved, in the joy of this meeting," the Duchess assured her. "I appreciate your concern, old friend, but I must insist that you keep still. The poor girl is confused enough. I will enlighten her. But first, a glass of wine — something to strengthen her —"

"A glass of wine will make her sick, or tipsy, or both," said a voice from the other side of the bed. Marianne rolled her eyes in that direction, feeling rather like a bird in a cage surrounded by cats. She was not surprised to see Carlton smiling down at her with his now familiar look of wry amusement. So bewildered was she that this first of her new acquaintances seemed almost like an old friend. She looked at him beseechingly, and he continued, "A bowl of soup might be more to the point. Sit up, Miss Ransom, and assure the Duchess of your good health. Then perhaps we can get on with this — er — discussion. I have an appointment this evening and would like to keep it. No, Duchess," he added, as that lady made a protesting gesture, "I beg you will not suggest that we leave you alone with the young lady. I, as your legal adviser, and Gruffstone, as your medical adviser, owe it to you and to ourselves to be present."

The Duchess agreed to this, but insisted on a brief interval of recuperation for Marianne first. The girl was certainly in need of attention. She had not taken the time to change her gown after the rough and tumble with Cyril, and the long dusty ride had improved neither her complexion nor her attire.

Under the lady's direction she was bathed, brushed, perfumed, and wrapped in a gown of the same delicate shell pink that filled the room. The unobtrusive luxury of her surroundings, from the huge marble bath to the gold-backed hairbrush wielded by the maid, were completely new to Marianne — but she found they were not at all difficult to get used to. She had never seen such a bedchamber. Pink, tulle, mother-of-pearl, and gilt covered every surface, and silk roses spilled in lavish profusion. It was obviously a girl's room, and as Marianne's strength returned she wondered who the lucky young lady could be. The wardrobe from which the maid took the pink tea gown was filled with equally beautiful garments. Though Marianne was too shy to voice the questions that had crowded into her mind, she began to formulate a hypothesis. Perhaps the Duchess had lost a beloved daughter or granddaughter, the original owner of the bedchamber and the lovely clothes.

Marianne's restoration was completed by the suggested bowl of soup; in fact, she was able to eat quite a respectable amount of the food presented by a neat parlormaid dressed in black alpaca, with long streamers hanging from her white lace cap. So gentle was the Duchess's fond regard that Marianne's appetite was not inhibited in the slightest. Turning to her hostess as the servant removed the tray, she started to speak. Smiling, the Duchess put her finger to her lips.

"I have promised my good friends, Carlton and Gruffstone, that I will tell you nothing until they are present. Do you feel strong enough now to receive them?"

Marianne, completely awed at receiving

such deference, indicated that she did.

The two gentlemen were admitted, and at the Duchess's suggestion they removed to an alcove at the far end of the room, which had been fitted up as a sitting room. The Duchess insisted that Marianne recline on a rose velvet chaise longue, and she tucked a fleecy shawl around the girl with her own aristocratic hands.

Though appreciating the kindness, Marianne was beginning to feel stifled by the unceasing attentions from a lady older than she and greatly her superior in rank. Having no longer any fears for her safety, she would have remonstrated, or at least demanded answers to the many questions that vexed her, but for one thing; her fear of distressing the Duchess. Her active imagination had by now filled in the details of the story she had invented to explain the peculiar circumstances in which she found herself. The dear old lady *had* lost a child, and her brain had been turned by the tragedy. Perhaps, Marianne thought pitifully, she believes I am her daughter returned from the grave! The doctor's concern confirmed this idea.

Convinced by the explanation she had woven from these hints — and ignoring the many holes in the fabric — Marianne allowed herself to be coddled. She was moved by genuine pity and gratitude, and was prepared to disillusion the unfortunate lady as gently as possible.

The doctor squeezed his large frame into a dainty little armchair It groaned as he shifted his weight. "Well?" he said belligerently.

"It is difficult to know how to begin," the Duchess murmured. "It will come as a shocking surprise to her."

"Allow me," Carlton said. Leaning in a negligent attitude against the window ledge, his arms folded, he viewed all of them with detached amusement. "How old are you, Miss Ransom?"

"Eighteen," Marianne replied, without thinking; and then, in surprise, demanded, "How do you know my name? And how did you find —"

"Never mind," was the reply. "The means by which I found you will be explained in due course; they are not important. You claim to be the daughter of a Squire Ransom of Yorkshire?"

"I *am* his daughter." Marianne sat upright. "What are you implying, sir?"

"Nothing to your disadvantage, I assure you." The young lawyer's eyes narrowed. Behind his constant, disconcerting amusement Marianne caught sight of another emotion, harder and more threatening. "The Duchess does not deny that you believe yourself to be the person you claim to be. What she denies —"

"Roger, you are doing this very badly," the Duchess exclaimed. "Naturally she would not remember any other life, having been adopted at such an early —"

"Adopted!" Marianne fell back against the cushioning pillows. "But . . . ma'am — Your Grace —"

"There can be no doubt about it." The Duchess patted the girl's limp hand. "You are the very image of my lost darling, my David."

Marianne felt as if her face had frozen into an expression of imbecilic surprise — mouth ajar, eyes wide.

"Your husband?" she asked.

A sharp intake of breath and a furious glare from the doctor warned her that she had made a faux pas. The Duchess merely smiled sadly. "No, my dear. David was my friend, my son in affection if not in name. I have mourned him for eighteen long years."

"It is impossible," Marianne stuttered. "I assure you —"

"David was in Yorkshire nineteen years ago; the Keighley circle was particularly prominent, and he —"

"He was all over England that year," the doctor interrupted rudely.

The Duchess waved a languid hand, dismissing this criticism. "I knew he had left a child. It Came To Me." Her impressive tone invested the statement with such significance that it might have been written in capitals. She turned to Marianne. "He would have married your mother had it not been for his tragic death. I am so happy that she found a good man to give her child a name; but now it is time for pretense to end. David's genius must not be lost."

Eyes alight, cheeks pink, she stared into space as if she saw a vision invisible to the others.

"Genius?" Marianne repeated.

"Have you never heard," the Duchess asked, "of David Holmes?"

She might have been asking, "Have you never heard of Ludwig van Beethoven?" Or "Mr. Charles Dickens?"

A vague memory stirred in Marianne's mind, but she could not pin it down. Gaping like a fish, she shook her head.

"Are you familiar," the lawyer inquired coolly, "with table turning? Spiritualism? The occult?"

"Charlatanism," the doctor added in a growl. "Hocus-pokery, paganism . . . Oh, very well, my dear Honoria, I will say no more."

"You have already said quite enough," the Duchess reproved him. She looked at Marianne. "Your father, my dear, was a man gifted with unique spiritual powers, a prophet equal to the great men of the Bible. The world's finest medium."

Marianne was familiar with the words the lawyer had mentioned. The spiritualist phenomenon had spread like wildfire from its humble beginnings in 1851, in a small town in Massachusetts. Five years later no fashionable London gathering was complete without an attempt at table turning. Ghostly hands and luminous trumpets pervaded the parlors of the wealthy, raps and thumps echoed through the darkened drawing rooms. Yorkshire had its own circle, and although the initial enthusiasm of devotees had been dimmed by exposures of flagrantly fraudulent mediums, giggling girls still played with planchettes and summoned the spirits of Julius Caesar and Pocahontas. As a clergyman's widow, Mrs. Jay disapproved of what she considered a frivolous, heathen practice. Whenever she ran across a newspaper story about haunted houses or spiritualism she gave Marianne stern lectures about the evils of dabbling in such matters.

Had she but known, her attitude was bound to inflame Marianne's curiosity as a healthy hoot of laughter would not have done; for, the girl reasoned, if spiritualism were merely an idle fad, the vicar's lady would not have been so angry about it.

Thanks to this clue she was able to remember that she had read about David Holmes in a magazine article devoted to spiritualism, but she was unable to recall the details of his career. She said as much.

The lawyer replied. "Mr. David Holmes was barely nineteen when he came to this country, after considerable success as a medium in his native land. He was the son of a coal miner and his wife, from the state of Pennsylvania —"

"His mother," the Duchess said, "was descended from the Dukes of Argyll."

"So she claimed," Carlton said dryly.

"The second sight," the Duchess murmured. "Her Celtic heritage . . ."

The lawyer waited politely for her to finish, but she did not go on. After a moment he continued, "David Holmes was a delicate boy, subject to fits of — er — fits. His person was handsome, his personality engaging. He took no money for his performances, but he never lacked wealthy patrons who gave him every luxury.

"When he came to England he immediately became the rage. Moving ever upward in society, he was the darling of the royal courts of England, and the imperial court of Russia. At one time he was actually engaged to marry a young relative of the Czar's. For reasons which were never made public, that affair fell through."

"He loved another," the Duchess murmured.

"Whatever the reason, Mr. Holmes left St. Petersburg," the lawyer went on. "He proceeded to Rome, where he was accused of heresy and expelled from the city. He had always been a devout Roman Catholic, and he was palpably distressed at learning that his religious superiors frowned on his activities. He lost his powers altogether. He announced to the world that his spiritual guides had departed for a period of one year. He was received sympathetically by his friends in England. . . ."

Here the lawyer shot a glance at his patroness, but she appeared not to notice. Her face had a rapt, dreaming expression.

"The year was almost over," Carlton said, "when Mr. Holmes went for a walk one winter night. He was never seen again. His cloak — have I mentioned that he habitually wore a long black cloak rather than an overcoat? — this garment was found next day entangled in the roots of a tree that hung over a rapidly rushing river near the spot where he had last been seen. Though inquiries were prosecuted with the greatest vigor, no other trace of him was ever discovered, and it was concluded that he must be presumed drowned. Since he left no heirs and no property, there were no legal complications. The coroner's jury agreed on a verdict of misadventure; but there were those who hinted that he had taken his own life, in despair over the failure of his spiritual powers."

"Never!" The Duchess had been listening after all. Her cheeks flushed with indignation. "Those were vile rumors, Roger. David's faith forbade suicide."

A violent creak of the doctor's chair preceded his comment. "My dear, many of his own friends felt he had killed himself. They accused the Church of hounding him to death."

"Equally absurd!" the Duchess cried. "These so-called friends were jealous of me, because I had his company and his confidence. He had been in cheerful spirits and was eagerly anticipating the return of his powers. Why, that very evening, he told me we would have a confidential chat about it after he returned from his walk."

"He was staying with you?" Marianne exclaimed. "Here?"

"No. Devenbrook Castle, in Scotland, was the scene of David's last days on this plane." She took the girl's hand in both of hers. "My dear, I hope this sad tale has not distressed you. Death, as David taught me, is only a doorway into a better world."

Marianne was not at all distressed — at least, not in the way the Duchess meant. It was difficult for her to feel any emotion over a father she had never known, particularly when she very much doubted that the relationship had existed. However, she squeezed the hand that clasped hers so kindly and tried to assume an expression of appropriate melancholy.

"Your Grace," she began timidly.

"You must not be so formal. My darling David called me by my name."

"I could not possibly do that!"

"Perhaps not. But something warmer, something closer. Aunt Honoria? Or . . ."

Marianne was overcome with a sudden shocking desire to giggle, as other alternatives popped into her mind. Grannie Honoria? Mother Honoria? Horrified at herself, she bit her lip. She had never been encouraged to indulge in fits of temperament and did not recognize incipient hysteria resulting from a series of stupefying shocks. She was, however, aware of the meaningful glances exchanged by the two men. It was clear to her now that not only did they doubt the Duchess's belief in her parentage, but that they suspected her of being an adventuress — quick to take advantage of an elderly lady's sad obsession. She resolved to do nothing to confirm such unworthy suspicions.

"Please," she murmured. "With respect — I don't feel just now that I can . . ."

"I quite understand." The Duchess squeezed her hand. "Time will solve that problem, as it will solve so many others."

Again the doctor and the young lawyer looked significantly at one another. As if that look had communicated their silent agreement, the lawyer said firmly, "Duchess, far be it from me to mar your happiness at this moment, but it is my professional duty to be practical. You are prepared to accept this young — er — lady as David Holmes's daughter, without proof, without the slightest evidence —"

"Only look at her!" the Duchess exclaimed.

Carlton shook his head. "You forget, I never knew Mr. Holmes. In my opinion the photographs of him show no striking resemblance to Miss Ransom. And even if they did —"

"Horace." The Duchess turned impetuously to her old friend. "You knew David, knew him well."

The doctor's chair had been emitting a series of alarming creaks — evidence, Marianne suspected, of mental perturbation displaying itself in physical discomfort.

"The only resemblance I can see is in her coloring," he growled.

"Precisely." The Duchess's hand brushed Marianne's hair. "That rare, unmistakable shade of pale gold. David was the only other person I have known who had hair of that color."

"No evidence." Again the lawyer shook his head. "Now, Your Grace, pray let me proceed without interruption. I admit that Doctor Gruffstone was struck, when he first saw Miss Ransom, by the resemblance you insist upon. This carries some weight, in view of his — er — personal feelings about the matter; he was the first to declare that such a fancied resemblance was not enough in itself. Therefore, I took it upon myself to make certain inquiries — or rather, since the doctor was then at liberty, he was good enough to make them for me. He has just returned from Yorkshire."

"You dared!" The Duchess half rose. There had been a certain regality even in her ordinary manner, but now Marianne saw the true nature of the result of centuries of noble ancestry. "Roger, you are my trusted adviser and the son of my old friend, but you have gone too far. How dare you act without my knowledge!"

"I dare because it is my duty. Will you wait to hear what I have to say? After that you may dismiss me. That is your privilege. But I request — nay, I insist — upon being allowed to carry out my responsibility toward you so long as I am in your service."

Marianne held her breath as the two confronted one another, the current of antagonism between them almost visible. Carlton's rocklike imperturbability was as impressive in its way as the flaming anger of the lady. And, as flame may touch a rock and then retreat, leaving it unscratched, the Duchess's anger subsided.

"You are correct, Roger. Proceed."

The lawyer's face relaxed into its habitual expression of bored amusement. He seemed almost embarrassed at his display of genuine feeling.

"I have not heard Dr. Gruffstone's report myself. I had hoped that we could wait to hear it before communicating with Miss Ransom —"

"You mean," the Duchess interrupted, with a note of humor, "you hoped you would not be required to communicate with her after you had heard it."

"Quite right." Carlton returned her smile. "As it turned out, I was forced to precipitate action. Learning that Miss Ransom had disappeared without warning or explanation from — er — her place of employment, I felt I ought to find out what had become of her. One of the persons at — er — that place was acquainted with her address —"

"Maggie!" Marianne exclaimed. "Was it Maggie? Did you see her? Is she safe?"

"I am not familiar with the person to whom you refer," the lawyer replied, looking at her in surprise.

"She helped me to escape. I have been so worried about her! If he learned that she had actually attacked him, struck him down, to defend me . . ."

"Attacked Bagshot?" The lawyer forgot his professional reserve and grinned broadly. Then, remembering himself, he covered his face with his hand and smoothed out the smile. "Never mind, we are wandering off the subject."

"But Maggie," Marianne insisted. "I must

find out where she is and make sure she is safe."

"Never fear, my child," the Duchess assured her. "Anyone who helped you can be sure of my goodwill. Oh, dear, I do hate to think of what you must have gone through! Who is this Bagshot person?"

"No one to whom you need give the slightest thought," Carlton told her. "I assure Miss Ransom that I will endeavor to locate this — er — Maggie person. I have the greatest interest in interviewing her." The gleam of malicious curiosity in his eyes assured Marianne that this was probably correct, and that Maggie would be assisted, if for the wrong reasons.

"If I may be allowed to resume?" Carlton asked. "Thank you, Miss Ransom. The person from whom I obtained your London address was of the male sex. You probably know to whom I refer."

Marianne nodded. She should have known Carlton could not have obtained her address from Maggie. Wilson was the only one who knew it.

Methodically Carlton resumed his report. "From Mrs. Shortbody, your landlady, I learned that you had recently come from Yorkshire. I was able to convince her of my bona fides, though naturally I did not explain the reason for my inquiries. She is under the impression that there is a small legacy involved." He added, with a meaningful look at Marianne, "Nor did I feel it was necessary to tell her where I had recently seen you."

Marianne's cheeks burned. "Thank you for that," she murmured.

"Oh, no thanks are required, I assure you. At any rate, I took Gruffstone with me the next time I visited the place to which we have been referring so obliquely; as things turned out, it was your last night there, though of course we did not know that. Having seen you, he rushed off to Yorkshire like a knight of old following the Grail, and I did my duty by returning nightly to — er — that place. It was a great sacrifice on my part, of course."

The wicked twinkle in his eye did not escape Marianne; but the Duchess took him quite seriously.

"I am deeply in your debt, Roger. I know your sober habits."

"Your Grace is too kind. To resume — when Miss Ransom failed to appear for two nights running, I returned to Mrs. Shortbody, and after a prolonged inquisition I managed to ascertain that she knows nothing of Miss Ransom's family history. She is a friend of a friend and has no acquaintances in Yorkshire."

"But she knows Mrs. Jay, and Mrs. Jay has known me since I was a baby," Marianne exclaimed. "If there were any mystery concerning any real parentage, surely Mrs. Jay —"

"I did not speak to Mrs. Jay, I spoke to her friend. I am convinced that if there is a secret concerning your parentage, Mrs. Shortbody knows nothing about it."

Marianne was forced to admire his impartiality. Though he was clearly against her, he had assessed the evidence fairly.

And why, she wondered suddenly, should I think of him as against me? I agree with him. I am not the daughter of that strange unknown man. I am my father's child. The Duchess has got it all wrong.

Seeing her absorbed in her own thoughts, the lawyer waited, with somewhat ironic courtesy, for her to return to the discussion. As Marianne continued to muse, trying to assess her real feelings, she recalled something the Duchess had said earlier, and all at once the true meaning of the casual comment dawned on her. The angry blood rushed into her face. She could not bring herself to accuse the Duchess, who had been so kind to her, so she turned her rage on a more suitable object.

"How dare you imply such things about my mother!" she shouted at Carlton.

He burst into a disconcerting shout of laughter.

"I wondered when that would strike you. No one really believes that your mother's honor is in question, Miss Ransom."

"Oh, no, my dear," the Duchess exclaimed. "Or, at least, if any such thought passed through my mind, let me apologize. I never knew the name of David's sweetheart. I am sure that if he had known about you, he would have married her at once. Perhaps only his passing prevented that. Finding herself alone in her pitiable state, your dear young mother must have been forced to give you up for adoption. That is all I meant."

The illogic of the statement and the apology failed to occur to Marianne. She could accept with relative complacency the idea that some unknown girl had committed the unforgivable sin, so long as Squire Ransom's wife was left with her reputation intact.

"Get on with it," the doctor said irritably.

"I will if I am allowed," the lawyer replied with some acerbity. "I trust there will be no further interruptions. To return, then, to what I was saying. Mrs. Shortbody, persuaded at last that Miss Ransom would hear something to her advantage, directed me to Richmond. Learning, to my surprise, that Dr. Gruffstone had — in my opinion most unadvisedly — let slip the state of our inquiries to Your Grace . . ."

"Stupid," the doctor muttered. He gnawed at his mustache. "Devilish stupid of me. Sorry."

"Now, Horace, when have you ever been able to hide something important from me?" the Duchess asked with an affectionate smile. "I knew you were trying to conceal something; and in view of the fact that I have been searching for David's daughter for several years, naturally I was able to guess the nature of the secret."

"However it came about, the fat was in the fire," Carlton said. "Her Grace insisted that I locate Miss Ransom at once. I found matters in Richmond in such a state that it seemed best to remove her. And so, here she is, and I am most curious to learn the results of the good doctor's investigations."

All eyes — including Marianne's — turned expectantly toward the doctor.

His chair gave off a perfect fusillade of creaks. Fearing for the dainty object — in which she had already, unconsciously, begun to have a proprietary interest — Marianne was relieved when he pulled himself out of it and began to stalk up and down the room. She realized that she was awaiting the doctor's statement with as much suspense as were the others. Which was ridiculous! She knew her own parentage.

"The evidence," Gruffstone said, "is inconclusive."

"What on earth do you mean?" Carlton demanded.

"Just what I say." The doctor continued to pace. "The young lady was born in York —"

"I was born at Wulfingham, in my — in Squire Ransom's house," Marianne exclaimed.

"Your mother was on a visit to York when — as she claimed — you were born a month before your time," the doctor said shortly. "I have here a signed affidavit to that effect, by a former servant, one of the housemaids." Irritably, as if he hated what he had to do, he flung a crumpled paper onto the table.

The young lawyer snatched it up and began to read. He had obviously not expected this development, and for once his countenance expressed his true feelings — chagrin and suspicion.

"It was difficult to obtain the facts," the doctor continued. "Particularly when, as I believed, it was necessary to conceal my reasons for demanding them. Few of the servants who were alive at that time are to be found. Mrs. Ransom's maid, who might have been useful, has been dead for ten years. Those few who remained in Mr. Ransom's employ departed for other positions after his estate was settled. Many of the older villagers remember Miss Ransom and her parents quite well, but naturally they were never admitted to the confidence of the Squire and his lady. If there was a secret, it was well kept."

"That is precisely the nature of a secret," the Duchess said. "It should not be common knowledge. If Mrs. Ransom desired to have the child adopted as her own, she would make sure that few people, if any, knew the truth."

"No doubt," the doctor agreed gloomily.

"Oh, nonsense," Carlton exclaimed. With a pettish gesture he threw the affidavit back onto the table. "It seems to be in order, but it tells us nothing. Why should Mrs. Ransom endeavor to conceal the fact that she had adopted a child?"

"I can think of many reasons," the Duchess retorted. "Women have strange fancies when the prospect of motherhood blesses them. If, let us say, the lady lost her own child and found another to take its place . . . Or if she knew the unfortunate mother and pitied the girl's situation . . . Oh, there are a dozen reasons! So you found no one, my poor Gruffstone, who could testify that the child was actually born of Mrs. Ransom?"

Her eyes sparkled with the anticipation of victory. The doctor's grim look softened into a smile as he bowed in sardonic acknowledgment.

"So far, my dear Honoria, you win. It was impossible even to discover the name of the physician who attended upon Mrs. Ransom in York."

"But there must be someone," the lawyer insisted angrily. "What of the friend or relative Mrs. Ransom was visiting at the time?"

The look the doctor turned on his young friend was comically like that of a large shaggy dog who has done something naughty.

"Dead," he replied.

"The nurse?"

"Dead."

The lawyer struck the table sharply with his clenched fist. "I tell you, this is absurd. We are going about it backward. The burden of proof does not rest on us, to find evidence that Miss Ransom must be her mother's child; it rests with her to prove she is —"

"With me?" Marianne exclaimed angrily. "I am attempting to prove no such thing, sir. I deny it. I do not believe . . ."

Her firm denials died on her lips as she encountered the Duchess's steady regard. The faded blue eyes were gentle, smiling, and confident.

"But you are the last person who would know," the Duchess said softly. Then, with apparent irrelevance, she went on, "I perceive, my dear, that you are wearing a pretty old-fashioned locket. Would it, by any chance, contain portraits of your parents?"

"How did you know?" Marianne exclaimed.

It was, in fact, a reasonable deduction. Such lockets were common, and those who had been bereaved often wore trinkets containing locks of hair or pictures of the deceased. The Duchess smiled complacently.

"It Came To Me," she said. "May I see it, my child?"

Marianne unfastened the chain and handed the locket to the Duchess, who pressed the catch that opened it. Her faint smile deepened. Still holding Marianne's locket, she drew from the soft lace at her throat a similar jewel, though this one, unlike Marianne's plain gold ornament, was a creation of jet and enamel and tiny diamonds. Opening it, she turned the two lockets and held them side by side.

The portrait of the Squire had been done years before by a local miniaturist, to match the painting of his pretty brown-haired wife. Even then he had been the epitome of John Bull — ruddy-faced, coarse of feature — and the questionable skill of the painter had not flattered him. Mrs. Ransom had suffered less in the process of being transferred to ivory, but the face might have been that of any young lady of fashionable prettiness.

Beside these two commonplace, if amiable, faces, lay that of a young man. No question, in this case, of the painter's skill; he had caught to perfection the blue eyes that shone like aquamarines, the halo of pale-golden hair, the delicate, almost feminine mouth.

There was no need to comment. After a moment the Duchess returned Marianne's locket and replaced her own in its hiding place next to her heart. Even the lawyer looked shaken.

"After all," the Duchess said calmly, "there is no need for all this fuss, is there? I am satisfied; Miss Ransom is entitled to her own opinion and shall not be forced to change it against her will; and as for you two silly men, I don't care what you think! If I had decided to assist some deserving young lady who found herself in difficulty, you would both admire me for my kind heart. Perhaps I may form an organization for that purpose. There is certainly need of it, if half the sad stories I hear are to be believed. I have chosen to begin my patronage with Miss Ransom. What is wrong with that?"

The effect of this speech on the two gentlemen amused Marianne. Unable to deny its killing logic, yet totally unconvinced, they exchanged looks of mutual disgust. The lawyer was the first to recover his speech.

"What is wrong," he said, "is your state of mind, Duchess. So long as you are convinced that this young person is David Holmes's child —"

"My state of mind is my own affair," the Duchess interrupted, with such cold dignity that even Carlton was silenced. Seeing the effect of her reproof she smiled at him in a kindly fashion. "Come, Roger, let us be friends. You have been most helpful, and I am deeply in your debt. Cannot we leave it at that?"

Such affable condescension, Marianne thought, must have its effect; and indeed the young man's lips twitched as though he wished to return the lady's smile. But he was more stubborn than she had realized.

He shook his head.

"I must point out to Your Grace —"

The Duchess cut him off by rising to her feet. "Very well, if you persist, there is one way of proving I am right. I had wished to give Miss Ransom time to adjust to the change in her condition, but in order to convince you two, I will beg her cooperation in a brief . . . experiment."

"I cannot refuse you anything," Marianne replied. "After your kindness . . ." She might have added, "and your insistence," for the force of the lady's rank and conviction were indeed difficult to withstand. Instead she finished, "But I do not understand what sort of experiment you mean."

The lawyer let out a heartfelt groan and slapped his forehead with his open hand. A lock of dark hair tumbled becomingly across his brow.

"I believe I do," he exclaimed. "For the love of heaven, Your Grace, you cannot intend —"

"Indeed I do, if Miss Ransom is willing. It is your own fault, Roger; if you were not so unreasonable, this would not be necessary. Let us adjourn to the White Room."

Carlton turned to the doctor. "Gruffstone, can't you forbid this farce?"

The doctor rubbed his nose with his

knuckle, apparently in order to assist the deep cogitation that wrinkled his brow. At last he said reluctantly, "Perhaps, after all, Carlton, this may be a way out, eh? You know my sentiments; they are in accord with your own. If the experiment should fail, as it must, why then. . . . Eh?"

This enigmatic speech left Marianne in deeper confusion than before, but the others seemed to understand. The Duchess laughed merrily.

"You are not a skeptic, Horace, you are completely close-minded. Come along, then."

She took his arm, making, at the same time, a beckoning gesture to Marianne, and the two older people left the room. Carlton, abandoned by his ally, swept his hair from his brow in a gesture positively Byronic.

"Curse and . . . er . . ." Meeting Marianne's wide, apprehensive eyes, he amended the remark, which would undoubtedly have been unfit for a young lady's ears. "What are you waiting for?" he demanded. "Let us go and get this disgusting business over with."

Marianne finished disentangling herself from the shawl that encumbered her limbs.

"I am perfectly willing to oblige Her Grace in anything she asks," she said. "I have not the faintest idea what all this is about, but if it will settle what I already know to be true — that I am my father's daughter — then by all means let us get on with it."

Ignoring the lawyer's proffered hand, she swept with dignity toward the door. She had to wait for him, however, since the others were nowhere in sight and she had not the slightest idea how to reach the room in question. With a gesture Carlton indicated the direction they were to follow, and they started along a seemingly interminable corridor. This terminated in a Grand Gallery, hung with oil paintings in heavy gold frames. So vast was this apartment that the Duchess and her escort, now visible at its farthest end, were well out of earshot. The lawyer spoke softly.

"I begin to wonder if I have done you an injustice. Either you are a consummate actress, deserving of a far better position than the one you left so abruptly, or you are genuinely bewildered by all this."

"How kind of you to give me the benefit of a doubt!"

She meant to stare steadily ahead, but could not resist a glance at him. His smile gave his thin face a kindness and charm it had not had before. He was very much taller than she; she had to tilt her head to look up into his face. Perhaps that is why she stumbled, so that it was necessary for him to catch her arm. He continued to hold it as they went on.

"Sarcasm does not suit you," he said. "Yet, if you are what you seem, you are certainly entitled to exhibit it. Well, to err is human; I am not often wrong, but . . . Tell me, Miss Ransom, have you ever played at table turning, or been present at a séance?"

The touch of his hand was warm and firm without being in the least presumptuous. It stimulated a current of heat that ran through Marianne's entire body.

"Why, yes," she replied. "Once, when Mr. Billings and his daughters came to visit, Amelia, the elder, proposed that we have a séance. It was most exciting. But then we found that Mary had been rapping on the floor with her shoe, and Amelia began to laugh, and . . . Oh! You don't mean to tell me that this experiment —"

Again she stumbled, and since they were at that time descending a staircase, the lawyer's grip on her arm prevented what might have been a nasty fall.

"Watch where you are going," he muttered.

Marianne began to feel dizzy again. She attributed this sensation to the latest shock she had received, but had no intention of using it as an excuse for sympathy.

"These slippers are too large," she said. "But I asked you —"

"Not surprising that they should be. Her Grace insisted on purchasing them and the other garments without having the least idea of the appropriate sizes. She seems to have done remarkably well, in general. I suppose she will pretend that she obtained your dress size from the ghost of David Holmes."

It was clear that he was trying to change the subject because he regretted the question that had given Marianne her first clue as to what was in store for her. Why, she thought, with a flare of anger, his soft words mean nothing. He does not trust me at all.

At the foot of the staircase they turned to the left and followed another corridor into the depths of the mansion, coming, at last, to an open doorway.

The first sight of the chamber within made Marianne gasp. It was not its magnificence that affected her, though the decor employed only the richest materials. There was not a trace of color in the room. Hangings, rugs, walls were of the same unrelieved white. Crystal chandeliers and sconces, ornaments of ivory and glass gave the room a frosty glitter that lowered the actual temperature by many degrees. Even the wood of the furniture had been overlaid in silver or mother-of-pearl.

Marianne did not need to be told that this was the scene of her purported father's occult activities in Devenbrook House.

A circular table in the exact center of the room, covered with snowy damask that fell in ample folds to the floor, was surrounded by several chairs upholstered in white velvet. The Duchess was already seated. With an imperious gesture she indicated that Marianne should take the chair at her right. The doctor moved along the wall loosening the heavy silver cords that held back ivory damask draperies. As each section of fabric fell into place across the window, the room sank deeper into an absence of light which was not so much darkness as an eerie, pallid shadow.

For a brief time the Duchess sat quietly, her head bowed as if in prayer. Then she lifted her eyes toward Marianne and the girl felt a cold, unpleasant thrill run through her. The strange light stripped colors of their warmth; the old woman's face was as bloodless as that of a corpse. Only her eyes burned with fanatical fervor. Not until much later was Marianne able to understand the emotion that filled them. It was hunger — insatiable, greedy desire. Though she did not fully comprehend, the intensity of that desire could not help but fill her with the gravest sensations.

"Do you understand what we are doing, my dear?" the Duchess inquired.

The gentle, familiar voice was reassuring — but it was also startling, coming from that frightening face. Marianne felt peculiar. The blood seemed to be slowing in her veins, her heart to beat less rapidly.

"No," she murmured.

"Open your heart," the Duchess whispered. "Invite *them* to enter. They are there, just beyond the veil of the senses — thronging, hoping for contact. Empty your mind and heart of all but thoughts of love."

Marianne did not find it difficult to empty her mind. Indeed, her thoughts seemed to be dissolving into an inchoate mass. It was rather a pleasant sensation.

"One moment." Carlton's deep voice cut through the fog that filled her head. "I would like to see Miss Ransom's hands on the table."

"Roger, Roger." The Duchess shook her head sadly. "Very well; we will clasp hands."

She extended her shapely white fingers. Marianne took one of her hands and the doctor took the other. The girl's right hand was clasped by Carlton.

Thinking thoughts of love was not as easy as Marianne had supposed. Dutifully she first considered her father and tried to squeeze out a tender memory or two. All she could conjure up was a vision of the Squire as she had last seen him, flat on his back in bed, with the counterpane rising to a hump over his stomach and his ruddy face peering around it like a harvest moon behind a winter hill.

Deciding that her father had not the face or the figure to inspire romantic visions, Marianne tried to think of something else. Very faintly, through the thickness of window glass and curtains, she heard a trill of birdsong. After that the silence was absolute. Her ears began to ring.

Two loud, distinct raps echoed through the stillness. The Duchess's hand contracted, squeezing Marianne's fingers painfully, but neither pressure nor sound disturbed her dreamlike reverie. In a voice vibrant with repressed emotion the Duchess said, "Is someone here?"

A single rap replied. Then the table began to move.

It tilted violently once and then settled into a steady rocking motion. Marianne had the sensation of swaying in tempo with it.

The lawyer's hand was like a vise, locking hers, but she scarcely felt his touch. Her head had become detached from her body. It was floating several inches above her neck. The sensation was very odd. She heard a soft moan and wondered if it had come from her neck or her head.

"She is going into a trance," the Duchess exclaimed, in a thrilling whisper. "Marianne, can you hear me?"

A sharp staccato creak replied.

"For pity's sake, Honoria," the doctor exclaimed.

"Be still! Marianne . . . *whoever you are* . . . speak to me!"

Marianne tried to oblige. No words came from her lips. She was floating in a crystalline underwater world, lifted up by the limpid liquid, swaying with the gentle current. The table continued to rock, until all at once, with the impact of a thunderbolt, something flashed in the dim light and fell, striking the tabletop with a solid thump. The table stopped moving. On it lay a small carved bust barely eight inches in height, with the frosty glitter of ice. Despite the dimness of the room and the transparency of the rock crystal, Marianne recognized the carved features. The empty eyes seemed to stare directly into hers; the delicate mouth was curved in a smile. The carving, which had apparently materialized in midair over the table, was of David Holmes.

Marianne made a rude, gurgling sound and, for the second time in an hour, fainted.

CHAPTER SIX

Her awakening was a nightmarish repetition of the earlier recovery, and she wondered hazily if the entire episode, culminating in that shattering materialization, had been merely a feverish dream. The same rosy draperies surrounded her, the same fingers touched her wrist, the same gruff voice demanded, "Drink this."

Here, however, the pattern changed.

"Oh, do stop fussing, Horace," the Duchess exclaimed. "She needs only peace and rest. Such exhaustion often follows the trance state; I have seen it before."

"Balderdash!" was the emphatic reply. "Today's young ladies fall into a faint on the slightest provocation. Sheer affection and tight lacing, that is all. If I have said it once, I have said it a hundred times —"

"Yes, my dear doctor, you have," Carlton interrupted. "Do you feel that this is not a counterfeit swoon, then?"

At this Marianne closed her eyes and kept them closed. She was still giddy, but beneath her physical distress, a feeble anger stirred. They were all talking about her as if she were incapable of hearing or responding. Even the Duchess treated her like a new toy.

The discussion continued. The Duchess insisted that Marianne had not fainted, but gone into a trance; the doctor declared that her pulse rate and pallor and other symptoms were suggestive of a faint; and the lawyer interjected skeptical comments and questions. Finally the doctor let out a roar. "This must stop. We are bickering over this unfortunate young woman as if she were a bone and we a pack of hungry dogs . . . I beg your pardon, Honoria!"

"No, my dear, you are quite right."

"Then I beg of you, leave the girl in peace! I have given her a mild sleeping draft; she will probably not wake until tomorrow morning. I propose to perform the same service for you. The excitement is very bad for you, Honoria, very bad indeed."

"I am a little tired," the Duchess admitted. "But very happy, Horace; very happy."

"All the same, you need rest. Please go to your room and lie down. I will come to see you shortly."

"Only let me call her maid."

"I will do that when I have made sure she

is sleeping. Promise me one more thing, Honoria."

"What?"

"No more of these experiments."

"You know I cannot promise that."

The doctor sighed. "Then promise you will do nothing without my prior approval. If you care nothing for your own health, you have no right to risk the health of Miss Ransom."

This appeal had the desired effect. The Duchess murmured an agreement. Marianne felt a light hand brush her forehead, but she kept her eyes obstinately closed.

After the Duchess had gone out, Carlton said, "Is she asleep?"

A finger lifted Marianne's eyelid. An alarming sight confronted her: the doctor's face three inches from hers, every vein and wrinkle and grizzled hair magnified by proximity into a caricature of late middle age. Still determined to remain unresponsive, she managed not to resist his touch, or change her expression, and after a moment the inquiring finger was removed. Marianne was aware of the faint odors of tobacco, bay rum, and brandy. She had never before been so conscious of her sense of smell and was, in this case, unable to analyze the constituent elements or understand why she suddenly felt more at ease. These odors were, in fact, the ones she unconsciously associated with her father. In the Squire's case they were usually overlaid with a stronger smell of horse; but even in this diluted form they were obscurely comforting.

The doctor answered Carlton's question. "No, she is not asleep."

"Just as I thought!"

"Keep your voice down. In fact, you had better go."

"When you do."

"Good Gad, man, do you suppose the young woman requires a chaperone? I will stay until she drops off. I prefer not to leave her until I am certain she has no adverse reaction to the medicine I have given her. I know nothing of her medical history."

"But I want to talk to you."

"Do so, then. She cannot hear us if we keep our voices down."

Marianne felt a childish surge of triumph. She had not fooled the doctor with her pretense of unconsciousness, but he had underestimated the keenness of her hearing. She listened with all her might.

"I can't understand your coolness," the lawyer exclaimed. "We must rid the house of this — this conniving female instantly."

"Impossible."

"But she is —"

"I don't know who, or what, she is," the doctor interrupted. "And neither do you. I do know that even if we could evict her the effect on the Duchess might be disastrous. You hotheaded young fellows make me tired. Your legal training ought to have made you more circumspect."

"She is a cold, calculating imposter," the lawyer insisted. "I admit I had my doubts; but after that bit of legerdemain —"

"That is certainly one explanation of what occurred."

"What other explanation can there be?"

In his irritation the doctor forgot his own injunction to speak softly. "I can think of several. Assuming that the girl is innocent of deliberate trickery — no, no, hear me out! Consider the room itself. Holmes was accustomed to use it for his performances whenever he stayed with Honoria; who knows what devices he may have installed, unknown to her? That crystalline bust normally stands on the mantel. How it traveled from there to the table I cannot explain; but at least we can be sure it did not come from the spirit world."

"I am relieved to hear you admit it. You used to be the most outspoken skeptic —"

"And still am, I assure you. Spiritualism

is a wicked, dangerous business. But the Duchess is not a skeptic, and it is her belief we must contend with. Only consider, young Roger, what one of the alternative explanations must be, and do not press me, I beg, to voice it aloud."

The silence that followed was so fraught with emotion that Marianne could almost feel it. She had no idea what the doctor meant; the drug he had given her was taking effect, and she was increasingly drowsy. But Carlton apparently did understand. After a moment he said, in tones of the most lively consternation, "You can't be serious."

"Only too serious. I tell you, we must proceed with caution. The health of our dear old friend must be our chief concern. Please allow me to be the judge of what is best for her."

"I must do so," the lawyer muttered. "But don't expect me to be civil to the wench."

"You needn't be civil, but if you speak of her in such terms to the Duchess, you will find yourself evicted from the house," was the doctor's dry response. "Be off with you now."

The lawyer's reply was unintelligible. Marianne felt as if she were being wrapped in blankets of soft wool, layer upon layer upon layer. Gradually hearing and touch were muffled; she could not have lifted her heavy lids if she had wanted to. Just as she was entering into the final failure of all sensation she seemed to hear a voice echo inside her head. "David," it said, and, "Father." Her lips shaped the words — and others — as she drifted away.

II

The following days were the happiest Marianne had known since her father's death. As in a fairy tale, she had been transformed from an impoverished orphan into the petted, pampered darling of a lady who possessed every possible charm — kindness, noble birth, and immense wealth. At first the girl objected when the Duchess showered her with gifts. The Duchess's reply was, "I am an old woman, my dear. Will you deprive me of what has become my chief pleasure in life?"

There was no possible reply to this but grateful acceptance. After all, Marianne told herself, even if the fairy tale ended like Cinderella's, on the stroke of some symbolic midnight, she would be no worse off than before. In this she was, of course, mistaken, but she was too inexperienced to know that the removal of luxury can be worse than the absence of that commodity, and even if she had known it she probably would not have had the strength of will to resist.

Her room was a bower of every pretty comfort money could buy. Delicate hothouse flowers filled the vases and were replenished daily. The sheets on the bed were of pale-pink silk, the toilet articles were backed with solid gold. Jars of steaming bathwater were hauled upstairs every evening by panting chambermaids — but of course Marianne never saw these unfortunates; the maid who attended her was a smart young Frenchwoman whose hands dealt magically with her luxuriant hair. Every evening she was bathed and dressed in one of her lovely new gowns; her hair was twisted with ribbons and posies, her throat and wrists hung with jewels. The only unpleasant part of this process was that she had to have her ears pierced. The squire had never thought of such a thing, and Mrs. Jay had not approved of vain adornment, so this operation had been neglected. But it was worth the pain to look forward to wearing the pearl and diamond and opal earrings the Duchess had given her.

One evening, several days after her arrival, she was seated before the fire wrapped in a dressing gown of pale-blue satin trimmed with feathers. Celeste, her maid, moved noiselessly around the room laying out the clothing she would presently put on. The gown was the most elaborate she had yet worn, voluminous folds of snowy tulle over a petticoat of heavy blue silk. A cascade of silk flowers fell from one shoulder across the front of the gown and down one side of the overskirt, which was drawn back in graceful folds over a soft bustle. Marianne's hair had been secured atop her head with a wreath of matching flowers; the skillfully arranged curls cascaded down her back. With this garment went long white gloves, a lace fan, and a parure of seed pearls. They were going to the opera. The Duchess had hailed Marianne's love of music as another proof of her parentage: "David was so sensitive to music!"

This was one of the few references she made to David Holmes. If she had not abandoned her belief in the girl's real origin, at least she had not dwelled on it. Whether this was calculation, avoiding a subject that might inspire her protégée to rebellion, or genuine indifference to the opinions of others, including the one most concerned, Marianne did not know — and did not really care, intoxicated as she was by the new pleasures of unlimited wealth. She managed to push the subject down to the uttermost depths of her waking mind.

She was less successful in managing her dreams. The bespectacled, bearded young Freud was still studying at the Institute for Cerebral Anatomy; he would not invent the subconscious for another fifteen years. It is possible, however, that even the great Sigmund in his prime might not have been able to account satisfactorily for the quality and frequency of Marianne's dreams of David Holmes. Some were of such a nature that her puritanical superego (assuming that Freud was correct in identifying this feature) suppressed them altogether, leaving only an uneasy sense of malaise when the girl awoke.

With a genteel murmur of inquiry Celeste knelt before her and Marianne lazily extended one slim bare foot. The first time the maid had put on her stockings she had been torn between embarrassment and amusement. She had never had a full-time personal attendant; one of the housemaids had helped her dress for special occasions, but most of the time she had taken care of herself. Now she accepted the service with complacent pleasure, so easily does one become accustomed to what one enjoys. Slippers, undergarments, layers of fine lawn petticoats tucked and frosted with lace; then the dress, which enveloped her in a cloud of soft white. Celeste hooked the dress up the back and fluffed out the skirt. Another murmur of inquiry; Marianne, turning to the full-length mirror, gave a kindly, patronizing nod.

"It looks very well. Now my jewelry . . . please."

She was still admiring her exquisite reflection when the Duchess entered, her little dog Pierre trotting along behind her. "You look lovely, my dear," she said.

"So do you." Marianne's compliment was sincere. The Duchess's color was high and her eyes sparkled. No wonder, Marianne thought, that the doctor was willing to tolerate anything that made his old friend so happy.

He was waiting for them when they entered the drawing room, looking quite distinguished in evening clothes. His mustache had been trimmed and his unruly hair ruthlessly subdued by an application of pomade. Pierre made straight for him and leaned against his ankles. White hairs adhered to the black broadcloth as if drawn by a magnet. An expression of mild anguish crossed the doctor's face, but he rose nobly to the occasion.

"Good boy; nice little doggy. . . . 'Pon my word, Honoria, you look no more than eighteen."

"What a pretty compliment! I wish I could return it; but you look as grumpy as a bear. I trust that your scowl is produced, not by present company, but by the prospect of the evening's entertainment?"

"You know I hate opera," was the candid reply. "Silly fools rushing about the stage shouting out secrets at the top of their lungs."

"But the music," Marianne said. "That is the important thing."

"Sounds like cats on a back fence, serenading the moon."

Pierre barked sharply, as if in agreement. The Duchess laughed. "Never mind, it won't hurt you to suffer for one evening. What do you hear from John?"

The doctor's face lit up. "Good news, I am happy to say. I received a letter yesterday. I had thought the wound was in his leg, where it might have been serious, you know, but it was only in his shoulder. He expects to be invalided home soon."

"Splendid. We speak of Dr. Gruffstone's son, my dear," the Duchess explained. "Following his father's example, he qualified as a surgeon and went out to India with the

Northumberland Fusiliers. He was wounded in the fighting in Afghanistan, and we were concerned about him. . . . But where is Roger? We shall be late."

Before she had time to become impatient the lawyer was announced. They went at once to the waiting carriage. Gruffstone and the Duchess walked ahead; that left Carlton with Marianne. He offered his arm. After a moment's hesitation, long enough to let him know she acted purely for conventional reasons, she took it.

"Let us declare a truce," Carlton murmured.

"Why should we? You obviously have the lowest possible opinion of me."

"Ah, but as yet I have discovered no evidence to substantiate my suspicions."

"No doubt you have tried to discover it."

"Yes, indeed, and I will go on trying. But why should that interfere with our truce? You don't want to distress Her Grace, and neither do I . . . unless it should become necessary. Who knows, perhaps that occasion will never arise. In the meantime, let us try to be civil."

"Very well," Marianne said sweetly. "You will find, sir, that I have covered my tracks with diabolical cleverness." Then, as they neared the other couple, she went on without even a breath, "Are you fond of opera, Mr. Carlton? The human voice is my favorite instrument."

The Duchess beamed to see her young friends on such good terms.

This was the first time Marianne had been out, except for occasional visits to shops, and these had been rare; most tradesmen were more than happy to attend Her Grace with whatever wares she cared to examine. She had been looking forward to the evening, and at first it lived up to her expectations. A luxurious carriage, a gorgeous gown, a handsome escort, a box in the select upper circle of the Opera House — no girl could have asked for more, and Carlton behaved impeccably. The Duchess liked to arrive early, so most of the other boxes were unoccupied when they took their places. Gradually these began to fill. So absorbed was Marianne in the decor and the fine gowns worn by the other ladies that it was some time before she realized that she was increasingly the focus of curious glances. Not until one ugly old lady wearing a coronet leveled an opera glass straight at her did she notice she was being watched. She shrank back.

Carlton, who was nothing if not observant, remarked, "That is Lady Morton. Looks like a horse, doesn't she? And has the manners of one."

He did not trouble to lower his voice. Marianne thought the Duchess must have overheard, but although she glanced quickly, almost furtively, at the girl, she did not break off her conversation with Gruffstone. Marianne had no one to appeal to but Carlton.

"Why is she staring at me?" she whispered.

"As I said, she had the manners of a plowhorse. She would wonder who you were even if she had not heard about you. And I fancy she has heard a great deal."

"From you?"

Carlton laughed softly. "Come, Miss Ransom, you can hardly suppose that I would sink so low as to gossip with Lady Morton. Nor can you be so naive to think that the Dowager Duchess of Devenbrook can take a beautiful unknown young lady into her household without creating a stir. Servants will talk."

Marianne's eyes grew round with surprise. "They will?"

The lawyer returned her stare. After a moment he shook his head. "You are too good to be true, Miss Ransom. Be still now and listen to the pretty music."

When the lights went up after the first act, Marianne sat in a daze of delight. She had never heard music so superbly performed before. She turned to the Duchess with her face alight and exclaimed, "It was wonderful! How can I ever thank you for such enjoyment?"

"Your pleasure is thanks enough," the Duchess replied affectionately. "Would you care for an ice? Or would you like to stroll, to stretch your limbs? Roger will accompany you."

"Alas, I fear that Roger will have no such opportunity," the lawyer replied with a sly smile. "The old lady was probably out of her seat before Patti hit her last high C."

With his enigmatic speech he rose lazily to his feet, just in time to greet the woman who had appeared in the door of the box.

In the days of Queen Victoria's predecessors the opera often served as just another social gathering. The gentry visited one another's boxes during the intervals and continued loud conversations during the actual performance, to the annoyance of the genuine music lovers present. The influence of Victoria's solemn young German prince, equally fond of music and of decorum, had halted this; but Lady Morton was a survival of an earlier age and, as the lawyer had predicted, she was at the door of her friend's box the moment the last strains of music died. Barely acknowledging the Duchess's greeting and introductions — "My young friend Miss Ransom" — she settled into the chair Carlton had vacated and fixed Marianne with a bold stare.

The stare was even more formidable at close range, and its effect was increased by Lady Morton's extreme strabismus. Not only did she squint, but one eye was turned so far to the left of its normal position that only a white orb confronted the victim. The only thing that saved Marianne from nervous paralysis was the fact that Lady Morton undoubtedly did look like a horse — not just any horse, but a wall-eyed, evil-tempered old stallion who had been the tyrant of the Squire's stables till he died of extreme old age.

The ensuing conversation — or rather, inquisition — was notable as an example of how rude an elderly titled lady could be without being reprimanded or cut dead. It began with an inquiry into Marianne's family.

"Ransom. I once knew a Harold Ransom. He was up at Christ Church with my brother."

"That would not be a connection of mine," Marianne replied.

"There are Ransoms in Devonshire."

Marianne shook her head. The lady's squint became positively malignant. "Then where the devil are you from, miss?"

There being no way of evading this demand without rudeness, Marianne replied, "Yorkshire, Lady Morton."

"What part of Yorkshire?"

Marianne had no legitimate reason for wishing to avoid these questions. Nevertheless, they made her squirm, and that streak of obstinacy which her golden curls and soft blue eyes masked so effectively rebelled against Lady Morton's impertinence. She gave the lawyer an anguished glance, but he merely smiled more broadly, enjoying her discomfiture.

Mercifully the Duchess herself came to the rescue, breaking up the tête-à-tête by introducing the other visitors who had crowded the box to bursting point. "Lord Ronald . . . The Honorable Miss Ditherson . . . Lord Willoughby . . ." All were of the Duchess's generation, and all were as curious as Lady Morton. But they were not so ill-bred, and the sheer number of them, which forced conversation to become general, saved Marianne from further questions. She saw that the Duchess had drawn Lady Morton away; they were speaking softly but urgently.

The warning bell sounded and the visitors

rose to leave. Lady Morton was, of course, the last to go, and thus Marianne was enabled to overhear a snatch of conversation between the two ladies. "I promise you I will arrange it; shall we say Thursday?" the Duchess asked.

Lady Morton nodded, and shot a glance at Marianne. "Don't forget, Honoria. If anyone has a claim to matters involving our dear departed —"

But instead of a name Lady Morton emitted a grunt of pain, clutching her side and glaring indignantly at Lord Ronald, who had passed her on his way out. The elderly nobleman went on, unaware. He, as Marianne could see, had never come within touching distance of Lady Morton. If the idea had not seemed so ludicrous she would have sworn that the Duchess's elbow had jabbed into her old friend's ribs.

"Dear me, what a crush," said the Duchess, her color a trifle high. "William" — addressing the footman, who was closing the door on Lady Morton — "deny us, please, in the next interval; this is really too much, it interferes with one's enjoyment of the music."

Thanks to this directive the remainder of *Lucia di Lammermoor* passed without interruption, and the second interval was spent in quiet conversation. Yet Marianne was increasingly distracted by an odd sense of being watched, not by the stares of casual curiosity seekers, but by something more intense and more inimical. So strong had her discomfort become by the end of the opera that she was scarcely aware of the music and could hardly wait to leave.

The crush down the stairs and across the lobby was so great that she had to cling closely to Roger Carlton's arm. He treated her as he would treat any rather boring young lady to whom he was obliged to be polite. They had almost reached the exit when she saw it — a face, distinct as a carved and tinted mask, staring directly into her eyes over the backs of the crowd ahead. The features had burned themselves into her memory: the sallow, lined skin, the piercing black eyes, the twisted, evil smile.

Marianne shrieked and clutched at her escort. Her voice was drowned in the general noise; only Carlton heard it and only he felt the frantic grasp of her hands. Thinking she had slipped or been rudely shoved, he tightened his grasp; but when he glanced at her he could see that something more serious had occurred.

"What the devil . . . ? I beg your pardon. Are you ill?"

"It was he," Marianne gasped. "I should have known. I felt him all evening, staring . . ."

"Who?"

"Mr. Bagshot."

"Where?"

"There, by the door." But when she looked again, the evil face had vanished.

Carlton surveyed the crowd. He shook his head.

"I don't see him. The opera is not his type of entertainment, Miss Ransom. Are you sure it was not your imagination?"

"No, no! I tell you, I saw him! And he recognized me!"

"Hush," Carlton said. "No talk of this before the Duchess, do you hear me? It would distress her. I assure you, you are in no danger from —"

"A figment of my imagination?"

Carlton shrugged. Marianne said no more. Bitterly she realized that she could not even relieve her fears by speaking of them. The Duchess must not be worried, the doctor was antagonistic to her, and Carlton was . . . probably right. Perhaps the fleeting, frightening glimpse had only been a phantom of her uneasy mind.

CHAPTER SEVEN

On Thursday evening Marianne went through the routine of dressing for dinner with less than her usual pleasure in that sybaritic exercise. It had been a dreary, wet day, and darkness had descended early. She could hear the steady beat of the rain against the curtained windows, though the bright lights and blazing fire created a small inner world of comfort.

Her gown had been finished that afternoon by a harried Madame LeFarge, the most fashionable dressmaker in London. It was of pale-blue brocaded tulle with panels of satin bordered with pearls across the bodice and down the full skirt. Marianne contemplated her reflection with satisfaction. She had never looked so well. Yet a tiny frown marred the smoothness of her white forehead.

Over her shoulder reflected in the glass, she saw the face of her maid. The Frenchwoman's unlined cheeks and neat dark hair did not in the slightest resemble that other face she had once seen similarly reflected;

but the memory stabbed painfully into Marianne's conscience, and she dismissed Celeste. After the maid had gone she did not sit down; to do so would have crumpled her gown, and besides, she was unaccountably restless. She began pacing up and down the room.

It was the first time she had been alone since early morning, and her thoughts were not pleasant companions. Guilt had haunted her since that night at the opera. The sight of Bagshot — if it had been he, and not a fear-inspired vision — had reminded her of Maggie. In the beginning she had been unable to help the woman who had risked so much to save her, that was true; but since the change in her fortune she had done little to locate Maggie, when she could very well have done more.

Not that it would have been easy. The Duchess hated any reference to that part of Marianne's past; an expression of pain would cross her face if Marianne referred to it, even obliquely, and she would change the subject. Yet, Marianne knew, she owed it to Maggie to risk the Duchess's displeasure, even the possibility of dismissal from her gilded cage. (Now why had she thought of that metaphor?) The truth was that the Duchess's gentle inflexibility was harder for her to combat than the antagonism of the two men. It was like a steel blade muffled in ermine.

The doctor was at least open and unsubtle. Besides acting as the Duchess's medical adviser he had the status of an old and valued friend — possibly, Marianne surmised. of an old admirer, who had accepted the crumbs of friendship in lieu of the forbidden fruits of love. (Marianne's figures of speech, like those of the age in which she lived, were often trite.) At any rate, the doctor was on a familiar footing in the household and was welcome at any time. Whether he had been coming more frequently on her account, Marianne did not know. For the first few days the Duchess had insisted that he stop by to make sure she had fully recovered from her fainting fits. The doctor did so without much enthusiasm; in fact his examinations consisted of peering into her eyes, listening to her pulse, and asking her to put her tongue out and say "ah." After three such visits he bluntly informed the Duchess that her protégée was in the rudest possible health and in no need of further attention. Yet somehow he managed to drop in for tea or some other meal almost every day. He had been in the house that morning. Marianne had not seen him, but she had heard him; he and the Duchess had been shut up in the library together for some time, and apparently they had had a disagreement, for when the old gentleman left he had stormed down the hall with the heavy stride of a charging elephant and had slammed the door before the butler could get to it.

Practicing in the music room next to the library, Marianne had heard these explosive expressions of annoyance and had been amused. Now, when combined with other hints, the incident took on a new and possibly alarming significance.

She had been told to wear her lovely new dress, but when she had asked what the occasion might be the Duchess had been evasive. "A few friends" were coming in after dinner. "No formal meeting," but "I want you to look your best."

Marianne might be young and easily intimidated, but she was not stupid. Today was Thursday; she remembered the snatch of conversation she had overheard at the opera and felt sure that Lady Morton would be one of the friends referred to. She had an equally strong suspicion of what might be expected of her. Despite the Duchess's promise to Dr. Gruffstone, Marianne was certain that she had not heard the last of spiritualism and the exercise of her own supposed psychic gifts.

She had tried not to think about the séance, which had ended with the startling materialization of David Holmes's face, cloudily crystalline as ectoplasm. The experience had been frightening — and yet it had had a certain fascination. Marianne had not been quite truthful about her own experiments with the occult. The encounter she had mentioned had been only one of many such attempts; table turning was a popular parlor game, with the additional thrill of the mysterious and forbidden. Marianne had also read all the articles on the subject in the newspapers and periodicals to which the squire had subscribed.

Not that anything had ever happened. Once, indeed, when she had tried to involve Billy and Jack in a midnight séance near the graveyard, they had been transfixed by a series of unearthly howls from the direction of the Ransom monuments. Jack had collapsed in a fit of speechless terror. Billy, a born skeptic, had investigated and found Mrs. Jay's cat atop a tombstone, summoning prospective lovers.

Yet Marianne had never quite given up a belief in the spirit world. Mrs. Jay, to be sure, denounced the practice as heretical. But Marianne could not see why. The Christian faith taught that the soul survived in a better world; why was it impossible, or evil, to reach such spirits? Perhaps she herself had psychic powers, even if she was not David Holmes's daughter.

She was interrupted at this point in her reasoning by the arrival of the Duchess, exquisitely attired and glittering with diamonds, who asked if she was ready to go downstairs.

The questions Marianne had been asking herself were fermenting in her mind. She did not dare interrogate the Duchess directly, so she tried an oblique approach.

"Are your guests coming for dinner, ma'am?"

Even that seemingly innocuous question had an unfortunate effect. The Duchess's brows drew together.

"Two only. The others will join us later."

"I beg your pardon for asking. I only wondered —"

"And you had every right to wonder." The old lady's sunny smile returned. "I was not vexed with you, child. My dear old Gruffstone has put me in a bad humor, and I hate being at odds with him. If only he were not so blindly prejudiced!"

"Oh, dear," Marianne said involuntarily.

Perhaps deliberately the Duchess misinterpreted her exclamation of distress.

"There is no reason for you to be disturbed. The other dinner guest I asked on your account, after Gruffstone had insisted. . . . Well. Can you guess who it is?"

It was not difficult for Marianne to guess. Her circle of acquaintances in London was very limited and she could not imagine that the Duchess would invite her former landlady or her former employer to dine.

"Mr. Carlton," she said.

"How clever you are! Aren't you pleased? Don't you think him very handsome?"

"He is certainly handsome."

"And he admires you. I saw that from the first."

"You did?" Marianne stared.

"Oh, yes. Like so many young men he affects a cynical manner that does not do justice to his good heart. But I could not be mistaken about his feelings. I know the dear lad too well. He is the son of one of my best friends."

"I see. Is that how he became your legal adviser?"

"It was quite the other way around. His mother was actually a distant connection of mine — a cousin. When she died I naturally took an interest in the boy, who was only six years old at the time. Later he showed some aptitude for the legal profession and I was able to apprentice him to my husband's solicitor. He has done very well."

A tall footman flung open the drawing-room doors.

The gentlemen were waiting. Carlton, looking indeed very handsome in evening clothes, rose to greet them. Marianne tried to catch his eye and succeeded, but found in his blank countenance no answer to the question she tried to project. The doctor was obviously ill at ease, and the coolness of the Duchess's greeting made him look even more hangdog. Finally she relented enough to allow him to offer her a glass of sherry and he brightened visibly.

Sipping her own wine, Marianne tried to think of a way to get Carlton aside and ask whether he had had any success in tracing Maggie or discovering whether it had really been Bagshot she had seen at the opera. The opportunity did not arise before dinner was announced. It was an uncomfortable meal, since at least three of the diners were preoccupied with their own thoughts, and conversation was spasmodic.

Marianne tried to nerve herself to speak to the Duchess. After all, if she was to be expected to take part in some sort of psychic performance that evening, she had the right to be told in advance. She hoped to find an opportunity when they returned to the drawing room, leaving the men to their port; but before she could begin, the Duchess asked her to play.

"Some of those charming ballads you do so nicely. I feel a slight headache; your music always relieves me."

Marianne had no choice but to do as she was asked. For once her good behavior was rewarded. The gentlemen were prompt to join them, and Carlton came at once to the piano.

"Ah, here is one of my favorites," he said, turning over the sheet music. "Do play it for me. I will turn the pages."

The selection was a Chopin polonaise; and Marianne suspected that its chief charm for Carlton was its volume. She played it rather badly, but did full justice to the fortissimo markings, and under cover of its passionate strains Carlton was able to say in a low voice, "He was there, all right. A friend of mine saw him too. No, don't stop! I am convinced the event was pure coincidence."

"But he knows where I am — with whom I am staying!"

"You little fool, that is your surest protection. No man in England would dare attack any dependent of the Duchess's. She has connections in the highest circles. Oh, I don't say that if our friend met you wandering the streets alone at night he might not try to carry you off, but I trust you will do nothing so foolish. So long as you behave properly you could not be safer in a cage."

"I wish you would not use that word," Marianne muttered. She brought all ten fingers down in a crashing chord.

"How interesting that you should feel that way."

The piece was coming to a ragged but resounding conclusion. There was very little time. Marianne said quickly, "The woman I mentioned to you — Maggie — have you found any trace of her?"

"I have not been looking," Carlton replied calmly.

"Then do so!" She did not dare look up from the music, she was playing badly enough with its aid; but she felt his reaction of haughty rejection. "If you do not," she continued rapidly, "I will speak to Her Grace about it. I owe that woman more than my life, and I have been inexcusably remiss in repaying her. She may be ill, she may be dead —"

"Calm yourself," Carlton said harshly. "I will do as you ask if only to prevent what you threaten."

Marianne's hands dropped in a crashing discord.

"Good gracious," the Duchess said gently. "What a strange sort of music that is! Give us something quieter, my dear."

Marianne spun around on the piano stool, ribbons and curls flying. The exchange with Carlton had worked up her courage.

"Duchess, I will play until my fingers drop off if it pleases you. But — forgive me — I am somewhat disturbed in my mind. What is it that you want of me this evening? Surely I can better assist you if I am prepared."

Even as she finished speaking she was afraid she had gone too far. But the Duchess did not appear to be angry.

"You have every right to ask," she said. "Please don't blame me, Marianne. It was at Gruffstone's insistence that I kept silent."

"And mine," Carlton added. "I too felt that if you insist on proceeding with the performance tonight, Miss Ransom should have no chance to prepare herself for it."

Marianne realized that her conjectures had been right. This disturbed her less than she had thought it would. Indeed, in her anger she wished that she were skilled in sleight of hand or some other form of trickery. Not that she would ever stoop to such deceit — but oh, what pleasure it would give her to confound the skeptics, to humiliate them as they wished to shame her. In her mind's eye she saw tables rocking, tambourines and trumpets and other mystic instruments flying through the air, shrouded spirit forms advancing on Carlton, who cringed and cried out in terror.

She tried to think of something profoundly cutting and sarcastic to say, but of course did not succeed. The Duchess said worriedly, "My dear child, I never doubted you. This was not my idea, I was forced into it by that ridiculous Clarabelle Morton. For years she has cherished the absurd notion that she was David's closest friend. She pursued him and bothered him mercilessly when he was in London."

"And," said the lawyer, "she entertained him lavishly when he first arrived. There was a certain gold cigar case, I remember, and a set of diamond studs. . . ."

"He returned those," the Duchess said quickly.

"After you had given him —"

"Enough," the doctor said, with the authoritative manner he could assume when he spoke professionally. "I will not have this unseemly bickering, Roger. No use crying over spilled milk; whatever Lady Morton's methods or reasons, she is coming here tonight, and I suppose we are in for it. I did my best to prevent it, heaven knows."

"You told me yourself that Marianne is in perfect health," the Duchess said.

"It is not *her* health that concerns me."

"Well, I assure you, mine will suffer more from being thwarted than from anything. Come now, Horace, don't be an old bear. They will be here at any moment —"

"Too late, they are here," Carlton intoned dramatically, as the door burst open. In Lady Morton's usual impetuous manner she had outrun the footman, whose scandalized face appeared behind her.

The two other visitors, who were some distance behind, were among those Marianne had met at the opera — Lord Ronald Limpetry-Theobald, an extremely emaciated old gentleman who looked as if he had scarcely strength enough to hold the quizzing glass through which he stared at her; and the Honorable Miss Ditherson, a lady whose mind had apparently become petrified at the age of seventeen, though her body most certainly had aged since that far-off day. It is no wonder that Marianne had only the vaguest impressions of these two, since neither of them got a chance to say more than three consecutive words all evening.

Lady Morton refused her hostess's offer

of refreshment. "No sense in wasting time. We all know what we have come for, so let us get to it at once." The blank white eye and its more mobile companion aimed themselves in Marianne's direction. "Can't see the slightest resemblance myself," Lady Morton said forcibly.

"But her hair," Miss Ditherson exclaimed.

"And her eyes," Lord Ronald whispered.

"Common as dirt," Lady Morton shouted. "You've been taken in again, Honoria; if you had consulted me I could have warned you. But that is just like you; you don't *look* stubborn, but you *are* stubborn, and no one knows that better than I. How many times have I —"

"Lady Morton." It was Carlton who spoke, and although his lips retained the faint smile that spoke of his contempt, his eyes were no longer amused. "Should we not, as you suggest, get to the business at hand?"

"Certainly. That is precisely what I have been saying. You young rascals never pay any attention —"

Carlton grasped her arm and assisted her to rise with such vigor that she staggered. He led her out of the room.

The others followed. Marianne, side by

side with the Duchess, could not help but admire Carlton for defending his patroness; but one word Lady Morton had used stuck in her mind. "Again." Again? Was she not, then, the first young girl whom the Duchess had taken in, under the impression that she was the child of her dear departed David? One delusion, based on a certain degree of physical resemblance, may be forgivable eccentricity. A series of such delusions smacked of something far more serious.

She was diverted from these thoughts by the sight of William the footman scampering (if a person of his impressive size could be said to scamper) along the hall, trying to keep ahead of Lady Morton. He just managed it, opening the door before the lady threw herself against it.

The white drawing room sparkled like an ice cavern. A blazing fire burned on the hearth, but its glow was lost in the dazzle of dozens of gas jets reflected from crystal and silver surfaces. No matter what the temperature, Marianne thought, this room would always be cold.

It was clear that all the guests were familiar with the room and the procedure. They took their places; Marianne, directed by the Duchess, took the chair at the lady's right. She did not need to be told that this had been David Holmes's accustomed place.

In the rustle of movement that accompanied these proceedings Marianne realized that her stomach was experiencing the same sensation she had sometimes felt just before performing. She turned impulsively to the Duchess. "I don't know what to do," she whispered.

"There is nothing to be afraid of." The Duchess's face was rapt; her voice seemed to come from a great distance. "Only open your mind to the influences that will come."

The curtains had already been drawn. The sound of the rain was a distant murmur, with the hiss of the burning logs as counterpoint. No one spoke until the doctor said heavily, "I must insist, Honoria, upon the usual precautions."

"Very well." The Duchess extended her hands, one to Marianne, the other to Lord Ronald, who sat on her left.

"Hold tight," said Carlton, on Marianne's right. "Your Grace, you will forgive me for mentioning the word, but . . . feet?"

"Feet?" Marianne repeated. Carlton winked. She wanted to exclaim aloud at this effrontery, but somehow the lawyer's open amusement made the whole business more endurable. The others were so solemn!

"Feet," Carlton repeated cheerfully. As he

spoke, Marianne felt a pressure on her left shoe and knew it must be the foot of the Duchess that touched hers. "Put your foot on mine," the lawyer went on. "We touch feet as we touch hands, around the circle. You would be amazed, my dear Miss Ransom, if you knew what a stockinged foot can do in the way of producing psychic phenomena!"

"Must that *person* be present?" Lady Morton demanded, glaring in Carlton's general direction. It was difficult to tell precisely where she was looking, but no one doubted to whom she referred.

"He is quite right," the Duchess replied. "David was always the first to agree to such controls. You should know that, Clarabelle."

"Humph," said Lady Morton.

Once these arrangements had been made, the silence descended. It seemed to continue for an interminable time. Marianne's nose began to itch. She felt she would go mad if she could not scratch it but did not dare ask to have her hand freed for that purpose. She sensed that everyone was watching her, either covertly or, in the case of Lady Morton, without concealment; and she felt all the discomfort of a performer alone in the spotlight who has no notion of what is expected of her.

After what seemed eons the Duchess said, "I think we had better extinguish the lights."

"But David never —" Lord Ronald was not allowed to finish the sentence.

"David was the master," the Duchess said. "I know of no other medium who performed in full light. The vibrations are painful to the spirits."

"Fair enough," Lady Morton said. "Let's give it a try."

Marianne was surprised at the lady's acquiescence until she realized that the one good eye was gleaming with anticipation. Lady Morton would not mind seeing her old rival's protégée fail, but she desired even more the thrill of communication with the dead. Marianne wondered what it was the woman sought — what message from the other side. Or was her interest only the sickly, feverish fascination of the unknown?

At a nod from the Duchess Dr. Gruffstone obediently rose to carry out the suggestion. The light diminished slowly, as if one veil after another were being dropped before their eyes. When finally the Duchess said gravely, "That will do, Horace; thank you," the room was enveloped in shadows. There was light enough to see the outlines of forms, limned in startling fiery silhouette where the fire was behind them. Details and expressions were lost in the gloom.

The doctor took his place again. The circle was resumed.

The Honorable Miss Ditherson let out a faint cry. "I felt something . . ."

"Um," Lord Ronald agreed.

The table began to sway.

"David!" Lady Morton emitted a whoop that made them all jump. "David, are you here? Speak to me, David!"

"You needn't shout, your ladyship," Carlton drawled. "Mr. Holmes was never hard of hearing."

"Hush," the Duchess said sharply.

As if in agreement, the table gave a coy little leap upward, against the hands resting on its top.

"Honoria," the doctor began. "I beg you —"

"Horace, hold your tongue."

"But," the doctor said piteously, "this is such absolute balderdash. . . ."

There was no transition, no gap in time. The doctor's last words had scarcely died away when Marianne heard him continue, in startling non sequitur, "Her pulse is normal. Speak to me, Miss Ransom."

"Marianne, my dear, can you hear me?"

The voice was that of the Duchess. Marianne turned politely toward her, blinking because the lights were so bright.

"Certainly, ma'am. Why do you ask?"

Then the truth struck her. The lights . . . Who had turned up the gas jets — and when?

So far as she knew she had not moved from her own seat at the table. But Carlton was no longer beside her; he was on his feet, staring in wide-eyed amazement. From across the table the visitors stared too; their open mouths and wide eyes gave them an absurd look of having been duplicated. Dr. Gruffstone held one of Marianne's hands. His fingers were pressed against her wrist.

Marianne's eyes returned to the lady at her left. The Duchess was the calmest of all those present, yet her face disturbed the girl most. Exultant, triumphant passion had taken the color from her cheeks and added a feverish luster to her eyes.

"Has something happened?" Marianne asked.

"You remember nothing? You do not recall what you said?"

"Said?" Marianne repeated stupidly. "The doctor said . . . something about nonsense. . . . Then all the lights were on."

The Duchess struck her hands together.

"What did I tell you?" she cried. "I was right; I was right! Oh, David, my darling — found at last!"

She covered her face with her hands.

"Oh, blessed assurance," Lord Ronald murmured.

"Let us pray," said Miss Ditherson. She bowed her head.

"Damn," said Roger Carlton.

None of those who might have objected seemed to hear this vulgarity, except Marianne. She glanced at Carlton. He looked back at her, not as if she were someone he had never met, but as if she were the sort of person he would never have any occasion to meet. "Do something, Gruffstone, will you?" he demanded. "If you don't, I will."

"Um," said the doctor. "Quite. Yes. Um . . . ladies and gentlemen — that is, Lord Ronald — why don't you all go away? Yes. Please do go away immediately."

Even Lady Morton left without comment or complaint. For the first time since Marianne had met her she seemed completely cowed.

When the guests had taken their departure the Duchess finally stirred. She removed the veiling hands from her face, showing a countenance once more under control.

"I do beg your pardon," she said in her

familiar gentle voice. "And I thank you, Horace, for taking charge so nicely. You need not worry about me, I have never felt better. Will you and Roger please excuse us now?"

The doctor started to expostulate. The Duchess cut him short. "You may call tomorrow if you like, though there is no need. But please come early. We will be leaving shortly after noon for Scotland."

CHAPTER EIGHT

The trip north was as far from Marianne's first experience of train travel as night is from day. The Duchess's private carriage had been attached to the engine of the Edinburgh express. It was furnished like an elegant drawing room, with soft sofas on which to sleep, and its own small kitchen. If Marianne had not felt the vibrations she would have found it hard to believe she was in a moving vehicle.

She had been in a daze all day. The Duchess had been too busy to answer questions; organizing a sizable household for a long journey on short notice had required considerable effort, and not until they actually boarded the train had the Duchess relaxed. At luncheon, served on board, they had been attended by two footmen, so there was no opportunity for private conversations. As soon as luncheon was over the Duchess announced that she intended to rest, and suggested that Marianne do the same.

Marianne was unable to follow this advice. Reclining on the couch she stared out the window, watching the landscape rush past, half obscured in a gray mist of rain. The grimy suburbs of London were replaced by green countryside, and then by the dark satanic mills of the industrial Midlands before the Duchess's regular breathing changed to a yawn and then to other sounds of waking.

Marianne turned. The car was quite dark. "Shall I call your maid, ma'am?"

"No, my child. Let us sit here in the shadows a while longer. Unless it troubles you?"

"Not at all," Marianne said. Indeed, she welcomed the darkness. It gave her courage for what must be done.

The Duchess anticipated her. "I know you must be full of questions. Believe me, the only reason why I have delayed this conversation was on your account. I want so much to have you understand and accept. It is necessary for us to speak at leisure, calmly; and until now there has been no proper time. Last night I was — oh, yes, I confess it! — I was overcome. This morning there was much to be done. But now the time has come. Ask, and I will answer."

It must be understood that although Marianne's father — or rather, let us say Squire Ransom, for the situation at present is far from clear — Squire Ransom tried to guard his speech in the presence of his daughter, Marianne was by no means ignorant of the more emphatic expletives of the English tongue. She had overheard a great deal. The Squire, in one of his rages, was audible at a considerable distance, and her playmates, Billy and Jack, had not always remembered to whom they spoke. Her self-control on this occasion can only be attributed to the respect she felt for the Duchess. What she really wanted to do was pound on the window with both fists and shout, "What the b— h— happened last night?"

Instead she said meekly, "Would you mind telling me, ma'am, what I said last night? You said then that I said something, but I don't remember what I said."

"What is the last thing you remember?"

"The table began to rock. And Dr. Gruffstone remarked . . . no. First you told him to be still. Then he said something about arrant nonsense. Then he said my pulse was normal . . . and all the lights were turned on."

"You went into a trance state," the Duchess said. "Do you know what that is?"

"I . . . Yes, ma'am. I think so."

"In that condition another entity — a spirit — takes possession of the mind of the medium — you. Many mediums have spirit controls. These controls are intermediaries between the blessed ones who have passed on and those of us who wait on this side of the veil."

"I have read of such things," Marianne said. "A control is like a master of ceremonies. He introduces the ones who want to speak to us."

"Very good, my dear. A spirit control is very much like a master of ceremonies. He performs the introductions, refuses admittance to disruptive, malevolent spirits, and warns us when the performance must come to an end. Last night your spirit control came to us. Her name is Pudenzia."

"Oh, dear," Marianne gasped. "You mean, ma'am, that I said —"

"Not you. It was Pudenzia who spoke to us with your organs of speech. You were not there. That is why you cannot remember what happened. It is common in the trance state."

"Oh, dear," Marianne said again. "But — but, ma'am — how do you know I wasn't making it all up?"

This ingenuous query made the Duchess laugh. "My dearest child, the fact that you could ask such a question proves you are above such wickedness. Not that I ever thought you capable of it! However, if it will relieve your innocent mind, I will tell you that Pudenzia gave me certain information that you could not possibly have known."

"What information? Oh, do forgive me; I didn't mean to pry —"

"There can be no secrets between us now. Would you like to know exactly what you said?"

"Oh, yes! If you can remember."

"Every word is imprinted on my heart." There was a brief pause, fraught with emotion. Then the Duchess resumed. "It took us some time to realize that you were in a trance. Mr. Carlton was the first to note that your hand had become limp; then I observed the change in your breathing. I asked if you could hear me; you did not reply. I then asked if someone else was present. Your voice said: 'I am Pudenzia.' "

Marianne was thrilled. She felt no alarm because she could not really imagine that this had happened to her. It was like hearing a story about someone else.

"Was my voice different?" she asked eagerly.

"Oh, yes. It was slower; you spoke with difficulty, as if in a foreign tongue, and at first your words were halting, your sentences incomplete. I asked who Pudenzia was, and received no reply. Then I asked if someone wanted to speak to me. And Pudenzia said . . ."

"Yes, ma'am?"

"Forgive me my emotion. You have such a sympathetic nature you must have suspected that I have long been awaiting a message from . . . from David. For years I have tried to reach him, and have met with one heartbreaking disappointment after another. You see, Marianne, I am not so gullible as some people believe. I know there are many fraudulent mediums. A number of times I had received what purported to be David's words, but they never rang true; they never passed the tests I applied to them."

"Did you apply such tests last night?" Marianne asked.

"There was no need. The proof was given me. Your control, Pudenzia, told me there was a spirit who desired desperately to reach me. Never before had he found a vessel pure enough. That is most significant, don't you think? Then she said — and this, my dear, is the proof I speak of — she said, 'He carries the golden heart.' My dear, I gave David a locket of that very shape! He was wearing it when he disappeared. Now, Miss Marianne Ransom of Yorkshire could not possibly have known that."

"I certainly did not," Marianne replied, awed.

"So you see, I am convinced. These things take time and experience; you are still unskilled, and it would never do to force you beyond your strength. But when you have become accustomed to the trance state, then I may hope to hear David himself speak to me through your lips."

"Oh, ma'am," Marianne began, not at all sure she liked this idea.

"You cannot imagine how great a gift you have given me. I was in despair. Heaven forgive me, I was beginning to doubt. I have you to thank for the greatest happiness I have known since my darling passed on."

"Oh," Marianne said.

She was unable to say more. Thrilling and mysterious as her new situation was, it carried such an awesome weight of responsibility that she felt unable to sustain it. The fact that she had no conscious control over her gift made the burden even more frightening. Torn between a pleasurable sensation of importance and the fear of failure, she was more inclined to fear than to enjoy. But there was no way for her to abdicate the responsibility. The Duchess's dependence made that fact impossible.

Now cheerful and refreshed, the Duchess

ordered tea and caused the lights to be lighted. As they sipped the fragrant beverage and nibbled on sandwiches, the older woman said thoughtfully, "I have been wondering who Pudenzia was, in this life. The name is Latin, of course."

"More tea, miss?" said Wilton, the parlormaid. Marianne glanced curiously at the woman's well-schooled, impassive face, wondering what the servants thought of their mistress's obsessive hobby. She did not doubt that the servants' hall knew every detail of what had transpired on the previous evening.

"We will serve ourselves, Wilton," said the Duchess.

The maid withdrew, her eyes respectfully lowered, and the Duchess resumed as if there had been no interruption.

"I think I remember hearing, when I was in Rome some years ago, of a Saint Pudenzia."

"A saint!" Marianne exclaimed. "I don't understand. I thought Pudenzia was a spirit."

"The spirit of someone who once lived. All those who have passed beyond were once on this plane. Perhaps next time she communicates she will tell us something of her history. The saint I am thinking of was a gently born Roman maiden who was martyred by Nero — or was it Diocletian? — because she refused to give up her — er — her maidenhood and her faith to marry a pagan."

"But," said Marianne doubtfully, "Mrs. Jay told me that the saints of the Roman church were pagan idols . . . or something of that sort."

"Mrs. Jay? Ah, yes, the vicar's wife. Well, my dear, I am sorry to say that many of our religious leaders are extremely narrow people. If they were not, they would not oppose spiritualism. Not that I believe in the Roman system of sainthood. That is a misunderstanding. Pudenzia was probably a sweet, innocent girl who is devoting her time in the next world to helping those less fortunate."

In such pleasant speculations they passed the time until dinner. Marianne knew very little of the complex hagiology of early Christianity; she found the legends enthralling. The number of beautiful maidens who had embraced martyrdom rather than submit to the embraces of pagan lovers was, if not legion, at least very extensive. After the Duchess had taken a glass or two of wine she even mentioned the word "virgin" in connection with the lovely young martyrs.

After dinner they played a few games of

cards, but Marianne admitted that she found the motion of the train made her drowsy, so they retired early.

Marianne dropped off to sleep at once; but sometime later she found herself suddenly and unaccountably wide awake. She felt quite cozy in the cunning little bed and could not imagine what had awakened her. Across the way she heard the Duchess's regular breathing. She did not wish to strike a light, for fear of disturbing her companion, but ventured to sit up in bed and draw the curtain from the window.

They were in open countryside. The night was moonless and extremely dark. Yet Marianne sensed a haunting familiarity about the dim landscape, and she realized that their journey north must lead through Yorkshire. Was she now looking upon the land hallowed by memories of childhood?

She was never to know the answer. Strain her eyes as she might, she saw nothing except an occasional village or town, distinguished only by a few lights. Surely, she thought, the main line to Scotland must pass through York. But although she sat by the window for quite a long time, she saw nothing recognizable.

Finally she drew the curtain and lay down, composing herself to sleep — and wondering why it had not occurred to her, till now, that she would be so near her childhood home. So quickly had old memories been replaced by new impressions.

This time, when she fell asleep, she dreamed — dreamed that she was standing pilloried against the door of the quaint old village church while her former friends and neighbors gathered stones to throw at her. Leading the mob, her kindly face distorted, her voice shrieking curses, was Mrs. Jay. "Virgin!" she shouted, and threw a stone that hit Marianne full on the temple.

II

The express was due to arrive in Edinburgh before daylight, but naturally no one expected Her Grace the Dowager Duchess of Devenbrook to tumble out into the cold gray dawn. Her railway car was respectfully shunted onto a siding, and when the two women emerged, after a leisurely toilette and a hearty breakfast, they found the Duchess's carriage waiting. This was a much more splendid equipage than the carriage the Duchess was accustomed to use in London. Indeed, the arms on the door were so large and so brightly blazoned with crimson and gold that the noble lady seemed slightly embarrassed.

"Oh, dear, Henry has had the arms repainted again," she said with a sigh. "It is harmless enough, I suppose, but I really do not enjoy having my presence proclaimed so — so emphatically."

"Henry?"

"The thirteenth Duke of Devenbrook." The Duchess settled herself comfortably against crimson velvet cushions and motioned Marianne to join her. "We have a long drive ahead of us; make yourself comfortable and I will tell you about the family."

But before this promise could be carried out Marianne was distracted by the sights of the city, which she had not seen before; and seeing her interest the Duchess good-naturedly pointed out various landmarks. Most impressive was the view of the Castle, its time-darkened stones brooding over the lower city like a great dragon.

Clouds gathered as they left the city behind them. A gentle drizzle began to fall. The Duchess then began the explanation she had promised.

"You must know that my husband was considerably older than I. He had been married twice before and had had several children. Only two of these survived, however.

The elder, Annabelle, is the child of Lady Helen Nicholson. This unfortunate lady produced only female offspring. All died in infancy except for Annabelle, and Lady Helen perished in childbirth. The Duke then wed the Honorable Miss Pilgrim, who finally presented him with a male heir. She passed on shortly afterwards. I often thought that if his mother had lived, Willy would have turned out differently. . . ."

Marianne listened in morbid fascination to this mournful history.

"What happened to him?" she asked.

"Well . . . One must not speak ill of the dead; and no doubt Willy has learned the error of his earthly life of dissipation now that he has passed on. A mother's kindly guidance might have wooed him from his wild companions. I, alas, was too young to assume this role; Willy was only a few years younger than I, and he resented me. Drink, drugs, Sunday driving and — er — other evils were responsible for his premature death. Fortunately, at his father's insistence, he had married, though I fear he led the poor girl a sad life. At any rate he lived long enough to produce a son of his own. This lad, Henry, is the present holder of the title. He is only ten years old."

"He doesn't live with you, then?"

"No, his mother is of Scottish birth and she prefers to reside at Devenbrook Castle."

"His mother is still living?"

"Oh, yes. She is a very retiring person. Her unfortunate deformity . . . I suppose I had better warn you about that."

"I wish you would."

"It is not much, really; one soon becomes accustomed to it. She has a harelip, poor creature, and is morbidly self-conscious about it."

"I will be very careful not to take the slightest notice of it."

"I felt sure you would. You probably won't see a great deal of her; she spends most of her time in her own rooms. The castle is quite large, so Violet and Annabelle do not have to meet."

"Annabelle? Ah, yes, your stepdaughter. She does not care for her . . . her . . ." Marianne gave up trying to decipher this relationship. ". . . for the Duke's mother?"

"Oh, they seem to get along amicably enough," the Duchess replied. "But Annabelle is also, in her way, something of a recluse. She . . . Yes, I had better tell you about Annabelle's peculiarity."

"Please do," said Marianne.

"Annabelle keeps quantities of cats."

"But there is nothing peculiar about that,"

Marianne said, relieved. "I am very fond of pussycats."

"I myself have no objection to them, in moderation. But Annabelle's collection cannot by even the most generous interpretation of the word be considered moderate. I am forced to leave my poor little Pierre in London when I come north; Annabelle's fierce felines quite overwhelm him."

"So then the household consists of Lady Annabelle, Lady Violet, and her son the Duke," said Marianne, trying to get the proper titles as well as the names straightened out. She assumed, from what the Duchess had said, that the ill-fated "Willy" had predeceased his father, and that therefore his widow did not hold the titles of a Duke's wife. In this she was apparently correct, for the Duchess nodded.

"Quite right. Then there are the servants, of course. Henry's dear old Nanny is something of a tart. She was also Willy's nurse, and I assure you, when I was a timid young bride she quite terrified me. Oh, and M. Victor, Henry's tutor. A pleasant-enough young man, except for his insistence on being French."

"Oh." Marianne was not quite sure what this meant. If M. Victor was French, as his name and title implied, there did not seem to be any harm in his insisting that he was.

"Oh, and I must warn you about MacDonald," the Duchess went on.

"Who is he?"

"The head gardener. He has been there forever; he grew up with my husband, so it is impossible for me to pension him off against his will."

"What is wrong with MacDonald?" Marianne asked resignedly.

"Pure senility, my dear. He talks to himself — or rather, to imaginary companions. It is quite harmless, but I admit it can be disconcerting to have MacDonald round on one and shout, 'Take yerself off, ye wearisome auld besom!' He wasn't speaking to me on that occasion, but to his deceased mother. And, since he occasionally forgets where he is, he is apt to turn up in the strangest places — in one's closet, for instance, or peering in the parlor windows at odd hours of the evening."

After this daunting description Marianne did not look forward to her stay at Devenbrook Castle. The only one who sounded comparatively normal was the young Duke, and Marianne knew only too well what ordinary lads of that age were apt to be like. A ten-year-old peer might be expected to be even more rowdy and undisciplined. Besides, she suspected that the Duchess might have omitted some flaw in the ducal person or personality — a passionate fondness for collecting snakes, or a withered arm, à la Richard III — in order to avoid overwhelming her guest with oddities.

Contrary to her expectations, her first impression was distinctly favorable. The clouds shed their load of rain as they proceeded, so that brilliant bursts of sunlight illumined an increasingly rugged and impressive landscape. The stark purple mountains laced by white waterfalls and girdled with trees impressed Marianne deeply.

Devenbrook Castle was framed by snowcapped peaks on three sides. The sun favored them with its appearance as they approached, and in its benevolent light the crenellated walls and pointed towers had the gaiety of a child's toy castle set on a bright-green mat and surrounded by trees and flower beds so improbably neat that they resembled paper cutouts. Marianne was unaware of the effort required to cultivate lawns and raise flowers in such rocky, infertile soil, but she was enough of a country girl to note that rocky promontories to the north and east protected the spot from the bitterest winter weather.

Somehow Marianne was not surprised

when the housekeeper, who hobbled out to greet them, turned out to be suffering from palsy and advanced deafness. She insisted on preceding them up the stairs to their rooms, which reduced their progress to the mournful solemnity of a funeral procession. Balancing on one foot as she waited for Mrs. Kenney to drag herself up to the next step, Marianne watched the Duchess's calm, deliberate pauses and advances with affectionate respect. Many employers insisted on only young, strong, well-favored servants, and ruthlessly dismissed any who succumbed to ill health or old age. Apparently any employee who served the Duchess faithfully could be sure of being kept on until he or she died of old age.

When they finally reached the chamber that had been assigned to her, Marianne had to admit that whatever her infirmities, Mrs. Kenney ran the house beautifully. Her room was rather dark and gloomy, with every inconvenience of the pseudo-Gothic style, but it was spotlessly clean.

"We must see to brightening this room," the Duchess said, with a disparaging glance. "It is enough to give one the shivers. You can help me select pretty fabrics, new carpets, furniture. . . . Do you enjoy doing that?"

"Oh, very much. But —"

"My rooms are just next door. That is why I had you put here, close to me. Now you will want to refresh yourself and rest a little. I will come and fetch you when it is time to go down to tea. One could get lost in this gloomy old pile without a guide."

She patted Marianne's cheek affectionately and started to leave. The housekeeper limped after her, but the Duchess waved her back. Putting her face next to the old woman's ear, she shouted, "My maid will take care of me, Mrs. Kenney; do attend Miss Ransom and make sure she has all she needs."

Marianne wanted nothing so much as to be left alone, in order to arrange her thoughts and consider the new impressions that had crowded so fast upon her. But Mrs. Kenney would have walked unhesitantly over the edge of a cliff if the Duchess had suggested that she do so; she had been ordered to attend Miss Ransom, and attend she would, whether or not it suited Miss Ransom.

Like a benevolent fairy godmother she summoned an army of little maids — who were most of them so young that they really did resemble the famous Scottish pixies or brownies — and set them to work. Marianne's trunks had already arrived. When every article of clothing had been neatly put away and a basin of steaming hot water awaited her ablutions, she tried to dismiss the housekeeper. She had a young, healthy voice and a good pair of lungs, and once she had gotten over her inhibition about shouting she had no trouble in making the housekeeper hear her.

"Thank you, Mrs. Kenney. That will be all."

The wrinkled old face split in a smile. "Why, miss, what a nice clear voice you have! It is amazing how some people will whisper and mumble their words."

"Thank you."

"Yes, indeed. A pleasure to have a nice young lady in the house."

"Thank you. And now —"

"I hope you will enjoy being here. You don't mind ghosts, do you?"

After her first gasp of surprise Marianne was strongly tempted to laugh. Since apparently her new mission in life was to reach as many of what Mrs. Kenney called ghosts as she possibly could, she could hardly complain of their presence.

"No," she shouted.

"That's good. Ours are very well behaved. They do not bother people at all. Just take no notice of them."

"How many are there?" Marianne asked.

"Let me see." Mrs. Kenney counted on her fingers. "There is the first Duke, of course, but one hardly ever sees him, he only stalks the battlements during thunderstorms. You will not want to go there in bad weather. And his daughter, Lady Lucy, whom he pushed down the stairs one night in a fit of temper. That is why he walks, you understand. And the young gentleman who was poisoned by the second Duke while —"

"Never mind," Marianne yelled. "I shall do just as you suggest and ignore them all."

"None of them come here." Mrs. Kenney stood firmly in the exact center of the room, as if she had taken root there. "This was the bedchamber of the former Duke — Her Grace's husband — and he would never allow that sort of thing."

"Oh." Marianne glanced uneasily at the heavy oak bedstead with its somber hangings of brown velvet. "He . . . he slept in that bed?"

"Aye, and died in it, God rest his soul," said the housekeeper, confirming Marianne's worst suspicions. "He was a hard man, but a good master."

If such a combination is possible, Marianne thought to herself. She had heard enough horrors; she doubted that she would be able to sleep in that dismal bed. Having tried every other means of dismissing the housekeeper, she calmly began to undress. This had the desired effect. When the old lady had finally backed out, Marianne blew out her breath in a long sigh. She removed her gown and hung it up. Standing in her chemise and petticoats, she began to bathe her face and arms, which were in need of attention after the long ride.

The warm water was soothing. She had begun to relax, even to contemplate the dreadful bed with wry amusement, when something like a small explosion made her gasp and shrink back, the dripping wash-cloth pressed to her breast. Her door had opened with a resounding crash. Standing in the opening was a child.

Marianne concluded, correctly, that this must be the Duke. He was tall for his age, but rather delicately built. Lank dark hair hung limply around his thin face. Big, wide-set brown eyes regarded Marianne with intense, unchildlike concentration.

The washcloth was dripping down Marianne's front. She tossed it back into the basin and reached for the dress she had taken off.

"How dare you enter without knocking!" she demanded.

"How dare you speak to me that way!" The boy marred the arrogance of his speech by stamping his foot like an angry child. "Don't you know who I am?"

"I assume you are the Duke of Devenbrook," Marianne replied. "If you are, you ought to know that no gentleman would burst into a lady's room uninvited."

"I wanted to see you. They say you are a witch. I have never seen a witch before."

"How absurd." Marianne could not help laughing. "Do I look like a witch?"

"No." The boy shook his head solemnly. "Witches are old and ugly. You are very pretty."

No female could fail to be disarmed by this speech. Marianne realized that the boy was more childish than he appeared. He was undoubtedly badly spoiled, but he seemed to be without malice; she was not confronting another edition of Cyril Pettibone. All the same . . .

"Really, Your Grace," she said. "You are too old to behave like this. I look forward to meeting you formally, but now —"

A voice was heard from the hall outside.

"Henri! Henri! to where have you gotten yourself? Come to me at once, Henry — *tout de suite!*"

Henry, Duke of Devenbrook did not move

or even turn his head; he simply took a deep breath and bellowed, "Here I am!"

Rapid footsteps thudded down the hall, and in the open doorway appeared, momentarily, the form of a thin young man with red hair and extremely large mustaches of the same color — obviously the French tutor in pursuit of his errant charge. Marianne had only a glimpse of this apparition before it let out a shriek of consternation and fell back out of sight.

"Ah, begorra. . . . Er — I should say, *mon Dieu, quel contretemps! Mademoiselle, pardonnez-moi.* . . . This *enfant terrible,* he has led me into a *situation très maladroit.* Henri, remove yourself, *immediatement!*"

Henry, knowing full well that his tutor would not dare to enter, grinned broadly. He looked like any normal, mischievous ten-year-old boy, and Marianne was tempted to join in his amusement. However, the situation had to be resolved; she could hardly stand there all afternoon in a state of dishabille chatting with Henry while his tutor shouted apologies and imprecations from beyond the door. She solved the problem by putting on her dress.

"Monsieur," she called, "you may enter now. I am . . . er . . . I have . . . That is to say, you have my permission to enter."

The tutor's head appeared around the doorframe. One eye was wide open, the other tightly closed — this, apparently, the best concession to the proprieties he could make. When he saw that Marianne was dressed, the other eye opened.

"Mademoiselle, you forgive — ?"

"Certainly, monsieur," Marianne replied graciously. "It was not your fault."

"I will hope for the honor of presenting myself in due course," said the tutor confusedly. "At the present —"

Marianne's patience was wearing thin. "Take him away," she said, gesturing.

"Mais certainement, mademoiselle."

Henry's triumphant smile had faded when he saw himself outmaneuvered. Now his lower lip protruded and his dark brows drew together.

"No! I am not finished talking. Leave me alone, Victor."

The tutor backed off a few steps. Marianne thought that if she were the boy's mother she would prefer to employ a more forceful person. Perhaps dukes were not subject to the rules that governed children of lesser rank. Well, she at least had no intention of putting up with any more of Henry's nonsense.

"This is quite enough, Your Grace," she

said firmly. "If you wish me to treat you like a gentleman, then behave like one. If you wish to behave like a child, I will take you by the ear and put you out."

Henry and his tutor gasped, in chorus. M. Victor's face took on a look of such horror that Marianne wondered if she had indeed committed a form of lese majesty, and would be condemned to the castle dungeons.

Then the boy's angry flush faded. He made Marianne a queer little bow.

"You are right, miss," he said gravely. "My apologies. Well, come, Victor, why are you standing there gaping?"

He stalked out, his head held high in a comical assumption of manly dignity. With a shrug and an apologetic gesture the tutor followed his charge. Neither of them bothered to close the door. Marianne did so, with a decided slam. Finding a heavy iron bolt on the inside of the door, she pushed it home. The servants might wonder, but she was past caring. Really, what a household!

She finished her ablutions in peace and put on a clean frock. She was then able to unbolt the door before ringing for assistance in finishing her toilette.

Celeste had been left in London on board wages, like most of the servants. Only the Duchess's personal maid and a few others who were needed to attend them on the journey had been brought along. The Duchess had been apologetic — "We quite rusticate in the country, my dear, I assure you; you will have no need of elaborate toilettes." But Marianne had been relieved to be rid of the French maid, whose sophistication made her feel awkward and immature. However, the fashions of the time necessitated some assistance in dressing; it was impossible for even an agile young woman to reach all the buttons and laces that held her clothes together.

When Marianne rang she was not sure who would answer. She was pleased to find that the respondent was not Mrs. Kenney but one of the young maids who had helped unpack for her. The girl was extremely shy, and her dialect was so thick Marianne could barely understand her, but she was deft and eager to please.

When Marianne was ready, Annie — for such was the girl's name — informed her that the Duchess was waiting for her in her own rooms, and indicated a door half hidden by a heavy tapestry, which Marianne had not noticed before. This led, by way of a small dressing room, into the Duchess's boudoir.

Bright chintzes, modern furniture, and a profusion of flowers made this chamber much more cheerful than Marianne's. The Duchess greeted the girl with a kiss and suggested that they go down at once.

"I think I have persuaded Annabelle to join us," she said. "She always requires to be coaxed, but of course she is curious about you."

"I hope that she does not believe I am a witch," Marianne said with a smile.

"My dear child, what an extraordinary thing to say! Oh — I see. Which of the servants has had the impertinence to say such a thing to you?"

"It was not one of the servants. It was Master Henry — that is to say, the Duke. But he —"

"Henry will do." The Duchess's face was stern. "How does it happen that you have met the boy?"

Marianne was sorry that her thoughtless speech had led into such unforeseen complications. But she had been forced to tell the truth, once the initial faux pas had been made, in justice to the innocent housemaids.

"He came to see me. He meant it as a joke, ma'am; I assure you, I was more amused than anything."

"Oh, dear. I trust there was no . . . unpleasantness?"

"We were both very pleasant," Marianne replied cheerfully.

"I hope you won't think badly of the lad for intruding. He is a good boy, but because of his delicate health he is not always disciplined as he should be."

"Of course. Do you think well of his tutor, then?"

"M. Victor? Did you meet him too?"

"He came in pursuit of Henry."

The Duchess laughed ruefully. "You are tactful, Marianne, but I can read between the lines. The boy is so high-spirited he leads poor M. Victor quite a dance. As for the other matter — I am afraid the servants, like all uneducated people, look on spiritualism as an exercise of the Devil. They were terrified of dear David. I have strictly forbidden them to talk of such things in front of Henry, but of course they do; and Nanny is one of the worst offenders. A strict Presbyterian, and you know how *they* are!"

Marianne was silent. In her innermost heart she sympathized with the superstitious servants. She had found table-turning very entertaining as a parlor game; but when unseen forces flung objects about and invaded her own body, it was hard to think of such influences as benevolent. The only thing that made the business endurable was the Duchess's attitude. The Duchess was older and wiser and very kind; the Duchess accepted spiritualism; so spiritualism must be all right. So ran the unconsciously formulated syllogism that was to keep her involved in a pursuit from which every other instinct recoiled.

Devenbrook Castle had been modernized thirty years earlier, when the Gothic revival was in full flood. It was therefore a bizarre mixture of genuine medieval features, imitation medieval misapprehensions, and a few remnants of seventeenth- and eighteenth-century elements, which had somehow escaped the twelfth Duke's remodeling eye. The small parlor into which the Duchess led Marianne was an example of the last category. Called the rose parlor because its tall, wide windows opened onto a walled garden devoted to the cultivation of those flowers, its decor reflected the same theme: soft, comfortable furniture covered with pink brocade, a magnificent molded ceiling with floral swags and medallions showing beautiful ladies of myth and history, and a carved marble mantel. A fire burned on the hearth; before it, several chairs and a love seat surrounded a table on which the teathings were already set out.

"Annabelle is not here, I see," the Duchess remarked. "We might as well begin; although she promised to join us I am never sure she will come."

Scarcely had she filled the cups, however, when the door was opened and a lady made her appearance.

She was so tall and so strikingly masculine in every physical aspect that if Marianne had not known whom to expect she would have taken the lady for a male in woman's garb. Lady Annabelle had heavy eyebrows that ran straight across her forehead, without a curve or a break between, and a perceptible mustache shadowed her upper lip. But instead of the tailored, mannish clothing such a woman might have favored she wore dainty, fragile garments dripping with lace and ruffles, which looked ridiculous on her tall, broad-shouldered frame. The ruffles were sadly tattered, and Marianne needed no explanation for this phenomenon, since Lady Annabelle was literally surrounded by cats.

One was draped over her shoulder, its paws resting on her flat bosom. Its tail bounced up and down with every step. She carried another in her arms, a red tabby with insolent yellow eyes; and Marianne's own eyes opened wide at the sight of it, for it was the largest cat she had ever seen, weighing a good thirty pounds. An indeterminate number of other felines accompanied this apparition, flowing in and out under her skirts like a living river of fur — gray, white, black, orange, yellow, and every conceivable permutation thereof. Eyes flashed and tails waved, and no one ever seemed to be stepped on, although Lady Annabelle paid no attention to her entourage.

Sitting down in an armchair she gave the Duchess an awkward nod and cradled the enormous red tabby in her lap.

"I am so happy you decided to join us, Annabelle," said the Duchess. "Pray allow me to present Miss Ransom."

"How do you do," said Lady Annabelle, in a deep bass growl. "Do you like cats?"

"I dote on them," Marianne replied promptly.

Lady Annabelle's wide mouth relaxed. "Sensible gel. So do I."

That fact hardly required mentioning. One cat was sharpening its claws on the lady's skirt and two others were sidling up to the tea table, their eyes fixed on the cream pitcher. The elephantine tabby in the favored position on Lady Annabelle's lap contemplated Marianne through slitted eyes.

"That is a very handsome creature you are holding," Marianne said politely. "I have never seen so large a cat."

"This is Horace. I named him after the doctor."

Marianne stared at Horace, who stared back at her with a look of profound boredom.

"Dr. Gruffstone?" she asked, wondering if the doctor had been pleased at the compliment.

"Yes. He does not resemble the doctor physically, but they have the same dignity of presence. Just push that plate of sandwiches closer to me, Miss Ransom. Horace is getting on in years — that is why I carry him — and he needs to eat frequently."

Marianne obliged. She was exceedingly diverted to see the lady feed sandwiches to Horace, who received the tidbits with an air of languid condescension. The lesser cats lined up and were rewarded with an occasional bite. Lady Annabelle continued to talk, explaining the genealogies, histories, and quaint habits of each cat in turn. Horace was the patriarch, having sired most of the other animals present.

After a while the Duchess interrupted; without such intervention Lady Annabelle would have gone on discussing cats all afternoon.

"Is Violet joining us, Annabelle?"

"Now the tabby with white paws, Angel Face. . . . What? Violet? How should I know, Honoria? I doubt it; she never comes down when there are strangers here."

"How is she? I have not yet had time to call on her."

"The same," Annabelle said with a shrug. "Now Hector — the black — not the black with the white bib, the other black — Hector was ill last week. I think he ate a bad bit of fish. I gave —"

"And you, my dear. What have you been doing since I saw you last?"

"I have been embroidering," Lady Annabelle said, in her queer gruff voice. "It was a pretty piece of Berlin work, Honoria; it had a basket of kittens on it. But Fluffy — that is the white one, Miss Ransom — Fluffy wound the yarn into a hopeless tangle. I feared for a time that she had eaten part of it, but —"

"Then your health has been good?"

"Yes, of course. I am never ill, Honoria, you know that."

"You are too thin, my dear. Won't you have a sandwich?"

"I believe," said Lady Annabelle, with great simplicity, "that Horace has eaten them all."

The door opened and the footman announced, "His Grace the Duke of Devenbrook."

The unkempt surly boy had undergone a surprising transformation. To be sure, he had outgrown his neat gray suit, so that his bony wrists protruded, and he was in need of a haircut, a fact that was even more apparent now that he had attempted to comb his hair. Still, Marianne appreciated the effort and thought complacently that it might be attributed to her cutting comments on Henry's manners. He made her a bow, then spoiled the effect by remarking, "You look much nicer in your frock."

In any other company this comment would have been the cause of spilled tea and exclamations of horror. The only one who appeared to be perturbed by it was the tutor, who had followed his charge at a respectful distance. He rolled his eyes heavenward. Then he bowed to the three ladies in turn. Each bow was a masterpiece of calculation, conveying abject reverence to the Duchess, courteous respect to Lady Annabelle, and respectful admiration to Marianne.

"Your Grace permits?" he inquired. "It were more *respectueux* to inquire first, but the Duke was anxious to pay his *devoirs* to Your Grace."

"I am sure he was," the Duchess said

dryly. "Well, Henry, have you been a good boy?"

"Yes." The Duke flung himself into a chair and reached for a piece of plum cake. M. Victor looked wistfully at the love seat where Marianne was sitting, but did not have the courage to sit beside her. Instead he lowered himself into a chair, where he sat perched on the very edge, as if the respect he showed the company were in reverse ratio to the amount of space he occupied.

Much later Marianne was to describe the occasion as resembling, in its spirit of genteel chaos, a similar tea party in *Alice's Adventures in Wonderland.*

"The Duchess kept asking Henry questions which he did not bother to answer; he never took his eyes off me and I felt sure he expected me to sprout bat wings and fly up the chimney at any moment. Lady Annabelle talked to the cats and to me about the cats and paid no attention to anything else that was said. As for M. Victor, the cats immediately converged on him. They must have sensed that he was terrified of them. But he was too much in awe of Lady Annabelle to say so. They climbed up his trouser legs and drank his tea and snatched the cakes from his hand as soon as he took them. He sneezed a great deal."

Henry finished off the cakes. No one reproved him for making a pig of himself or for scattering crumbs all over the carpet. When the food was gone he jumped up, interrupting the Duchess in the middle of a question.

"I'm going now. This is dull. I thought she would do something exciting. Come on, Victor, I want to play chess."

"I shall retire as well," Lady Annabelle announced. She rose, still holding Horace, who had not moved during the entire affair except to open his mouth when food was placed next to it. "The pussycats need their exercise; and I fear Fluffy is going to be sick."

Fluffy promptly proved her premonition to be correct.

After they had gone and a footman had tactfully dealt with Fluffy's misdemeanor, the Duchess sighed. "Poor Annabelle. Being accustomed to her I forget how eccentric she must appear to a stranger. But there is no harm in her. And we all have our foibles, don't we?"

"Very true," Marianne agreed. To her, Lady Annabelle had appeared to be not merely eccentric but almost simple-minded. However, spinster ladies of peculiar habits presented no problem to a family that could afford to keep them safely tucked away somewhere. The girl wondered whether the Duchess's real concern was not for the boy, whose behavior also left a great deal to be desired. It would indeed be a tragedy if the last heir to one of the oldest dukedoms in England were lacking some of his wits.

"If you will excuse me," the Duchess said, "I believe I will dine in my room tonight. I have letters to write and business matters to deal with. Would such an arrangement suit you? We do not usually dine *en famille;* Henry is really too young, and his mother . . ."

"A tray in my room would suit me admirably. I am a little tired."

"Amuse yourself as you like," the Duchess said. "The music room and the library are in this wing, but I advise you not to explore farther than that tonight. The older parts of the castle are dreary and a little frightening after dark."

"Please don't worry about me."

"Then I will say good night. Oh — I usually attend church in the village. The people like it; but you need not join me tomorrow unless you like."

"I would be glad to go to church," Marianne said eagerly. Indeed, her variegated career in London had prevented her from attending divine service, and her conscience was troubling her on that point.

When the Duchess had gone, Marianne wandered about the room examining the paintings and the pretty ornaments. She had not been strictly accurate when she said she was tired; mental and emotional fatigue she did indeed feel, but physically she was more in need of exercise than of rest, after a long, cramped ride. Deciding to walk in the garden for a while, she found that the long windows were actually French doors, and so let herself out onto the terrace.

Here she walked for some time, admiring the changing sunset light on the high mountains that could be seen beyond the wall.

The Duchess's abrupt decision to leave London for this remote Scottish castle had not troubled her initially. She had no idea what matters, business or personal, might have motivated such a decision. Now that she had met most of the members of the household she was ready to eliminate natural affection as a motive. The Duchess was not related by blood to any of them, so it was no wonder that her strongest emotion toward one and all was a sense of responsibility. Certainly duty might have prompted this visit, but the more Marianne thought about it, the more she was inclined to suspect another reason. This was where David Holmes had died. Now that the first tenuous contact had been made, the Duchess hoped that proximity to the scene of his last days on earth would strengthen the tie.

Marianne shivered. The sun had dropped behind the mountains. The air was chill. She turned back to the house, finding that during her absence someone had lighted the lamps in the parlor and in the corridor beyond. No more modern form of lighting would reach this remote place for years to come, Marianne supposed; she found the familiar candles and oil lamps comforting, reminding her as they did of the home of her youth and of Mrs. Jay's cottage.

A now-familiar pang of guilt touched her as she remembered her old friend. Really, she must write Mrs. Jay. Roger Carlton had mentioned that he had spoken with Marianne's former landlady and — what was the phrase he had used? — "assured her of his bona fides." But that was no guarantee that Mrs. Shortbody had been relieved of concern on her behalf, or had written to reassure Mrs. Jay. Really, Marianne thought guiltily, it is too bad for me. Mrs. Jay had always told her that one of her worst faults was procrastination. "You seem to think if you postpone a difficulty long enough, it will disappear," she had remarked sarcastically. "It is much more likely, Marianne, that the difficulty will grow larger and less amenable to a solution."

I will write tonight, Marianne promised herself. Perhaps in the library I may find writing materials.

This apartment was not difficult to find, for the comforting lights ended abruptly just beyond its entrance. The door had been left open, no doubt on her account, and the room was adequately lighted. It was like a fairy tale "Beauty and the Beast," in which the captive maiden was attended by thoughtful but invisible spirits.

This was not entirely a comfortable thought, nor was the chasm of blackness at the end of the hall a comfortable sight. The Duchess had not exaggerated when she said the castle was a dreary place at night. As Marianne stood looking curiously into the dark, wondering what lay farther along the corridor, she heard a faint dry rustling and fancied the darkness shifted as if something lumbered stealthily toward her. She fled into the library.

It would have taken a thousand wax tapers to illumine the vast room properly; it was two stories high, with row upon row of books on both levels, the upper one reached by an iron staircase. Chairs and tables of all kinds were scattered about, but the room was so large it looked scantily furnished. There was light enough, however, for Marianne to see that a nearby table held an assortment of volumes which, by their neat bindings, appeared to be more modern than the crumbling leather tomes on the shelves.

Sure enough, she found among these books several familiar authors, and finally selected *Persuasion* and *Wuthering Heights* to take upstairs with her. She also looked for writing paper, but found none. Then it occurred to her that she had only to ring for a servant and ask for anything she desired. She was not yet accustomed to this luxury. The management of the squire's household had been anything but efficient, and the servants had had a tendency to treat their young mistress with more affection than deference.

With a bright fire on the hearth and dozens of candles, her room looked less forbidding than before. Marianne settled herself in a chair and opened *Wuthering Heights.*

Marianne's reading had been more catholic than her old friend Mrs. Jay suspected. That good lady had kept her supplied with moralistic tales. The only modem writers of whom she approved were Scott and Dickens and Miss Austen, and the only essays Marianne was allowed to read were sermons of stupefying dullness. She had never been exposed to "that pernicious doctrine of women's rights," or to the novels of Balzac or George Eliot. But she had picked up certain other novels from her governesses. None of these were really pornographic, they were merely sensational, ranging from *Lady Audley's Secret* and the Gothic horrors of Mrs. Radcliffe to *Jane Eyre*, which latter volume Mrs. Jay had condemned as unwomanly and immoral.

Marianne had loved *Jane Eyre*. She had been at a loss to understand her friend's condemnation, for it seemed to her a wonderfully moral story. Indeed, she was not at all sure that she would have had the strength to resist Mr. Rochester. But she had never managed to lay her hands on *Wuthering Heights*.

Yet this volume is not, perhaps, the most soothing fare for a young lady of imaginative temperament alone at night in an ancient castle. So immersed was Marianne in the fatal love of Cathy and Heathcliffe that she jumped and let out a shriek when the door opened, admitting Annie and a footman carrying her dinner. This was laid out upon a table, and the pair were about to withdraw when Marianne remembered she wanted to write a letter. She asked Annie to fetch pen and ink, adding that the girl need not return at once; she could bring the writing materials when she came to carry away the tray.

When Annie returned she was accompanied by the same young footman, who was carrying a heavy can of hot water for Marianne's bath. In other households this work was properly that of a housemaid. This was not significant in itself; but Marianne noticed that Annie kept as far from her, and as close to the young man, as she possibly could. The girl had been friendly enough, in her shy way, before; Marianne wondered what had happened to change her. But she thought she knew. The story of her being a witch had spread through the servants' hall.

So she let Annie go instead of requesting that the girl help her prepare for bed. Assuming a warm woolen dressing gown, she sat down at the table, dipped her pen in the inkwell, and began to write:

"My dear Mrs. Jay. Knowing that you must have been concerned about me, I take pleasure in writing to inform you that I am well, and am now in the most fortunate situation. The Dowager Duchess of Devenbrook — a lady of the highest character — has taken me into her household. . . ."

The words had flowed fluently until then; but Marianne came to a sudden halt as she realized she would have to be more specific about her role in the Duchess's household.

To tell Mrs. Jay the truth was out of the question. The vicar's widow had condemned the awful heresy of spiritualism in no uncertain terms. On the other hand, lying was a sin.

Marianne nibbled the end of her pen in considerable agitation, seeking a compromise between unpalatable truth and out-and-out falsehood. Finally her worried frown smoothed out and she began to write again.

". . . as her companion. Her Grace is a widow and childless; she treats me quite as a daughter, and I hope I am of service to her."

Upon rereading this, Marianne was satisfied. She had spoken the literal truth, and if a few salient facts had been omitted. . . . Well, surely it would also be a sin to worry poor Mrs. Jay unnecessarily.

The difficult part of the letter having been dealt with, she wrote on easily, describing the appointments of the London house and the private railway carriage with considerable enthusiasm. She was pleased to be able to add, "We attend church services tomorrow. I will be thinking of you, dear Mrs. Jay. I hope your health is good and that you will find time to write me. A letter addressed to Devenbrook Castle will find me for some weeks to come, I believe."

With a feeling of virtuous accomplishment she sealed and addressed the letter. Tomorrow she would ask the Duchess how it could be sent to the post.

Rising to return to her chair by the fire, she was suddenly aware of how quiet the room was. There was no clock, so she had no idea of the time. The fire was dying and the candles had burned low. She felt a chill for which the cooling air was not entirely responsible, and reminded herself that she was not alone and isolated; the Duchess's room was next door.

A sound from the direction of her own door made her whirl around. In the silence the slightest creak was magnified. The source of the noise was not hard to find: the heavy iron handle was moving. Transfixed, Marianne stood glaring as the handle reached its lowest point and the door began to open. The aperture was no more than the merest slit, however, before the door closed again and the frightened girl heard soft footsteps retreating.

It was several seconds before she could move. Now that the unseen visitor had departed, she thought of several innocent explanations for its presence; one of the servants, coming to see if she required anything more; or the young Duke, hoping to find her engaged in mysterious rites. She ran to the door and threw it open. If the boy had ventured to peek into her room she would give him a good lecture.

The corridor was empty of any human presence. Most of the candles had gone out. At the far end, where a window slit admitted a flood of moonlight, something moved. A pale diaphanous substance veiled a more solid but indistinguishable form; it flashed briefly luminous in the bleached light, and then was gone. Marianne's straining ears heard a ghost of sound, like a faint sigh of wind. But there was no wind. The night was calm.

Marianne bolted her door. But she lay awake a long time, with the covers over her head, until exhaustion sent her to sleep.

CHAPTER NINE

Marianne would have preferred not to admit her foolish fancies of the night, for reason came with the dawn and assured her that what she had seen was no disembodied spirit from beyond the grave, but one of the eccentric denizens of Devenbrook Castle — possibly the Duke's unfortunate mother, too shy to show her face, but quite humanly curious about the newcomer. However, she slept late and did not manage to unbolt her door before the maid arrived with her hot water. So the Duchess was notified, and the story came out, for the Duchess leaped to the conclusion that the Duke had been paying unauthorized calls again and Marianne felt she had to admit the truth.

"It probably was Violet," the Duchess said. "She will become accustomed to you in time. I know I can trust you, my dear, to greet her with no show of surprise or distaste."

With her mind at ease on this point, Marianne prepared for church. She chose one of her old black gowns, remorsefully acknowledging to herself that she had neglected this obligation while in London. On this day and on this occasion at least she would behave properly. Had not Mrs. Jay often admonished her that worldly vanity was out of place in the house of the Lord?

The Duchess was ready for her when she came downstairs, and they started off without waiting for any of the others. Marianne could understand that the Duke's mother and the eccentric Lady Annabelle might not attend church, but she wondered at the absence of the boy and his tutor. Naturally she did not ask why he was not present, and no explanation was forthcoming.

The village was small, with only an inn — the Devenbrook Arms — and a general shop besides a collection of grim-looking houses built of unadorned gray granite. The church was surprisingly large for such a poor place. Its rough Romanesque exterior struck Marianne as plain and unattractive, but she admired the interior, which, the Duchess explained, had been "restored" by her late husband. The restoration consisted of bright gilt paint on all the monuments, susceptible to this treatment and a series of garish stained-glass windows.

Marianne noticed several monuments of reclining knights — Devenbrook ancestors, no doubt. One conspicuous memorial had a life-sized effigy of a gentleman in Elizabethan ruff and hose leaning nonchalantly on his elbow as he faced the congregation, ignoring the meek-looking wife who lay beside him. Before him, like a frieze, ran an astonishing row of miniature kneeling figures, presumably his children. While waiting for the service to begin, Marianne counted them — there were sixteen altogether — and felt she could understand why the Lady Devenbrook of that era had not the strength to lift herself up on her elbow.

Seated as they were at the very front of the church, under the pulpit, Marianne's back was turned to the rest of the congregation, but she knew they were staring. They had certainly gaped openly as she walked down the aisle to her place. Yet the holy quiet of the church gave her a feeling of peace such as she had not known for many days. She relaxed, her eyes fixed dreamily on the worldly carved face of the Elizabethan Duke. His faint, cynical smile assured her that the mysteries of life and death were known to him; if she would only listen a little harder he would impart them to her. She was not at all surprised to hear a grave voice pronounce the words, "The wages of sin is death."

The Duchess shifted position and coughed. Marianne woke from her daze. The statue had not spoken; that was absurd. Yet surely she had heard the words. . . . She looked up. The clergyman had mounted into the pulpit.

If Helen's face had launched a thousand ships, with all-male crews, this man might have inspired an equivalent female effort. His was the classic beauty of a face on an antique coin. To be sure, Marianne had never seen such a coin or such a profile, but she had read the phrase somewhere and it had struck her as the quintessential summary of what perfection must be. In fact, the pastor's good looks were not at all Greek. His forehead was broad and white, but instead of carrying on the straight unbroken line demanded by Attic notions of beauty his nose jutted out like the prow of a ship. His firm, chiseled lips might have been those of a sculptured Augustus or Alexander, but the shape of his chin was too pronounced for perfect handsomeness. Still, he was undeniably good-looking, and when a ray of sunlight struck his golden hair, giving it a glow like a halo, Marianne caught her breath.

She could never remember the content of that first sermon. She only knew that his solemn exhortation made her yearn to attain the Christian virtues he urged — whatever these might have been. Her suppressed feelings of guilt about so many of her recent actions would have made her receptive to any sincere sermon. The combination of male beauty, religious appeal, and a warm, passionate voice was almost too much for her. If the meeting had taken place in a revival tent, and the pastor had urged all sinners to come forward to the arms of Jesus, Marianne would have been the first one to reach the altar rail.

The dignified Church of England service allowed no such catharsis, so Marianne was forced to repress her feelings. After the service was over and the congregation began to disperse, she was scandalized to hear one parishioner remark, "Aye, aye, the laddie has a powerful call, nae doubt, but Ah niver know just what he's talking aboot."

Once again she had to run the gauntlet of staring eyes, for the other parishioners waited for the lady of the manor to exit before they left their places. Marianne scarcely noticed. Still in a daze, she took her place in the carriage.

"Well, that is done," the Duchess said. "Mr. St. John gives a good sermon, don't you think? But I fear he is over the heads of most of his hearers."

Mr. St. John. Marianne locked the name away in her memory. "I found him most inspiring," she murmured.

"Oh, I don't doubt his ability, or his fervor. They tell me he has made quite an impression on the congregation, particularly the young women." The Duchess smiled indulgently. "Ah, well, I would be the last to deny that truths are more palatable when they are pronounced by such well-shaped lips. I do hope he decides to take a wife soon, though. I do not believe in a celibate priesthood, and a bachelor clergyman is unsettling to the neighborhood."

It had never occurred to Marianne that this Christian hero might be a married man. The fear having been aroused and dispelled in the same breath, she tried to tell herself that it did not matter in the least to her. One might admire a man's eloquence, even his physical appearance, without being suspected of having vulgar designs upon him.

"I suppose I must ask him to dine one day soon," the Duchess continued. "Tomorrow evening, perhaps."

It was as well for Marianne that she had this new interest on which to exercise her thoughts, for without it she would have been very bored. The Duchess observed the Sabbath with strictness. No profane music was permitted, only hymns; no entertainment or travel to places of amusement was allowed. Marianne spent the day walking in the garden and listening to her hostess read aloud from a book of vaguely heretical theology. She was happy when evening came and she could retire to her room and the (probably illicit) pleasures of *Wuthering Heights*. No secret visitor disturbed her and she slept soundly.

When she awoke next morning she could not at first understand why she felt like leaping out of bed and dancing around the room. Then she remembered. Today the clergyman was coming to dine!

Though he could not be expected for hours, she took forever over her morning toilette and snapped at Annie because her hair would not curl properly. When she went down to breakfast she found M. Victor there and expressed surprise to find him lingering so late over his coffee.

"I was — er — that is, I had hopes of meeting you," the young man confessed, with a betraying blush.

The blush made the freckles that starred the bridge of his nose stand out vividly, and his blue eyes studied her with anxious interest. Marianne had never seen a visage that spoke so unmistakably of its owner's origin, and in her good spirits she could not resist teasing him.

"Ah, begorra, had you indeed?"

M. Victor's prominent jaw dropped. For a moment he looked as if he would protest. Then he let out a long sigh.

"Ah, faith, and it's found me out you have. And surely ye won't be betraying me to the Duchess, angel of kindness that you must be, with a heavenly face like the one you have on you?"

"I am sure Her Grace already knows," Marianne said, laughing. "*She* is the angel of kindness; if she has not objected to your masquerade so far, I don't see why she should now. But why pretend? Are you ashamed of being Irish?"

"Indeed it's proud I am to be a son of Erin! But . . . the world is a foolish place, bedad, and there's no denying that an Irish tutor does not have the prestige of a Frenchie."

"That may be true, monsieur. . . . What am I to call you then?"

"Victor is me name; indeed, me lie is only a wee bit of a half-lie, for me dear mither was French. Call me Victor, without the monsieur, and you'll honor me for life."

"Thank you. But why were you hoping to meet me?"

"I wished to offer me services as a guide. I know this crumbling old bin like the back o' me hand. Bedad, there's little enough to do here but read the old histories of the place. So, if you would enjoy a tour of the premises, consider me your man."

"But aren't you supposed to be teaching?" Marianne asked innocently. "I would not want to take you from your duties."

Victor's eyes twinkled slyly. "All work and no play makes Henry a dull boy. It's a dull boy he is altogether, hardly worth me talents as a teacher."

"It is kind of you," Marianne said. "But not today. I have — uh — duties to perform."

She left the young man looking downcast. Even if she had not had other things on her mind, she would not have been eager to go wandering off with him. His comment about his pupil's dullness had struck a sour note. He had no right to feel himself on such confidential terms with her.

As the day wore on, however, she almost regretted she had not accepted the tutor's offer, for the hours had to be filled somehow, and the Duchess was busy with household matters. There were always details of this nature to settle when she came north, since neither of the other ladies had the interest or the ability to deal with them. So Marianne read a little, walked a little, and looked at her pretty enameled lapel watch — the Duchess's latest gift — every fifteen minutes.

The day was unusually mild, so she finally settled down under the rose arbor with a piece of needlework. In that sheltered spot, situated to the south of the castle and shielded by plantings of firs, a few late roses lingered. Marianne passed an hour there. She had just decided that she could now go in and begin dressing for dinner when the sound of footsteps on the gravel path made her look up. For a moment she could hardly believe her eyes. What was Roger Carlton doing here?

So thoroughly had her new idol filled her thoughts that she studied the lawyer with a cool dispassionate eye and wondered how she could have found him handsome. Not that he was actually ugly. His height, his form, and the vigor of his walk were attractive enough. But dark-brown hair was so dull, compared to golden locks.

He came to a stop before her. "The servants told me I would find you here."

"Did they?" Marianne's voice was cool. "But I shan't be here for long. In fact, I was just about to go in."

"That would be a pity. You make such a

charming picture — a golden-haired lady in a white gown, framed in clusters of roses. The roses are almost gone, of course, but a romantic imagination like mine can easily supply them."

"You are making fun of me," Marianne said, plunging her needle vigorously into the linen fabric and gathering her silks together.

"Not at all. I have as keen an eye for beauty as any man."

"What are you doing here? Business, I suppose."

"Your business." Carlton adjusted the crease in his fawn trousers and took a seat.

"Mine? But I have none."

"Perhaps business is not quite the right word. Your affairs, I should say."

"Well?"

Carlton reached out his hand and plucked a rose. He let out a little exclamation as the flower came into his hand. "A pity such beautiful flowers have thorns," he said, looking with mock dismay at a tiny bead of blood on his thumb.

"I am in a hurry," Marianne said. "What do you want to tell me?"

"But it can't be told in a sentence. I want to talk with you at length."

"Then it will have to wait. We are having a guest for dinner, and I must go and dress."

"Quite a royal 'we,' I must say. Who is this guest?"

"The . . . the clergyman," Marianne said. She would have given anything she owned not to blush, but she felt the warm, betraying tide of blood move across her cheeks.

"St. John?" To her annoyance Carlton threw his head back and let out a loud hearty laugh. "Where did you. . . . Ah, but of course; yesterday was Sunday, and you —"

"And you," Marianne interrupted, "must have left London yesterday. Sunday travel, Mr. Carlton? How shocking!"

"Duty called," Carlton said solemnly.

"You are impossible! Please excuse me."

"Don't you even want to know what business I meant to discuss with you?"

"No. Unless . . ." Marianne had risen to her feet and started forward. Now she stopped. Quite without warning a terrible picture had flashed into her mind. She seemed to see Mrs. Jay lying on her bed, her hands crossed over her breast, and her eyes closed. The mental apparition was so vivid that she spun around, her curls flashing in the sunlight, her skirts billowing out. "Has something happened? Have you bad news?"

For once she was unaware of the lovely picture she presented, with emotion darkening her eyes and the sunlight caressing the graceful lines of her body and arms. The young lawyer took a long, shaken breath before replying.

"No, no. Not the sort of news you are dreading. It can wait."

"Well." In her relief Marianne smiled. Dimples, fluttering lashes, curving lips came into full play. "We will talk later, then. Tomorrow, perhaps."

Carlton nodded dumbly. With another gracious smile Marianne left him.

He sat under the rose arbor for some time, his brow furrowed, meticulously stripping the petals from the rose, careless of its thorns. When he finally returned to the house the ground beside his chair was strewn with the soft pink petals of the murdered flower.

II

It need not be said that Marianne dressed for dinner with unusual care. By the time she left her room she had tried on all the dresses she owned and reduced Annie to a state of quivering nerves. The results, however, were magnificent. Perhaps those few days in the theater had taught her something about creating an effect, or perhaps the basic instincts of a woman had warned her that the pastor would be more struck with virginal modesty than with ostentation. Her gown was the same one she had worn that fateful night at the opera, but with the trailing flowers and coquettish blue ribbons removed. It was now stark unadorned white, and Marianne's only ornament was a black velvet ribbon that supported the locket with the pictures of her parents.

Her lateness was not a matter of calculation, but the inevitable result of prolonged primping. Most of the others were assembled in the drawing room when she made her entrance.

The room was extravagantly lighted by lamps and candles and by two great fires. Such light is flattering; Marianne knew she was the cynosure of all eyes as she stood in the doorway. Her own eyes went straight to *his* face, ignoring all the others.

In the white collar and unrelieved black of his calling he was as handsome as ever. His pale skin and fair hair looked like a faded watercolor above the stark black, but there was nothing faded about his eyes; they caught fire as they met hers.

But the formalities had to be observed. Her first duty was to the Duchess; then a mocking curtsy to Carlton. Then came the moment she had been waiting for. He was much taller than she. She tipped her head back and gazed up at him as he took her hand.

The atmosphere was changed from pulsating romance to sheer farce by the entrance of Lady Annabelle.

"I am dining," she announced. "Heard you were here, vicar. Good to see you. Fluffy's been sick again."

"Her old trouble?" the vicar asked interestedly.

"Looks that way." Lady Annabelle pushed him down onto the sofa; took a seat beside him, and launched into an explicit description of Fluffy's symptoms.

St. John looked at Marianne. "I share Lady Annabelle's interest in our animal friends, Miss Ransom. Not a sparrow shall fall, you know."

"I am fond of animals too," Marianne assured him eagerly.

"So am I," said the Duchess. "But their ailments are not a suitable subject for drawing-room conversation. Later, perhaps, Annabelle. Mr. St. John, I believe you have done a great deal of good here since my last visit."

A courteous but decisive inquiry into parish charitable matters followed. Marianne sat in demure silence, admiring the animation of the young pastor's face as he described various needy cases. Finally, when the Duchess had finished her questions, Marianne said shyly, "I much enjoyed your sermon, Mr. St. John."

"Thank you, thank you." He beamed at her. "I hope I did not dwell too long on the Amalekites?"

A snort from Carlton won that gentleman a freezing stare from Marianne. She turned back to the vicar. "Not at all. I found it . . . inspirational."

"Inspirational of what, precisely, one wonders?" Carlton mused aloud.

Any reply Marianne might have been tempted to make was forestalled by the announcement of dinner. As the youngest lady present, she was forced to bring up the rear; but this offered her the opportunity to admire the back of Mr. St. John's neck. It was an admirable neck, sturdy without being fleshy, squarely set on his fine shoulders.

After the meal was concluded, the ladies returned to the drawing room, leaving the gentlemen to their port. Marianne wondered, as she often had, why men had to be left alone and what they talked about on such occasions. It seemed unlikely that

Carlton and the vicar would have much to discuss.

At the Duchess's request Marianne went to the piano. She was still playing when the gentlemen came in; they had not lingered overlong. Though she continued to make her fingers ripple over the keys, she saw that St. John started toward her, his face alight with the appreciation of a genuine lover of music. However, he was caught by the Duchess, and it was Carlton who joined her at the instrument.

"Just give me a nod," he said, touching the music. "I am the most accomplished of page turners."

"There is no need," Marianne said sweetly. "That is the last page."

"Dear me, how embarrassing. I ought to have seen that, oughtn't I? Let us try a duet, then. I must do something to win back your respect."

"Do you sing?" Marianne asked.

"Magnificently. Here — do you know this?"

After a false start — for Marianne's attention was not entirely on the music — they launched into the song. Carlton had a pleasant baritone voice, rather deeper than she would have expected, and he sang with taste and feeling. The power of music over Marianne's sensibilities was strong enough to overcome her, even on this thrilling occasion; she was as startled and surprised as the others when the vicar jumped to his feet, exclaiming, "No!"

Seeing the sensation he had created, the vicar's cheeks darkened. "I beg your pardon," he said quietly. "Perhaps, Your Grace, we should discuss this another time."

The Duchess appeared quite calm, but those who knew her could tell by the rigidity of her pose and by the deadly courtesy of her voice how angry she was.

"There is nothing to discuss, if you meant what you said. I have asked you to perform your clerical duties and you have refused."

"Not that — never that." The burning sincerity of the young man's voice could not be denied. "Never, I hope, will I refuse to do my duty. What you wish, Your Grace, are prayers for the repose of a man's soul. That is a popish practice. I cannot condone it."

"Your are quite mistaken, Mr. St. John," the Duchess replied. "My beliefs also deny the existence of those myths, Hell and Purgatory; and if I were foolish enough to believe in them, I would never believe that the soul of David Holmes required my prayers to escape them. He is in heavenly bliss. I asked only for a memorial service. What can you object to in that?"

St. John had himself well in hand now. Only his clenched fists betrayed his emotion. "I object," he said, in a low, thrilling voice, "because Holmes was a heretic, condemned even by his own church."

"Then," said Carlton, leaning negligently against the piano, "you only bestow your prayers on the saint, Mr. St. John? Is there not more rejoicing in heaven over one sinner redeemed than —"

"I know my Bible as well as you, Mr. Carlton," the vicar interrupted. "I will gladly pray for that unfortunate, that misguided man. What I will not do is lend my countenance to a mockery of the Christian faith."

"You have not reconsidered, then," the Duchess said. "You do not believe in the principles of spiritualism?"

"I have reconsidered," was the reply. "I do believe." His voice rose. "I believe that the manifestations produced by such men as Mr. Holmes are actually moved by a spirit from Hell, sent by the Devil, for the purpose of deluding the credulous, and doomed to return to Hell when its evil intent is accomplished!"

"How dare you!" The Duchess, vibrating with wrath, rose to her feet. "Sir, the hour is late. You will, no doubt, wish to leave. I will order the carriage."

"I am deeply sorry to have offended Your Grace."

"It is too late to apologize."

"I do not apologize for my belief, I only express regret that the truth must harm those I respect and admire."

His sincerity was evident. The Duchess relaxed; she even smiled faintly.

"Well, well; I too was at fault. I should be more patient with human weakness. 'They have eyes, but see not . . .' David tried to teach me that."

The vicar's lips tightened. "Your Grace is too kind," he muttered.

"Only think of what I have said. It would please me so much, Mr. St. John; try, can't you, to find a way to reconcile with your conscience?"

The ghost of her old beauty and coquetry touched her as she held out a reconciling hand, and the young man's face showed that he was not unmoved.

"I will consider it, Your Grace. I will pray."

"I could not ask more. And now, good night."

Lady Annabelle followed him out; Marianne heard "Fluffy" and "sick" before the door closed on the pair.

The Duchess passed a hand over her brow. "Intolerance! None so blind as those who will not see! Sometimes I despair. . . . Marianne. Come with me, child."

"Now?" Marianne's voice rose to a plaintive wail.

"Yes, now. I have waited long enough. I am perturbed. I need reassurance. Please."

"I'll try," Marianne mumbled.

Carlton was not invited to join them, but he went along anyhow, to a room which was in all essentials a replica of the white-swathed chamber in the London mansion. The Duchess's decision had been so sudden that the servants had not had time to prepare the room. Here Carlton proved his usefulness, for he had had the foresight to carry with him a candelabrum. This was set on the mantel, some distance from the table in the center of the room, and they all took their places. As soon as the silence demanded by the exercise descended, Marianne heard a sound that was certainly not supernatural.

"Someone is here," she exclaimed.

The sound, a sly, scuttling, ratlike scrabble, was repeated. Carlton leaped up and made a dash for a far comer of the room. A brief scuffle ensued; then Carlton pulled the wriggling form of the young Duke from behind the window draperies.

"How long have you been there?" he inquired in a conversational tone.

The calm voice had its effect on Henry; he stopped thrashing around and hung limp from Carlton's fist, which was clamped on his shoulder.

"All evening. You've been long enough about it, I must say."

"How many times have I told you . . ." The Duchess closed her mouth without finishing the sentence. She shook her head. "What a sad little snoop you are, Henry. Go to bed. Roger, call one of the servants — that wretched Victor — someone to take the boy away."

So Henry was handed over to a burly footman who promised to deliver him to his own room.

"You aren't faaaaair." His long howl echoed along the corridor.

They sat again. But there was no message, no mobility of the furniture — nothing — though they remained until the room grew cold and Marianne was nodding with fatigue.

The Duchess was disappointed but not distressed by their failure. She attributed it to the influence of a hostile mind. She referred, of course, to the vicar; but Marianne, catching Carlton's mocking eye, felt sure he radiated enough hostility to rout a regiment of friendly spirits, including that of David Holmes.

CHAPTER TEN

"I do not suppose," Carlton said, "that you are any sort of horsewoman, Miss Ransom."

"Why should you suppose that? I dote on riding."

They were sitting at the breakfast table, together with M. Victor, who remained resolutely in his chair nibbling on petrified toast, even though Carlton ignored him completely after the first curt greeting.

"Will you join me in a hearty gallop, then?" Carlton inquired.

Marianne gave him a sweet smile. "Unfortunately I am engaged. M. Victor has promised to show me the castle and tell me thrilling tales about the family."

M. Victor choked on a crumb and turned crimson in the face before he got his breath back. Finally he managed to gasp, "Honored . . . I had hoped, indeed," and a few other phrases indicative of pleasure — and surprise. Marianne did not mind. She wanted to make sure Carlton knew he was being snubbed.

To her annoyance he did not appear to be at all hurt.

"After luncheon, then. You cannot mean to spend the entire day roaming these dusty halls; a few hours of it will make you anxious for some fresh air, I assure you."

Marianne was forced to agree to the appointment. She knew the lawyer's sudden interest in her equestrian skills was only a device to get her alone so he could discuss the business he had mentioned. She assumed he had discovered, or believed he had discovered, something to her detriment, so she was not particularly anxious to hear it.

At Victor's suggestion she changed her fresh muslin gown for something more practical. The uninhabited parts of the castle were dusty and unheated.

At first Marianne rather enjoyed the tour. The Great Hall of the old keep, with its minstrels' gallery and ten-foot fireplaces, was thrillingly Gothic in character. It was in the Portrait Gallery, beyond the Hall, that she first noticed a change in Victor's behavior.

Most of the pictures were old, the newer portraits having been scattered through the other rooms. Some were so ancient that the features of the fifteenth- and sixteenth-century Devenbrooks could scarcely he made out. Victor had not exaggerated when he boasted of knowing the family legends. Many were tales of desperate deeds and desperate men, dark rumors of revenge, treachery, and murder.

They came to a full-length portrait of a woman, or rather a sort of Scottish Fury; a voluminous plaid draped her stately form, her dark hair writhed around her head as if blown by a gale, and in her upraised hand she held a trunkless head. Gouts of painted blood dripped from this ghastly trophy, whose eyes were fixed in a horrid stare.

"Good heavens," Marianne exclaimed. "How dreadful!"

"The fourth Duchess, née Lady Flora MacMonihan," said Victor. "Known before her marriage as the Iron Maiden of Monihan. The reference is to an antique device of torture —"

"I have heard of it." Averting her eyes, Marianne would have moved on. Victor caught her arm.

"Don't you want to hear about the lady? The head is of her former lover, Angus MacGonigal, who had annoyed her by abandoning her for another. They say she had it sent to the home of his betrothed and served up to the girl at dinner. She went raving mad."

"No wonder." Marianne shuddered. Victor casually slipped an arm around her waist.

"Ah, they were barbaric times, to be sure. Not like —"

"Sir!" Marianne pulled away from him. "What are you doing?"

" 'Tis begging your pardon I am. The place is chilly and I thought —"

"You thought wrong. I have seen enough." She turned and started back the way they had come. With an agile leap Victor barred her path.

" 'Tis shorter by the way I'll be showing you. Ah, now, don't pout at me, that's a darling; I'll be behaving myself after this."

His manner left a great deal to be desired, but he did not try to touch her; and since Marianne was uncertain of the precise path they had taken, she decided to follow him.

They passed through the heavy oak door at the end of the Portrait Gallery. Victor shut it carefully behind them and proceeded along a stone-flagged corridor lighted only by narrow slits high in the wall.

" 'Twas the passage to the old kitchens and scullery. Indeed but the food must have been icy cold before it reached the Banqueting Hall."

He continued to chatter, interspersing bits of historical information with courteous warnings about broken flagstones and other impediments to walking. The darkness imperceptibly thickened as they went on, but Marianne was caught completely off guard when he suddenly turned and folded her in his arms, pressing her against the cold stone wall.

"Come, now, it's private we are, and no one to see us at all, at all. Give us a little kiss to start, me darling, and then we'll —"

Momentarily Marianne was paralyzed, not so much by what was happening but by her memory of what had happened in the past. However, the tutor's breath, though far from pleasant, was not heavy with wine fumes; his fumbling hands had not the maniacal strength of Bagshot's. Turning her head to avoid his wet lips, Marianne freed one hand, doubled it into a fist, and brought it down on Victor's cheek.

He let out a howl of pain and relaxed his hold. Marianne twisted away. Three quick steps brought her to the door which she could dimly see through the gloom. She threw her weight against it; after a moment's resistance it yielded, admitting a flood of light from the windows in the hall beyond. This she recognized as a portion of the more modern wing, not far from the main staircase. This path had indeed been the shortest way back; Victor had been truthful on that score, at least.

"Wait." The tutor's voice, close behind her, made her turn quickly. She was no longer afraid, for a hearty scream would undoubtedly fetch help. What a contemptible-looking creature he was, nursing his cheek with one hand, his shoulders bowed and his eyes narrowed.

"Stand back," she said. "I don't want you near me."

"And no doubt you'll be off to Her Grace and tell her what happened."

"No doubt."

Victor made a sudden move. Marianne opened her mouth, prepared to cry out for help. But he made no attempt to seize her. In a way, what he did was worse. He dropped to his knees and clasped his hands. Marianne saw, with a thrill of disgust, that his eyes were overflowing with tears. He burst into a tempestuous appeal, of which, between his brogue and his sobs, she understood only the gist. He groveled, he apologized abjectly, he assured her no such thing would ever happen again. It was her fault, because her beauty had driven him mad; but it was his fault since nothing could excuse such vile, unmanly conduct. He begged her not to have him dismissed from his position.

The young Duke needed him, his "poor old mother in Killarney" would die of starvation and heartbreak. . . .

"Oh, do stop it," Marianne exclaimed. "Stand up and act like a man instead of a baby, and perhaps . . ."

Victor's sobs cut off. His tears had been genuine enough; his face was drenched, and when he wiped at his eyes with his dusty hands, trails of mud ran down his cheeks.

"Is it granting me mercy you are?"

"Well . . ." Seeing his eyes again overflow and his lips tremble, Marianne said disgustedly, "I will say nothing of this so long as there is no repetition of it. Only keep away from me in future."

She left him still on his knees babbling protestations of undying but respectful gratitude.

Ludicrous as the performance had been, Marianne had no impulse to laugh. She had been thoroughly repelled, and when, on reaching her own room, she saw that the sleeve of her dress bore the marks of the tutor's dirty hand, she stripped it off so quickly she burst half the buttons.

It was later than she had thought. She was still scrubbing vigorously at her face and arms when Annie knocked to tell her luncheon was served.

She had not expected that Victor would have the effrontery to appear for luncheon, nor did he. This was an informal meal when no visitors were present; the family came or not as they pleased. Lady Annabelle was always accompanied by one or more cats when she attended the meal. Today Marianne was glad to see that her companion was the enormous red Horace. He at least could be trusted to remain in his mistress's lap.

The Duchess studied Marianne with an expression of concern, and the girl squirmed self-consciously. Perhaps the Duchess did have psychic powers and could read her mind! But, as it turned out, the lady was thinking of another matter entirely.

"I fear this is dull for you," she said. "We will have to plan some outings. I only wish there were young people in the neighborhood with whom you might associate. Dr. Gruffstone is coming today or tomorrow, but he is not the gayest of companions. Roger, cannot I persuade you to stay for a few days and help entertain Marianne?"

"Thank you," the lawyer replied smoothly. "You tempt me. In fact, I had already arranged to go riding with Miss Ransom this afternoon."

Marianne had forgotten this arrangement, and she might have tried to get out of it but for the Duchess's response.

"What a splendid idea! I had thought of suggesting it, but it would be quite unsafe for her to venture out alone. Of course one of the grooms could accompany her, but this is much more suitable."

With the scheme thus approved, Marianne had no choice but to smile and say she was looking forward to it.

After the meal she went up to change into her riding habit. She was halfway up the stairs when a head popped out from between two of the carved banisters, with such an unnerving effect that only a firm grip of the handrail kept her from falling. She was irresistibly reminded of the painting of Lady Flora and her dreadful trophy. Then she saw that the head belonged to the young Duke, and that he was standing on a chest in the hall below.

"I gave you a start, didn't I?" he inquired complacently. "I did that to Annie once and she fell all the way down the stairs backwards. It was great fun."

"Annie did not find it great fun," Marianne replied with some asperity. "Nor will you, if you get your head caught between those posts and can't remove it."

"I got it in. I can get it out."

"So you think. I once saw a young rascal

get caught in just such a way, between two iron railings. He got his head in, all right, but it required two large constables and a crowbar to get him out."

"Oh." Henry tried to withdraw his head. An expression of alarm crossed his face when he found himself momentarily caught; Marianne watched with un-Christian satisfaction. Then the boy turned slightly, freeing his ears, and made good his escape. He looked thoughtful, however, and Marianne hoped she had put an end to this particular sport.

She continued up the stairs. Henry swung over the rail and followed. "Where are you going?" he asked.

"Riding, with Mr. Carlton."

"I will come along."

"Shouldn't you be at your studies?"

"Oh, I don't have to study. I am really quite clever, you know."

"I am sure you are." Marianne paused at her door, knowing that Henry would follow her in unless she dismissed him in no uncertain terms. "But you cannot come with us."

"Why not?"

"I don't want you."

Henry's lower lip began to swell like a rising blister.

"You had better let me come. If you don't,

I will tell my grandmother that you let Victor hug you and kiss you."

"What?" Marianne gasped. "You dreadful little . . . Were you following us this morning?"

"I do that a lot," said the Duke. "I'm very good at it. I practice in the woods, walking like Natty Bumppo; not a twig snaps."

"But sneaking — eavesdropping — that is most dishonorable!"

"But very interesting. People do the most amazing things when they think they are alone. This place is full of secret passages, you know. I have explored them all."

He took an apple from his pocket and juggled it as he spoke. Something about the restless gesture and the animation of the boy's face gave Marianne an unexpected feeling of sympathy. He seemed to have no companions of his own age and very few occupations; and if Victor was his preceptor it was no wonder Henry's notions of honorable behavior were deficient.

"If you followed us you must have seen that I did not *allow* M. Victor to do anything," she said.

"You hit him a good one," said the Duke admiringly. "I didn't know you were so strong. But Victor is a poor weak sort of fellow. I'd have come to rescue you if you had needed rescuing," he added. "The place where I was . . . it's a little hard to get out of it in a hurry."

"I appreciate the thought," Marianne said. "I promised, you know, that I wouldn't tell anyone about that."

"I won't tell either," said the Duke, tossing his apple high.

Marianne thought he was probably speaking the truth, not because of his noble nature but because the incident gave him a hold over his tutor. She considered admonishing him about the evils of blackmail but decided that if this thought had not already occurred to him she would only be putting ideas into his head.

"I would like very much to ride with you another day," she said. "I will need an escort after Mr. Carlton has returned to London. But today we must talk about certain business matters. It is a private talk. You would be bored."

"No, I wouldn't."

"Another time," Marianne said. Moving quickly, she got inside her room and bolted the door.

She wondered, as she changed, whether she had been wise to tell Henry that she and Carlton would be discussing private matters. His curiosity would certainly be piqued by that. But she felt sure they could find a place removed from any possibility of eavesdropping, even by the ingenious Duke.

Her spirits rose as she studied her reflection in the full-length mirror. The riding costume, made of the usual dull black cloth, set off her fair coloring and fit snugly around the waist before billowing out over a small bustle. Simple as the gown was, it had the unmistakable air of superb tailoring, and the hat was delicious — a dashing cavalier style with a broad brim and sweeping plumes.

When she came downstairs Carlton was waiting for her. He carried a leather crop, which he switched impatiently against his boots as he strode up and down.

"You were long enough," was his only greeting.

"A gentleman would say that the wait was well worthwhile," said Marianne, conscious of how pretty she looked.

"That depends on what one is waiting for. Come along. I have selected a mount for you and only hope you are up to it."

"I would have preferred to select my own."

"The choice is not that great." A footman hastened to open the door for them, and Carlton went on, "There is only one horse in the stable suitable for a lady. The head groom assures me she is gentle and tractable."

From this Marianne fully expected a timid old mare or a fat pony. She was agreeably surprised when she saw the horses a groom was leading up and down along the drive. One was a tall bay gelding which was stamping and blowing, impatient to be off; the other, which carried a lady's sidesaddle, was an elegant gray. Mild brown eyes turned to study Marianne as she approached, and a velvety soft mouth nuzzled the hand she extended.

"But I have nothing for you," she whispered. "Next time, I promise. How beautiful you are!" She turned to the groom. "What is her name?"

"Stella," was the reply. "Ye'll hae no trouble wi' her, miss; she's gentle as a lamb."

Marianne was about to reply that she was not at all afraid when she saw Carlton looking superciliously down at her from his saddle and a wicked impulse came over her. When the groom offered his hands to help her mount she made a clumsy business of it and wriggled around as if she were having difficulty finding her seat.

They started off at a walk, with Carlton leading. As soon as his back was turned Marianne settled herself more comfortably.

Carlton stayed on the path until they were out of the grounds. They went out a back gate instead of following the main drive to the road, and found themselves on the open moors, with the mountains forming a magnificent backdrop. The terrain was not too unlike the moors of Marianne's home, and as a fresh breeze tugged at the plumes in her hat she felt a rush of delight flood her veins. She had not realized how much she had missed the open air and the joy of finding herself on the back of a good horse.

She knew she rode well; had not her father, the best horseman in the West Riding, taught her? Indeed, these lessons had been the only occasions when Marianne felt close to her father — because only then was the squire unselfconscious with her. He had taken pride in her aptitude and made no allowance for her sex, except to insist that she ride sidesaddle after she grew too old to let her bare legs dangle. Noting the eager arch of the horse's neck, she knew Stella was yearning to run. The mare was too well trained to do so without an order from her rider, but her muscles quivered with desire.

So when Carlton said, "We might try a trot, I suppose, if you think you can stay on," Marianne yielded to her evil angel. It was only necessary to raise her hands and make a soft wordless sound of encouragement, and Stella was off.

Marianne heard Carlton's cry of alarm far behind her and tried to look as if she were being run away with; but after the first moment she forgot her intention in the sheer rapture of speed. The squire had owned some fine horses, but she had never ridden an animal that moved as well as Stella. Marianne urged her on with a shout, and lost her hat. The wind tore her curls loose from their net.

It was not repentance or fear that finally made her slow the horse's reckless pace, but awareness that she did not know the terrain and had no right to endanger the splendid animal by risking a stumble or a fall. Only then, as the whistling of air in her ears diminished, did she hear the pound of hooves behind her. Glancing over her shoulder she saw Carlton urging the gelding on at a desperate pace. He rode like a centaur, but the sight of his taut, anxious face made her want to burst out laughing. As he drew closer he shouted, "Hold on, don't let go the reins! Try to pull her in."

Marianne did so. The obedient Stella stopped, so suddenly that Carlton went shooting past. He turned his mount with ruthless strength and rode back more slowly.

The truth had dawned on him by then, and his expression was too much for Marianne. She doubled up over Stella's neck. Carlton waited until she had controlled her mirth. Then he said grimly, "I hope you enjoyed that."

"I did. So did Stella." Marianne stroked the mare's neck. Stella turned her head and curled her lips back as if joining in the girl's amusement. "Oh, it was wonderful," she went on exultantly. "I didn't realize how much I had missed it. And she moves like a dream — she is a wonder!"

"She is," Carlton agreed. "And you are a thoughtless, reckless young idiot." He studied her laughing, unrepentant face with its frame of tumbled curls, and after a moment the corners of his mouth twitched. "I suppose I sounded very smug, didn't I?"

"Yes, you did. I could not resist."

"I can't say that I blame you. All the same, you took a risk you should not have taken, and frightened me half to death. My heart has not stopped pounding yet."

"I didn't know you cared," said Marianne, lowering her eyes and looking up at him through her lashes.

"The Duchess would never forgive me if I let anything happen to you," was the cool reply. "Now, if your sense of humor is satisfied, shall we go on?"

"Well," said Marianne, after they had proceeded for some distance side by side, "what was it you wanted to talk to me about?"

"First I want you to tell me something. What precisely happened between you and Bagshot?"

Marianne's hands tightened. The intelligent Stella rolled an inquiring eye back at her, decided that the movement had not been meant for her, and proceeded onward at the same steady pace.

"I don't want to talk about it," Marianne muttered.

"I fear you must if you want me to trace your Maggie. I was unable to discover what had become of her. I must have more information if I am to proceed."

"You tried to find her?" Marianne's pique evaporated. She gave him a look of sincere gratitude. "That was kind."

"But ineffective, so far. I learned something of her history from the performers at the club, but none of them knew her well, and no one admits to having seen her after that night. Did she ever mention where she lived, or the name of a friend with whom she might have taken shelter? I must know everything she said."

"I didn't know what sort of place it was!"

Marianne burst out. "You must think me very stupid . . . but there are respectable theaters. I only wanted to earn my living singing. I see now that Mr. Wilson must have taken pains to keep me from finding out that the Alhambra was . . . And Maggie said something . . . what was it? Something to the effect that she should have known what he — what he was after. She watched over me, and I never realized. I believe he had sent a false message of some sort, that night, to lure her away."

"She would know of Bagshot's reputation," Carlton agreed dryly. "It is notorious, to say the least. And I myself observed him watching you the first night I attended your performance."

"You probably thought I would encourage his attentions," Marianne mumbled abjectly. "*He* certainly did. He walked into my dressing room as if he owned the place — and me. At first I think he could not believe I was sincere in rejecting him. Then he became very angry. His face was like a devil's! I wish I could forget it."

She closed her eyes and shivered. After a moment Carlton said gently, "I am sorry to put you through this. If it is any comfort to you, I believe you were as innocent as you claim."

Marianne opened her eyes and looked directly at him. "But you don't believe I am innocent now. You think that when I learned of the Duchess's fantasy I determined to take advantage of it."

"That is not the issue. Finish your account, please."

"But . . . Well, it is soon finished. He seized me. I resisted. My resistance only enraged him more. I did not see Maggie come in; I was — I was on the verge of fainting, I think. I felt his grasp relax; then he fell at my feet and I saw Maggie holding the stick with which she had struck him — his own gold-headed cane."

"Hoist with his own petard," Carlton said, his lip curling. "That stick is as notorious as its owner; it is lead-filled, and has often been employed as an offensive weapon. What happened next?"

"I was too dazed to think," Marianne confessed. "But Maggie was wonderful. She escorted me out of the place and hailed a cab. She told me never to come back, to leave London if I could." As she spoke, the events Marianne had tried to forget came back with a peculiar vividness. Once again she seemed to stand shivering in a fog-shrouded street, with the distant gaslights glimmering through the mist. Again she heard Maggie say, " 'E didn't see me, but 'e'll know who done it. 'E allus knows. They say 'e's in league wif the Devil. Old 'Arry'll take me in . . ."

She repeated the words. Carlton nodded thoughtfully.

"Old Harry. Well, it's not much, but it is more than I had. Don't worry; I inquired at the hospitals and the police stations, and no one answering her description has turned up."

"Why are you taking so much trouble?" Marianne asked. "She is only a poor ignorant woman —"

"My motives need not concern you," was the curt answer.

But Marianne thought she knew. Carlton believed that Maggie was more than a casual acquaintance and that she might give information about Marianne's real background — information that would prove to the Duchess that she was the fraud and the cheat Carlton believed her to be.

She tried to be angry, but the memories of her folly had so lowered her opinion of herself that she could only feel chagrin and remorse. How could she blame Carlton for thinking the worst of her? And the clergyman. . . . Marianne's heart sank when she thought how that saintly man would receive her story. She imagined the handsome face hardening with revulsion and she felt like bursting into tears.

"Perhaps it would be better to forget it," she said in a stilted voice. "Trying to trace her might only call attention to her. Mr. Bagshot seems to have dismissed the incident."

Carlton did not reply for a moment.

"Possibly he has," he said at last. "But . . . I don't want to frighten you, but you are so incredibly careless and naive! The man is well known for harboring grudges, and it would not be difficult for him to trace you if he cared to do so. His presence at the opera that night may have been a coincidence. Or he may have heard a description of the Duchess's protégée and followed her carriage to see if you were the girl he was seeking. Are you all right? You are not going to faint?"

"Certainly not," Marianne said, though her lips were so stiff with terror she could scarcely shape the word. She had convinced herself that she was safe from that danger, at least.

"You are very pale. Mind you, I think it unlikely that Bagshot would dare pursue you here. I only mention the possibility to warn you. Don't wander about alone."

"No. And you will look for Maggie?"

"I have people in London searching for her. I will telegraph the information you have given me at once."

In her distress Marianne had not been aware of her surroundings. Now she realized that they were approaching a ridge of low but jagged hills, harbingers of the more distant mountains. Bare granite spurs stood up between the pines that clothed their slopes.

"Are you recovered?" Carlton asked. "Do you wish to return, or have you strength to go on a little farther?"

"I would prefer to ride awhile longer."

"Follow me, then. We must go single file for a time."

Before long they were among the trees and riding along a narrow path blanketed with fallen needles. As they proceeded the going became more difficult. The trees closed in and the silence was profound. When Marianne heard a burst of song from a lark winging high and unseen above the overhanging boughs, it was as startling as a shout. Then she became aware of another sound, a distant murmuring, and she realized that the path had taken a downward angle. Ahead she caught glimpses of sunlight and was glad to see it; the green gloom around her was depressing.

They came out of the trees and Carlton's arm shot out like a bar, grasping Stella's bridle and stopping her.

They were on a rocky ledge, wide enough to make Carlton's gesture a needless precaution, though an unskilled rider or a frightened horse might easily go over the brink. Below, a wide mountain stream ran murmuring over peaty brown rocks. So steep was the gorge through which it ran that although the sky above was visible, the sunlight would only strike down into the depths at midday. Now the oblique rays cast a strange light over a scene of wild grandeur — the rocky slopes and twisted tree trunks, the bubbling water, the glistening stones in its depth.

The murmur she had heard was now a roar. Looking for its source Marianne saw that some distance to the left the water dropped over a small waterfall, no more than ten feet high, but narrowing so that the stream dropped with considerable force into a dark pool beyond. The pool and the portion of the stream below it seemed quite deep. She could not see bottom there. A brooding silence hung over the place. She would not have been surprised to behold a brown, inhuman face crowned with twisted horns peer out from behind the rocks.

And then, as unmistakably as if he had spoken, she knew why Carlton had brought her here.

"Is this where it happened? Where he died?"

"It seems that your claims of clairvoyance are not entirely unfounded," Carlton said. "Yes, this is the place. Holmes's cloak was found caught among the rocks beyond the waterfall. He was a great walker, and this was one of his favorite spots. The stream is comparatively shallow now. When there are heavy rains — as there were that autumn eighteen years ago — the water rises and the current is extremely swift. Gruffstone told me he had never seen it so high as it was that year; one of the men in the searching party he led came close to being swept away himself."

"But his body was never found," Marianne mused.

"That is not surprising. This stream is a tributary of the Tay, which it flows into a few miles downstream. The body might have been swept down all the way to the sea, or it might have been caught under some rocky bank."

"Yet I find it hard to believe no trace was ever found. The Duchess must have had every inch of the area searched."

"I believe she still harbors the belief that Holmes was snatched bodily into heaven like the prophet Elijah," Carlton said. "Don't start imagining things, Miss Ransom. If he had survived, even wounded and suffering from that convenient device of novelists, temporary amnesia, he would have been found eventually. The Duchess offered incredible rewards."

"I suppose so." Marianne tugged at the reins and turned Stella. "The place is uncanny. Let us go back — unless you have any other unpleasant news or ugly encounters for me."

"No, I have done my share. No doubt Gruffstone will have more to say."

Marianne grimaced. She had forgotten that the doctor was due to arrive shortly. She wondered what his specious excuse for coming might be. She knew the real reason, for it was also Carlton's. They feared her influence over the Duchess. She wished the doctor did not regard her so inimically, for she felt the need of someone she could confide in and lean upon. Carlton had his moments of kindness, but if she tried to lean on him he was just as apt to step back and let her fall to the ground.

Instead of going back the way they had

come, they followed a great circle that led to the main road beyond the village. Before long the church spire came into view. Conscious of her disheveled state, Marianne slowed Stella to a walk and tried to effect repairs, not an easy task without comb, mirror or . . .

"My hat!" she exclaimed in dismay. "Oh, dear, I have lost my beautiful hat."

"You can hardly blame me for failing to retrieve it," Carlton said. "I was too concerned about your breaking your head to worry about its covering."

"But it had real egret plumes," Marianne mourned.

She struggled with her windblown hair, trying to bundle it back into the net that dangled from a few pins. As he watched her, Carlton's face assumed its most disagreeable expression, eyes narrowed, lips curled in a sneer.

"One would think, after the serious matters we have discussed, that you would have no time for egret plumes or hats. But women's minds are incapable of intellectual concentration; and yours is really one of the most —"

If he was attempting to provoke her, he succeeded; the quick temper Marianne had acquired from her father flared up, and she interrupted Carlton's insult with a wild swing. He avoided the blow with an easy turn of his head.

"Temper, temper," he said. "You'll fall if you continue to bounce around that way."

Marianne became aware that her lacings were too tight. She could not get enough breath to shout. This was just as well, since she might have used some of the words she had heard the squire employ when he was in a rage. Finally she managed to say, "I would rather dispense with your escort, Mr. Carlton. Leave me."

"I can safely do so, I suppose, since we are in sight of the village. Remember my advice, Miss Carlton, and don't go dashing off after your egret plumes."

He lifted his hat, made her a genteel bow, and trotted off down the road.

Realizing that Stella was moving uneasily as she sensed her rider's agitation, Marianne calmed herself. She did not regret trying to slap Carlton; she only regretted missing. She waited until he had vanished around a turn in the road before following. By the time she reached the first houses of the village he was out of sight.

There were few people abroad, despite the unseasonably mild weather. The cottage windows were tightly sealed. Presumably the hard-working peasants had no time to enjoy nature. The men would be at work, the women tending children and preparing the evening meal. The only signs of activity were at the Devenbrook Arms. Marianne could see through the open gates into the innyard, where a coach and horses stood waiting for some traveler. This reminded her of Bagshot and of Carlton's warning. Ridiculous, she told herself angrily. Bagshot would not dare to show his face in such a small place as this, where every stranger was immediately observed.

The houses thinned out; only the church and the vicarage, a neat stone house somewhat larger than the others, remained to be passed before she turned into the drive leading to the castle. Though she had convinced herself she was in no danger, she felt nervous and had lifted the reins, preparatory to urging Stella into a trot, when she saw the church doors open and a familiar form appear. The sunlight caught its cap of golden hair and set it aglow.

Without any conscious intent on her part, Marianne's hands tightened and Stella came to a stop. The vicar saw her at the same time. Lifting a hand as if to ask her to wait, he quickly descended the steps and came toward her.

He had to speak to me, Marianne thought, her heart pounding. He saw me stop — why was I so forward? — and felt obliged to greet me. But the glow of pleasure on St. John's face made her hope that this depressing idea was wrong.

"What a welcome and unlooked-for surprise," he exclaimed. "If I thought the Almighty concerned himself with such trivial matters, I would almost believe this meeting to be an answer to prayer."

Marianne did not quite like being considered trivial, but the speech was otherwise so gracious she decided to overlook that part of it.

"It is a pleasure to see you, Mr. St. John. I hope you are well?"

"Splendid, thank you. But you are wondering why I stopped you."

"Not at all," Marianne murmured.

"I wished, first, to apologize for the unpleasantness that marred what was otherwise a delightful evening."

"You have no need to apologize. I am only sorry —"

"No, no, the fault was mine. I was too abrupt. Her Grace was quite right in accusing me of a lack of tolerance. I assure you, I have been berating myself ever since."

Indeed, Marianne could now see the delicate strains of sleeplessness and worry marking his eyelids. They only made him look more romantic.

"I hate to see you in distress," she said impulsively. "The Duchess is the kindest woman in the world; if you go to her and tell her you have changed your mind —"

"But I cannot. I have not." He looked up at her, his hand resting on Stella's neck. "That is where my trouble lies, Miss Ransom. You do understand, don't you?"

"I am not sure —"

"Prayers for the dead — that is sheer popery!" His eyes glowed with a fiery light. "Her Grace may call it a memorial service, but she wants more, more than I can in conscience give. Yet I might be tempted to do something of the sort if I sincerely believed that she had abandoned her heathen practices. Oh, Miss Ransom, I must say this, hard as it is — I must warn you. Do not, I beg you, participate in those actions which can only endanger your immortal soul."

Before the burning intensity of his look Marianne's eyes fell. She would like to have disclaimed any knowledge of what he meant, but she could not; those clear eyes seemed to see straight into her heart.

"I owe her so much," she murmured.

"She took me in when I was friendless, poor —"

One more minute and she would have confessed the whole shameful story. But Mr. St. John did not give her the opportunity.

"You owe her gratitude, companionship, devotion. But your soul you owe to no man — or woman," he added punctiliously.

Marianne wanted to promise anything he asked. His voice thrilled her; mind, heart, and soul responded. But her buried streak of obstinacy made her say, "I can't see that there is any harm in it."

"I tell you these manifestations are of the Devil! Have you read that splendid pamphlet, *Table-moving Tested and Proved to be the Result of Satanic Agency*? Or *Tableturning, the Devil's Modern Masterpiece*?"

"No," Marianne admitted.

"The table confessed," Mr. St. John said solemnly, "that it was moved by the spirit of a lost soul sent from Hell."

"Oh, dear."

"Will you read these books if I give them to you?"

"Yes; but —"

"Wait here. Wait only a moment."

Any other man would have looked foolish running at such a pace, his coattails flapping; but Mr. St. John — his admirer thought —

even ran beautifully. He vanished into the parsonage; in a moment he came pelting back, waving several small volumes.

"Here," he panted, pressing them into her hand. "Read and heed the blessed words in them. Read and pray, my dear Miss Ransom. And if you should ever require spiritual guidance, I am at your service — at any hour of the day or night."

A thrill ran down Marianne's spine. "Thank you," she said. "I . . . I must go now."

"Yes, you must." The young man stepped back. "I have kept you too long. But it was well done, if my words bear fruit. Remember."

"I will."

He looked as if he would have said more, but a burst of distant laughter from the inn made him recollect himself. He made her a formal bow and turned to return to the house.

Stella looked inquiringly at her new mistress. "May we go on now?" she seemed to say. Marianne said absently, "Yes, Stella, go on, do," and they trotted sedately off, with Marianne's head craned to watch the vicar until he disappeared inside.

Stella knew her way home, which was fortunate, because her rider was daydreaming.

They had passed into the drive before Marianne realized it would never do to let the Duchess see the books the vicar had given her. She thrust them into the front of her jacket. They made an unseemly bulge, but at least their titles were not visible.

She found one of the grooms waiting by the front steps, sent, he said, by Mr. Carlton, who had promised she would be along directly. After an affectionate farewell to Stella, Marianne crossed both arms awkwardly over her breast to hide the books and made a dash for her room. She thrust the dangerous little volumes into her wardrobe under a heap of undergarments, and just in time — a tap at the connecting door heralded the arrival of the Duchess.

"Well," she exclaimed, smiling, "from your appearance, my dear Marianne, I would conclude that you have spent a happy, busy day."

"I lost my hat," Marianne said.

The Duchess laughed outright. "I heard about that. Roger pretended to be annoyed at the trick you played on him, but I could tell he was greatly entertained. Don't concern yourself, child; he has sent one of the menservants out to look for your hat, and if it is not found we well get you another. I would sacrifice a dozen hats to see you looking so bright and healthy."

"You are too kind," Marianne said miserably. She felt as if the offending volumes were out in plain sight, blazoning their messages aloud.

"Not at all." The Duchess patted her cheek. "What do you say to a cup of tea here in your room, and a little rest? My dear old Gruffstone has arrived, so we will be seven for dinner. I sometimes allow Henry to dine when Horace is here; they are so fond of one another. And one can't exclude M. Victor, he is so sensitive. . . . And Annabelle, of course. I only hope she will not bring half a dozen cats. *À bientôt,* then, my child."

She went out, leaving Marianne no opportunity to speak even if she had wanted to — which she did not. As she watched the maids running in and out with trays of tea and cakes, buckets of hot water, warm towels, and other luxuries, she felt like a racehorse being groomed — and bribed — for the evening's performance.

CHAPTER ELEVEN

Marianne was not looking forward to the dinner party. The presence of one man whom she had tried to slap and another whom she had not only slapped, but struck with her fist, was enough to promise discomfort. Add to them Dr. Gruffstone, who thoroughly disapproved of her, the Duke, the most accomplished little Paul Pry of all time, Lady Annabelle and her cats . . .

Yet the meeting turned out to be surprisingly successful. Dr. Gruffstone met her kindly, taking her hand and asking with concern how she felt. "Have you been sleeping?" he inquired. "You appear a little pale."

"This is not your consulting room, Horace," the Duchess said with a smile. "You medical men, always seeing symptoms where there are none! Marianne has had a long day in the fresh air and feels splendid, don't you, my love?"

Carlton's greeting, too, was pleasant. "I am happy to report that the lost treasure has been found," he said lightly. "Your hat is being refurbished and will be returned to you by morning, plumes and all."

To be sure, Victor sulked, but he did not dare do it ostentatiously. Marianne thought she was the only one who noticed his reproachful and pleading looks until Carlton said sotto voce, "Have you been forced to put our Irish Frenchman in his place? I trust he did not make rude advances to you."

"How absurd," Marianne said haughtily.

But the big surprise was Lady Annabelle, who appeared on time, without cats, and wearing quite a nice gown from which most of the cat hairs had been removed. It was obvious that the doctor was the cause of her transformation. To say that she fawned on him or flirted with him would be inaccurate; rather, she courted his approval and hung on his pronouncements. There was no denying that the plain, aging man radiated a strong aura of fatherly authority when he chose. Even Henry was on his best behavior.

When the ladies retired to the drawing room, Marianne felt an immediate change in the atmosphere. It originated with the Duchess, who showed signs of increasing agitation as time wore on and the men lingered in the dining room. Marianne offered to play, but was refused, though in a kindly fashion. Lady Annabelle, removed from the doctor's presence, relapsed into a peaceful doze.

Finally a burst of laughter from Carlton heralded the appearance of the gentlemen. They sauntered into the drawing room with the smug sleepy look of men who had drunk quite a quantity of good port.

"What a long time you have been," the Duchess exclaimed. "I hope you were not telling stories — you know the kind I mean — in front of Henry, or that you did not let him drink with you."

"He had a single glass of port," the doctor said, giving Henry a paternal pat on the shoulder. "He must learn to handle his wine like a gentleman, Honoria; he is growing up."

Henry's chest swelled visibly.

"Well and good; but it is time for him to go to bed now," said the Duchess.

"Oh, no, not yet! I'm too old to be sent off to bed like a baby. Besides, I want to see the table turning."

The doctor's face lost its good humor and became thunderous. "Honoria, you gave me your word —"

"I did nothing of the sort! In any event I refuse to discuss it in front of Henry. Monsieur Victor, assert your authority."

"Certainement, madame la duchesse," said

Victor, with a look of utter incompetence. "Henri —"

"No, I won't. I want to stay."

"Off with you, young man," the doctor said. "I intend to test your progress in Latin tomorrow, and I promise you you will need your wits about you."

"But . . . Oh, very well."

The doctor beamed approval. Marianne was not so sanguine; she had caught a familiar expression on Henry's face and suspected he had some scheme in mind.

He went off quietly, however, with Victor trailing after him. Then Gruffstone turned to the Duchess.

"Honoria, have you been up to your tricks? I told you —"

"You told me and I chose to dismiss what you said. What — am I some dependent of yours, that I must obey your every whim? Are you Socrates or Solon, always right? Either you participate or you remove yourself, Horace. There are no other possibilities."

"I do participate then," said the doctor heavily. "With profound misgivings. I warned you, Honoria."

"So you did. We will adjourn to the other room now. Annabelle, will you join us?"

"Yes, I think so," Lady Annabelle replied,

yawning. "That is, if Dr. Gruffstone approves."

"Certainly," the doctor said with a sigh. "The more, the merrier."

The White Room had been prepared. A fire blazed on the hearth and the draperies had been drawn. A screen shielded the firelight.

Marianne's pulse was fast as she took her place, and Carlton must have felt it when he clasped his fingers around her wrist; he gave her a strange look, but said nothing. The circle of hands was formed, Lady Annabelle participating as if this were no new thing for her.

She was the calmest of them all, and for once Marianne found her bovine placidity soothing.

"What is going to happen?" she inquired. "Will David come at last, do you suppose?"

"Perhaps," the Duchess replied.

"Well, if the girl is his daughter —"

"Please, Annabelle. You know the rules. No more talking."

Scarcely had this last request been made when there was a sharp rap, seemingly from under the table. The Duchess's fingers clamped down on Marianne's hand.

"They are strong tonight," she murmured.

"They are," Carlton agreed. "Your Grace,

may I suggest that we take the usual precautions to make sure no one is tapping with his, or her, foot? Unconsciously, of course."

The Duchess nodded impatiently and moved so that the sole of her slipper rested lightly on Marianne's left foot. Carlton placed his foot, not so lightly, on her right shoe.

Two more raps echoed. The table lifted and dropped down.

"We will communicate in the usual way," the Duchess said. She began to recite the alphabet, intoning each letter slowly and solemnly, like a litany. When she reached the letter *G*, another rap sounded. By this means the phrase "Good evening" was spelled out. A snort from the doctor's end of the table greeted this courteous remark.

"Be quiet," the Duchess snapped. "Will the spirit who is present indicate its name?"

This time the alphabetic method produced the letters "puden," and the Duchess exclaimed, "Pudenzia! Is it you?" A vehement rap confirmed this.

"Who the blazes is that?" Lady Annabelle inquired.

"Never mind. This takes too long," the Duchess said. "I trust you skeptics will have no objection to our reverting to written letters so long as we all keep our hands in plain sight?"

No one objected, though it was clear that the men were not in favor of the suggestion. Marianne flexed her fingers. Her left hand had gone quite numb from the pressure of the Duchess's grasp.

From a drawer under the table the Duchess produced a printed list of the letters of the alphabet and an ivory stylus. As she began to run the point of the stylus down the list, Marianne saw the advantage of the process. The stylus could move much more quickly than the voice could pronounce the letters.

After the first few letters had been designated by means of the familiar raps, Marianne lost track of what was being spelled. The affair confounded her; it was so brisk and matter-of-fact, rather like writing out a telegram; yet she could not understand where the raps were coming from. Carlton's suggestion that someone was tapping with a foot was ridiculous. The sounds were too sharp and distinct to have been produced by leather on wood or carpeting.

"Most interesting," the Duchess said, after an interval. "Did the rest of you follow that?"

"No," Carlton said.

"It is as I thought," the Duchess said, repressed excitement coloring her voice. "Pudenzia says she was a Christian maiden in early Rome under Diocletian, to be precise."

"Poor old Diocletian," said the incorrigible Carlton. "He and Nero are blamed for everything that went wrong with the Christians. I suppose the lady was martyred?"

"If you cannot be serious, Roger, you will have to leave."

"I beg your pardon."

"Pudenzia refuses to speak of the manner of her death. Quite understandable. She says that we must think of love, not hate; of life, not death."

"A very pretty, pious, pointless sentiment," Carlton muttered under his breath.

Apparently the Duchess did not hear this. She went on. "She is your control, Marianne."

"My what?" Marianne looked alarmed. Up to that point she had found the process only mildly bewildering. She was not the focus of attention; all she had to do was sit and listen. "I don't understand. I don't know what to do."

"You have done very nicely so far," said Carlton, in the barely audible murmur he had adopted, designed for her ears alone.

"I think we have spent enough time on the alphabet," the Duchess said. "If you will darken the room, Roger, we will try for more direct contact."

The lawyer did as he was directed, extinguishing one candle after another until the only light came from the fire. At the Duchess's order he drew the screen closer, so that the room was in almost total darkness. He stumbled over something on his way back to the table, and Marianne thought she heard a rude word, quickly stifled. He had barely taken his place before the Duchess said, "We are waiting, Pudenzia. Show us a sign."

At the rim of the table a pallid glow appeared and gradually took form. At first it was only a thick, short column of pale luminescence. Then, with a bizarre suggestion of sprouting, five stumps appeared and lengthened into fingers and thumb.

Lady Annabelle coughed. "Quite nice," she said approvingly. "May I touch it? Will it shake hands with us?"

The table began to rock wildly, as if offended by the suggestion. Carlton swore again without bothering to muffle his voice; Marianne deduced that he had tried to leave his place and had been soundly rapped by a table leg. Her mouth was dry with excitement and fear. In the darkness she seemed to see the vicar's earnest face with its halo of sunlit hair. "I beg you, Miss Ransom, that you will not take part. . . ." Was she responsible for the raps, for the phantom hand?

"Sit still," the doctor's voice exclaimed. "I tell you this is sheer delusion — absolute balderdash!"

Marianne heard someone screaming. *She* was screaming. Varied sensations pounded at organs that had been shocked into renewed life after a period of interminable and chaotic darkness. In that darkness she had struggled, lost and alone, with some detestable adversary.

A glass pressed to her lips and a sharp burning liquid filled her mouth. She choked and pushed the glass away, but the liquid etched a path down her throat and helped to restore her.

She opened her eyes. An oil lamp stood on the table, casting eerie distorted shadows over the faces of the others. The doctor held the glass of brandy that had been forced against her lips. She recognized the taste now; the squire's breath had often smelled of it. Carlton held her by the arm.

"What happened?" she whispered.

"Her Grace would call it a trance, no

doubt," Carlton said. "But this was not such a smooth performance as the other; were the questions too difficult for you?"

"Enough, Roger," the doctor broke in. "Miss Ransom, can you remember nothing of what you said?"

"No. It was horrible! Like dying . . . and being forced back into my body."

The Duchess started to speak; her old admirer cut her off with a forceful gesture. "Be still, Honoria. Miss Ransom. You were in obvious distress from the first, writhing and moaning. Suddenly you began to shout, No, no, and went on until Roger here caught hold of you. Did something occur to upset you?"

"It is wrong," Marianne said confusedly. "He told me . . . The Devil . . ."

"*Who* told you?" the doctor demanded sharply.

"Some other entity, obviously," the Duchess said. "There are elemental spirits, soulless creatures of chaos. . . . Pudenzia is inexperienced, no doubt she has not yet learned to keep such intrusive spirits away."

The calm description was so like an appraisal of a new housemaid that Marianne felt a hysterical desire to laugh. The sound came out as a moan, however, and the doctor said firmly, "Bed for you, young woman.

I will come in to see you later. We will tell your maid you were taken ill, a fit of giddiness —"

"Always thinking of appearances, Gruffstone," Carlton said with a sneer. "You fool, every servant in the house knows quite well what is going on. It's a wonder they haven't fled screaming into the night."

The attitude of Marianne's maid, when she finally answered her bell, substantiated the lawyer's suggestion. Annie rolled her eyes till the whites showed every time Marianne moved, and once Marianne was in bed she literally ran from the room. The doctor had been waiting in the hall. Marianne heard him speak and Annie answer. She could not make out the words, but after an exchange or two, the maid's voice lost its nervous stammer. She even giggled.

The doctor went through the usual routine, checking Marianne's pulse and inspecting her tongue. He then made her take a dose of a mild sleeping medicine.

"You do believe me, don't you, sir?" Marianne asked pathetically. "I wasn't pretending; really I wasn't."

Gruffstone's grim expression softened.

"In all honesty, child, I don't know what to make of it. I assure you I am not leaping to conclusions. There is such a thing as . . .

But I do not want to frighten you."

It was the second time that day someone had expressed that sentiment; on the first occasion Carlton *had* frightened her, rather badly. Marianne looked apprehensively at the doctor.

"Have you ever heard of a condition called hysteria?" Gruffstone asked.

"Yes, of course. I *was* hysterical, for a few minutes, but I never —"

"You don't understand what I mean. I use the term in its medical sense. It is a pathological nervous condition which may occur when there is a conflict between the natural impulses and the demands of duty, loyalty, or moral standards. Is that clear?"

It is doubtful whether Marianne would have fully comprehended this description even if she had been fully alert. Now, with the effects of the sleeping draft creeping over her, she replied drowsily, "No, sir."

"Well, well, never mind; perhaps," the doctor said, half to himself, "perhaps it is just as well you don't. Sleep, child; rest. You are at peace and need fear no harm. Do you believe in your heavenly Father and His abiding love? Do you say your prayers?"

"Yes, sir. Always . . ." Marianne felt herself drifting off.

"Then you know he will watch over you.

Say with me: 'Our Father which art in Heaven . . .' "

The doctor sat with her for some time after her voice had died away. When he left she was sleeping peacefully, with a contented smile on her face.

II

Next morning she felt perfectly wretched. Squire Ransom could have told her what ailed her: the aftereffects of a combination of wine, brandy, and laudanum, which would have affected even a practiced toper. Marianne did not know why she felt so terrible, but she forced herself to dress and go down to breakfast. After a few cups of strong tea and a piece of dry toast she began to feel that she might live through the day. But she was still tired and queasy when she crept out to the garden and took her seat under the rose arbor. She had slept late, the morning mist had been burned away by the sun and it was a fine, brisk day.

Marianne had brought her needlework with her, in the pretty embroidered bag she had made under Mrs. Jay's supervision. But the bag concealed a less innocent object than her Berlin work. She had brought it to this distant spot, braving the chilly air, so that she could read without fear of discovery. There was no way of approaching her without crossing a stretch of gravel, and she hoped the sound would alert her in time for her to hide the volume.

Her sense of guilt and shame about participating in the séances had not been entirely dispelled, but she appreciated the doctor's attempt to restore not only her body but her distracted mind. Most reassuring of all was her memory of praying with him. Surely no one possessed by a devil could repeat the Lord's Prayer. Once she had had a nursery maid who had told her horrible stories about ghosts and witches. The girl had been dismissed when her exercise in sadism had been discovered, but Marianne had never forgotten the gruesome tales. One of the worst had concerned a demon who had taken possession of a poor farmer's body and had occupied it without suspicion until a clergyman had spotted the intruder and forced him to betray himself by repeating the Lord's Prayer. The demon had said it backwards.

Folktales, repeated by an ignorant, superstitious woman? Oh, certainly; but in the past weeks Marianne had seen things she would once have dismissed as fiction. Perhaps the vicar's books would help to explain them. She opened the one she had brought with her and began to read.

"Can it be, that this is the beginning of Satan's last struggle, that on the imposition of hands the table is endued with power from the Devil? I merely ask, can it be?"

But the author obviously thought he knew the answer. Marianne read on, puckering her forehead over some of the more ponderously illogical sentences. So absorbed was she that, after all, she failed to hear the crunch of gravel. A shadow fell across the page; she looked up, with a startled scream, to see Carlton looming over her.

She made a belated attempt to hide the book. Carlton's eyebrows lifted and he twitched the volume neatly out of her hands.

"Good heavens," he said disgustedly, after a glance at the title, "where did you get this rubbish? No, let me guess. Who else but St. John?"

"How can you call it rubbish? You said yourself you do not believe that the spirits of the blessed dead return —"

"I don't believe anything returns," Carlton replied irritably. "But this is even worse than the Duchess's theories."

He turned over a few pages, scanned the print, and burst into a shout of laughter.

"Here we have the interrogator asking the spirit where Satan's headquarters are. 'Are they in England?' A slight movement of the table. 'Are they in France?' A violent movement. 'Are they at Rome?' The table seemed literally frantic. . . . Really, Miss Ransom, how can you read such bigoted trash with a straight face?"

Marianne ought to have been offended. Instead his laughter made her feel better.

"Do you really think it is trash?"

"Of course. This is the worst possible thing for you, huddling here in the cold straining your eyes and your poor little conscience. Come for a ride. The exercise will do you good. At least it does me good, after a night of overindulgence."

"How can you say such a thing?" Marianne protested. But she took the hand he extended and allowed him to raise her to her feet.

"You had too much brandy for someone who is not accustomed to spirits," was the reply. "I suppose Gruffstone concluded that it was better for you to be tipsy than hysterical. However, the morning after is not pleasant. Hurry now; I will meet you downstairs in ten minutes."

It took Marianne longer than ten minutes, for she had to go to the kitchen to beg some carrots. Stella received the offering graciously.

"What a glorious day," Marianne exclaimed, removing her hat and lifting her face to the sun. "Thank you, Mr. Carlton. This is just what I needed."

"I have had considerable experience in these matters," Carlton replied.

They rode on in comfortable silence, side by side. Then Marianne asked, "Have you had any word about Maggie?"

"Hardly; I only dispatched the new information yesterday. I also requested my people to find out what Bagshot is doing just now."

"I am sure your concern on that point is unnecessary," Marianne said, with more confidence than she really felt.

"No doubt. At this moment I am much more concerned about another matter. Miss Ransom, have you considered what you are doing? How long do you plan to continue this masquerade?"

"You still think me a cheat, then." Marianne felt more weariness than anger.

"I don't know what you are! Gruffstone has another theory. I am forced to admit there may be some truth in it."

"Theory? Oh, yes. He said something to me last night, but I did not understand his meaning — something about hysteria. He was very kind."

"He is too inclined to take people at face value," Carlton replied cynically. "However, I respect his medical knowledge, and he tells me that there has been considerable research into this phenomenon of hysteria. Some fellow at the Salpêtrière in Paris — Charlot? . . . Charcot, that was the name — at any rate, he and some others have learned that illnesses of certain patients are purely mental in origin, and can be cured by suggestion. These patients believe themselves to be ill, so they become ill. I suppose I am explaining it badly, for he bombarded me with medical terms I didn't understand; but the gist of it is simple enough. People believe what they want to believe, and some people are more susceptible to self-delusion than others."

"But there is nothing scientific about that! In any case," Marianne added haughtily, "I am not deluding myself."

"My dear girl, we all do, to varying degrees. The doctor believes that all men — and women — are basically good; the Duchess believes the spirits of the dead talk to her —"

"And what makes you so sure they are wrong?"

"That is my form of self-delusion," the

lawyer said wryly. "That I know better than they. See here, Miss Ransom, I am not such a pompous fool as I sound. Most of what I have seen and heard about spiritualism strikes me as absurd, but I am not so dogmatic as to insist there may not be a germ of truth in it. Would you be willing to let me subject you to some kind of physical restraint the next time Her Grace insists on a performance?"

"What did you have in mind?" Marianne asked doubtfully.

"Nothing more than most mediums now accept. That you be bound to a chair — I promise I will only use the softest of cloths — which is bolted to the floor."

"Certainly," Marianne replied. "That seems reasonable."

"Also . . ."

"Well?"

The lawyer coughed self-consciously. "That you be searched. Oh, not by me! Lady Annabelle will oblige, I am sure."

"It sounds most disagreeable," Marianne grumbled. "However, if it will settle your doubts, I agree. Not that I am anxious to repeat the performance. Do you think the Duchess might give up —"

"Her séances? Never! Believe me, I would not ask you to go through another one solely to satisfy my curiosity; I only propose these means because I know you have not the strength to resist her demands. Those demands will not stop. Don't you realize that the anniversary of Holmes's death is less than a fortnight away? She will not rest until she receives some message from him."

Marianne shuddered. "It is wrong. I can't help but feel that."

"It is," Carlton agreed. For once his face and his voice were quite serious. "Wrong not to accept God's will; wrong to call those who are at peace back from their rest. Whether one believes that they come or not, the very demand is mistaken and harmful. Ah, I've had enough of this somber talk. Come, I will race you back to the road."

Marianne took off her hat and reveled in the wind's strong fingers running through her hair; but as she urged Stella on, she was pondering a new and startling idea. What if the Duchess were to receive a message from David Holmes telling her to abandon her attempt to reach him, to let him rest? Marianne had not the capability to perform such a trick; but if she had, she would have been sorely tempted to try it, as much for her kind friend's sake as for her own.

III

As the party assembled in the White Room that evening, Marianne was struck by the difference in atmosphere from the preceding night. Then darkness and mystery and distress had filled the air. Tonight, thanks to Carlton, the affair had the brisk efficiency of a scientific experiment.

Lady Annabelle had agreed to cooperate, even though her offer of the cat Horace, as a sniffer out of evil spirits, had been firmly declined. In the music room next to the parlor she searched Marianne, while the Duchess looked on. She was surprisingly efficient, shaking out each petticoat as it was handed to her, and running light fingers over Marianne's body once the girl had removed all her clothing except her drawers and bodice. She even asked Marianne to unpin her hair.

"That is that," she announced, motioning Marianne to resume her clothing. "I can testify, Miss Ransom, that you have no infernal devices about you. How silly this is! No self-respecting animal would engage in such a performance."

"Animals have no souls," the Duchess said.

"I am not convinced of that," Lady Annabelle retorted. "I can tell you, at any rate, that if my cats don't go to Heaven I won't go there either."

She stalked out of the room. The Duchess smiled apologetically at Marianne.

"She is such a strange mixture of child and woman. Thank you, my dear, for taking this so well."

"Candidly, it is a relief to me," Marianne replied, tying the strings of the last petticoat. The Duchess helped her into her gown, it having been decided that the servants should not be involved in the affair.

"I don't blame you for being confused," she said. "Or for doubting your own powers. It is frightening at first, and I would not have pushed you as I have, but . . . There is a reason, Marianne."

"The anniversary?" Marianne asked.

She had no need to be more specific. For the tormented woman there was only one date in all history worthy of remembrance.

"You know, then," the Duchess said.

"Mr. Carlton told me."

"Marianne, I must hear from him — I must! I will go mad if that day passes without some word. I know this is hard for you; but I will repay you, child, never fear. I will make sure you have —" She caught sight of Marianne's face and began murmuring apologies.

"No, I didn't mean that. I know you need no reward. Forgive me."

"Of course. Please don't distress yourself."

There was a knock on the door — Carlton, impatiently demanding whether it took all night to tie a few ribbons and button half a dozen buttons.

The Duchess had accepted Carlton's suggestion of restraints. She had insisted on only one point: total darkness. It was well known, she said, that the vibrations of light were hurtful to the discarnates.

Marianne was led to an armchair, upholstered in the seat and back, but with legs and arms of plain wood. After asking if she was comfortable and receiving an affirmative reply, Carlton proceeded to fasten her wrists to the arms of the chair. Her ankles were tied together and bound to the cross-piece. When Carlton rose after performing this last task, his face was redder than usual. Marianne had felt herself blushing too; it was the first time since childhood that a man's hands had touched her lower extremities, and although Carlton had been quick and respectful, the pressure of his fingers had felt . . . strange. Marianne wondered what the vicar would have said about that slightly indelicate act. She forced the thought from her mind.

It would not do to think of the vicar now.

Carlton turned to the doctor, who had been watching morosely. "Would you like to test the fastenings, Gruffstone?"

"My dear boy, don't be ridiculous. You are sure the chair itself is firmly anchored?"

"I did not have the heart to ask that bolts be driven into this beautiful old flooring," Carlton replied. "But the chair is extremely heavy; I doubt that a slight woman like Miss Ransom could budge it. However, I intend to remove any doubts on that score by sitting here beside her." And he drew up a low stool with a petit-point floral scene and sat down at Marianne's feet.

"Quite satisfactory," the doctor replied. "Er — Honoria?"

The Duchess was flushed with excitement. "Quite, quite," she said impatiently. "Get on with it, Horace. The lights, if you please — and draw that screen closer to the fire."

She took her place at the table, turning her chair slightly so as to face Marianne. Lady Annabelle took another chair; her hands moved restlessly, as if stroking an imaginary cat. The doctor dealt with the lights.

"Curse it," came his plaintive voice, from the darkness that followed the extinction of the last candle. "I can't see a thing, Honoria.

Can't we have just one light so I don't fall and break a limb?"

"Sit down there, where you are, and stop fussing," the Duchess said sharply.

Marianne was nervous, but it was no more than the nervousness of a performer before she goes on stage — a sensation with which she was tolerably familiar. She feared only one thing, a repetition of the horrid trance state, if that was what it was. To lose control of one's body is frightening in itself, but the experience of the previous evening, the bodiless struggle in darkness with some unseen force, was an experiment she did not care to repeat.

The silence continued for a long time, so long that it was at last broken by the unmistakable sound of a soft snore. Carlton emitted a snicker of amusement, but he did not speak, and Lady Annabelle continued to snore until the well-known rap was heard. Annabelle snorted. "What?" she began sleepily.

"Quiet," the Duchess ordered.

A perfect fusillade of cracks replied. A creak from somewhere in the darkness was followed by Annabelle's exclamation. "The table is moving. It is lifting, tilting . . . Ow!"

"Really, Annabelle, if you cannot refrain from crying out you will have to leave the room," the Duchess said.

"It came down on my foot," Annabelle replied angrily.

"Then tuck your feet under your chair. I warn you, one more word . . ."

But the apparitions did not seem to be inhibited by conversation. The cracks reverberated from all corners of the room, and others pieces of furniture began to creak and sway. At least Marianne assumed that was the cause of the sounds she heard. Her eyes had become more accustomed to the darkness, but since her back was to the scanty illumination of the well-screened fire, she could not even make out dim shapes.

A faint glow heralded the appearance of a mandolin, outlined in fire, hanging unsupported in midair. A strain of soft music sounded.

"David," the Duchess whispered. "David, is it you?"

The mandolin swooped up and down, still playing.

Hands fumbled at Marianne's feet, touched the bonds on her ankles, and moved up to her wrists.

"I beg your pardon," Carlton whispered. "I only wanted to make certain —"

"Your head is in my way," Marianne answered, straining her neck to watch the gyrations of the flying mandolin.

"Stop squirming! How can I be sure —"

"Move your head! Oh — oh, it is gone."

The luminous mandolin had indeed disappeared.

A medley of music followed — bells rang, chords sounded on the piano, a tambourine jingled. They were pleasant-enough sounds, though they formed no pattern and no recognizable tune.

Then there was a brief pause, as if the spirit needed rest after its strenuous efforts. In the silence Marianne heard the Duchess's breath coming in quick, sobbing pants, and her initial fascinated interest faded. She felt sad and a little giddy, and wished she had not taken quite so much wine at dinner.

The next demonstration was of a luminous hand that appeared suddenly in midair. Marianne could see it was not the same shape as the one that had materialized on the previous evening, being long and slim with delicate fingers.

This time the Duchess's cry was one of recognition.

"David — it is you!" A scrape of wood and a rustle of skirts told Marianne that the distraught woman had left her chair to pursue the phantom hand. As if to tease her, it darted back and forth. Panting and gasping, the Duchess stumbled after it.

"Stop her," Marianne exclaimed. "Oh, stop her; this is dreadful! She will fall and hurt herself —"

She pulled against the bonds that confined her hands, but Carlton had tied the knots too well. The struggle made her dizzier than before; she felt herself on the verge of swooning.

The grotesque, pitiful chase had only lasted for a few seconds, in fact, and Carlton was rising to his feet when the voice came.

"Silence. Be still. Silence."

It was hardly more than a whisper, but it had a hollow, penetrating quality that echoed as if the words had been pronounced in some other place, much larger than the parlor.

"Honor," the whisper came again. "Honor, listen and do not speak. I have little strength. I may not stay. The day approaches, be ready for me then. Now let me rest. I must have rest. . . ."

The final sibilant turned into an insect buzzing that went on and on. Marianne felt as if it sounded inside her head. She shook that member and at once regretted the movement, for the darkness blazed with colored cartwheels and rings of fire. An icy wind touched the back of her neck.

With an effort she kept her senses. The eerie effects seemed to be over. The cold wind ceased to blow, the whispering voice was no longer heard, and she was beginning to relax when a new outburst brought her upright and shaking. This was the worst yet: a cry of wordless, almost animal, rage, a crash, a thud as of a heavy body falling — and then a horrible choking rattle and drumming.

Brightness flared, and she realized that Carlton had had the foresight to provide himself with a lamp and the means of lighting it. He held it high.

Writhing on the floor, his heels pounding in jerky spasms, foam issuing from his mouth, was a form Marianne scarcely recognized as that of the Duke. The tutor stood over the boy, wringing his hands and looking half-witted. Marianne could only think of the vicar's warnings and the old horror tales of men possessed by demons.

Then Carlton said sharply, "Don't stand there gaping, man; you know what to do"; and Victor, after a startled glance, dropped to his knees beside the boy.

" 'Twas dark; I could not see," he stammered, forgetting his French accent in his agitation.

Scarcely had this crisis been dealt with —

Marianne realized that it had, though she still did not understand its precise nature — than a stifled cry from the Duchess drew her attention in that direction just in time to see the lady's slender form crumple to the floor, one hand pressed against her heart.

The doctor, who had started toward the fallen boy, wheeled around and hurried toward her. Marianne tugged against her bonds.

"For pity's sake," she exclaimed. "Mr. Carlton, please —"

Carlton did not move. He stood staring at the Duchess's still form.

"What is it?" he mumbled. "What?"

"Her heart." Gruffstone's hands moved with deft quickness, quite unlike his usual clumsy motions. "Fortunately I brought my bag with me. Annabelle! On the table by the window — step lively —"

So admonished, Annabelle moved quickly, and after a few moments the doctor looked up. His face was shining wet in the lamplight, whether with perspiration or tears or a blend of both Marianne could not tell.

"She lives," he said. "We must get her to her room now. Call the servants. Victor, how does the boy?"

"As usual," the tutor replied.

Marianne did not know which way to turn. She continued to wriggle and protest, and finally Carlton broke through his paralysis and untied her.

"At any rate," he remarked, with a ghastly attempt at jauntiness, "I can testify that you did not free yourself. These are my knots, no question about it. I'm sorry to have left you so long, but a string of horrors like this is really a bit much, even for me."

"The night is not over," the doctor said. "Annabelle, ring again; where in heaven's name are those worthless servants? One of the footmen can carry the boy, but I want a thin mattress or cot for Her Grace; she must be transported as gently as possible."

It was done as he directed. Before long Marianne found herself alone with Carlton. The Duke had recovered from his fit and seemed better although he was sobbing softly — possibly with embarrassment, for a damp stain on the Persian rug indicated that he had suffered an accident more explicable in a much younger child.

"Will she be all right?" Marianne asked.

Carlton shook his head. "If anyone can save her, Gruffstone can. I knew her heart was weak, but . . . I suppose seeing the boy was the final straw. She has seen it before, but it seems to grow worse each time, and after the emotional strain of this evening . . ."

"What is wrong with Henry?"

"He is an epileptic, of course." Carlton gave her a derisive look, though he was still pale and his disheveled hair had tumbled over his brow. "Did you think him a victim of demonic possession?"

"You could hardly blame me if I did, after all the other things that happened."

Carlton flung out his arms in a gesture of despair that was nonetheless genuine for looking so theatrical.

"For heaven's sake, let us not even think of that! My brain is reeling; I cannot think sensibly. You look as if you could do with a restorative. A glass of wine, perhaps?"

"I have had too much wine," Marianne said faintly. "I don't seem to be accustomed to it."

"You only had two glasses," Carlton said. "I wonder . . . Never mind that now. Let me help you upstairs."

Marianne was glad to take his arm. "I could not possibly sleep," she insisted.

"Nor I. Perhaps we could both do with that universal nursery panacea, a cup of good strong tea. There is a little sitting room upstairs, not far from your bedchamber; the Duchess meant — means — to have it refurbished for you, but it is habitable. We will wait there for news."

The Duchess's illness had roused the household. The servants seemed genuinely devoted and concerned; they hovered anxiously about the stairs and jumped to obey Carlton's orders. A fire was lighted in the sitting room he had mentioned, and the housekeeper herself brought tea and biscuits. The poor old creature's eyes were suffused with tears when she asked about her mistress, and Carlton patted her hand as he tried to find some answer that would combine truth and comfort.

"We know everything is being done, Mrs. Kenney. Dr. Gruffstone is a first-rate physician."

"He won't let her die," the old woman quavered; and Marianne realized, from her upturned glance and clasped hands, that she was not referring to the doctor. "What will become of us if she goes? Oh, sire, I don't want to sound selfish —"

"I know, I know. I'll tell you what, Mrs. Kenney; this may be a long night and we are all tired; why don't you put together some food in case the doctor requires refreshment? A good mutton roast, or salmon, or one of your magnificent trifles."

Despite the absurd selection he had found

the way to distract the housekeeper. Her face brightened.

"And some soup," she exclaimed. "Her Grace might fancy some nice strengthening broth when she feels a little better. There is nothing like it, I always say. I'll do it right away, Mr. Carlton."

She hobbled out.

"What *will* become of them?" Carlton muttered, staring after her. "All the misfits, the unemployables, whom she has taken in? Who else would find a place for them?"

"I am sure she has made provisions for them," Marianne said absently. "A woman so kind would not neglect old servants. Mr. Carlton, can we not tiptoe down the hall and look in? I am so anxious."

"Gruffstone said he would send for us if . . . if we could be useful," was the reply, made in an abstracted voice, as if the lawyer had something else on his mind.

"Whatever possessed you to order that ridiculous amount of food? It would be impossible to eat anything."

But when, sometime later, trays of sandwiches and salad were brought up, she found that she was ravenous. The food and the strong tea removed the last traces of her dizziness; she felt keyed up and alert and too restless to sit or be silent. Talking seemed to relieve her mind. Unfortunately Carlton did not share this weakness, if weakness it was. He sat hunched in his chair staring into space and responded to her irritable comments in monosyllables, if at all.

It was almost dawn before the doctor came to them. "She will do now," he said. "It was not as serious as I feared, but I stayed with her till she slept."

"You look very tired," Marianne said. "Can you take some food before you retire, or a cup of tea? I have kept the water hot."

"I have no appetite." But he began to nibble on a sandwich and Marianne poured him some tea. "You realize," he continued, with a severe look at the girl, "that she must have quiet and rest. The least excitement —"

"And how do you propose to accomplish that?" Carlton demanded. Now that his anxieties were relieved he had reverted to his old snappish manner. "The Duchess creates her own excitement. After that purported message tonight she will be on pins and needles till she hears the great revelation."

"We have a little time to prepare," the doctor replied heavily. "If, as I suppose, the reference was to the anniversary of that scoundrel's death, it is almost a fortnight away — the thirteenth of November, to be precise. Perhaps by then I can persuade her . . ."

"To do what?" Carlton seemed determined to be objectionable. "Give up hope of contacting that scoundrel, as you call him? Never believe it. Or have you some other scheme in mind? I warn you, Gruffstone, that any frustration of her hopes will prove as severe a shock as the message itself."

"Don't try to teach me my own profession! I know that as well as you do. I have an idea . . ." This time Carlton did not interrupt him, and after a moment of hesitation and a sidelong glance at Marianne, the doctor continued, "I can at least hope to strengthen her, to prepare her for the inevitable disappointment."

"Why should you suppose she will be disappointed? The agency that produced those obscene demonstrations tonight is quite capable of doing it again, unless we can discover how it was done and prevent it. Ah — your face is too open, Doctor; it gives you away. That is what you plan, is it not? What do you have in mind?"

The doctor did not reply.

Marianne said quietly, "Dr. Gruffstone prefers not to speak in front of me. I will go."

"No, no, it doesn't matter." The doctor

waved his arm and gave a great yawn. "Only you will have to let me express my ideas without regard for your feelings, Miss Ransom, and not take offense. At the present time I have no plan, I have only theories — too many of them."

"You can dismiss Miss Ransom from consideration," Carlton declared. "I will swear she could not have freed herself."

"Are you sure? You did your best, but you have not studied, as I have, the tricks these charlatans employ. I made it a point to investigate them when the Duchess became so infatuated with — with spiritualism. Not that it was any use, exposing the tricks to her; she merely replied that because a thing *could* be done in a certain way did not prove it *was* done in that way. This, despite the fact that phenomena such as we saw tonight can be duplicated by any clever conjurer."

Carlton shook his head. "I don't believe Miss Ransom could have managed it." But he sounded less certain.

"I am not accusing her. I am merely pointing out a possibility. There are others. Young Henry, for instance, is quite bright enough and mischievous enough to perpetrate such antics. I am not convinced that Holmes did not install mechanisms of various kinds in that room. Even without such aids Henry could have crept in, by means of one of the secret passages he boasts of knowing so well — or hidden himself in the room beforehand — and done everything that was done under cover of darkness. His seizures are brought on by excitement; it would not be surprising if one followed a performance such as that."

"Hmm." Carlton nodded. "That is a possibility that did not occur to me. Though I believe the seizures began when that idiot tutor, trying to recapture him, laid violent hands on the boy. And what of M. Victor himself? He's a wretched creature, capable of playing tricks for the fun of it."

"He is," Marianne declared.

"I won't ask how you know that. . . . Well, Doctor, you are a clever fellow, you have given me much to think about."

"I am not done," the doctor declared. "I cannot wholly discount the operation of some unknown force — not the sentimental twaddle about spirits, but a form of animal magnetism that can move objects at a distance. Certain cases of haunted houses suggest that possibility; the agent is usually a young person, who is quite unaware of his, or her, abilities. Well." He put his cup down and rose to his feet. "I must have a few hours' sleep before returning to my patient. Good night."

Carlton also said good night. Marianne went to her bed, but she did not fall asleep immediately.

She knew why the doctor had not voiced one of the theories that must have been in his mind. She, too, was reluctant to admit it; yet to an objective observer, the Duchess had to be considered a suspect. It was absurd, of course, to suppose that she would deliberately play tricks on herself, but the doctor's theory of hysteria, if Marianne understood it correctly, could explain a great deal. "We believe what we want to believe," Carlton had said. He might have added, "Some of us will go to any length to prove that what we believe is true."

There was one other suspect. Perhaps the doctor had reasons for dismissing her from consideration, or perhaps he had simply forgotten about her, for she was a shadowy figure at best. Marianne had never set eyes on her, unless the retreating figure she had seen the first night had indeed been the Duke's mother.

I will make an effort to meet her tomorrow, Marianne thought drowsily — if she exists at all, and is not another of the Duchess's fantasies.

CHAPTER TWELVE

The following day brought answers to some of the questions that had troubled Marianne, but they were not the answers she had hoped to hear.

She slept late, and upon arising went to see how the Duchess was. Her soft knock was answered at once, and when she entered she saw the patient propped up on lace-trimmed pillows and looking quite herself. She greeted Marianne with a smile.

"My dear girl, what a night you must have had!"

"Nothing compared with yours. I am so glad to see you looking better. But perhaps you should not talk, or have visitors," Marianne added; for as she came closer, the Duchess's high color and sparkling eyes did not look so much like signs of recovered health as of unhealthy excitement. "I won't stay. I only came to ask how you were."

"I feel splendid. Horace is an old fuss-budget. It is you I am concerned about. I will ask him to have a look at you."

"I assure you, my health has never been better. Is there anything I can do for you? Write letters, or read, perhaps?"

"You are a sweet child," the Duchess replied, with an affectionate smile. "Later, perhaps, if you would care to join me for tea, I might ask you to write a letter or two. Now I want you to get out into the fresh air. I am sure Roger is waiting impatiently to go riding with you."

"I imagine he is still sleeping."

"No, no; he was here only a few minutes ago. Have you had breakfast? You must eat; it is essential to your health."

"You are not to fuss," Marianne said, patting the thin hand that moved restlessly on the counterpane, as if seeking to take up the reins of authority once again. "I will leave you to rest now, and return later. I hope you will sleep."

She had no particular desire for food, or for Carlton's company, but she sensed that her presence was keeping the Duchess from the rest she needed.

Carlton was in the entrance hall, turning over a heap of papers and letters.

"The post has come," he said, glancing up. "And here is a letter for you."

"For me?"

"Why do you sound surprised? We are not

cut off from civilization. This was forwarded from London."

Even before he handed it to her, Marianne suspected whom the letter was from. There could be only one correspondent. The sight of the handwriting confirmed her assumption.

Carlton, frowning over a letter he had just opened, did not appear to be paying attention, but when she thrust her mail, unread, into her bag, he inquired, "Don't you want to read it? Pray don't let my presence deter you."

"It can wait," Marianne replied. Mrs. Jay could not yet have received her letter, so this epistle, written when she was probably still in doubt as to her young friend's whereabouts, could hardly contain anything she wanted to hear. It was probably full of admonitions and advice.

"The Duchess has ordered me to take you riding," Carlton said, still glancing through his mail.

"You need not consider it an obligation."

"Ah, but I do. Run along and change; that will give me time to finish looking over my correspondence."

Marianne did as she was bid. When she had put on her riding habit she sat down to open Mrs. Jay's letter. There was no sense putting it off — and really she had no reason except her own uneasy conscience to anticipate that the contents might not be to her liking.

They were, however, even worse than she had expected. Mrs. Shortbody had apparently peppered her old friend with daily bulletins about Marianne's activities. Naturally she knew nothing of Marianne's brief career in the theater, or of Bagshot; but Mrs. Pettibone had reported her quondam governess's "insolence and brutality" to the employment agency, which had passed the report on to Mrs. Shortbody. The good landlady was too fair-minded to take this account at face value; Mrs. Jay acknowledged that she had reported Mrs. Pettibone to be an impossible woman, who could not keep help of any kind. All the same, Mrs. Jay felt bound to lecture Marianne at some length on the advisability of controlling her temper and facing adversity with Christian meekness.

"But this," she went on, "is of small consequence compared with the latest news I have from Mrs. Shortbody. She was unaware when Mr. Carlton first called upon her that he was in the employ of the Dowager Duchess of Devenbrook. Had she known, she would not have been a party to connecting you with such a person. Naturally you would not be aware of Her Grace's reputation, but, Marianne, you ought to know enough to inquire of those older and wiser before entrusting yourself to anyone not known to you personally! Heaven knows I am not one to give credence to vulgar gossip, and Her Grace's relationship with a certain gentleman now deceased was never proved; in any case that subject is not fit for your ears. What concerns me even more is the fact that she is known to be involved with a pagan cult condemned by all true —"

At this point Marianne crumpled the letter in her hand and threw it at the fireplace. Her cheeks were burning. Really, Mrs. Jay was outrageous! If she was so concerned about me, Marianne thought angrily, why didn't she offer me a home? Not that she had wanted to stay in that Yorkshire backwater, and as things turned out it was fortunate that she had not. But she had been hurt, at the time, that Mrs. Jay seemed so willing to be rid of her.

Outside the library she stopped and forced herself to wait till her temper had cooled. Not for all the world would she want Carlton to see her in a flaming rage. When her breathing had slowed down she turned the knob, and as she did so a voice boomed out, uttering a phrase that made her stand motionless and listen intently.

". . . she will leave that wretched girl every penny she has. Her personal fortune is enormous, you know that."

The speaker was Roger Carlton, angry enough to speak more loudly than was his wont. The voice of the doctor replied.

"You don't know that she will do that. Surely you can remind her of her obligations toward the servants and charities she has always supported. In any case, my young friend, your duty is to see that she makes a will; it is not to approve or disapprove her choice of beneficiaries."

"Curse it, Gruffstone, don't remind me of my duty — even if I did the same to you!" Carlton's voice was calmer now. "Are you really sure that — that the situation is serious?"

"Her heart has been deteriorating for years," was the grave reply. "She has made a remarkable recovery from the last attack, but the end may come any day."

Silence ensued. Shocked and distressed at what she had heard, Marianne tried to decide whether to retreat as silently as she had come, or to warn the men of her presence by making a noise. Much as she resented Carlton's implication that she was a cold-blooded, consciousless fortune hunter, she was ashamed of eavesdropping. She could not even throw the words back in his face without admitting that she had been listening.

"I suppose I knew it," Carlton said finally. "Instinct told me — but my feelings denied the truth. Of course you are right, Gruffstone. I have tried before to convince Her Grace to make her will. I will try again, more forcefully."

"But without frightening her," the doctor warned.

"I shall do my best. It won't be easy."

"I know that, my boy."

Marianne eased the door open a little farther. The two men were at the far end of the long room, their backs to her. Carlton sat with head bowed, his hands over his face. The doctor was patting his shoulder.

Marianne pulled the door closed, then rattled the knob vigorously. When she entered Carlton was sitting upright, his face a calm mask. The doctor's coattails were just disappearing through a door at the other end of the room.

"Ready?" Carlton asked coolly.

"Yes. I hope I have not kept you waiting."

"Not at all. I entertained myself by reading

the papers. You may be interested to know that you have become famous, Miss Ransom."

"What do you mean?"

Carlton handed her a newspaper. "You are not familiar with this offensive publication, I daresay; only those of us who are brave enough to admit we enjoy scandal dare read it openly."

Marianne *was* familiar with the *Daily Yell*, though she should not have been; it was the squire's favorite newspaper, and he had not always remembered to remove it from her path.

She took the newspaper with a fine display of fastidious distaste. "Are you telling me that my name appears in this — this —"

"Rag," Carlton supplied. "Not your name, no. But there is no doubt as to who is meant. See here."

He folded the paper back and indicated a column with the charming title of "Aristocratic Antics." The paragraph in question did not, in fact, mention names. It referred, in the most revoltingly coy terms, to "a lady of decal degree, known for her probings into spiritual matters" and "the young and beautiful handmaiden of the occult, reputed to be descended from a gentleman well known to the royal courts of Europe as well as the boudoirs of the noble ladies of London. . . .”

For the second time Marianne crumpled a sheet of paper and flung it away. “It suggests that I am the Duchess’s . . .” She could not finish the sentence; her face was as hot as fire. “How dare they? Are there no laws?”

“There is no violation of law when no names are mentioned. Besides, would you care to fan this nasty little flame of innuendo into a roaring blaze of scandal by bringing the publisher to court?”

“Good heavens, no!”

“Most of his victims feel the same. As for the implication, surely you must have realized that evil minds would place that interpretation on the Duchess’s kindness to an unknown young woman. There was considerable scandal regarding her relationship with Holmes. I need not add that there was no foundation for it —”

“You need not. I could never believe such a thing of her! Why, she thought of him as a son.”

“As to that . . .” Carlton’s eyebrows lifted. Then he shook his head and made a sour face. “Listen to me! Her Grace’s feelings are none of my business, and her actions are beyond criticism. Oh, the devil with this; let us go out and let some fresh air blow the filth from our minds."

Marianne enjoyed the ride, but it did not free her mind of the discomfort induced by Mrs. Jay's letter, and reinforced by the newspaper column. What a sad world it was, when a woman like the Duchess could be suspected of such things. Though it went against all her instinct of natural affection and common sense, she could admit the bare possibility that she might be the daughter of David Holmes. The suggestion that the Duchess might be her mother never took the slightest hold on her imagination, much less her reason. Yet the suggestion made her feel contaminated.

Carlton was also abstracted — and no wonder, Marianne thought. Fond as she was of the Duchess, she knew her affection was nothing compared to the feelings of someone who was virtually a foster son and who must face the imminence of the final parting from one he loved. She could not even give him, and herself, the comfort of sharing grief without confessing her reprehensible behavior.

Even more distressing was the thought that the Duchess might be planning to leave her money. It surprised her a little that a woman of such efficiency in other matters should not have made her will, but she supposed there were reasons; it was not a subject to which she had given any thought. Under happier circumstances she would have been pleased and grateful for a small remembrance. Now she could not accept so much as a penny without incurring the scorn of those who suspected her.

Eventually Carlton roused himself from his reverie and sought relief in baiting her.

"I wonder," he said guilelessly, "what has become of poor Pudenzia?"

"Who? Oh." Rallying, Marianne replied haughtily, "Since I was never aware of that — er — person's existence, I can hardly be responsible for her actions."

"Oh, yes, I had forgotten. A medium is not supposed to be conscious of remarks made by her control. That is the right word, is it not?"

"So I have been told."

"But I am afraid that poor girl has met with some unpleasant fate. She did not turn up at all last time, and on the previous occasion, when the Duchess called on her, you went into a fit before she had a chance to say more than a word or two. I wonder why."

"I have not the faintest idea."

"I wonder if the vicar's lecture could have had anything to do with it," Carlton mused.

"You had, I think, been impressed by that silly notion of demonic possession?"

"What on earth could that have to do —"

"Ah, well, no doubt I have got it all wrong." His eyes wide with assumed innocence, Carlton tried without success to look humble. "When Gruffstone was talking about hysteria and autosuggestion, I thought of an interesting hypothetical case —"

"Hypothetical!"

"Oh, purely hypothetical, I assure you. Imagine an amiable young woman who is asked, by someone she admires and respects, to produce a certain effect. With the best intentions in the world she obliges. But when another person whom she also admires and respects suggests that her actions might be wrong, even dangerous —"

"That is a ridiculous suggestion! How could I have invented such a name as Pudenzia, or concocted a history for her?"

"Such things are common in the spiritualist trade," Carlton replied. "Red Indians are the most popular controls, I admit, but any pathetic story —"

Marianne loosened the reins and left her tormentor far behind. He had not caught her up by the time she reached the castle.

However, the day had one pleasant surprise in store for her. After she had tidied herself and changed, she went to the Duchess's room. And whom should she find, sitting by the bed, but Mr. St. John.

"We two have made it up, you see," the Duchess explained with a smile. "Mr. St. John very kindly called when he heard that I was taken ill, and we have had a pleasant talk. Now, my dear Marianne, you are just in time to take him downstairs and give him some tea."

It must be recorded, to Marianne's credit, that she demurred, although the smile of the young man showed her how much he approved this idea.

"I had hoped to take tea with you, ma'am, and perhaps write those letters we spoke of."

"You may come up later, my dear. Just now you can serve me best by doing as I ask."

"But first," St. John said, "let us pray."

It was a beautiful and very affecting prayer; Marianne's eyes were piously lowered, so she did not observe that the Duchess grimaced once or twice at pointed references to the Hereafter. But she thanked the vicar prettily when it was done, and said he had helped her.

Once outside the room the vicar heaved a deep sigh. Marianne glanced at him, but was too shy to ask why he looked so serious all at once. Not until they had reached the rose parlor did she venture to speak.

"It was good of you to come," she said, tugging at the bellpull.

"I could do no less," was the reply, made in gloomy tones, and accompanied by an equally lugubrious look. "Her Grace has been an angel of kindness to the poor. If only . . . Oh, Miss Ransom, may I relieve an overburdened heart by speaking frankly?"

"Oh, sir," Marianne exclaimed, startled by his agitated look.

"Thank you. Thank you. I knew I could depend on your kindness. I do not know what —"

The parlormaid entered and Marianne asked for tea to be served. As soon as the maid had gone the vicar resumed exactly where he had left off.

"— what to do. I can do Her Grace no good unless I am in her confidence. Yet I cannot subscribe to the very doctrine that gives her peace of mind. A false peace, a dangerous peace. Can I see this kind but misguided woman sink into eternal fire because I —"

"Sir!" Marianne bounced up from her chair. "How dare you suggest that the Duchess is going to Hell . . . Oh!" The vicar's horrified expression made her clap her hands to her mouth. "Oh, I didn't mean that! I have never said that word before — except, of course, in church . . . you know — 'He descended into Hell; the third day He rose again from —' "

"Do not fear the word." St. John advanced toward her, shaking a long finger vehemently. "Fear the reality! Do you think I am unaware of what evil transpired here last night? The devilish spirit that moved furniture and played on Satan's instruments finally found a vehicle in that unfortunate boy — but it might have been you, Miss Ransom. It might have been you!"

In his agitation he actually took her by the shoulders. Like a rabbit mesmerized by a snake, Marianne gazed up into a face transformed by spiritual fervor. No longer did he resemble a gentle saint, but an archangel with a fiery sword of eloquence.

"I don't think . . ." she began weakly.

"Do not think! Let the love of God enter your heart." The vicar's hands drew Marianne closer to him. His face bent low over hers. "That heavenly love . . . that divine affection . . ."

"Oh," Marianne breathed. "Oh, yes!"

"No earthly love can compare with it," St. John said, without conviction. His lips were only inches from hers.

The doorknob rattled. The vicar pulled his hands away as if the surface they touched had turned red-hot. Marianne collapsed into the nearest chair. The door opened, admitting the maid with the tea tray. She was followed by Roger Carlton.

"Ah, Mr. St. John," Carlton said. "How nice to see you. I hope I have not interrupted some tender exchange of — er — religious exhortation?"

"I was warning Miss Ransom," the vicar said stiffly, "about the performance that went on here last night."

"Oh, was that it? I congratulate you for having the courage to expose yourself to such dreadful dangers."

"That is my duty. I only wish I could persuade Her Grace how dangerous it is."

"For heaven's sake," Carlton exclaimed. "You didn't rant at her and threaten her with hellfire, I hope? If you did —"

"Of course I did not." St. John passed a slender hand across his brow. "I want to help Her Grace. I only wish I knew how to go about it."

"Pray," Carlton suggested, taking a chair and a buttered scone.

"I have," the young vicar replied simply. "And I will return to the church now to pray again. No, thank you, Miss Ransom, I really cannot stay."

His mouth filled with scone, Carlton waved a casual hand in farewell, and the vicar left the room.

"You were very rude," Marianne said. "You drove him away."

"No, not I. It was God who drove him — his God, who is not, I thank Him, mine. Has he seen the Duchess?"

"Yes, and she seemed cheered by his visit."

"Oh, he has his points," Carlton admitted grudgingly. "He is pompous, stupid, priggish, and conceited, but I believe at heart he is sincere. If he were not cursed with those girlish good looks —"

Before Marianne could reply to this outrageous remark the door opened and the vicar's handsome head reappeared.

"I hope he did not hear you," Marianne muttered to Carlton, who merely grinned in an aggravating manner. Aloud she exclaimed, "Have you changed your mind, Mr. St. John? Do have a cup of tea, at least."

The vicar closed the door behind him and came toward her with an air of portentous gravity. "I will return, Miss Ransom, if I can persuade someone else to join me. I met her in the hall and I think I have persuaded her to come in; but I ran ahead to warn you and ask you to welcome her."

"Is it Lady Violet of whom you speak?" Marianne asked eagerly. "Poor lady, this is her house and I am only a guest, she does me a favor by joining me."

"You are an angel of goodness," the young man said, with a look that made Marianne's bones melt. "I will go and fetch her."

He ran out. Marianne turned defiantly to Carlton, expecting some sarcastic comment. She was not disappointed.

"Angel of goodness," he repeated, mimicking the vicar's deep voice with devastating effect. "Good of you to let the lady take tea in her own parlor from her own teapot."

Marianne was saved from a rude reply by the opening of the door. The vicar's tall body towered over the form of a woman so slender and small that she looked like a child playing at dress-up in her mother's clothes. She had very pretty, soft brown hair, which fell loose in a style more appropriate to a young lady than a mother and a widow. Marianne suspected that she wore it so in an attempt to veil her face. That face was turned aside and her hand, toying nervously with a stray lock of hair, further concealed her features.

Marianne rose and curtsied. "It is an

honor to meet you, Lady Violet. Not knowing you were coming, I fear I have taken your place. Will you not sit here?"

Her voice was so sweet and her manner so genuinely anxious to please that the rigid little figure in the doorway relaxed and took a few timid steps forward. The vicar beamed approval over her head; even Carlton's eagle glance softened, though Marianne missed this rare sign of approval, so eager was she to make the lady feel at ease.

"Thank you," was the reply, in tones so soft they could scarcely be heard. "Please don't get up; I will sit here." And she indicated a chair as far removed as possible from the window.

"May I pour you a cup of tea?" Marianne asked.

"Thank you."

Carlton had risen too. "May I say how well you are looking, Lady Violet. Have one of these little cakes."

Lady Violet had to lower her hand, which she had kept before her face, in order to take the proffered cake. She had big, expressive brown eyes. They darted rapidly from one face to the next, as if trying to judge the effect of her disfigurement.

Marianne was glad she had been warned. The harelip was more pathetic than terrible, but without some preparation she might have allowed some demonstration of surprise to escape her. The vicar smiled on all and sundry and bounced up and down on his heels, his hands clasped behind him like a proud father watching his child's performance.

The conversation was easy, thanks primarily — Marianne had to admit — to Roger Carlton, who babbled on about the topics of the day. Once Lady Violet actually laughed at one of his jokes. Finally the vicar, who had consumed quite a quantity of tea and sandwiches after all, rose to take his leave.

"This has been a most pleasant meeting. It has been too long since I have seen you, Lady Violet, Now —" he lifted an admonitory finger — "I expect to see you on Sunday. Promise you won't fail me."

A look of terror clouded the lady's fine brown eyes.

"Perhaps," Marianne said quickly, "Lady Violet will be good enough to let me accompany her to church. I don't suppose," she added, with a cold glance at Carlton, "that anyone else in the household will be attending."

"The very thing," St. John exclaimed, with rather excessive enthusiasm. "It is settled then; I look forward to seeing you both."

The door had hardly closed behind him when Lady Violet rose.

"It has been pleasant," she murmured. "Thank you, I must go now — I will see you again —"

She left with a gliding, rapid movement that reminded Marianne of the elusive figure she had seen in the dark hallway.

"That was kindly meant," Carlton said, resuming his seat and taking the last scone. "But it was a mistake. She won't go."

"To church? But why not? It is terrifying to walk down that aisle with all the villagers staring; I thought companionship might make it easier for her. It certainly would be pleasanter for me. My offer was not entirely unselfish."

"I cannot contradict that, since you insist upon it. Good heavens, Miss Ransom, just think a moment; with her sad misfortune, to be seen beside a girl radiant with youthful beauty — why, the contrast is too pitiful."

Marianne felt herself blushing. Did he really think her "radiant"? He had never paid her a compliment before.

And he seemed to regret having done so now, for he went on rapidly, with a self-conscious look, "I know many people with similar difficulties — birthmarks, withered limbs, wens, and so on — some try to hide, others make the best of it and face life with a smile and a jest. Perhaps it is more difficult for a woman who might, but for that, be beautiful."

"You are right," Marianne said, wondering at his perception. "She would be beautiful; she has lovely eyes and skin, beautiful hair, a pretty figure. Life is very sad."

"How profound." Carlton's eyes shone with amusement over the rim of the cup he had raised to his lips.

"I must go to the Duchess," Marianne said coolly.

Curse the man, she thought, stamping up the stairs. Why was he so gentle and sympathetic one moment and so sarcastic the next? It was as if he wanted to win her confidence only so he could make fun of her. He had been so kind with Lady Violet. Was it possible that he could feel . . . ? She must be years older than he, Marianne told herself, not realizing that she was paying Carlton the highest compliment in her power by assuming that Lady Violet's pitiful looks would not affect his feelings.

At least she had finally met the mysterious figure she had seen wandering in the night like a lost soul. She could not believe such a shy, timid woman would play malicious tricks. Cross one off her list of suspects.

She had hoped to find the Duchess resting, but such was not the case. The lady was wide awake and ready to be amused. So Marianne stayed with her, sharing her dinner and reading from *Pride and Prejudice* until the Duchess began to nod.

"What a good child you are," she murmured drowsily, as Marianne bent over her to bid her good night. "Giving up your evening to entertain an old woman . . ."

Much as she would like to have thought of herself as noble and self-sacrificing, Marianne could not really feel that she had given up much. An evening with Carlton and Gruffstone grumbling at her, or Henry asking impertinent questions and his tutor glowering . . . Of course, there was Lady Annabelle and the cat Horace.

On leaving the room she was surprised to see Dr. Gruffstone sitting in a chair in the hall, his legs stretched out in front of him, his hands folded over his stomach, and a series of snuffling snores coming from his parted lips. He woke the instant the door closed and blinked drowsily at her.

"She is not asleep yet, is she?"

"Not quite; but she was dropping off when I left."

"I want to have another look at her,"

Gruffstone said, rising with a grunt. "I hope you said nothing —"

"The subject is as unpleasant to me as it is to you, sir," Marianne answered quickly. But the doctor looked so weary and so sad, like a tired old bear, that she regretted her sauciness. "She did not mention that subject and neither did I," she said more gently. "Truly, sir, she seems much better."

"Good, good." The doctor peered at her over his spectacles. "You look a little peaked yourself, young lady. I will just drop in for a moment after I have seen the Duchess. I promised her I would look after you. Go on and prepare for bed; an old man like myself cannot endanger your reputation."

He smiled as he spoke, and looked so amiable and avuncular that Marianne could not refuse his offer, though she had no particular desire to be poked and prodded and made to say "ah."

When she reached her room she found her bath waiting, her bed turned back, and all the other duties of a maid performed; but Annie was not to be seen. Marianne tested the bathwater and found it still hot. She made a sour face. Annie was trying to emulate the little elves who had helped the shoemaker, but her motive in remaining unseen was superstitious fear.

So Marianne did not ring for help in preparing for bed. Since the bath was neatly concealed behind a screen, she had no hesitation in hopping into it; if the doctor came into the room, she would still be private. She took her time, enjoying the comfort of the hot water, and then put on the flannel nightgown she had to warm before the fire, covering it with a heavy dressing gown.

She was toasting her feet and reading *Wuthering Heights*, which she had neglected for the past few days, when the doctor knocked.

"Nothing much wrong with you," he said, after examining her. "Have you trouble sleeping?"

"Not often."

"A glass of wine, perhaps, if you are wakeful."

"I can't drink wine," Marianne said. "The other evening I felt quite faint and giddy after dinner."

"During the séance?" The doctor laughed shortly. "No wonder."

"I don't think it was that. Indeed, the symptoms improved as the evening wore on; but it was not until much later, when I had taken some food and several cups of tea, that I felt quite myself again."

"Hmph. Let me see your tongue once more."

Gravely he examined the protruding member and then shook his head.

"If you have an ailment it is not of the body. Did you take any wine tonight?"

"Yes; the Duchess insisted that I take a glass with her."

"And you feel no such symptoms as you felt last night?"

"No."

"Then it cannot have been the wine," the doctor said. "No doubt you are suffering from nervous strain; that would not be surprising. The Duchess wants me to give you some medicine, so . . ." From his bag he took a bottle of dark-brown liquid. "A mild sedative in case you find yourself wakeful. You probably will not need it; but at least I can tell Her Grace, when she asks, that I duly prescribed for you. It will be our little conspiracy, eh?"

He smiled and took his leave. Marianne was not as reassured by his comments as she ought to have been. The big brown bottle on the table seemed to wink and grimace at her as the firelight reflected dully from its glass surface. Having medicine prescribed suggests that medicine is needed, no matter what the verbal disclaimers.

She read for a little longer, but found that the descriptions of desolate heaths and wailing ghostly voices did nothing to relieve her nerves. So she got into bed and blew out the candle, and fell asleep almost at once.

Later, however, she seemed to wake — or rather, to come halfway out of slumber into a state midway between unconsciousness and dreaming. The fire had died to a bed of coals that gave no light, but the room was alive with small sounds and movements — rustlings and soft creakings and a distant whistling wail, like that of a rising wind.

Marianne could not decide whether she was awake or dreaming of waking. She tried to remember whether she had locked her door after the doctor left. Somehow the question did not seem important. She concluded that she must be dreaming, stimulated by the eerie prose of Miss Brontë, and was about to woo slumber again when the bed vibrated with the fall of a heavy weight upon it.

Fully, shockingly awake, Marianne tried to pull her body up and away from the object that pressed the bedclothes tight against her lower limbs. She was on the verge of hysteria — not the medical state the doctor had described, but a good, old-fashioned screaming fit — when one particular sound reached her ears and produced a miraculous cure for her nerves. It was a low, rumbling purr.

Marianne stretched out her hand. It brushed a soft, furry surface.

There is no more soothing sound than a cat's purr; when the animal walked up the length of the girl's body and settled down next to her she wrapped both arms around its warm bulk and let the purring sing her to sleep.

CHAPTER THIRTEEN

Until the following morning Marianne did not know, or care, which of Lady Annabelle's pets had given her such a fright. She was awakened by a small head pushing against her chin and claws kneading her chest. She opened her eyes. The face confronting her had a pink nose, blue eyes, and white fur.

"Fluffy," Marianne said drowsily.

Fluffy meowed. She jumped off the bed and marched to the door, where she meowed again and stared demandingly at Marianne. The girl lost no time in responding; she was well aware of Fluffy's delicate constitution, and did not want to be responsible for any untoward accidents.

She let the cat out and watched it saunter down the hall, its tail waving.

The room was so dark she thought it must be very early, but when she looked at her watch she saw that it was after eight o'clock. The sounds she had heard in the night had not been the product of nightmare after all; the wind still howled around the eaves and drove rain against the windowpanes. The air felt damp and chilly. Marianne hopped back into the warm bed and gave the bellpull a determined yank. She had let Annie off often enough; this morning she wanted hot tea and hot water and a hot fire.

Annie was in no hurry to respond, however. The warmth of the blankets and the monotonous, soothing beat of the rain made Marianne drowsy. She was remembering her nocturnal fears and smiling at her own fancies when a thought occurred to her — one that should have occurred long before. How had the cat gotten into her room?

That alarming question dispelled the last vestiges of drowsiness. She could not remember whether she had locked her door, but it had most certainly been closed. Or had it? Perhaps the latch had not caught and the cat had pushed the door open. Marianne found that hard to believe, though. The doors were several inches thick, of wood so hard it was almost petrified. Fluffy was not a massively muscled cat like Horace, she was one of the smaller of Lady Annabelle's pets. Furthermore, Marianne realized, the door *had* been firmly shut that morning; she had had to twist the knob to open it for Fluffy. There seemed no way around the conclusion that at some time during the night the door

— or a door — had been opened by a human hand.

She was about to ring the bell again when Annie finally came. Amusement mingled with Marianne's annoyance when she saw that Annie's companion was the same stalwart young footman. He was carrying an armful of firewood as well as a bucket of steaming water. Annie had a breakfast tray, which she handed Marianne at arm's length.

After the fire was blazing, Marianne asked the young man his name. He started as if she had shouted at him, but managed to answer that his name was John.

"Thank you, John," Marianne said. "You may go now. I want to talk to Annie."

Annie's eyes opened so wide the white showed all around her dilated pupils. Twisting her hands in the folds of her apron, she backed off until she was as far from Marianne as she could get without actually leaving the room.

"Stop being so silly, Annie," Marianne said impatiently. "You look as if you expect me to sprout horns and a tail. I am only human, like yourself. Why are you afraid of me?"

"They say . . ." Annie began. Words failed her.

"They? Who? The other servants? Who is

spreading wild stories about me?"

Annie shrugged, her eyes rolling wildly, and Marianne realized it was useless to try to get anything coherent out of her. If those who listen to rumors were capable of analyzing their origins, they would not believe them in the first place.

"The Duchess has been conducting séances for years," Marianne persisted. "You aren't afraid of her. Why me?"

Annie knew the answer to that one. "You're his daughter, miss. The wizard's daughter."

"No, I am not!" The vehemence of the statement startled Marianne almost as much as it did Annie. It was the first time since the suggestion had been made that she had denied it with perfect conviction. She went on, "I am a poor orphan from Yorkshire whom the Duchess has befriended — not so different from you, you see. I would like to be your friend."

"Yes, miss." Annie continued to crumple her neat white apron, but she appeared less nervous.

"All right, you may go," Marianne said with a sigh. She had done all that she could. "I am sure your sweetheart is still waiting for you outside, to protect you from me."

"Oh, miss, he's not my sweetheart." Annie giggled.

"If he is not, it is your fault; I saw how he looked at you. Run along, now."

Annie bobbed a curtsy and obeyed. Cheered by what appeared to be at least moderate success in overcoming the girl's fear, Marianne ate her breakfast with good appetite and then washed and dressed. She put on one of her old dresses, for she had a project in mind.

It was possible that someone had opened her door during the night, allowing the cat to slip in. The sighing of wind and rain would have concealed any sound. But there was another possibility. As she knew from her reading, old castles were replete with secret passages, hidden rooms, and other such features. Indeed, young Henry had bragged of his familiarity with the passageways that honeycombed the castle walls.

Marianne set about the search with the optimism born of ignorance that is characteristic of the young. An older, wiser person would have told her she had little chance of success. Even if such devices existed, a certain degree of expertise was necessary to discover them. Older, wiser persons are constantly annoyed by the unwarranted success of the young and ignorant; and such was the case in this instance. Since the entire room was paneled, the search took quite some time and Marianne was beginning to be bored when one of the Tudor roses on a panel by the fireplace yielded to the pressure of her fingers and the panel itself slid quietly to one side.

More excited than frightened, Marianne lighted a candle and thrust it into the aperture that had opened before her. The light showed the beginning of a flight of stone steps leading sharply downward. The steps were less than six inches wide and so steep that only a cat could have used them comfortably.

She was not a cat — or a careless, agile, small boy; the steep pitch of the stairs was more than she cared to attempt. Furthermore, she had no idea where the steps led. She might find herself in some cul-de-sac from which exit was impossible. And what if the door closed and she was unable to discover the catch that would release it? Marianne shivered dramatically, picturing herself pounding desperately on the locked panel until lack of air finally overcame her and she sank into a deathly sleep. This contingency was, of course, most unlikely. The Duke could not be the only one who knew the network of secret passages, and if she turned up missing, a search would certainly be thorough and immediate. All the same, Marianne was not inclined to risk it. Even a few minutes in imprisoning, dusty darkness and she would scream herself into a fit. No, she would not explore. But she could try to make sure no one else used that entrance.

With some difficulty she dragged a table in front of the panel and put a bowl of flowers on top of it. If someone tried to come in, table or bowl or both would fall, and the crash would awaken her.

Complacently pleased with her morning's work, she changed her dusty frock and went to see how the Duchess was doing.

II

The long day dragged. Since it was too wet to ride, Marianne spent most of the time with the Duchess, reading and talking and embroidering. The doctor had forbidden card games as being too exciting. Dismissed while the Duchess napped, Marianne was so bored she even went looking for Henry, thinking she might offer to play a game with him. The schoolroom was deserted; one of the servants told her His Grace was with his mother.

She did not look for Carlton. She went to the library thinking she might find an entertaining book, and peeped into the billiard room — solely out of curiosity, to see what it was like — *not* looking for Carlton. When one of the footmen, mistaking her intentions, informed her that the gentlemen had gone out, Marianne replied haughtily that she had no interest in the whereabouts of the gentlemen. She went into the music room and relieved her feelings by banging out a series of emphatic polonaises and marches.

By the time she finished practicing, the gentlemen had returned, or so she was told by another overzealous servant. Marianne told him that she had not the slightest interest in the subject. She returned to the Duchess's room, hoping that the vicar might have been moved to make another pastoral call. But apparently the rain had dampened his ardor, for he never came.

The Duchess urged her to join the gentlemen for dinner. She refused, feeling that if she could not be amused she might as well be useful, but she was glad to be dismissed when the doctor came up to sit with his friend. She was so bored she was even beginning to think regretfully of the séances. They had been alarming, but they had not been dull.

Moving aimlessly around her room in search of something to occupy her mind, she picked up her writing portfolio and sat down with it on her lap. She was sorry she had not kept a diary, as so many young ladies did; at least she would have more interesting things to write about than who danced with whom at the last ball, and what color ribbons she had selected for her new gown. But perhaps, she reflected, the only people who have time to write in their diaries are the ones to whom nothing ever happens.

The rain hissed against the windows. It was just the sort of night to write a long, intimate letter to a friend. But she had no such friends. The only girls she knew were casual acquaintances, daughters of the squire's friends and neighbors.

Marianne yawned. Tomorrow was Sunday. She could look forward to that, at any rate. She wondered whether Lady Violet meant to go to church with her. The next move was certainly up to the lady; it would be rude of her to press further.

Absently she opened the portfolio, and there before her, like a scrap of her conscience that had taken visible form, was the letter from Mrs. Jay, which she had crumpled and hurled at the fire.

Her receptivity toward suggestions of the uncanny was now so keen that she stared at the paper with dilating eyes. Then common sense asserted itself. So her aim had not been as good as she thought. The letter had fallen to the floor, Annie had found it, had smoothed it out and put it neatly away. That was the explanation, of course.

Still, the reappearance of the letter was a salutary reminder of her duty. She owed Mrs. Jay an explanation that would relieve the old lady's fears and justify her own behavior. She had been wrong to respond to its criticism with anger. Mrs. Jay was moved solely by concern for her, she knew that.

She forced herself to finish the part of the letter she had left unread. It was more of the same — lectures on the evils of spiritualism. Mrs. Jay did not use the vicar's arguments. Hers was a robustly rational attitude that deplored the activity because it was a denial of the quite adequate and comforting explanations offered by traditional religion. Naturally she said this at much greater length, and it was not until the very end of the letter that she added a single sentence that caused Marianne to uncurl her pretty mouth (a gesture she had unconsciously acquired from Carlton) and pay close attention.

"I find myself not so well as I would like;

but at my age, Marianne, one must expect some infirmities."

To do Marianne justice, this statement made her feel bad for a full thirty seconds. To do her even more justice, she would have been thoroughly overcome if she could have seen Mrs. Jay, or known the hours of agonized debate that had resulted in that single understated comment. Mrs. Jay had finally concluded that the shock to her darling's sensibilities might be lessened if she received a well-chosen hint about the event that could not now be far away. But the words conveyed nothing of the physical pain or mental distress that had prompted them; and perhaps Marianne cannot be blamed for dismissing the sentence with a shrug. To be sure, Mrs. Jay was no longer young. Some infirmities had to be expected. . . .

However, she was moved to pick up her pen and dash off a few lines of reassurance. The letter was a skillful blend of candor and tactful omissions. She admitted that the Duchess dabbled in spiritualism, but did not mention her own participation. She assured Mrs. Jay that she herself had not the slightest belief in that pernicious doctrine. She described the vicar at length without going into detail about his reasons for condemning table turning, for some instinct told her that

Mrs. Jay would be as disgusted by demons as she was by spirits. All in all, Marianne was pleased with the letter when she read it over. She added a final sentence. "I do hope your rheumatism is better; you must take care of yourself and not do too much."

With a pleasant consciousness of duty done, she prepared for bed. Whether it was the idea of the approaching Sabbath — when no evil spirits are allowed to walk abroad — or the thought of her good old friend, she felt a peace of mind that had been foreign to her for many days. Still, she did not neglect to lock her door and, after a moment of silent debate, to leave a candle burning. The small, valiant flame dipped and swayed in the draft. Its vagrant movements were the last thing she saw before she fell asleep.

She woke with a start to find the room in darkness. At first she thought the unpleasantness of a bad dream must have roused her. It had been a horrid, confused mixture of the varied miseries she had suffered since arriving in London. In it she had seemed to pass, with the swift, unhindered movement of a bodiless spirit, through a dreadful twilight country of bare twisted trees and half-seen monsters, all wearing human faces:

Mrs. Pettibone and her sadistic son; Bagshot, mouthing curses; Wilson, the sinister manager of the supper club; and, worst of all, dear Mrs. Jay, who had shaken her fist and shrieked out threats of hellfire and eternal damnation.

This last terrible vision lingered even after she awoke. The limp white hands of her old friend still hovered above her head.

Marianne felt the bedclothes pressing down on her. She was awake . . . and the hands still hung luminous in the darkness. A clammy sweat dampened her brow. She was too frightened to move or scream.

A low, wavering moan sounded, mounting to a scream. It came again, louder and more peremptory; and then, all at once, Marianne was fully awake and furious. With a lunge she sat up and snatched, not at the pale spectral hands, but at a point just beyond where they ended in darkness. Her fingers closed over a solid, human arm. She pulled with all her strength.

The moan ended in a yelp of surprise and pain, and something fell heavily across her lap. In fumbling for a better hold, Marianne lost her grip on the intruder, who immediately rolled off the bed. She heard him blundering around the room, but made no attempt to recapture him. Instead she found her candle and struck a light.

She had known, as soon as her fingers touched the thin, boyish wrist, who her tormentor was. The flaring candlelight caught the young Duke on his way to the hidden passage. It gaped open. The table she had placed before it stood to one side, and Marianne cursed her own stupidity; anyone coming by way of the stairs would naturally carry a light, and as soon as the panel slid to one side he would see the obstacle.

Remembering the boy's propensity to fall into a fit when he was startled, Marianne did not shout at him, as she wanted to do, but spoke in a firm, quiet voice.

"You are fairly caught, Henry. Sit down, if you please."

Henry hesitated long enough to make her wonder what on earth she would do if he fell to the floor frothing and writhing. Then, with a sullen swagger, he threw himself into a chair, crossed one leg over the other, and stared at her defiantly.

"You weren't frightened at all," he said. "How did you know it was me?"

"It was I," Marianne corrected. "I wasn't frightened, but I might have been; it was a cruel, malicious thing to do. Why did you do it?"

"I thought it would be fun."

"And how did you evade M. Victor? He should not allow —"

"He has gone out. I suppose he is down at the Devenbrook Arms, getting drunk, as usual."

"Getting . . ." Marianne decided not to pursue this line of investigation. Curiosity got the better of her, and she inquired rather ingenuously, "How did you do that?"

"Gloves, coated with phosphorus," Henry answered readily. He pulled these objects from his pocket and dangled them from his hand. In the gloom they had a perceptible glow; but, like all enlightened viewers of a conjurer, Marianne wondered how she could ever have been deceived by such a simple trick.

"I got the idea from *A Young Person's Guide to Science*," Henry went on. "There are lots of other good things in that book. Would you like to see it?"

"Yes, I would." Marianne was decidedly interested; but seeing that Henry was now quite at ease, and indeed rather proud of his ingenuity, she thought she had better not encourage him any more. Returning to her lecturing tone, she asked reproachfully,

"What would your dear mama say if she knew you had done this?"

A singularly unpleasant, unchildlike smile

came over Henry's face. "She would like it. She hates you."

"Hates me? You must be mistaken. Why should she hate me?"

"You are very pretty," Henry said. "And the vicar admires you."

Marianne was silenced momentarily. Consternation, lingering anger, pleasure at the compliment, and hurt — for she had really hoped that the unhappy Lady Violet would be her friend — gave way to an overwhelming pity.

"I am sorry if she doesn't like me," she said gently. "I like her very much, and would like to be of service to her. And to you, Henry. I know it is dull for you here. I am bored too, sometimes; perhaps we could do things together. I am very good at playing ball, and marbles."

"Girls can't play ball," Henry said.

"I can. Before I had to become a proper young lady I played with Billy Turnbull and Jack Daws, at home. Why don't we make a pact? I won't tell anyone about this if you will try to be my friend."

Henry was wise enough to see that this offer was to his advantage, since it committed him to nothing specific.

"All right," he said ungraciously. "Can I go now?"

"Yes. But if you ever use that passageway again I will not hold my tongue."

Henry departed as he had come, without further comment; but the last glance he gave Marianne held an inquiring, almost wistful quality that gave her hope that some good had been done. She had deliberately refrained from questioning the boy about any other tricks he might have played. If she could gain his confidence he might confide in her of his own free will.

III

To Marianne's surprise Carlton accompanied her to church next morning. He was waiting for her in the hall when she came down and handed her into the carriage with a solemn air perfectly suited to a Sunday morning. It was still raining.

"So Lady Violet changed her mind," Marianne said.

"No; she remained of the same mind. She never intended to go."

"I am sorry."

"You have been reading too many tracts," Carlton said. "You earnest Christians seem to feel that a single noble gesture from you should bring about instant conversion, and you become highly indignant when there is no such result. A long-seated timidity like that of the Lady Violet is not to be overcome in a day; if you really wanted to befriend her you would persist and not be discouraged by lack of immediate success."

"And what makes you suppose I will not persist? You do have a poor opinion of me!"

"Now you are becoming angry," Carlton said gravely. "Tut, tut, Miss Ransom. Try to adopt an attitude more becoming to the day and the occasion."

So Marianne had to swallow her wrath. "Why is not Dr. Gruffstone with us?" she asked. "I hope the Duchess is not worse."

"No, she does quite well. Gruffstone is a rational deist, or some such thing; he does not approve of organized religion, except for the lower classes."

Marianne had no comment to make on this absurd statement. With Carlton she could never be sure whether he was reporting a fact or embroidering it in his own peculiar way.

Going down the aisle of the church on Carlton's arm was almost as much of an ordeal as going alone; her self-possession was not improved when he said out of the corner of his mouth, "Practice, Miss Ransom, for the day of your nuptials. Aren't you glad the groom will be someone else?"

Nor was the sermon soothing. To be sure, the vicar was as handsome as ever, and he seemed to smile directly at her; but the text was the famous exhortation that had led to the hideous deaths of thousands of innocents: "Thou shalt not suffer a witch to live." Naturally St. John did not advocate such a fate for those who dabbled in forbidden arts, but by the time he had finished painting a vivid picture of the flames singeing the screaming sinners, Marianne was almost inclined to think that being burned alive would be preferable. At least it had an end, whereas according to St. John the fires of Hell never went out.

The congregation found this sermon much more to its taste than the last one had been. Several of them were beginning to sway and groan in chorus by the time St. John finished with a thundering condemnation.

Carlton, who had sat with folded arms and impassive face throughout, did not comment until they had squelched through the mud and taken their places in the carriage.

"Ah, the comforts of religion. It is as well Her Grace was not well enough to attend. I fully expected some of the elderly faithful to suffer heart attacks on the spot."

"He would not have delivered that sermon if the Duchess had been there," Marianne said.

"No doubt you are right. He has enough self-interest to avoid such an error."

"Compassion, you mean."

"No, that is not what I mean. But you and I will never agree on that subject; enough of it. Have you given any thought as to what you will do a few days from now, when the Duchess calls on you to summon up the spirit of David Holmes?"

The seemingly abrupt change of subject left Marianne momentarily at a loss for words. It was not, in fact, a non sequitur; the fiery sermon had revived her distaste for spiritualism and reminded her of something she had tried not to think about.

"She may not ask it of me."

"Don't cherish that illusion. She lives for that moment. Indeed," Carlton added, his expression thoughtful, "I think she lives only for that moment. If she believes that Holmes waits for her on the other side . . ."

"Are you by any chance suggesting that I invent a message to that effect?"

"Little Miss Innocent is not quite so naive as she appears," Carlton jeered. "I was not about to suggest that, no; but don't be too surprised if the doctor comes to you with some such request."

"He would never do such a thing!"

"Don't be too sure. However, I admit that you are in a devilish difficult position. If there is no contact at all, the disappointment might literally break her heart. If Holmes greets her with the usual vague meandering about flowers and sunshine and peace on the other side, she may decide to join him forthwith. In fact, if you are considering a literary invention along those lines, I suggest you say that, while Holmes is happy to see her, he does not expect to meet her in heaven for many years to come."

"I could not do that," Marianne said wearily. "Even if I wanted to, I would not know how to make it convincing."

Carlton's hand, resting on his knee, clenched into a fist, as if he were trying to keep it from making a gesture foreign to his will.

"Something must be decided before the day comes," he said. "I cannot — I will not! — endure a repetition of what happened the last time."

"Which of the doctor's theories do you follow?" Marianne asked. "No doubt you have decided, despite the evidence of your own eyes — and hands — that I was responsible after all."

She thought Carlton flushed faintly at the reference to his fumbling at her skirt, but in the dim light it was hard to tell. Certainly his voice held no trace of embarrassment as he replied, "I have as yet reached no conclusion. But I am working on the problem, make no mistake about that."

Marianne was tempted to tell him about her nocturnal visit from Henry. However, it seemed unworthy to try to lift suspicion from herself by casting it on another. Besides, she had given her word not to tell.

Carlton said no more, and when they reached the castle he went off with only a brusque nod of farewell. Marianne went up to change her damp shoes. When she opened her door the first thing she saw was Henry, comfortably curled up in a chair by the fire.

"You were a very long time," he remarked. "I've been waiting for hours."

"You have no business being here at all," Marianne replied. "I thought I told you never to come into without knocking."

"I did knock."

Marianne could not help laughing. "Then let me amend my statement. You must not come in unless I answer your knock."

"I'm sorry." The apology, which she had

not expected, and the ingratiating tone, warned Marianne not to pursue the lecture. "You said you would play something with me," Henry went on.

"Yes, but this is Sunday."

"Please. You said you would."

Marianne's childhood was not so far in the past. She could well remember the appalling dullness of Sunday afternoons, after Mrs. Jay had taken over her education. She could also remember the squire's foul temper on the mornings after all-night drinking sessions with his cronies, and she imagined that Victor was in no state to be useful to his pupil — assuming, of course, that the boy's account of his tutor's Saturday-night amusements was correct.

After all, she told herself recklessly, I am probably doomed to Hell anyway. What does one more small sin matter?

"Very well. Wait outside for me while I change."

Henry obeyed so promptly and with such a beaming face that she realized what a nice boy he could be, under the right circumstances. She put on her oldest gown, suspecting it would probably sustain some damage.

The dress was certainly not improved by the activities of the succeeding hours. First she was taken to admire Henry's new velocipede, which he was allowed to ride indoors on wet days. The old castle had plenty of abandoned corridors suitable to this exercise, and it amused Marianne to think how shocked the former dukes would have been to see the boy racing at full speed along the passages where they had paced in solemn dignity. She even took a turn on the velocipede herself, with Henry shouting encouragement.

"I really think," she said, dismounting, "that I had better go and see if the Duchess needs me for anything."

"Oh, not yet!" Henry snatched her hand. "There are lots of things we haven't played. I want to show you my room."

Marianne was unable to resist his shining face. Besides, she was enjoying herself.

They climbed the endless flights of stairs that led to the upper regions, where the young were tucked away in the pious hope that they would be neither seen nor heard. It occurred to Marianne that M. Victor's room must be near that of his pupil. She hoped she would not see him. She did not mean to let the fear of such a meeting deter her, however; after all, she was the injured party.

Henry showed off his rooms with pardonable pride. They contained every comfort, and most of the luxuries, that money could provide. The night nursery was a cozy little chamber with a quaint turreted roof, hung all around with tapestries to keep off the chill. The former day nursery, which Henry preferred to call his schoolroom, had a pair of desks and a bookcase in one corner, but playroom might have been a better term, for the rest of the long, lofty chamber was crowded with an assortment of expensive toys, including the latest mechanical wind-up trains and fire engines. A huge wooden Noah's Ark contained almost as many pairs of animals as the original must have done; and Marianne was child enough to be enchanted with a large toy theater with curtains of real red velvet and enough wooden figures for an entire repertoire of Shakespeare. She wanted to play with this, but Henry dragged out boxes of lead soldiers and proposed a battle. They were in the middle of the last charge at Waterloo (Marianne, of course, had to take the French side) and she was so absorbed in avoiding Wellington's assault that she failed to hear the door open. Looking up through her tumbled hair she saw M. Victor.

Marianne scrambled to her feet. Victor stepped forward to offer his hand; she ignored it. The smile faded from the tutor's face, to be replaced by a singularly ugly look Marianne wondered how she could ever have thought him pleasant or amusing. He showed all the signs of the dissipation Henry had accused him of: sunken eyes, pasty complexion, and a perceptible tremor in the hand he now withdrew.

"What do you want?" Henry demanded. "We are busy. Go away."

"I am sorry to interrupt Your Grace in such an edifying Sunday activity," said Victor, with a sneer. "But Miss Ransom is wanted."

"I want her!"

"Sure, and you'll not be the only one! I was referring," Victor explained, smirking at Marianne, "to her noble Grace. Now you can't be letting her wait, can you?"

"Certainly not," Marianne said coldly. "Henry, I have enjoyed this. Tomorrow, after your lessons, perhaps we can finish the battle. This time the French may win after all!"

Henry's sulky look was replaced by a smile. "No, they won't."

"We shall see. Thank you for letting me come."

She walked straight toward Victor, whose outstretched arm barred the door. At the last possible moment he stepped aside and followed her out into the hall.

"Will you not wait a tiny little minute? It's wanting to speak with you I am."

"I have nothing to say to you," Marianne snapped, continuing on her way.

"Have you not then? Yet we could be the best of friends, I'm thinking; having so much in common, one might say."

Trotting along beside her he put out his hand with what he obviously believed to be an ingratiating smile.

"We have nothing whatever in common," Marianne replied. "And as for being friends, that is not only ludicrous, it is insulting. I warn you" — as he seemed to be about to take her by the arm — "if you touch me I will complain at once, not to Her Grace, who must not be troubled with such things, but to Mr. Carlton. He will see that you are dismissed, and possibly thrashed."

Victor looked as if he might have said more, but Marianne did not wait to hear it. Increasing her pace, she went on as rapidly as she could. The tutor did not follow.

Once she was out of sight, she paused for a few moments to compose herself, since she did not want the Duchess to ask the cause of her flushed lace. She was half tempted to carry out her threat of telling Carlton. Surely the tutor was not the right person to be in charge of a boy like Henry. Yet she hesitated to complain of him. It seemed so mean-spirited.

When she reached the Duchess's room she found Dr. Gruffstone pacing along the corridor, glancing impatiently at his watch.

"Is something wrong?" Marianne asked. "I came as soon as I could."

"No, no. Her Grace simply wondered what had become of you, and since she is not to suffer the slightest worry I sent the servants to look for you. Will you sit with her awhile? She has been resting and now wants to be amused. You may even play a game of backgammon if you promise to lose badly, so there will be no suspense to the play."

"Of course," Marianne said, returning his smile. "I will go in to her at once."

She found the room in semidarkness and at first thought the Duchess had gone to sleep. However, she roused when Marianne tiptoed in. In a dazed, drowsy voice, she said, "I have had the most beautiful dream. . . . At least Horace would call it a dream. David . . . He smiled at me and held out his hands and called me 'Honor.' He was the only one who ever called me that."

"Dreams can be very real," Marianne said

gently. "Would you like to sleep again?"

"It was not a dream. I saw him as plainly as I see you." Marianne did not point out that in the shadowy twilight she must appear insubstantial and ghostly too. The Duchess went on, "I could even make out the furnishings of the room where he was. It was a shabby, homely little place, a bedchamber of some kind. There was rain pouring down the windowpane. Blue hangings on the bed. . . . Or were they gray?" The Duchess sighed. "It is fading now, but it was very real."

A superstitious shiver ran down Marianne's limbs.

"It is cool here," she said. "Shall I put more wood on the fire, and light the lamps? What can I do to amuse you? The doctor says we may play backgammon if you would like."

"What, on Sunday?" The Duchess laughed. "Horace is a frightful old pagan, but I know better. Yes, light the lamps if you will, child. Tea will be coming up shortly."

Marianne poked up the fire and lighted all the lamps she could find. With the curtains drawn the room took on a warm, cheerful look that was much more to her taste.

The Duchess also seemed more cheerful,

though she complained, half jokingly, of having a hard time keeping her eyes open.

"It must be the weather. The sound of rain always makes one sleepy. Never mind, a cup of tea will wake me up. Tell me what you have been doing all day."

Marianne gave her a spirited account of the battle of Waterloo and the activities that had preceded it. The Duchess laughed aloud at her description of herself on the velocipede, her knees high, scraping first one wall and then the other as she raced.

"I know I should not have allowed the Duke to play on Sunday," she said apologetically. "But I did want to be friends with him, and he seemed at loose ends —"

"And that wretched Irishman sleeping off his overindulgence," the Duchess broke in. "Don't look so surprised, child; I am not incompetent yet! I began to question his influence over Henry last time I was here, and what I have seen on this visit confirms my feelings that he must be replaced. Don't apologize for breaking the Sabbath. You committed a minor sin in doing an act of kindness, which is much more important. Now tell me. . . . Ah, here is Rose with our tea."

Marianne was happy to see that the tray the maid carried appeared to be heavily laden. She had worked up an appetite playing with Henry.

All at once the maid came to a dead stop, her eyes bulging. The cups and saucers on the tray rattled. Marianne jumped up and seized it as it tilted; she was just in time to prevent the contents from sliding off onto the floor.

She put the tray on a table. "What on earth is the matter, Rose?" she asked.

The maid tried to reply. The muscles of her throat bulged, but no sound came from her parted lips. Her staring eyes were fixed on some object behind Marianne.

Marianne turned, following the gaze, which was almost as explicit as a pointing finger.

The wall between the windows blazed with letters of fire. A large oil lamp on the table below them allowed her to read the message they spelled.

"The time is near. Come to me then."

The maid began to scream. Marianne swayed, not through faintness, but through indecision. She did not know whether to run to the Duchess, or silence the shrieking maid, or summon help, or seize the nearest cloth and wipe out the fiery letters . . . assuming they could be wiped out by something so ordinary as a cloth.

Before she could decide, the door burst open and Dr. Gruffstone appeared. She had never admired his quickness so much; a sudden bound took him to Rose; he slapped her briskly on the cheek. Her shrieks stopped. Then the doctor turned to his patient.

"It is all right, Horace," the Duchess said calmly. "I am happy. I am at peace."

Indeed she looked quite beautiful. Smiling, flushed, except for her snow-white hair she might have been a young girl.

Gruffstone turned to Marianne.

"Watch that fool woman," he snarled, gesturing at Rose. "She is about to swoon. Get her into the next room, don't let her talk to the others." As she spoke he pulled his handkerchief out of his breast pocket and with one vicious sweeping gesture removed the first line of the glowing inscription. The second followed, just as a rush of footsteps heralded the arrival of Carlton.

"What in heaven's name —"

Rose proved the doctor a true prophet by collapsing into an untidy heap on the floor. Marianne bent over her.

"What —" Carlton began again.

"My smelling salts are in the cabinet," the Duchess said calmly. "Do what you can for her, Horace, and then please join me in a cup of tea."

CHAPTER FOURTEEN

The hour that followed was one Marianne would never forget. Drinking her tea, the Duchess contributed little; she sat smiling with dreamy detachment while the others argued about what had happened.

Rose had been given a sleeping draft and was snoring on a sofa in the boudoir.

"Though heaven knows it is only postponing the inevitable," the doctor groaned, running his hand through his wildly ruffled hair. "The moment the wretched woman wakes up she will tell every servant in the house what she saw."

"If you had not seen it too, I would think —" Carlton began. He broke off, with a sidelong look at the Duchess.

"There are enough witnesses," the doctor said gloomily.

"Then someone wrote it while the Duchess was asleep," Carlton said. "There was a period of time after you left, Gruffstone, and before Miss Ransom came in."

"I was outside the door the entire time," the doctor said.

"What about the secret passages?" Marianne asked. "The Duke said . . ." Then she remembered her promise to Henry and could say no more. "However," she went on, "the wall was unmarked when I lighted the lamps. I am sure of that, because one lamp, one of the largest, was on the table just below that section of the paneling."

A long discouraged silence followed, while they stared at one another. Marianne felt slightly sick. She knew the finger of suspicion pointed at her. She could have written the message in phosphorous paint, or some similar chemical, while the Duchess dozed. Only she knew she had not done so.

Finally the Duchess spoke. "You are all behaving very foolishly. There is nothing to be afraid of. Go down to dinner, all of you. I would like to be alone for a while. After you have dined, Roger, will you come up to me? I will not keep you long, I promise."

The dismissal could not be ignored. Carlton rose uncertainly, and Marianne followed suit. The doctor remained seated.

"Honoria," he began.

"Dear old friend." She held out her hand and the doctor took it in his. "I am perfectly well. I only want to think about . . . matters I have put off too long. You may come and say good night, later."

The doctor raised her hand to his lips. When he turned away Marianne saw his eyes held an unnatural shine, as if they were filled with tears.

Not until she glanced at herself in the mirror in her own room did Marianne realize she was still wearing the dusty, crumpled frock in which she had played with Henry. She dropped wearily into a chair. This latest and most bewildering phenomenon had exhausted her strength. She did not know what to make of it, and she was too tired to think.

If she had obeyed her own desires she would have remained in her room. However, the Duchess's command had been explicit, and besides, not to put too fine a face upon it, she was hungry.

Dinner could not be called a success. The doctor spoke but little; Carlton made inane comments at random, and several times Marianne caught him staring wildly at her, as if she had changed into a person he had never seen before. Not feeling in spirits enough for the finish of *Wuthering Heights* (she had peeked at the ending and read just enough to curdle her blood), she went to the library to find another book. Rejecting any work of fiction that smacked even slightly of the sensational, she selected a volume of

Carlyle's essays and went dispiritedly up to her room.

The volume did what she hoped it would do; it put her to sleep, in spite of a rising wind that made uncanny sounds behind the drawn draperies. And if a hand opened her door and a shadowed face looked in, Marianne was unaware of it.

II

The wind that had howled so drearily had not been an evil portent but the reverse. Not only did Marianne sleep through the night, but she awoke to find her room bright with sunlight. The lift to her spirits was tremendous. She dressed as quickly as she could and without waiting for breakfast put on her coat and ran outside.

The air was cold, and frost whitened the grass. Puddles of water had fringes of ice. It would have taken more than cold to discourage Marianne; she felt like an animal freed from a narrow cage. Swinging her arms and striding briskly, she set off down the driveway. As soon as she was out of sight of the house she broke into an undignified run, for the sheer joy of it. The distance from the front steps to the iron gates was a good mile.

Still exhilarated, she turned onto the foot-path and walked toward the village.

The smoke of the cooking fires rose up into a cloudless sky. There were few people abroad; early as it was for the pampered upper classes, most of the villagers had been up for hours and had gone to their work. Marianne saw only a few housewives, baskets on their arms, on their way to market, and one gentleman enjoying his morning constitutional.

She had intended to go as far as the church — for no particular reason, just to have a goal in mind — but the sight of the stroller ahead of her made her self-conscious. She turned and started back.

Before long she heard rapid footsteps approaching; then around a curve in the drive came Carlton, trotting along like a man who is late for an urgent appointment. He was hatless; his dark hair blew in the wind. Marianne was about to hail him with a joking reference to his passion for early-morning exercise when he caught sight of her and came to an abrupt halt. A formidable scowl darkened his face. "Where have you been?" he demanded.

"Walking. The sun was so welcome I could not wait to enjoy it."

"You have no business rushing out like

that. If one of the footmen had not seen you I would have had no idea where you were."

"Why should you concern yourself about my whereabouts?" Marianne demanded. "Ah, I know; you thought I had run off with the Duchess's jewels. You suspect me of every mean and contemptible act; why not that?"

As her anger grew, Carlton became cooler. He smiled in a superior way and replied, "Oddly enough — that had not occurred to me. I hope you have no such scheme in mind; I am far too busy to be forever searching your room."

"I don't see you actively engaged in anything," Marianne retorted. "In fact, I wonder that a busy lawyer like yourself can spare so much time for one client. Shouldn't you be in your office?"

"As a matter of fact, I am leaving almost at once."

"Oh," Marianne said flatly.

"But I shall return."

"When?"

"Ah, you do care!" Carlton exclaimed, clasping his hands in mock rapture. "I don't know when, Miss Ransom. Hopefully in two or three days. Now I want you to promise me something before I go."

"What?"

"You are monosyllabic today — and wary, too. Couldn't you have said, 'Anything,' instead of pronouncing that flat, skeptical 'what?' I merely want your word that you will not leave the house until I return."

"Impossible! I will lose my mind cooped up any longer. Surely a ride, with one of the grooms —"

"No. Not even a walk in the garden. I have postponed discussing this matter with you because. . . . Well, for a variety of reasons which need not concern you. But now I must speak out. There is a stranger staying at the Devenbrook Arms."

"The man I saw this morning?"

"Ah, you saw him. Then it was not Bagshot?"

Marianne gasped. Strolling side by side, they had reached the castle; in her agitation she turned away from it and began pacing back and forth.

"I . . . I cannot say for certain. I saw the man at a distance; his back was to me and he wore a broad-brimmed hat and a long cloak."

"I have not been able to get a look at him," Carlton said. "He keeps very much to himself. But even if I had seen him I might not know him; there are such things as disguises. I do not really believe this man is Bagshot.

He probably is not. But I learned a few days ago, from my informants in London, that Bagshot is not to be seen in his usual haunts, and that he is rumored to have left the city."

"Days ago! Why didn't you tell me?"

Carlton shrugged. "You would not believe my reasons," he said enigmatically. "I am telling you now only because I am going away and you will have to watch out for yourself."

"But it is so vague," Marianne said obstinately. "I cannot imagine that he would have the audacity to come here, even in disguise. You are starting at shadows, Mr. Carlton . . . and the sun is shining."

"If you take that attitude I will be forced to tell you another fact I had meant to keep from you, because of its distressing nature. I have found Maggie."

Marianne clapped her hands with joy. "You have found her! Oh, how cruel of you not to . . ." Carlton's grim look gave her a hint of the truth. She caught her breath. "She is dead. Oh, good heavens, is that it?"

"Not dead, no; but she was badly beaten and left for dead. Precisely when the attack happened is uncertain; but she finally managed to reach the man she had mentioned to you, old Harry. A scavenger and ragpicker by trade. He took her in and did his best for her, but when my people found her she was delirious and sinking fast. She is now receiving the finest care," he added quickly, seeing Marianne's stricken face. "Her prospects are good, Marianne, indeed they are. Such women are tough. They must be, to survive the lives they are forced to lead."

Marianne covered her face with her hands. "I cannot bear it," she sobbed. "It was on my account, I know it was; it is all my fault."

Carlton took a quick, impulsive step toward her, his hands extended; but caught himself before he actually touched her. When Marianne took her hands from her face he was standing several feet away, his pocket handkerchief held out. She took it, sniffling, and Carlton said composedly, "You are leaping to unwarranted conclusions. We do not know that it was Bagshot who instigated the attack; in that section of London there are men who would murder for a few coins. I assure you, Maggie is in good hands. You had better think of yourself. Will you give me that promise now?"

Marianne nodded submissively. She mopped her wet forehead with the handkerchief.

"Good. Let us go in now. I will return as soon as I possibly can. Take sensible precautions, but don't let your fears get the better of you."

Marianne might not have been able to follow this excellent advice; but the rest of the day was so busy, it left her little time for moping. In spite of the remonstrances of Dr. Gruffstone, the Duchess decided she had been in bed long enough. Marianne found her up and dressed and declaring her intention of returning to her duties.

Precisely what those duties were Marianne could not make out at first, though she was kept fully occupied in assisting them. The Duchess spent hours at her desk writing and sorting through papers. She also instigated what appeared to be a limited and belated kind of fall housecleaning; the maids were required to turn out her wardrobes and her dresser drawers, and under her crisp orders the various garments were sorted into piles, some of which were returned to their places, while others were packed into boxes and carried away.

Not until this last activity was in progress did Marianne guess at a possible explanation; and she felt a chill of foreboding. The Duchess seemed composed, even happy; she hummed quietly to herself as she wrote letters and lists. But Marianne thought the delicate white hands had a new transparency, and the face an unearthly look of peace.

Late that afternoon Marianne returned to the boudoir after looking in the library for a book the Duchess had requested — a book of sermons. This in itself meant nothing; the Duchess often read devotional works, both spiritualist and conventional. But when Marianne entered the dainty sitting room she found her friend reclining on a chaise longue sorting through the contents of a velvet case. She held up one piece of jewelry after another; the lamplight shone upon the sullen blood-red of garnets, the limpid glow of moonstone and opal, the variegated blues of aquamarines, sapphires, and Persian turquoise.

"Do sit down, my dear," the Duchess said, indicating a nearby chair. "How tired you must be, after running my errands all day long. And on such a fine day, too, when you must have longed to be out."

"I had a nice brisk run this morning," Marianne replied. "Besides, after all you have done for me, I am only too happy to be able to help, even in such small ways." The Duchess held up a gold chain hung with dangling multicolored gems, and Marianne exclaimed involuntarily, "Oh, how pretty!"

"It is only an inexpensive trinket; the

stones are citrines and amethysts and other semiprecious gems. Like most of the pieces in this case, it is a personal memento of mine. The valuable family jewels are in the bank in London. Do you really like it? Take it, then."

She handed it to the girl, whose hand moved automatically to receive it, and continued to sort through the other ornaments, inquiring calmly, "What else would you care to have? These garnets are pretty, but perhaps they are too somber for a young girl. Ah, this is what I was searching for."

The jewel was a ring shaped like two small golden hands, the fingers curved around a central aquamarine. To Marianne its deep-blue color and sparkling clarity were prettier than many of the more valuable stones.

"Just the color of your eyes," the Duchess said with a smile. "No" — for Marianne, confused and apprehensive, tried to hand it back — "I want you to have that now. And any of the others that appeal to you."

The stress on the word "now" had been unmistakable. Marianne's eyes filled with tears.

"Please don't speak as if . . ." She could not finish the sentence.

"Now your eyes are as bright as the stone," the Duchess said, with a little laugh.

"My dear child, don't be distressed; I am not being morbid. I am merely facing a fact I have refused to face before. We are all immortal; but none of us remains on this plane forever. The ring is not valuable, but I know you will cherish it as a memento. And who knows? I may see you wear it for many years yet."

"God grant that it may be so," Marianne exclaimed.

"Now there is one more little task you can perform for me, and then we will take a well-deserved rest. I want a list of all these trinkets. Suppose I give you the description and you write it down for me."

Marianne's fingers were willing; but her heart was heavy as she made out the list in her very best handwriting. There was no longer any doubt about the Duchess's state of mind. She had accepted the imminence of death and was disposing of her worldly possessions.

And why, Marianne wondered, should the idea of receiving a few of these treasures repel her? She had complacently accepted expensive clothes and pretty ornaments, and the attentions of servants; she had enjoyed borrowed luxuries as if they were her own. Ah, but that was the point — she had never really thought of these things as hers by right. They were only lent to her, and in her heart she had known that one day they would vanish, as fairy gold turns to dust when the spell is wound up. Besides, she was no longer the careless, selfish child who had arrived in London. Since then she had experienced the most profound human emotions — terror and love, gratitude and pity. She had grown up — and she almost wished she could have remained a child forever.

Finally the list was finished and the Duchess dismissed her.

"Put on your prettiest dress," she instructed. "Then you may come back and sit with me while I dress. I am dining downstairs tonight. I wish to enjoy the company of my dear friends as much as possible."

Marianne managed to get outside the door before she broke down. Leaning against the wall she wept silently, wiping her eyes with her fingers. She knew she should not be distressed; the spectacle of a Christian preparing tranquilly for the long-awaited meeting with her Saviour and God ought to have been edifying. Marianne believed in the immortality of the soul. Why, then, should she feel so sad?

Lost in her illogical but overwhelming grief, she did not hear the soft footsteps approaching till they were almost upon her.

Turning, with a choked gasp, she saw Victor standing a little distance away. The lamps in the hall had not yet been lighted and the air was shadowy with twilight; she could not make out his features. But when he spoke his voice left no doubt as to his state of mind.

"So you spoke to the old besom after all, and I've lost me position. I'll be getting no references, after what you said; what the devil will become of me now?"

Marianne knew the Duchess had seen Victor that day, but he had been only one of a number of servants and dependents who had come and gone on various errands. Until now she had not known why he had been sent for.

"I said nothing," she protested.

"Indeed! I'll not be taking your word for that."

"I don't care whether you believe me or not. Your drunkenness and incompetence have led to your dismissal, and it serves you right! Now let me pass."

He came so close that she could see his face, set in an ugly sneer. She had never felt any real fear of this contemptible creature and she was not afraid now; but she was glad to see a light approach, for she was not anxious for any further unpleasantness.

"The maids are coming to light the

lamps," she said. "You had better take yourself off before you get into more trouble."

With a muttered Celtic curse Victor pushed past her and walked away. Marianne went into her room. The meeting had annoyed but not alarmed her; she was unable to regard Victor's veiled threats with any stronger emotion than contempt. Furthermore, the solemn knowledge that had come upon her left no room in her heart for transitory fears. All her thoughts were now bent on the great Mystery — and on what she could do to prevent its happening. She considered some such action as Carlton had suggested, though she could not believe he had been serious about the idea of fabricating a message from David Holmes. Thank heaven Carlton would be back before the fateful day. Perhaps together they could invent some scheme.

With Annie's reluctant assistance she made an elaborate toilette. Since the most recent manifestations the maid had reverted to her original wide-eyed terror of Marianne, and the latter had given up trying to soothe her. After dressing she looked into the mirror only long enough to make sure she had been able to manufacture a cheerful expression. Then she went next door.

The Duchess was seated at her dressing

table while Rose tried to arrange her hair. The poor woman's hands trembled so much they had lost their usual skill, and her face was swollen with weeping. So, Marianne thought sympathetically, she too understands the meaning of what has happened today.

"There you are," the Duchess exclaimed, catching sight of Marianne's reflection. "Just in time, too. Rose is pulling the hairs out of my head, she is so clumsy tonight. Would you replace her?"

"With pleasure," Marianne replied. "Rose, you look unwell. Why don't you go and rest?"

This kindly offer was received with a look of unconcealed hatred. Putting her apron to her eyes, Rose stumbled out of the room.

"Ridiculous woman," the Duchess said, as Marianne began to brush her white locks.

"She is jealous of me, I think. And she has had a bad shock, you know."

"So have you. It is amazing how shocked people are when the things they have always believed to be true actually happen. Rose knows her Bible, she is devout; but when she sees evidence of the survival of the spirit she loses her wits. Ah, that feels splendid. How gentle your touch is."

They went downstairs together to find the

others waiting. Even Lady Violet was present, dressed in her usual gray, a lace veil covering her pretty hair and shadowing her face. The evening was not a success, despite the doctor's spasmodic attempts at cheerful conversation; in between his comments his face would sag like that of a sad old bloodhound.

After dinner, at the Duchess's request, Marianne went to the piano. The music soothed her, and it seemed to comfort the Duchess, who listened with a dreamy smile. Lady Annabelle did not stay long. Remarking that music always made Horace the cat start to howl, she departed, carrying the said animal, who did indeed give Marianne a pained stare in passing.

The night and the next day were a repetition of the nights and days that had gone before — quiet sleep, hours of sorting and making lists. By midafternoon the Duchess had finished her self-appointed tasks and declared she intended to rest awhile.

"My dear Marianne, run out and enjoy the sunshine," she said. "We will not have many more such days before winter comes; make the most of them. Only, if you ride, do take one of the grooms so you don't risk getting lost. That selfish Roger and his mysterious business! I am really vexed with him for being away just now."

Marianne was sorely tempted to follow the suggestion. She went to the rose parlor which overlooked the garden, and stood at the window looking wistfully out. All the roses were brown and withered now, and most of the trees were bare. The clear light and wide blue skies drew her, but she had promised Carlton not to go out; and, although she was sure his fears were groundless, she would not violate her word. Feeling very sorry for herself, she went to the music room and practiced for an hour on some of the pieces she most disliked.

Upon leaving the room she was surprised and annoyed to see Victor standing by the stairs, apparently intent on the design of a handsome Ming vase that stood on a table there. She would rather not have seen him, but she had no intention of going out of her way to avoid him, so she advanced resolutely toward the stairs. Victor looked up.

"Ah, Miss Ransom. You don't ride today?"

"No."

"But the weather is *très beau, n'est pas?* What a pity to stay indoors."

Marianne did not reply. She ascended the stairs without looking back. She sensed that he continued to stand there watching her, and she had an equally strong impression that if she had turned she would have found that his obsequious smile had changed into an expression more indicative of his real feelings.

She was sufficiently upset by the encounter and by Victor's belated attempt to ingratiate himself to ask the Duchess how much longer the tutor would be with them.

"Only until I can find a replacement," was the reply. "I have written to friends in Edinburgh asking for recommendations and with luck I shall begin interviewing applicants this week. Why do you ask? The man has not bothered you, I hope?"

The serenity of her tone showed how far this possibility was from her mind. Marianne saw no reason to disabuse her. "I was only wondering," she said; and so the subject passed.

Another uneasy evening followed. The party broke up early. As Marianne was leaving, the doctor asked for a private word with her.

"I am sorry to keep you from your rest," he said formally, closing the parlor door. "I assure you I will not keep you long."

"Indeed, you need not apologize. I have been so anxious to talk to you! Only, I did not want to intrude."

The doctor smiled sadly. “You understand what is happening, don’t you? You are fond of her too, I daresay.”

“I love her,” Marianne said simply. “It breaks my heart to see her accepting — nay, embracing . . .”

“Death. Strange, how hard it is for us to pronounce the word. Or perhaps not so strange, since we fear the actuality so much. I am afraid that in my own grief I have been selfish. I ought to have talked with you earlier. The position is difficult for you.”

“Is there nothing we can do? Mr. Carlton suggested —”

The doctor’s eyes flashed. “Carlton! Where is he, when I need him? He went off without so much as a word or a by-your-leave; most heartless and inconsiderate of him! Any suggestion of his would be absolute balderdash. . . . But now you had better go to bed. You are very tired, I see.”

Marianne put her hand to her head. “I do feel dizzy.”

“Small wonder. Your nerves are under a great strain. We will talk again — tomorrow, perhaps. It will comfort both of us, I think.”

He patted her hand. So natural was the gesture that Marianne could not even remember when he had taken her hand in his.

"Sleep well," he said softly. "Sleep well and soundly."

Marianne was so tired she had to drag herself upstairs. She got ready for bed without bothering to summon Annie, tucking her hair helter-skelter under her nightcap and kicking her slippers carelessly into the corner. As she reached for the candle, to snuff it, the light caught the gem on her finger and set it into a blue blaze. The ring fit her perfectly. She decided she would never take it off. It would always be a reminder of the dear friend who had given it to her.

Perhaps it was the thought of one kind elderly lady that recalled Mrs. Jay to her mind, with such vividness that she actually turned, half expecting to see the familiar, black-gowned form sitting in the armchair by the fire. The chair was, of course, empty. Marianne rubbed her eyes. She was becoming fanciful. Small wonder, as the doctor might have said.

She was about to get into bed when she remembered she had not locked the door. Foolish it might be, but she was determined to neglect no precaution, though she was now so weary she could barely force her limbs to walk to the door and back. She left one candle burning. Scarcely had her nightcap touched the pillow than she was asleep.

* * *

Deep in the grasp of nightmare, Marianne moaned and turned, flinging her arm free of the bedclothes. It was the same dream that had haunted her before: the eerie dream landscape, dim with fog, the jeering, hating faces. But this time Mrs. Jay did not scream curses at her. Marianne seemed to see her leaning against a column of rough dark stone whose top faded into the lowering mist. Her face was so thin and drawn the girl scarcely recognized it, and she wrung her gnarled hands. Her lips parted; but instead of the well-known, incisive tones Marianne heard a hollow, distant wailing, in which only a few words were audible. "Danger . . . care . . . beware. . . ."

The mist curdled and lifted and Marianne saw that the support against which her old friend leaned was not a column but a cross, and that the tormented figure it bore was a living man, twisted in agony, the dark blood streaming from His pierced hands and feet.

She felt her lips part and a scream form in her throat. Before she could utter it, something was forced into her mouth, something coarse and crumpled that tasted, bizarrely, of tobacco. Gagging, she tried in vain to spit it out. The dream landscape had dissolved and blown away; darkness was all around her. Rough hands touched a body that belonged to her, but over which she had no power of control. She felt cold air on her bare legs and tried to move her hands, to adjust her nightgown. They would not respond. Something came over her head, down the length of her body and limbs; hands fumbled at her ankles. With an effort that made perspiration spring out all over her, she tried to break through the nightmare by opening her eyes.

They were already open.

She was close to fainting, then, and indeed the smothering gag and the muffling folds that enclosed her would have given her good cause to lose her senses. But as she was about to succumb, something peculiar happened. It was almost as if the failure of her normal, waking senses had freed some other entity that lay curled, silent and unsuspected, in the deepest recesses of her mind. A small, cool voice pointed out that there was no point in fainting; better to keep her wits about her — such of them that remained — and try to understand what was happening.

So Marianne lay still and listened; and she heard a voice growl, "Be quick about it, can't you?"

"Ah, that's better," was the reply. "The

gel must've swooned; she's stopped squirming."

Marianne now realized that she had been enclosed in a blanket or a bag or something of the sort, which covered her from the top of her head to her feet and was tied around her ankles. Scarcely had she deduced this when she was hoisted up, bag and all, and tossed over a hard surface, from which she dangled ignominiously, her head hanging down on one side and her bare feet on the other. It took little exercise of intelligence to know that she was lying over a man's shoulder. The hard bone and muscle cut painfully into her diaphragm, making breathing even more difficult.

"Hurry, hurry," a third voice urged.

Marianne would have uttered an exclamation then, if she had been able. She knew that voice, though it was almost as high as a woman's. Victor! He sounded as if he wanted to scream. How on earth had such a limp custard of a man gotten the courage to abduct her, or the money to hire confederates? For there were at least two other men present.

Even as these thoughts passed through her mind she was carried swiftly across the room. The man stooped, but not quite far enough, for something scraped across her back. She knew then where she was being taken, and braced herself for an unpleasant journey, for she well remembered the narrowness of the passage she had seen. The succeeding moments were as uncomfortable as she had feared; the men had to pass her on from hand to hand, like a sack of potatoes, since it was impossible for them to descend the stairs carrying her.

In spite of her resolution she fell into a sort of half-swoon, as a result of the stifling air and the rough handling. A sudden blast of icy air roused her and she began to shiver. The sack was not very warm, and it was her only covering, besides her nightgown. Again she was transferred to a man's shoulder. The man began to run, jolting Marianne painfully. Her bare feet tingled with cold.

She had now reached a plateau of complete detachment and was surprised at her own control — although the doctor could have told her that this was not an unusual symptom in cases of emotional shock. The man who was carrying her came to a stop. Hearing horses stamp and snort, and the creaking of springs, Marianne postulated a conveyance of some sort. Then another voice spoke, and her abnormal self-control shattered.

"Damn you, what took you so long?

You've bungled it somehow; there are lights springing up all through the house. Here, hand her up and be quick about it!"

The voice, the arms that grasped her shrinking body and flung it down onto a soft, yielding surface . . . Bagshot!

Very well, said the small silent voice, no longer so cool; very well, you may as well faint now. So Marianne did.

She was awakened by a tingling, sharp discomfort in her nose and instinctively turned her head away. She kept her eyes obstinately closed; but she imagined the enclosing bag had been removed, or slit open, for she could see dim light through her lids.

"Clever of me to have had the foresight to bring along smelling salts," said a familiar, hateful voice. "I know you are awake, my love; don't pretend." Fingers grasped her chin in a tight grip and forced her head around.

Marianne opened her eyes. The sight of the yellow, unhealthy face and twisted smile, only inches from her own face, made her stomach lurch. She could still taste tobacco, though the muffling gag had been removed, and her lips were dry and stiff.

"You will not escape," she said faintly. "You cannot hope to succeed in this —"

"Vile plot?" Bagshot grinned wolfishly.

"How very unoriginal, my dear. But then I never was interested in your mind, you know." His smile turned to a grimace of utter malignancy. "No one plays tricks like that on me with impunity. I'd have tired of you soon enough if you had been sensible; but after what you did, I'd have followed you to the ends of the earth." Marianne shivered, and he added, with a return to his suave manner, "Sorry to have removed your warm sack; I wanted to make sure those bungling idiots had snatched the right girl."

He leaned toward her. Marianne shrank back into the corner as far as she could. Her hands and feet were still bound, so she could not move easily.

"How much did you pay Victor to help you?" she asked, with some forlorn hope of distracting him from his obvious intention.

"Much less than I was prepared to offer for such a prize," was the gloating reply. "He patronizes the local tavern; one of my men heard him complaining in his cups and fancied he would be the tool we were looking for. What did you do to the poor fool? He seemed quite bitter about you. But I can understand his feelings; you really are a delicious little morsel. I'm not sure I can contain myself till we reach the cozy nest I have prepared for us."

With a horrid parody of delicacy he put out his hand and untied the ribbon at the neck of Marianne's gown. She could retreat no further. She bent her head and bit him on the finger.

With a howl of pain he pulled back, shaking the wounded member. Then he lifted his hand and would have struck her if the trap on the ceiling had not opened to show the coachman's face. Marianne could not make out the words he shouted; but Bagshot understood. His face turned even blacker with rage, if that was possible, and with a muttered oath he opened the window and put his head out. Then Marianne heard it too — voices shouting, a distant rumble of hoofbeats. Her heart pounded with hope and excitement.

Bagshot banged on the trap. "Faster, damn you," he shouted.

They were already traveling at considerable speed, but now the coach began to sway wildly as the coachman urged his steeds on. Bagshot paid no more attention to Marianne. Drawing a pair of pistols from his pocket, he stationed himself at the window. Marianne bit her lip to keep from crying out. Common sense warned her not to attempt any foolhardy act of heroism, bound and helpless as she was; and really it seemed unlikely that Bagshot could hope to hit a moving target when the coach was going at such speed.

Suddenly a dark mass rushed past the open window. Marianne caught only a glimpse of it, since Bagshot's head and shoulders filled most of the space. Swearing obscenely, he let out a fusillade of shots. Then, with a rending crash, the coach reeled to one side, rocked violently, and overturned. Marianne was crushed by the weight of a heavy body; her ears were deafened by cries and curses and the screech of cracking metal.

Bagshot had been thrown against her, but he had not been rendered unconscious. He moved almost at once, scrambling out the window, which was now directly over their heads, since the coach was lying on its side. As soon as he was gone Marianne felt it would be safe to scream, which she did with extreme vigor. The sounds of struggle continued outside. Between screams she strained her ears, trying to discover what was happening, but heard only indistinguishable cries of rage and pain.

The sounds finally died away. Marianne emitted a final scream, the loudest of the lot, and sank back, breathless. For an interval nothing happened; she had time to wonder, despairingly, if her rescuers had lost the fight, before the square of light marking the window was obscured by the black silhouette of a head and shoulder.

"Marianne," a voice said. "Speak to me! Are you conscious? Are you unwounded? Are you — er — unharmed?"

The voice was the last one Marianne had expected to hear. Dizzy with surprise and joy she managed to croak, "I can't talk. I am hoarse from screaming."

The door was wrenched open and with some effort Marianne was extracted, rather like a very large puppet from a deep packing box, for she could do nothing to help herself. Her feet had barely touched the ground when she felt herself clasped in Roger Carlton's arms.

CHAPTER FIFTEEN

As all admitted, the real hero of the evening was the thirteenth Duke of Devenbrook. When the rescue party reached the castle they found the boy dancing up and down on the steps in a frenzy of frustration at not having been allowed to join the pursuit; but the praises of the men and the admiring comments of Marianne restored his self-esteem, and he was delighted to explain how he had discovered the plot — too late to prevent its being carried out, but just in time to make rescue possible.

After the housekeeper had tended Marianne's bruises and wrapped her in a dozen blankets, they settled down to discuss the adventure. The Duchess alone had slept through it all, and it was unanimously agreed that she should know nothing of what had transpired.

"For it is settled now," Carlton said. "Bagshot will be some time recovering from the thrashing he received, and he knows that if he tries another trick of that nature, he will be charged and imprisoned."

His speech was not as crisp as usual, thanks to a swollen lower lip. The satisfaction with which he gazed at his scraped knuckles left Marianne in no doubt as to who had administered the thrashing referred to. Feeling that his ego was in no need of reinforcement, she turned to Henry.

"Now tell me, Your Grace, of how you discovered the plot."

"He drugged my milk," Henry explained, swelling with delight at the drama of it. "I knew he was up to something when he kept telling me to be sure I finished it; so naturally I poured it into the slop pail when his back was turned."

"You always do that with your milk, you young rascal," Carlton said, giving him an affectionate slap on the back.

"Well, but I suspected he was up to no good," the boy insisted. "He was very angry at being dismissed; I would hear him muttering to himself. I thought, perhaps he is going to steal something — Granny Honoria's jewels, or the plate. He never cared before whether I drank my milk."

"It was very clever of you," Marianne said.

The Duke beamed. "So," he resumed, "I pretended to be asleep. And I went on pretending, even when he pulled my hair and prodded me — and stuck a pin in my arm!" He cocked an eye at Marianne, who responded with an exclamation of outrage and admiration, before he resumed. "Then he opened the secret door — there is one in my bedroom, you know. He wasn't supposed to know about that, but . . . well, to be honest, he caught me one day. At any rate, then I was *sure* he was up to no good! I got up and followed him. But before I had gone far I heard him coming back, and I really had to run to get into bed before he returned. Those two frightful ruffians were with him; and I can tell you, when I saw them, I . . . Of course I wasn't afraid, but it made me feel very serious, I can tell you."

Carlton laughed. "If I had been in your shoes, Henry, I would have been terrified."

"Well, perhaps I was a little bit afraid. Just a little. One of them looked at me and said, 'Is the brat safe?' and Victor said I had had enough laudanum to down a grown man. Then the other man said, 'What about the girl?' and Victor said if they couldn't handle one small woman they ought to be looking for other employment, begorra."

Carlton's scraped hands clenched when he heard this. "I wish that rascal had not gotten away," he muttered. "But we'll track him down, never fear, and then . . . I beg your pardon, Henry. We are hanging on your words."

Though the Duke's narrative style lacked elegance, being too heavily interlarded with phrases like "Then he said," and "Then the other one said," his hearers were indeed enthralled. On hearing the words he had quoted the boy realized, with a thrill of horror, that the plot his imagination had invented had a much more serious aim than theft. It was all he could do to lie motionless until the men had left his room, by way of the secret passage. Leaping from his bed, he had had the good sense to go for help instead of trying to overcome the villains single-handed.

"I am hurt that you did not waken me," the doctor exclaimed with a look of mock reproach. "Thought I was too old and fat, eh?"

"Oh, no, sir," the Duke exclaimed. But it was clear that this *was* what he had thought. The doctor broke into a rumbling laugh.

"Never mind, my boy. I don't blame you. But I am glad young Roger got me up. I wouldn't have missed that chase for worlds. Made me feel twenty years younger, by Gad!"

The Duke had, in fact, gone to rouse some of the menservants. He had not known of

Carlton's return, since the lawyer had only reached the castle after most of the residents had gone to bed. Reading in the library, Carlton had heard Henry rush past on his way to the servants' wing, and had gone to find out what was wrong. Though Carlton was too tactful to say so, Marianne realized that the rapid organization of the pursuit was due to him; even so, it had taken an agonizingly long time to awaken two of the grooms and get the party mounted. Henry had continued to play a leading part by going through the secret passage to Marianne's room after it was discovered that her door was locked.

Marianne groaned. "And I thought I was being so prudent!"

"It would not have mattered," Carlton assured her. "When Henry reached your room he found that the deed had been done and the villains had departed. However, there is only one road through the village and we knew they must take it; and thanks to Henry's quickness we were in time to see the carriage lights. If we had been a few minutes later, we might not have known which direction to take."

That seemed to wind up the essential parts of the story; but in deference to Henry they talked it all over a while longer and let him go into more detail about his heroism, before the doctor suggested that the victim of the kidnapping should be allowed to get the rest she needed.

Marianne was glad to obey. "I think I will take a dose of that medicine you gave me," she said, accepting the doctor's arm. "Now that it is all over, I am almost too nervous to sleep."

"Sleeping medicine?" Carlton asked alertly. "Perhaps we should all take a dose. I am keyed up myself, and so is Henry. Will you share, Miss Ransom?"

Marianne looked at his face. Shadowy bruises were now apparent, and his lip had swollen to grotesque proportions. "Are you in pain?" she asked.

"Does it look that bad?" Carlton fingered his jaw and made a wry face. "I will have to tell the Duchess I fell off my horse. What a humiliating admission."

Marianne had assumed he was joking about the medicine, but he came to her room almost immediately and repeated his request. She had not, in fact, taken any, and had almost forgotten where she had put it; but Carlton soon discovered the bottle on her dressing table and made off with it. She was sorry, after he had gone, that she had not taken a dose herself, for she was some time in falling asleep.

She woke early the next morning and dragged herself out of bed, tired though she was; for it was imperative that the Duchess should not suspect that anything had happened.

And yet, Marianne thought sadly as the day wore on, the Duchess's failure to notice Carlton's bruises and the Duke's febrile excitement was a portent of her absorption in the event that was fast drawing nigh. She accepted the news of Victor's disappearance with abnormal indifference. "I suppose he has made off with some odds and ends," was her only comment. "It is a small price to pay to be rid of him."

Carlton suggested a ride that afternoon. Marianne agreed; she was glad of the exercise and hoped for a confidential talk. In this she was disappointed. The relaxed, laughing young man who had slapped Henry on the back and called Marianne by her first name had been replaced by the old Carlton, surly and sarcastic and withdrawn.

The Duchess, too, seemed to be withdrawing a little further every day. She had acquired a habit of sitting with her head tilted, as if listening to voices the others could not hear, and she did not seem to care whether anyone was with her or not. After trying to rouse her by suggestions and amusements and receiving only vague replies such as "Whatever you like, my dear," Marianne gave up and went in search of Henry.

They spent the rest of the afternoon out of doors playing lawn tennis. This was a new sport to Marianne, who had read of it but had never played, and the Duke was delighted to play the role of teacher. They returned to the house arm in arm, and Henry, still heavy-eyed from lack of sleep the preceding night, was easily persuaded to go up to his supper and the attentions of his Nanny. The good creature was, he reported, quite delighted at the absence of M. Victor, whom she had always considered a slippery sort of foreign body, not at all the kind to look after her wee laddie.

Henry's imitation of the old lady made Marianne laugh heartily. He had a wicked gift for mimicry; she had noticed it the night before, when he parroted Victor's brogue. But when she went to her room to repair the damages of vigorous exercise, a thought occurred to her that removed her amusement. She was becoming quite fond of Henry and was inclined to attribute his weaknesses of character to overindulgence and lack of discipline; but there was no denying the boy had a mischievous streak and that he was quite intelligent enough to plan complicated tricks. The weird whispering voice at the last séance could well have been Henry's, and he was too young to comprehend what a terrible effect it might have.

The evening passed without incident, except that once again Marianne enjoyed a brief comforting talk with Dr. Gruffstone. She had always found the doctor helpful, even when he seemed suspicious of her; he radiated reliability and authority as a stove radiates warmth. On this occasion she felt that he was really beginning to consider her a friend, for he spoke, as he had never done before, of personal matters, especially of his son, who would soon be coming home. Though obviously proud of the young man's gallantry, he had nothing but criticism for the way matters had been handled in Afghanistan; he denounced the fighting there with his favorite phrase, "absolute balderdash!"

As Marianne started upstairs she heard the click of billiard balls from the room devoted to that entertainment and surmised that Carlton was working off whatever annoyed him in a typically masculine manner. He had hardly spoken all evening.

If she dreamed that night, she did not remember the dreams. But she woke with a strange feeling of heaviness and lay pondering the matter for some time before she realized what was troubling her. Today was Tuesday. The fateful anniversary was only three days off.

When she went to pay her morning call on the Duchess, she found her up and dressing, with the faithful Rose in attendance. The maid had evidently conquered her grief, but she had not gotten over her resentment of Marianne; her greeting was barely civil. The Duchess did not seem to notice.

"Enjoy the sunshine while it lasts, my child," she murmured. "It is all too brief. . . ."

So Marianne left. Henry was lying in wait for her in the breakfast room. He barely allowed her time to eat before he demanded a repetition of the lawn-tennis game.

"A few more days of practice and you will be quite good at it," he remarked patronizingly. "For a girl, that is. Do hurry. I have been waiting ever so long."

Having nothing better to do, Marianne passed the morning with him. They returned to the house in time to see a hired carriage leaving. Henry craned his neck to see who was inside.

"My new tutor, I expect," he said. "Grandmother Honoria said one would be coming. That means I shall have only a few more days of holiday, Miss Ransom; we had better have another practice this afternoon."

"Impossible," Marianne said, laughing. "You know I am not as young as you; I have done quite enough for one day."

They were standing by the front steps, and as Henry argued his case Marianne fancied she saw a curtain in one of the upper windows move aside and a face peer out. Whether she was correct in identifying it she did not know; but it reminded her of poor timid Lady Violet, and she interrupted Henry with a firm "No, I really cannot. As for you, you ought to spend some time with your dear mama. That should be a pleasure as well as a duty."

"Oh." Henry thought a moment. "All right. She likes to read to me, and I don't mind it much. . . . Thank you for your company, Miss Ransom. We must do it again sometime."

With a very dignified bow, he offered his arm and led her into the house.

The Duchess did not come down to luncheon, but Marianne found the doctor and Lady Annabelle deep in conversation. Lady Annabelle had taken advantage of the Duchess's absence to introduce several cats into the room, and Marianne was amused at the doctor's calm forbearance; he devoured his lunch quite unperturbed by the chorus of meows and by the sight of his namesake's tail waving like a banner above the edge of the table.

They were on the second course when the door opened and Carlton came in. He was wearing riding clothes and seemed to be in a particularly evil temper; with a sketchy bow toward Lady Annabelle and a gruff greeting to the others, he threw himself into a chair and demanded food.

The doctor stared at him in mild surprise. "Where have you been all morning? I had intended to challenge you to a game of billiards."

"I had an errand," Carlton replied, stabbing viciously at the piece of sole the footman had placed before him.

"Satisfactory, I hope?"

"Not at all."

The doctor raised his eyebrows and then turned to Lady Annabelle, inquiring politely about the health of Fluffy.

Since Marianne was not especially interested in Fluffy's health she ate in silence, wondering what Carlton was up to. He had taken several mysterious journeys lately. No doubt, she thought cynically, he is trying to find out something to my discredit.

Lady Annabelle never followed conventional social usage, and this occasion was no exception. Instead of giving the nods and winks that indicated to the ladies that it is time to retire, she rose abruptly midway through the last course. Remarking, "You are in a wretched mood, Carlton; you are making Horace the cat quite nervous; I shall go now," she took her departure, with the spoiled Horace in her arms. Caught unawares, Marianne started to rise too, but was waved back into her chair by the doctor.

"No need for ceremony," he grunted. "Eat your meal, child. What the dev— er — what is wrong with you, Roger? You may not be affecting that animal's nerves, but you are doing mine no good."

"Sorry." Carlton pushed his plate away. "To be candid, Gruffstone, I have taken a certain liberty and I don't know how you will react. I hope you will not be offended."

"What have you done?" the doctor inquired calmly.

"I have summoned Sir Walter Bliss to see the Duchess."

Carlton dropped the words like bullets and looked as if he expected an explosion to follow. Instead, after a look of unconcealed astonishment, the doctor's face broke into a broad smile.

"Splendid, my boy, splendid! How did you persuade Honoria to see him? I have been trying for months."

"I have not yet told her. I thought she could not send him away after he had come so far on her account."

"That was well thought of." The doctor tugged thoughtfully at his mustache. "It never occurred to me. Well — fools rush in, if you will forgive me, my boy. I could not be more pleased." Seeing Marianne's bafflement, he explained, "Sir Walter is probably the best heart specialist in England. I am mightily relieved to have a second opinion, I can tell you. When does he come?"

"This afternoon. I learned from an article in the *Times* that he was to be in Edinburgh this week, so I sent a telegram. I have just now received the answer."

"Splendid, splendid," the doctor repeated. "Who knows, perhaps he will have good news for us. I am only a simple general practitioner; I could be wrong. I hope I am."

Carlton seemed to be cast into even greater gloom by this genial pronouncement. Marianne waited until the doctor had left, to prepare for the visit of the specialist; then she said, "I suppose you will not care to ride this afternoon."

"Not with Sir Walter expected. I wish to

hear what he has to say."

"You have no objection if I go alone?"

"Suit yourself," was the ungracious reply.

The dignified butler, obviously confused by the unconventional division of the luncheon party, brought in the port. Carlton gestured for his glass to be filled, and Marianne left him with the decanter before him.

Thinking Henry might like to join her in a ride, she went to the schoolroom. Nanny, nodding by the fire, told her the boy was with his mother, so Marianne was forced to request the company of one of the grooms. The menace from Bagshot had been removed, but she had not forgotten the Duchess's warning about getting lost.

The presence of the manservant, trotting respectfully behind her, took some of the pleasure from the ride and she cut it short, returning by way of the village. If she hoped to catch a glimpse of the vicar she was disappointed; but she did see something that surprised her — the black-clad visitor whom Carlton had suspected of being Bagshot in disguise. As on the previous occasion, he was walking away from her. Marianne urged Stella into a trot, hoping to overtake the man and see his face, but before she could catch him up he turned into the inn and disappeared. So she returned to the castle.

The Duchess's carriage, waiting before the castle, made her wonder who was about to go on a journey before she realized that it must have been sent to fetch the famous medical man. Handing her reins to the groom and giving Stella an affectionate pat, she hurried in. She found Carlton in the library, pacing back and forth between the open door and the fireplace.

"What news?" she asked. "He has come, has he not? I saw the carriage —"

"He is with her now. I am waiting to catch him before he goes; he must return immediately to Edinburgh."

Marianne was tempted to join him in his agitated walk, but forced herself to take a chair.

"By the way," she remarked, "the gentleman who was staying at the Devenbrook Arms is still here. He was not Mr. Bagshot after all."

"I know. You were right in supposing that Bagshot would not venture into the neighborhood. The preliminary work was all done by his hired cutthroats; he did not come until the final hour."

His tone made it clear that he had nothing more to say on that subject, so Marianne did not break the silence again. It went on for quite some time before they heard footsteps and low voices, one that of Dr. Gruffstone, the other unfamiliar.

Carlton bolted out the door without bothering to close it. Marianne remained where she was; she did not feel she had the right to intrude on such a meeting. However, she listened intently, and when she heard the front door open and close, she ran out.

Carlton was alone. He stood with his back toward her, but she did not need to see his face to know that the news had been bad. The droop of his shoulders, his hands clenched on the newel post, were eloquent enough.

She had not realized until then how much he had hoped for a reversal of Gruffstone's diagnosis. As she stood staring at Carlton, who had obviously not heard her approach, and wishing she dared comfort him, the front door opened and Gruffstone entered.

"I have seen Sir Walter off," he explained. "And thanked him again for coming so far."

"Then —" Marianne began.

Gruffstone shook his head. "He was kind enough to commend my medical knowledge. It was small comfort to me, I assure you. Excuse me; I must go to her now."

He went heavily up the stairs. Carlton straightened but did not turn, and something in the set of his shoulders told Marianne she had better not speak to him. So she went to her room and wept.

Later the Duchess summoned her, and Marianne was struck by the fact that of all the people in the house the dying woman seemed least concerned with her fate. The Duchess was, in fact, in a cheerful mood, which was explained when she remarked casually, "I have seen David. He does not seem to have aged at all, but then that is to be expected."

Rose, arranging the tea-things, dropped a saucer.

"Take yourself off, you clumsy creature," the Duchess said amiably. "After all these years, one would think . . ."

"You dreamed," Marianne said, as poor Rose stumbled toward the door.

"Oh, yes; that is the common term for such visions." After the door had closed she added rather irritably, "I find Rose a trial of late. If she is not dropping things, she is crying."

"She is devoted to you," Marianne said. "And, like the rest of us, she is deeply concerned —"

"But why? I am happier now than I have been for many years. If you could only have faith! Gruffstone particularly — he is a medical man, he of all people should be able to accept the fact that I must die sometime."

"But not now!" Marianne exclaimed. "You are willing yourself to die! You might live for months, years —"

"I don't want to," the Duchess said simply. "I want only one thing — the knowledge that David will be there to guide me over the threshold." Suddenly and alarmingly the look of peace faded from her face and was replaced by an expression of a most pitiful terror. "My faith is weak," she said rapidly. "I am afraid — I confess it. I know what awaits me, I believe in Paradise . . . but my body trembles in the fear of dissolution. If I could see David, feel his hand reaching out for me. . . . You won't deny me that, Marianne? You could not be so cruel. Promise — promise me —"

In her agitation she struggled forward, and Marianne realized in horror that she was about to fall to her knees. She caught the thin, shaking shoulders and forced the Duchess back into her chair.

"I will promise anything you like. Anything. Be calm, I beg you. You have my word."

"Thank you." After a few seconds Marianne felt the old woman's rigid limbs relax.

"I will fetch Dr. Gruffstone," she said.

"No." The Duchess forced a smile. "I am

better now. Horace can do me no good. You alone can help me. You *have* helped me."

"A glass of brandy, then," Marianne said desperately.

"A cup of tea will be splendid." The Duchess brushed her hand across her brow and spoke in almost her normal voice. "There. I am quite myself again. Let us eat all those delicious little cakes and drink our tea and have a game of backgammon. What do you say?"

Marianne felt as if the rich pastry would make her sick, and she went down to ignominious defeat in the game. The Duchess ignored her mood. She laughed and ate and moved the pieces with her old animation. To Marianne the spectacle was dreadful. The promise she had made lay like a heavy weight on her heart.

She knew now that she had clung to the hope that she would not be forced to go through the next — perhaps the last — attempt to reach the spirit of David Holmes; that the Duchess would not ask it of her, that Gruffstone would forbid it, that Carlton would think of some means of preventing it. Now she was committed. That agonized plea could not be denied. Only how on earth could she produce the evidence the Duchess longed for? Should she attempt to produce it by trickery? It seemed that whatever she did was bound to be disastrous.

The Duchess decided to dine in her room, and Marianne did the same. She simply could not face the glum looks of the two men, or Lady Annabelle's idiot indifference. After she had crumbled her bread and pushed the food around her plate, she decided to see what Henry was doing. Perhaps she could read him a story, or play chess with him.

She was wearing soft house slippers and her feet fell lightly on the carpet of the corridor. As she approached the door of the schoolroom, she saw light and realized that the door was open. Standing unseen in its shadow she beheld the scene within.

Lady Violet sat by the fire. For once she wore no veil or cap, and her hair was pushed back from her face, which wore a look of such peace and happiness that to Marianne it appeared quite beautiful, despite its physical defect. Perched on a stool by the lady's side, leaning against her skirts, sat the young Duke. He was reading aloud to her, and her hand rested lightly on his dark hair.

"So the prince said, 'Oh, lovely lady, I have been searching throughout my kingdom for a maiden who can wear this slipper.' "

Marianne felt tears prick her eyes. Pressing her skirts close to her sides, so that no betraying rustle would give her presence away, she retreated as silently as she had come.

II

Next day Marianne had to force herself to pay her usual morning call on the Duchess. One of the worst features of the whole affair was the growing ambivalence of her attitude toward her kind patroness, for she felt an increasing resentment, almost anger, at being forced into such an impossible position. She made her escape as soon as she could.

Henry was waiting for her, and they had another strenuous game of lawn tennis. Marianne finally called a halt when her fingers, in their thin kid gloves, became too numb to hold the racket. The day was much colder than the one before, and toward the end of the morning the sunlight vanished behind rolling gray clouds.

"It looks like snow." Henry said gleefully. "We will build a snow fort and go sledding. I know a splendid place for it."

Marianne was amused at the boy's bland assumption that she had become his permanent playmate. There was no reason to disillusion him, she thought; reality would come soon enough, in the form of a new tutor, for the Duchess had told her she expected to interview another candidate that morning.

Looking for something to distract her mind from the dread event that was coming even closer, she lingered in the hall hoping to catch a glimpse of the prospective tutor. Any new face would be a welcome change.

She was about to give up and go to her room to change when the door of the library opened and Carlton appeared. He gave an exaggerated start of surprise at seeing her and exclaimed, "Oh, there you are. I was about to . . . that is . . . where have you been?"

Marianne gazed at him in astonishment. His incoherent speech, his flushed face, and a certain air of suppressed excitement immediately aroused the suspicion that he had been drinking. Before she could answer he took her by the arm and fairly dragged her into the library.

"This is Mr. MacGregor," he said, indicating the young man who had politely risen from his chair. "Miss Ransom, Mr. MacGregor. Perhaps you would — er — entertain him, I must . . . I must go on an errand."

Upon which he rushed out, leaving Marianne staring. An amused chuckle from Mr. MacGregor made her turn.

"What an excitable, enthusiastic fellow!" he exclaimed. "But I can't complain of the change; may I offer you a chair, Miss Ransom?"

Marianne sat down. Mr. MacGregor must be the newest applicant for the position of tutor, she decided.

She took an immediate liking to him. He was a tall young man with an open, freckled face. One of his front teeth was chipped, giving his smile a boyish, lopsided charm. His speech was educated, with just a trace of Scottish burr.

"What was that all about?" she asked, nodding at the door through which Carlton had disappeared.

"I cannot imagine. We were talking about this and that, when all at once he bounded up and rushed away. I take it he is not always so impulsive? It is an attractive quality in itself, but I should think it would be a disadvantage in a man of the law."

His eyes twinkled with such frank amusement that Marianne could not help smiling. "I take it," she said, "that you are the new tutor."

"I hope I may be. The position appeals to

me very much. My home is in Sterling, only an hour's ride away, and I have a widowed mother who would like to have me so close. Also, I find the Duke a most appealing little chap. There is a good brain there; it would be a challenge to work with it."

Marianne liked him more and more. The enthusiasm glowing in his eyes was that of a dedicated teacher.

"You know of His Grace's — difficulty?" she inquired.

"Yes, the Duchess was very candid with me. It merely makes me more eager to take the position. Epilepsy is a much misunderstood illness. I was a medical student before I turned to teaching, so I feel I can be of help there."

"Why did you give it up? It is a noble profession."

"Healing the body? Certainly! But healing the mind, developing its gifts, is surely just as important. Besides," he added, with a grin, "I had no aptitude for medicine. Every time a knife cut into human flesh, living or not, I fainted dead away. It got to be a joke, and my fellow students enjoyed dragging me out of the room by my heels, but the professors began to be irritated by my crashing down unconscious in the middle of their demonstrations. So I gave it up."

Marianne was enjoying the conversation, and would have gone on with it, had not the ringing of the luncheon bell reminded her of the time.

"Are you joining us for lunch?" she asked.

"No, I thank you." MacGregor rose. "I have a cold ride ahead of me, and the weather threatens. I hope we may meet again, Miss Ransom."

"I hope so too," Marianne said sincerely.

She went in to luncheon and immediately demanded of Carlton what Mr. MacGregor's prospects were. "I liked him very much," she declared. "I think he would be good for Henry."

"Do you indeed," said Carlton, with a malevolent look. "You favor freckles and a Scottish burr, then?"

"I was not speaking of his personal attributes," Marianne said in a dignified manner. "But of his qualifications for the post."

"The Duchess was most impressed with him," Dr. Gruffstone said, forestalling another rude comment from the lawyer.

His efforts to keep the conversation pleasant were in vain, however. Carlton was in a perverse mood and kept interjecting remarks that seemed designed to be inflammatory. He contradicted almost everything that was said, and found matter for insult in the most innocuous subjects. He even provoked the doctor by derogatory remarks about his profession.

"After all," he said, at one point, "it has been a good many years since you qualified, doctor. 'Thirty-eight, was it not?"

"You mean to make me an old fogy, do you," said the doctor, with perfect good humor. "No, no, my lad; 'forty-five was the year. A long time, but not so long as you would have."

"Where did you study?" Carlton asked.

The doctor looked surprised at his inquisitorial tone, but replied readily enough, "I took my degree in London, after studying for several years in Edinburgh."

"Ah, Edinburgh."

"A beautiful city," the doctor said reminiscently.

"With such wonderful people. Major Weird, Deacon Brodie, Burke and Hare. . . ."

"Come now," the doctor protested. "Is that how the legal mind operates? To define a charming old city in terms of the murderers who plied their trade there? If so, I am glad I think otherwise."

"But Burke and Hare were in your own profession, Doctor," said Carlton, leaning back in his chair.

This sally finally pierced the doctor's armor. "What an outrageous thing to say!"

"Well, at least their friend Dr. Knox was. He bought the bodies from them." Carlton closed his eyes and began to chant,

> " 'Up the close and doun the stair,
> But and ben wi' Burke and Hare.
> Burke's the butcher, Hare's the thief,
> Knox the boy that buys the beef.' "

"Knox was never charged," said the doctor, red as a turkeycock. "The whole dreadful situation would never have arisen had it not been for the antiquated laws forbidding medical students to obtain cadavers for dissection. How can a surgeon possibly learn —"

"What?" Marianne exclaimed in disgust. The sense of the discussion had finally become clear to her. "Surely, gentlemen, this is not a suitable subject for luncheon conversation."

"I quite agree, Miss Ransom," the doctor said. "And I beg your pardon for my part in it."

"But wouldn't you think Dr. Knox might have noticed that some of the corpses were still *warm* when they were delivered to him?" Carlton inquired sweetly.

Marianne made a protesting sound and fled from the room, followed by the doctor's indignant response.

During the afternoon the snow began. Delicate, fragile white flakes drifted against the windowpanes and danced in the wind. Marianne took a book and went to the rose parlor, which was the most cheerful room in the bleak old place on such a day. Tired after a hard morning's exercise and a disturbed day, she was drowsing over the pages of Carlyle's *French Revolution* when the butler announced a caller.

"Mr. St. John, miss."

Marianne rose and tried to smooth her hair.

"I am afraid I woke you," the vicar said, advancing with outstretched hand.

"I am glad you did. I ought to have been improving my mind instead of dozing. The Duchess is in her room, Mr. St. John; shall I ring and —"

"I asked to see you. You do not mind?" Still holding her hand, he stood so close that with her disadvantage of height Marianne had to crane her neck at an uncomfortable angle in order to meet his eyes. He appeared very serious.

"No, no, of course . . . I am happy to see you. Would you care for tea, or sherry, or —"

She made as if to tug on the bellpull. St. John forestalled her.

"I want nothing, except your attention. I did intend to pay Her Grace a pastoral visit, but I was denied. Is it true that she is sinking fast?"

"Who told you that?"

"Gruffstone and Carlton." The vicar smiled faintly. "Two faithful dragons, guarding her door. Faithful, but oh, how terribly, tragically misled! Now of all times does she need the consolation only I — that is, only my Master, through me, His humble servant — can give."

Marianne indicated a chair, but he refused with an agitated shake of his head. So she sat down, thinking that in this case Carlton and the doctor had acted correctly. The vicar's brand of salvation was not suited to the Duchess even when she was in good health, and she needed no more reminders that her end was near.

"You have done all you could," she said. "Please sit down and let me give you a cup of tea. You are upset —"

"Upset!" The vicar whirled and crossed the space that separated them in a single bound, his coattails flying out like the wings of a big black bird. Marianne was so startled that she emitted a faint yelp of alarm. Before she could do more the vicar took her by the shoulders — it seemed to be a favorite gesture of his — and lifted her clean out of her chair. Holding her at arm's length, with the tips of her slippers barely touching the floor, he cried out, "Yes, I am upset! I confess it. But I will not yield. I will snatch one brand from the burning. Miss Ransom, will you. . . . No, I will not ask, I will command — purely in my pastoral capacity, of course. Miss Ransom, you must be mine!"

Marianne could only conclude that she had lost her wits, or that the vicar had lost his. One of them must be mad.

Seeing her consternation, St. John grew calmer. "I have frightened you," he said.

Marianne nodded dumbly.

"My zeal overcame me." St. John lowered her into her chair. But then he lifted her again, having transferred his grasp from her shoulders to her waist. "I do not ask this," he explained carefully, "out of selfish lust."

"Oh, indeed?" Marianne had at last recovered her breath. She put her hands against the young man's chest and pushed. For all the effect this had she might have been pushing at a stone.

"No," St. John said. "I do it in order to save a soul. You are doomed to perdition, my dear Miss Ransom, if you remain here.

I offer you sanctuary — redemption — everlasting bliss! I realize the ambiguities of your position: your doubtful heritage, your lack of a dowry, your scandalous past. I overlook them. At heart you are honest, I am sure. We will leave this house at once. I will take you to an aged relative of mine, where you will remain until the wedding."

Throughout this speech his actions had been somewhat at variance with his lofty sentiments; for his arms clasped Marianne closer and closer and he made a very determined effort to reach her lips with his.

Sad to say, Marianne's reaction was not indignation or the sense of spiritual shame the vicar had hoped to inspire. It was, simply and solely, boredom. She wondered how she could have gone out of her way to catch a glimpse of this singularly dull, pompous young man.

Finally, realizing that she was losing ground in her effort to keep him from kissing her, she freed one hand and slapped his face as hard as she could. St. John let her go. Nursing his wounded cheek with one hand, he stared at her in shocked surprise.

"You are distraught," he suggested.

"I am insulted — and amused. Let me advise you, Mr. St. John, the next time you propose to a lady, do not begin by listing all her negative qualities. Can you find your way out, or shall I ring for Jenkins to show you out?"

St. John found his own way out.

Marianne collapsed into a chair. She did not know whether she wanted to laugh or cry or swear. She was only certain of one thing: what a blessing it was that Carlton had not come in upon that dreadful, farcical scene!

Even as the thought came to her mind a voice remarked, "Very nicely done, upon my word. I would not have believed you had it in you."

Carlton's head appeared above the back of the sofa.

"You listened!" Marianne cried furiously. "You are the most disgusting — the most reprehensible —"

She was so angry she stumbled over the last word, pronouncing it "rehensibubble," and Carlton burst out laughing. Marianne fled, her hands pressed to her burning cheeks.

After that misadventure it was time to force herself to face the Duchess.

At first all went smoothly. The Duchess appeared bright and calm. They spoke of Mr. MacGregor, and Marianne expressed her enthusiastic approval. The Duchess agreed. She had one more candidate to interview next day, but unless he proved to be extraordinary she thought the nod must go to the young Scot.

When Marianne rose to dress for dinner, the Duchess caught her hand and, with a startling change in manner and tone, said, "You have not forgotten? You will keep your word? It will not be long now. . . ."

"I know." The fingers clasping hers were so thin and cold they felt like fleshless bone. Marianne repressed a shudder. "I — I will do my best. Are you not coming downstairs tonight?"

"No, I think not. I am a little tired. I want to save my strength for tomorrow." The Duchess smiled — a strange, shadowy smile. "We will have a grand dinner party and all dress in our best. Won't that be splendid?"

"Yes, indeed," Marianne managed to say. When she was outside the room she wiped her fingers with a fold of her skirt; but the icy touch still lingered on her flesh.

CHAPTER SIXTEEN

At two o'clock in the morning Marianne finally abandoned her effort to sleep. She had been tossing and turning for hours, watching the shadows lengthen as her candle burned down, and listening to the hiss of sleety snow against the windows.

Dinner had been a miserable affair. The brisk north wind had found cracks and crannies in the paneling of the dining room that had never before been apparent, and Marianne had shivered in her formal gown until the doctor sent a maid for her shawl. She could not meet Carlton's eyes. Whenever she tried, they narrowed with such diabolical amusement that she was afraid he would say something about the encounter between herself and the vicar. He was in a particularly exasperating mood, baiting the doctor, insulting Horace the cat until Lady Annabelle finally threw her napkin at him and retired in a high dudgeon, and even committing the unspeakable faux pas of speaking to the footmen as they passed the dishes. And after dinner, when Marianne tried to speak alone with the doctor, longing for the solid comfort of his conversation, Carlton refused to be dismissed. He suggested music and made her stay at the piano until bedtime.

She had hoped the dreary weather would help her sleep, but it was no use; the knowledge of what the next day would bring twisted in her mind like a sharp knife, destroying peace. Twenty-four hours from now, she told herself, it will be over. But that was no comfort, for who knew what the denouement would bring, and what unwilling role she would play in bringing it about?

She got up at last, lighted a fresh candle, and started to look for the doctor's brown bottle. She did not like sleeping medicine, but tonight she would have been tempted to swallow a cup of hemlock if someone had assured her it would bring temporary forgetfulness. She searched in increasing frustration until she remembered that Carlton had made off with the medicine and had never returned it. That made her stamp and use some of the squire's swear words. If the hour had not been so late she would have gone after it, but she could imagine Carlton's comments if she crept into his room in the dead of night.

Parting the window curtains, she peered out into the dark. There was nothing to be seen but a blowing curtain of snow. An icy draft blew against her through cracks in the molding and she let the curtain drop.

There was no sense in going back to bed. Wrapping herself in a comforter, she poked the fire up and settled down with Carlyle. He had put her to sleep once before, perhaps he would perform the same office again.

Sleep came upon her so subtly that she did not sense its approach. It seemed to her that she was still sitting by the fire, her head bent over her book, though its print had become a meaningless blur, when a smoldering brand in the fire broke and sent up a last spurt of flame. In the brief illumination she saw a figure sitting in the chair opposite hers.

Such is the nature of dreams that they carry an emotional atmosphere independent of their content. The most innocent-seeming dreams can cause the dreamer to wake in a sweat of terror, and nightmares of death and horror do not always alarm. So Marianne was not frightened, even when she recognized the neat black skirts and little lace cap and the face of Mrs. Jay.

The vicar's widow was smiling. She looked vigorous and healthy and many years younger than she had looked when Marianne last saw her. As Marianne started to cry out, in pleased greeting, the elderly lady lifted a warning hand. Nodding almost coquettishly, she sketched a brief gesture in the air . . . and disappeared.

Marianne rubbed her eyes. Her lower limbs, which had been tucked up under her, had gone quite numb. She staggered to her bed. This time she fell asleep at once.

Dreams are all very well, but their influence does not last long. Marianne awoke with a lingering memory of happiness and peace; but as soon as she came fully awake the knowledge of what was to happen that night swept over her like a great salty wave.

The weather was so bad that even Henry had to admit it was not a good day for sledding, so they spent the morning in the schoolroom finishing the battle of Waterloo. This time the victory almost went to Napoleon, thanks to Roger Carlton, who turned up in midbattle and demanded to be allowed to play. He was given the Austrian troops and managed them so successfully that the Iron Duke had to fight for his life. At last, however, the British lion roared triumphant over the field, and Henry sat back on his heels with a sigh of delight.

"That was splendid! Let's do it again."

"Not until my wounded have recovered,"

Carlton replied. On hands and knees, his hair hanging over his brow and his sleeves rolled up, he had entered into the game with enthusiasm, shouting orders in fractured German and imitating the agonies of the wounded. "They need nourishment, and so do I; it is time for luncheon. You are coming down, are you not, Miss Ransom?"

Before Marianne could answer, Henry scrambled to his feet with a glad cry. "Mama! I won, Mama; the British won!"

"Wonderful," Lady Violet said, smiling. "Miss Ransom, Mr. Carlton — how good of you to play with Henry."

"I enjoyed it," Marianne said truthfully.

"Run along and wash for lunch, Henry." Lady Violet ran caressing fingers through her son's hair. "Mr. Carlton, if you will excuse me, I would like to speak to Miss Ransom for a moment."

So that is how you do it, Marianne thought, as the two male creatures obeyed without an argument or a backward look. I wonder if I could learn. But perhaps it takes generations of aristocratic blood, or some such thing.

She started to scramble to her feet, but Lady Violet put a hand on her shoulder.

"Don't stand, I beg you. I will not keep you long; I only wanted to apologize for not accompanying you to church Sunday. You are a kind person. You have been very good to my son. I hope . . . I hope that from now on we can be friends."

"I would be so glad," Marianne exclaimed, quite overcome. "I need a friend, Lady Violet, I do indeed."

"I wish I could help you." The lady sank into a chair and looked thoughtfully at Marianne. The girl was pleased to see that she had abandoned the defensive gesture of hiding her face with her hand. "I know what is happening; but I do not know what to do about it."

"Did you know him?" Marianne asked.

She did not have to name names. They both knew to whom she was referring. Regretfully Lady Violet shook her head.

"I have heard a great deal about him, of course. But he had been dead for over five years when I married Henry's father and came here to live."

"I wish I knew what to do," Marianne murmured.

"I am hardly the proper person to ask," Lady Violet said, with a faint smile. "I have not managed my own life so well as to venture to offer advice to others. But if I *were* to advise you, Miss Ransom, I would tell you to leave this place. There is a curse on the Devenbrook family. No one knows it better than I. You will only fall victim to it yourself if you attempt to fight against it."

This statement was made in such a calm, reasonable tone that Marianne stared, hardly able to believe her ears were not deceiving her. Lady Violet nodded at her.

"I wish you well, Miss Ransom. You have been kind to Henry. But you cannot combat the curse of the Devenbrooks."

Well, Marianne thought dismally, as she made her way to her room, that is a sad end to what began so well! She could not blame poor Lady Violet for adding to her worry instead of relieving it; but she wished the lady had stopped after her thanks and not mentioned curses.

The last candidate for the tutor's post never came. Marianne was not surprised; as the day went on, the storm mounted in fury. By three o'clock it was as dark as night and the lamps were lighted. Soon thereafter Marianne was summoned to the Duchess. She obeyed, trembling with apprehension.

Seated before her dressing table, the Duchess greeted her warmly. Flaring candles on either side of the tall mirror illuminated her face. Marianne was reminded, not pleasantly, of her brief theatrical career. So must she have looked on those evenings when she performed, with a mixture of excitement and stage fright alternately flushing and whitening her cheeks.

"I have sent Rose away, she was of no use whatever," the Duchess said. "It is your company I want, in any case. Will you stay with me and help me dress? I want to look my best."

Marianne assumed the Duchess was primping in order to leave her friends with a lasting and beautiful memory. It was a morbid-enough idea, but when the girl turned, to see the dress that was laid out across the bed, she knew that until that moment she had never fully understood the truth.

The gown was one she had never seen the Duchess wear. But it was not new; the style was years out of date and the white fabric had begun to yellow. There were even a few faint cracks along the stiff folds. The bodice was trimmed with the softest, most exquisite of handmade lace, like a drift of snowflakes. There was no other ornament. On the table beside the bed stood a vase of waxy white gardenias, the prized products of MacDonald's conservatory. A draft rattled the windows and carried the flowers' sweet, overpowering scent to Marianne's nostrils.

For an instant she thought she was going

to be sick. Then — from what cause she never really knew — the last of the many changes of mood she had undergone took place; it was to stay with her until the end. It was plainly and simply pity.

"How perfectly beautiful," she said in a steady voice. "I must do my best to do justice to that gown."

She brushed the Duchess's hair till her arms ached and shaped it into a masterpiece of soft waves and curls, crowning it with the waxy flowers. She took her time; there was no hurry. At the Duchess's suggestion she brought her dress from her own room and they primped and laughed and admired one another like two young girls preparing for a ball. When all else was ready she slipped the white satin gown over the old lady's head and fastened the long row of tiny buttons. Then she stood back and clasped her hands.

"You are lovely," she said.

"One more thing." Around her neck the Duchess hung the gold locket that contained David Holmes's picture.

Then they went down together.

Marianne's new calm was sorely tested when she saw Roger Carlton's face change, at the sight of the satin wedding dress. But the doctor was magnificent. He behaved as if nothing out of the ordinary was happening, or was expected to happen. He talked, he told bad jokes, he flirted with the Duchess. Somehow he got them through the first bad minutes until Carlton revived and made spasmodic attempts to join in. Lady Annabelle did not make her appearance until they were ready to go in to dinner. She looked almost undressed without a cat in her arms; the orange hairs clinging to the front of her green velvet gown suggested that she had held Horace until the last possible minute, and Marianne had a sudden insane vision of a maid wrestling the animal away before allowing her mistress to leave the room. Perhaps it was the absence of her favorite companion that made her so ill at ease; she sat in silence, moving her hands restlessly and blinking her eyes until Marianne yearned to shake her.

She was unable to eat. The time had come upon her so quickly that she felt cheated; she wanted more time to think, to plan. But perhaps it was just as well. How could one plan for the unimaginable?

When the port was brought in, the Duchess rose. "Tonight we will go out together," she said in a calm, clear voice. "Horace, give me your arm, please."

Speechless, the doctor complied. The two went out, arm in arm.

Marianne turned to Carlton. "What are we going to do? We must do something."

"Do nothing." His eyes held hers. "Say nothing, do nothing. Whatever impulse may strike you, whatever force may compel you — resist it. Do you understand?"

"Yes, but —"

"Always 'but.' " He smiled at her. He seemed in the grip of some strange excitement, but his smile was free of malice, the smile of a friend.

"Roger," Lady Annabelle said plaintively, "I don't feel well. Something is going to happen. Something bad. I don't know how I know that, but I do. Must I come with you?"

"I would like you to. Do you mind? You never have before."

"But this is different. At least let me bring Horace."

"Now, Lady Annabelle . . ." Carlton let out a brief, unamused laugh. "After all, what does it matter? They say cats are in tune with occult forces; why not?"

"Thank you, thank you." Lady Annabelle trotted out.

Carlton offered Marianne his arm. "Cheer up," he said. "The worst is yet to come."

"You have some scheme in mind," she said, as they walked along together. "Tell me what it is. I am half insane with worry."

"You have some distance to go before you break," was the seemingly callous reply; but Marianne sensed that it was not meant in a derogatory sense, and she was pleased. "I can't tell you," he went on rapidly — for they were approaching the White Room. "I do have an idea — but it is so wild, so unlikely that I can scarcely believe it myself; and even if it is true, it gives me no real guidelines by which to act. . . . Trust me."

She had no opportunity to reply. They were at the door.

The room felt cold, despite a blazing fire and the illusory warmth of lamps and candles. The doctor pushed aside one of the draperies and looked out.

"It is a wild night," he said gravely. "God help any poor soul abroad in this winter darkness. Honoria, in the presence of your friends, I make one last plea. Do not do this."

"I will and I shall," was the calm reply. "Horace, dim the lights."

Lady Annabelle's breathless arrival added a touch of comedy to the otherwise macabre scene. She came in sideways, her shoulders hunched, though Horace's huge orange tail hanging down over her arm made futile any attempt to hide his presence. The Duchess did not comment, however, and Lady Annabelle sidled crab-fashion into a chair.

No one suggested forming a circle or holding hands or any of the other controls usual to such meetings. As the light gradually dimmed, Marianne watched Carlton. His face grave, his eyes abstracted, he seemed deep in thought. She had not often seen him in a serious mood, and she thought it became him.

The doctor put out the last light and shifted the heavy screen before the fire. Marianne heard the creak of leather and deduced that he had taken a chair next to the screen rather than stumble across the room in the dark.

In the silence she heard the wind crying like a lost child. Remembering Carlton's warning, she clenched her hands and determined to follow his advice.

The doctor's voice suddenly exclaimed, "Nothing is going to happen. Honoria, I beg —"

A long, drawn-out sigh broke into this speech. It was followed by a loud intake of breath that went on and on until Marianne thought it would never end. When at last the expiration followed, it too was abnormally extended. The deep, slow breathing continued for several seconds before Marianne realized that it issued from Roger Carlton. His head had fallen forward onto his breast.

"Roger?" the Duchess exclaimed in utter astonishment.

"What?" the doctor cried. "What is it?"

"Be still! Not another sound!"

Carlton's body jerked convulsively. His head fell back against the high carved back of the chair.

"He is entranced," the Duchess exclaimed. "I never knew —"

From Carlton's lips came a voice that did not sound like his — a strained yet penetrating whisper.

"Murder . . . will out. After years . . . murder. . . ."

Somewhere in the room someone's voice caught in a harsh gasp.

"Vengeance . . ." Carlton's voice droned. "Vengeance is mine. . . ."

"What are you saying?" the Duchess whispered. "Who are you? David — David, is it you?"

A breath of icy air blasted the room, sending the heavy draperies billowing furiously. With a blasphemous oath the doctor leaped from his chair and sent the screen toppling over. The fire leaped up, fanned by the wind; and in its light Marianne saw a tall figure standing in the window. It might have been male or female; it wore a long, shrouding black garment, and its head was covered. With the snowflakes swirling madly around it, it resembled some elemental spirit, born of the darkness and the storm. It lifted one arm and swept off its hat. The light shone on a cap of silvery fair hair.

The doctor shrieked like a mortally wounded animal. "Damn you! Have you come from Hell to haunt me? How many times must I kill you?"

Arms extended, fingers crooked, he plunged in a headlong rush toward the figure in black. It stepped nimbly to one side as he came at it; still shrieking curses, the doctor rushed out into the storm and was gone.

The man in black closed the windows and put out an arm to stop Carlton, who had gone in pursuit.

"You will only endanger your own life, my friend, by following. You had better stay."

Calmly, like a well-trained servant, he moved along the wall lighting the lamps. In their swelling glow Marianne saw him clearly: a tall, thin man, no longer young; his hair was not fair, but completely white.

When he removed his cloak, tossing it carelessly toward the chair, she saw that he was wearing the collar and cassock of a Catholic priest.

Carlton pressed his hand to his head. "I could not find him in this storm," he muttered, looking at the window. "It is too late now."

"It was already too late for him, long before this," the stranger said. "You will find him in the morning. It will be soon enough. You know where he has gone."

"To the waterfall, you mean?" Carlton said dazedly. "He did not kill you, then?"

"He tried." The stranger brushed the clustering curls from his high white forehead. A livid scar twisted from hairline to temple. "He did me a service, though he intended harm. My doubts and questions ended. All was made clear to me. I had found my true vocation and I followed it."

Smiling, he looked down at something at his feet; and Marianne saw that Horace the lethargic had at last found an object worth moving for. The cat was rubbing his head against the black-clad ankles and purring loudly. Holmes bent to stroke him.

"I knew your grandfather," he said whimsically. Horace let out a hoarse meow as if in response. With a final caress, Holmes straightened. "Lady Annabelle, I hope all is well with you."

Annabelle nodded. "It is. But . . . but —"

"I know." Holmes nodded gravely. "I came only for that."

He crossed the room, moving with the grace Marianne had heard described. The Duchess sat upright in her chair, her eyes wide open, her hands resting on the arms of her chair. Her lips were curved in a faint smile.

Holmes passed his hand over her brow, closing her eyes. Then he knelt by her chair, crossed himself and bent his head.

II

Not until after the funeral was Marianne in a fit state to untangle the final riddles. There had been much to do, for Lady Annabelle had retired with her cats and refused to come out, and Lady Violet, though she tried to help, was too obsessed with the latest evidence of the Devenbrook curse to be very useful. To Marianne, with Carlton's full assent and cooperation, went the mournful task of dealing with the Duchess's personal possessions.

When she left the church with Carlton

after the simple service, they turned in silent accord away from the ducal carriage and walked slowly along the road. It was a mild winter day; the sunlight was muted by mist; the air was still.

"I thought he would be here today," Marianne said, after a long silence.

"He returned to Rome yesterday. He had already said goodbye to her, you know."

"I am still bewildered," Marianne said. "That he should be alive after all . . ."

"Did you think he was a ghost when he made that theatrical appearance?" Carlton asked with a smile.

"No. No, strangely enough, I never thought that. He does not convey an aura of ghostly terror. But it was cruel of him to leave her to grieve all those years."

"The saints are often cruel," Carlton said quite seriously. "Having their minds on higher things, they care little for the transitory agonies of this life. But do the man justice, Marianne. He must have suffered greatly. And, with all respect to a good, kind woman . . ."

"I know. She would never have let him go."

"You don't blame her?"

"Oh, no! Nor can I truly grieve for her. She had what few people have — the attainment of her fondest wish." Marianne was silent, remembering that desperate and oddly prophetic prayer: "David's hand . . . guiding me over the threshold."

Then she said, with a sudden change of mood from melancholy to vindictive, "It is the doctor I cannot forgive. How could he? And how in heaven's name did you come to suspect the truth? That was what you meant, was it not — to accuse him, with your melodramatic groans about vengeance and murder?"

Carlton looked somewhat sheepish. "It was not a good performance," he admitted. "But I had to act fast, before Gruffstone could begin his playacting, and I counted on the atmosphere supplying any deficiencies in my talent. Yes, I suspected Gruffstone — not of murder, in the beginning, but of being responsible for the tricks at the séances. I should have seen it long before I did; for if you will think back over all that happened, Marianne, you will realize that he was the only one who could have engineered everything."

"Yes, I see it now. In London, when the thing began, there were only the four of us. For a time I suspected the Duchess of tricking herself."

"So did I. But during the last séance but

one Gruffstone became overconfident. I was seated next to the Duchess and I knew she never left her chair. The doctor, on the other hand, made sure he sat at some distance from us."

"I had an advantage you did not," Marianne said slyly. "I knew I was innocent."

"You were certainly the most obvious suspect," Carlton said. Then, as if to keep her from asking the question that came next to mind, he hastened on with his explanation. "I could see how the doctor might have engineered the majority of the tricks; remember he actually boasted of having studied the devices those 'charlatans' used in their séances. Phosphorescent paint on gloves and other objects, a chemical that became visible only after heat was applied — the lamp under the 'mysterious' writing was one of the largest, if you recall, and he could count on your wishing to brighten that dismal room; even the bust of Holmes, which he took from its place as he was closing the draperies and flipped dexterously onto the table while I was staring suspiciously at you. That made his task all the easier, the fact that no one thought of watching him. But the biggest stumbling block was your astonishing trance state."

"I cannot recall that, even now."

"No wonder. You were mesmerized."

"What?" Marianne stared in disbelief.

"Or hypnotized, if you prefer that term; it was coined by Dr. Braid of Edinburgh, who experimented with the procedure in the early forties. You may thank Mr. MacGregor, who will be joining our establishment tomorrow, for giving me that vital clue. I was so desperate by that time that I tried to pump him about drugs or other substances that could cause a person to fall into a seeming trance. He mentioned Braid, and Charcot, and a lot of other fellows I had never heard of, and it was like a light in a dark room. I saw how it might have been done. I interrogated Gruffstone and, sure enough, he had studied in Edinburgh when Braid was there. The technique is considered questionable by most physicians, so he never used it openly, but I have no doubt that many of his patients benefited by his experiments along those lines."

"I was very stupid," Marianne said. "But he seemed so kind, so strong —"

"That is why he was such a successful hypnotist. Especially," Carlton added, with a sidelong glance, "with a young, orphaned, impressionable, frightened —"

"Ninny."

"Not really," Carlton said tolerantly.

"You had a great deal on your mind. I don't believe I have ever met a young woman who has crowded so many adventures into such a short period of time."

"But why did he do it?" Marianne asked. "He was the last person I would have suspected of wanting to harm her."

"He didn't want to. He knew she was mortally ill and doomed to die soon, so . . . Really, his motives are too complicated for a simple person like myself to understand. Hatred and jealousy of Holmes were part of it. After all his years of devotion, to see himself supplanted in her affections by an upstart like that . . .

"The night Holmes disappeared he was half mad with jealousy. Remember, Holmes's supposed psychic talents had been quiescent for a year and they were due to return soon. Gruffstone saw him gaining more and more of the lady's confidence; she had already spoken of making him her heir. The doctor did not know that Holmes was fighting a profound mental and emotional battle of his own. He believed in his powers and felt they were for good; but his church condemned him for using them. He was in an impossible dilemma.

"Gruffstone had no idea of this. He followed Holmes that night and demanded that he end his relationship with the Duchess. Holmes refused, saying he must follow his own conscience. In a fit of fury Gruffstone struck him and pushed him into the stream. He survived by a miracle — he uses that word quite literally, I assure you — and found, when he dragged himself from the water, that his path lay clear before him. He entered the priesthood and has served ever since.

"I did not begin to suspect Gruffstone of murder until quite late in the proceedings, when I was desperately seeking a means of forcing him to confess his antics in the séance room. The idea was so dreadful I could scarcely believe it; yet if the rest of my theory was correct, Gruffstone had every reason to wish Holmes dead. You see, his basic motive was the common shabby one of greed. You were there when I read the will."

"She left him ten thousand pounds," Marianne exclaimed. "Such a paltry sum!"

"You can afford to sneer at it, since you were left almost two hundred thousand."

"I have no intention of keeping it. I told you that." Marianne twisted the ring on her finger. "This is the only keepsake I want."

"How high-minded you are! Ten thousand pounds is a great sum of money for a poor doctor, I assure you, especially when he has a wounded son to take care of. But therein lies the greatest irony of all, to my mind; the only way Gruffstone could get his inheritance was by getting someone else much more. He knew the Duchess had put off making a will; it was likely that she would never do so. Hence the mad, brilliant scheme occurred to him — why not supply an heir whom she would wish to benefit, and so be inspired to do what she had postponed so long? He knew she would remember him, she had often expressed her intentions of doing so. And — mark the irony — the only heir who might rouse such an interest in her was another David Holmes. Holmes could not be resurrected — so the doctor believed, little knowing the truth — nor would he want to do so. But the Duchess had often mentioned her fantasy about a child of Holmes — that was all it was, her desire to believe that something of the man she loved remained on earth. Gruffstone hit on this as his means to an inheritance, and subtly fanned her vague hope into a burning obsession. He of all people knew how seriously ill the Duchess was. Time was growing short. So he began his search for a girl who could pass as Holmes's daughter. It took him almost two years, for finding the right person was difficult. She had to be an orphan, without kin who could prove her true parentage. And she had to be a lady of breeding; the Duchess would never accept a common girl of the streets as her dear David's child. He even used me in the search," Carlton added, with a disgusted look. "When I mentioned you —"

Here he came to a stop; and Marianne said sweetly, "I wonder why you did. What was it about me that struck you?"

"You were only one of many young — er — ladies whom I have had cause to mention to other men," Carlton replied. "And admit it, my dear; you were an anomaly in that place, it was part of your charm. To proceed — if your vanity is satisfied? — Gruffstone was growing desperate by the time you so providentially appeared. Your appearance and manners suited his requirements, and by a skillful use of drugs and mesmerism he managed to get some rather nice performances out of you before your conscience, exacerbated by St. John's threats of damnation, rose up in arms and overcame Gruffstone's suggestions.

"Unfortunately, though you were an orphan, there were people who could prove beyond a doubt that you were Squire Ransom's daughter. Gruffstone could not afford to wait any longer. So he lied about his investigations. Naturally I did not think of doubting him at first, but when my suspicions awoke I made a journey there myself and discovered he had been less than candid. It was not at all difficult to trace your mother's personal maid, who had been with her when you were born. Emily Bateson is an old woman now, but her mind is perfectly clear, and she certainly is not dead.

"So then I knew Gruffstone was guilty. But I had a frightful time getting proof. Every clue I investigated failed me; I even found it was exactly what it purported to be. I suppose that when he wanted to drug you he slipped the stuff into your glass of wine or your cup of tea. But he did not resort to such means often; he had already established his mesmeric power over your mind, and so long as he did not ask you to do anything contrary to your moral sense you slid in and out of trances very obligingly."

"You went to Yorkshire!" Marianne exclaimed, ignoring the remainder of his speech. "So that was where you were when I was so nearly stolen away. Whom else did you see, besides my mother's maid?"

"I saw Mrs. Jay." Carlton looked seriously at her. "Marianne, I had not wanted to tell you this so soon after. . . . but perhaps you are strong enough to bear it now."

"You need not tell me," Marianne said quietly. "I know. Mrs. Jay is dead."

"She was a dying woman when I saw her. The doctor gave her only a short time. But she may still —"

"No. She died last week. I expect I will receive a letter today or tomorrow."

"How do you know?"

"I saw her. One night, in my room, as I sat by the fire. She smiled at me and made a gesture of farewell. You needn't raise your eyebrows and look skeptical! There has been a great deal of hocus-pokery in this affair, but that does not mean some true visions have not occurred. She loved me and she was deeply concerned for me; and she came."

"I would not for all the world destroy such a comforting idea," Carlton said. "So what will you do now?"

"Go back to London. Mrs. Shortbody will take me in, I daresay; I will find another post. Surely there cannot be two Mrs. Pettibones looking for a governess."

She spoke cheerfully, but she could not bring herself to look at Carlton. Knowing her heart at last, the thought of leaving him was almost more than she could bear. However, she was not totally despondent; for some of the things he had said, she thought she could guess why he had arbitrarily removed her from the unenviable position of chief suspect.

"Then you were sincere when you spoke of giving up your inheritance?" Carlton asked.

"Certainly."

"That makes things more difficult. I don't know that I could marry a girl with less than two hundred thousand pounds."

Then at last Marianne looked him in the face. But only for a moment; he caught her in his arms, and her eyes closed as his lips found hers.

He let her go at last, but only to fold her close and press her head against his breast.

"I will give you the spirit of Mrs. Jay," he said, breathless with laughter and another, more satisfactory, emotion. "But I really must insist on no more experiments with the occult. It is all nonsense, my dear; absolute balderdash, as the doctor used to . . . What is the matter with you?"

Marianne shook her head dizzily. "But that is what he said," she stuttered.

"I know he did. I was quoting him."

"No, no. That is what he said just before I went into one of those spells you were talking about. I remember now. For an instant, when you spoke the words, I felt quite giddy."

"Ah, so that was it. Posthypnotic suggestion, according to MacGregor; and that was the key phrase that would send you tumbling into your trance. All explained rationally and scientifically, you see. No spirits."

"All but one thing," Marianne said. They linked arms and began strolling up and down before the castle, reluctant to resume the mundane duties that awaited them.

"Oh? And what is that?"

"Mr. Holmes. How did he know to come back just when he did?"

Carlton looked utterly taken aback. "The anniversary of his death?" he hazarded.

"Why this one? There have been many others. Oh, I know what you are going to say — the newspaper story. But can you imagine Mr. Holmes, or any of the other priests, reading that scandalous sheet?"

"He had been staying at the inn for some days," Carlton muttered.

"That only makes his presence more remarkable. He knew, Roger. And you must admit that, but for him, the doctor would still be free and enjoying his legacy. You could never have proved him guilty of anything."

"Curse it." Carlton scowled. "Give me time. I'll think of an explanation."

"I am sure you will," Marianne said.

We hope you have enjoyed this Large Print book. Other Thorndike Press or Chivers Press Large Print books are available at your library or directly from the publishers.

For more information about current and upcoming titles, please call or write, without obligation, to:

Thorndike Press
P.O. Box 159
Thorndike, Maine 04986 USA
Tel. (800) 223-2336

OR

Chivers Press Limited
Windsor Bridge Road
Bath BA2 3AX
England
Tel. (0225) 335336

All our Large Print titles are designed for easy reading, and all our books are made to last.